THRONE
OF THE
HORDE KING

ZOEY DRAVEN

Throne of the Horde King

Horde Kings of Dakkar

Book Six

Zoey Draven

The final book of the *Horde Kings of Dakkar* series is here...

High in the icy northlands of Dakkar, I've lived a sheltered, predictable, and safe life. My days are spent caring for an ancient temple and staying out of the priestesses' way. My nights are spent pouring over the great stories of warrior kings and the queens that stole their hearts.

But I have a secret.

I'm a hybrid female. Half-Dakkari, half-human, the first of my kind. The priestesses have risked everything to keep me hidden from the dangerous hordes that roam the wild lands and the greedy king that sits on the throne in *Dothik*. I am the secret they could never let free.

Then a horde king—with molten eyes and the body of a battle god—shows up at the temple's gates, demanding entry.

He's the one I see in my dreams, all ruthless, merciless strength and a tempting smirk to match. Only, he's not the gentle male I always imagined. He's cunning, sensual, cruel...and he thinks that everything has a price. Even me.

With a growing danger in the east and a precarious throne in the west, he steals me away from the sacred temple with daring plans all his own.

He thinks I'm a naive temple girl, who will bend easily to his demands. Instead, I fight him at every turn, showing him claws of my own. Instead of fear, lust begins to rise between us—hot, addicting, and *forbidden*. His teasing touch makes me tremble. His stolen kisses make me weak.

But the horde king of Rath Serok is as mysterious as he is devilish.

And he has his own secret...one that will forever change the future of Dakkar.

CHAPTER 1

The whispers of the priestesses rose and spread. Ancient words that tingled up my arms, that made my head feel dizzy and light. For a moment, I felt like I was floating. I was entranced. Enchanted.

I was not meant to hear them. However I'd already finished with my chores. Beyla had already shooed me from the kitchens. And there was a book I wanted from *Kalloma's* library. The only way to reach it was through the sanctum—the *sa'kilan.*

Creeping along the wall, I made certain my footsteps were silent. The Dakkari had incredible hearing. While that was not a gift I had inherited from my father, I *had* been sneaking around quiet hallways and ancient rooms since I was a child.

In another life, I'd make a good thief, I thought. But for now, all I wanted was that book. My favorite book. One I'd read nearly a hundred times.

There were twelve priestesses in prayer, standing in a circle around the pedestal in the very center of the sanctum. On that pedestal was a heartstone of Kakkari. Lovely and shimmering. Colors swirled underneath its surface with the prayers. I could almost feel the beat of it, the *heat* of it.

A wave of dizziness had me reaching out a hand, sliding it against the stone wall to steady myself. The whispers swarmed my mind, mingling with my thoughts until I thought they were not my own. I shook it off, as I often did, before a crack could appear. A crack in my vision that would show me something I didn't want to see.

Plugging my ears, jamming my fingers against the small flap of flesh, I took another shuffled side step. And then another. Another.

I'd made it to the middle of the circular room. The door to *Kalloma's* private room was only a short distance away. The golden door gleamed, and my heart was full of trembling *want*. *Kalloma* would chastise me if she knew what I was thinking. But all I was thinking was that I wanted to read about Bekkar, the ancient Dakkari warrior turned king, and his campaign across the West Lands. I wanted to read the account of his fateful meeting with his future queen, Lessa. The daughter of his enemy. The daughter of an enemy horde.

Enemies that became lovers. I nearly sighed.

I wanted to read their love story again. I wanted to read about their adventures as they grew a great kingdom together. I wanted to—

A flash of red had me freezing.

Avala had spotted me. Her eyes pinned me in place though I could see her lips were still moving in prayer. Subtly, she shook her head, her expression pointed as she tilted her head to the opposite door of the sanctum, a clear message: *get out*.

But I was determined. She must have recognized the look on my face because she closed her eyes once more, tossing her head, her shoulders moving with a barely concealed huff, as she pretended she hadn't seen me.

I could almost hear her thoughts: *Don't come crying to me when the* Seta Kalliri *makes you clean out the chamber pots for a week.*

Chamber pots would be worth it. Grinning in triumph, I took another shuffled step to my right.

However, I'd forgotten my plugged ears.

As such, my sharp elbow rammed into one of the steel fire pillars, one of ten that stood around the sanctum to illuminate it.

Vok, I thought, cringing as the pillar rocked. Its motion seemed to slow as it toppled. I watched with a thundering heart, and a lump in my throat as it crashed to the marble floor, sending embers flying and skittering toward the priestesses. The chaotic echo continued to reverberate around the massive room, climbing higher and higher into the darkness above our heads.

Abruptly, the whispered prayers ceased.

Silence descended.

Then a loud shriek came, out of place and jarring.

One of the embers caught on the bottom hem of Trissa's dress. The delicate silk burst into flames, and I gasped, rushing forward before sliding to my knees across the marble. Sounds of alarm boomed against the halls. I slapped at the silk around her ankles, trying to put out the flames before they burned her, trying to stop the fire's path up her legs.

I felt the dizzying rush of familiar energy swarm toward me. I was shoved back, sliding away. I saw Trissa's dress warp and bunch. Then the flames grew smaller and smaller until they were no more. Not even tendrils of smoke rose from her destroyed dress.

Then that energy retreated as quickly as it had appeared.

No one moved.

My gaze met Trissa's.

"I'm so sorry, *sika,*" I breathed, my eyes widened in disbelief and shock. "I'm sorry, I never meant to—"

"*Kara,*" came the sharp bark.

I cringed and tensed. Briefly, my eyes darted to Avala's. Her expression was one of pity, but there was also knowing in her eyes. *I told you so*, those eyes said. Later, we'd likely laugh about this, but right then, I wanted to cry.

Then I rose from the floor, meeting the eyes of the *Seta Kalliri*.

Her black hair was gathered in a neat braid down her back, not a hair out of place. Her dress was a waterfall of flawless blue silk, skimming over the curves of her breasts and hips. She was striking in appearance. Golden eyes, dark skin, and she towered over the rest of the priestesses. And it was only through the strength and quickness of her power that Trissa's legs weren't burned.

Behind her, Kakkari's heartstone had stopped swirling.

"My library. *Now*," the *Seta Kalliri*, the High Priestess of Dakkar, ordered.

<hr>

Kalloma called it her library, but truthfully, it was her home within the temple. It was where she studied, where she met with the priestesses, where she took her meals, where she slept. I'd slept here too, once upon a time.

The room was large—though smaller than the sanctum—with a sea of books and stacks of ancient scrolls lining the walls. It was well lit. There were floor-to-ceiling windows that lined the far wall. The view they revealed...well, it was one that always took my breath away. The majesty of the North, as cruel as it was beautiful.

To the right of the room were the living quarters. Her bed was neatly made, not a wrinkle adorning the white furs. A goblet of water was perched on the small table where she took her meals. Only on occasion did she eat with the rest of the priestesses.

When the heavy door swung shut, sealing us inside, the

whispers of the priestesses ceased. I heard nothing in the sanctum. When I was a baby, even if I cried all night, *Kalloma* would tell me that none of the other priestesses were disturbed in their rest. This room was separate from all the rest. It was a world of its own.

"*Kalloma,*" I began, drawing in a deep breath. "I—"

She had the book in her hands when I turned to regard her.

My book.

Kalloma was standing near her library wall, next to the modest steel desk where she studied the ancient histories and painstakingly repaired crumbling scrolls.

Gently, she placed the book on her desk. Though it was my favorite, it was the only copy in existence—for now. I was working to transcribe it, was nearly done, and—

I knew the look in *Kalloma's* eyes. Against the marble floor, my tail twitched. I brought it up, my fingers playing with the small tufted end.

"I finished with my chores," I told her softly. "I finished. With the sweeping, the dusting. I hauled in the water from the well. I polished the statue of Drukkar. Beyla didn't want my help for the evening meal, so I just thought…"

"I regret ever having given you this book to study," she said, the mask falling away. She was the *Seta Kalliri*—the High Priestess. An esteemed, respected, powerful position. The highest position a priestess could ever hope to achieve on Dakkar.

And yet…she was my *kalloma*.

I'd called her that when I was a child. I'd mashed together *kalliri*—which meant *priestess*—and *lomma*—which meant *mother*.

Because that was what she'd been to me. A mother. The only one I'd ever known though she was not mine by blood.

My *kalloma* was different than the *Seta Kalliri*, but I knew that there was a fine line between the two. A very fine line that

I had navigated carefully my entire life. Or at least, I had tried to.

"I'll mend Trissa's dress," I told her. Because I *did* feel terrible about that. Trissa had worked hard on that dress. She'd been so excited when the material came in from *Dothik,* though I knew she'd tried to hide that excitement from the others. "I will work all of tonight to make her a new one."

"Kara," *Kalloma* sighed. "It is not just about the dress. You are not allowed in the sanctum in the evenings. You are not allowed to touch the ancient books without my permission. You are not a priestess."

And you never will be, was the unspoken message in her tone.

It wasn't intended as a barb, but like always, it stung like one.

"What do you want me to do?" I asked *Kalloma,* meeting her gaze. Her smooth skin glittered in the sunset's light. "Do you... do you want me to dust the *sa'kilan* and scrub dishes and wash bedding and polish floors for the *rest of my life?*"

Kalloma's expression contorted into one of pain, her brows drawing together, her lips downturning.

"Is that my only purpose here?" I asked, rehashing an old argument, one we'd had for *years.* "To serve?"

"You serve like we all do. Just in a different way, and just for now," *Kalloma* said, rounding her desk to stand in front of me. The last words were spoken as a whisper. Her hand came to my cheek. "The path of the *kalliri* is not for you, Kara."

I'd been restless my entire life. Achingly, clawingly so. That restless boredom ate at me. It buzzed under my skin. Knowing that I'd likely never see anything beyond the Orala Pass, knowing I'd likely die within these walls...it scared me like nothing else ever had.

And worst of all was that I was not allowed to make the vow. I was not allowed to be like *them,* to serve like *them.* Because *Kalloma* would not allow it.

I stepped away from her touch.

"Let me transcribe the oldest of the scrolls, then," I pleaded, my heart in my throat because I feared she would deny me again. For the hundredth time. "Let me *do something*."

"*Nik,*" she clipped.

"*Why?*" I demanded, letting my tail fall from my grip when I threw my arms wide. "None of the others like transcription. Avala says it bores her to tears. *I like it.* And at least the work will *mean something*."

That morning, I'd wiped down Drukkar's statue. The handsome god, glittering gold—the only male allowed to stay within the temple. I talked to him as I worked—foolish, silly conversations that no one would overhear. But that morning, as I wiped dust from the crease of his mouth, I was struck with a numbing realization. That tomorrow there would be more dust. And the next day. And the next day.

My work didn't *matter*. In another thirty years, would I be within the same walls, doing the same tasks—wiping dust from ancient statues because it was the only thing I was good for?

I'd been overcome with grief so potent I'd nearly fallen to my knees at Drukkar's feet.

Then, moments later, I stood, wiping the tears from my cheeks. I finished my task. I did my next task. And the next.

Then I'd set my sights on the book. Because at least in a book, I could live a different life entirely. How many nights had I lain in bed, pretending to be Lessa, Bekkar's wife? How many nights had I wondered how she *felt*—how it felt to be on the cusp of something *more*? Something *great*?

"You are not a priestess, Kara!" the *Seta Kalliri* repeated, and her voice rose, which it hardly ever did. "And you never will be!"

I bit my tongue, disappointment crashing into me. My mind flickered to the memory of the dust, especially when I saw pinpricks of it floating in the shafts of light coming in through the windows. I watched it swirl and sway as *Kalloma* bit out a sigh.

Gentling her tone, she said, "I do not know your path, Kara. I have never been able to see it. All I know is that—"

"I am not allowed to be a priestess because I'm only half-Dakkari," I finished for her bitterly. "Because my blood is mixed. Because my mother was human. And Kakkari will not allow that."

She sucked in a breath. "*Nik*, that is not—"

"*Lysi*," I breathed. *Yes.* "It is. And because of that, I will never be *enough*. Not for Kakkari. Not for the *kalliris*. Not even for *you*."

It had been made apparent to me my entire life.

Never maliciously so, never with cruel intent. But it was a truth that was always present.

Against the floor, *Kalloma's* tail whipped restlessly. I listened to the soft swish of it against the rug.

"*Nik*, Kara," she finally said, her voice pained. "You are *more* than enough, my dear. I rejected your vow not because you are half-Dakkari."

I froze. I heard something in her tone that I'd never heard before.

Fear.

Resignation.

"Then why?" I pleaded. "Tell me."

Her jaw set. She seemed to draw herself up, bit by bit, growing taller before my very eyes.

Finally, she said, "I rejected your vow because I know that you are meant to *leave*."

"*Neffar?*" I whispered. *What?*

Kalloma looked at me. For a brief sliver of time, she looked miserable. She looked as restless as I often felt. She looked heartbroken.

"And soon," she continued. "Soon. I have felt it."

Licking my lips, I asked, "Is this about the…is this about the things I see? Or is it about the *thesper* messages from the hordes that I know you hide away?"

Despite her misery, I saw her lips lift slightly.

"Perhaps I should have taken you to *Dothik* when you were a child after all," she said. "The *Dothikkar* would have likely made you his spy by now. How do you know about the messages?"

"I haven't read them," I assured her. "But I see the *thespers* flying in from my tower. Dozens of them in the past months. From all different directions, so I know they are not from *Dothik*."

I had studied maps endlessly. I knew Dakkar like the back of my hand, though I would never see it for myself.

Kalloma went to the shelves lining the wall. She pulled down an ancient tome, one with a sturdy spine. When she opened it, I saw leaflets of loose paper. She stared down at the messages and then, with great hesitation, as if someone else was controlling her hand, she plucked one out.

She replaced the book on the shelf. Her eyes were unseeing as she gazed down at the lone message in her hand. The paper was nearly transparent, and I could make out a strong script scrawled across it.

"I have prayed," she told me quietly. "I have sought answers within our shared knowledge, within these books and words, and I have found none. Except in you."

My brow furrowed. I took a small step toward the desk. What was she talking about?

"*Kalloma*, what's wrong?"

I had sensed something had been plaguing her these last months. We all had. Oftentimes, I'd find her staring at me, an expression of worry, of concentration, of loss on her features. But then she'd blink and the expression would vanish.

Avala had told me that a few weeks ago, *Kalloma* had nearly collapsed during their evening prayers. The others thought she'd had a vision from Kakkari, but I knew that her gifts did not work in that way. It was something else.

She held the message out to me.

Her expression was grim as I took it, my hand slow with hesitation. But the moment it was in my grip, my eyes ate at the words, hungry and curious.

What I read, however, made disbelief infuse my veins.

"What...what is this?" I asked.

My eyes caught on different words when I read it again.

Red fog.

Dead Mountain.

Setava Terun.

We seek your aid.

The seal at the bottom was that of the horde of Rath Kitala.

The *Vorakkar* of Rath Kitala.

The messages *were* from the hordes.

"You've hidden this from us?" I rasped, looking up to meet *Kalloma's* eyes. Shock. Fear. Disbelief. And *anger* came next. "But why?"

"Not from the others," she told me. "We have been in discussion for months."

I stumbled back, nearly stepping on my tail in the act. Betrayal cut deep.

"So you've hidden it just from me," I said softly, my fingers gripping the message tight. Avala and Trissa had never said a word, though I thought we shared everything.

Kalloma was staring at me, but her eyes were assessing. When she looked at me like this, I felt like I was being plucked apart. I wasn't her daughter. Instead, I was a specimen. A crumbling tome on her desk that needed to be studied.

"Have you seen him?" she demanded. "Have you seen him at all? In your dreams? Or in your visions?"

Him.

My lips parted.

"This...this isn't about him!" I protested. "I don't even know who he is! What this is about is that the hordes have been asking for your help and you have turned your back on them. You have turned your back on Dakkar!"

"That's where you're wrong, Kara," *Kalloma* said, shaking her head, a fleeting expression of despair crossing her beautiful face. "Something more is happening. Kakkari has set it in motion. It was set in motion long before now. Maybe even at your birth. Or...perhaps a year after it."

She turned to look out over the North Lands. The *orala sa'k-ilan*. The frozen haven. Time seemed to stop here. The ice was finally beginning to thaw after the frost season, however, and it would create passage to the temple. A road.

"This *is* about him," she told me. "About Dakkar. And this is about you too."

My breath ceased.

"Everything is connected," she murmured quietly. "And whatever this fog is that lays waste to the East...both of your fates are tied to it. I feel it. The heartstone showed it to me, though I did not ask it to."

Kalloma took a deep breath, her shoulders rising with the huff. Her eyes were unseeing, however, when they met mine.

"He is coming for you, Kara," she said. "And soon."

CHAPTER 2

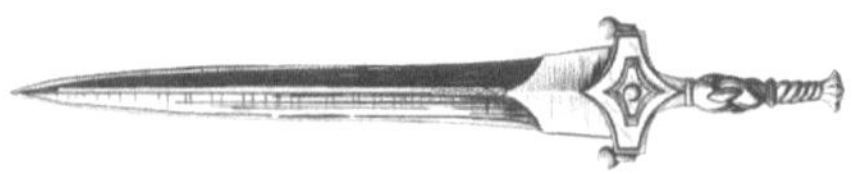

"*V*orakkar*," came Nassik's voice, his tone holding a hint of a smile.

When I turned to regard him, he gave me a nod of confirmation, though he was huffing from the exertion to reach me on the peak.

"The road is still icy, but we can travel it by *pyroki*."

"A day's ride to the temple," I mused aloud, returning my gaze to the Orala Pass. "Though perhaps longer if we encounter any blockages."

"*Lysi,*" Nassik said, coming to stand at my side, his hands sliding to his hips as he caught his breath.

From up on the mountain's ledge, we had a clear view of the North Lands. The *orala sa'kilan* and beyond. The only thing we couldn't see was the priestesses' ancient temple.

"Do you think it's true?" Nassik asked quietly. His eyes were pinned on the last section of the pass we could see.

"Do I think what is true?" I asked, turning to him with a grin though I felt a curl of rage in my chest. "Do I think the priestesses knowingly ignored our messages, our calls for aid? Do I think the priestesses are in the pocket of the *Dothikkar*, that they only serve him and not *all* of Dakkar? Do I think that they are cowards for hiding away from the world in their sacred, *precious* temple while the hordes try to clean up their goddess's mess?"

Nassik blinked, lazy and slow. He rocked forward on his heels as he pondered my words. He'd done that since we were children.

"You know," he started quietly, turning to me with an equally wide grin. "I don't think I'll ever get used to calling you *Vorakkar*."

A laugh rose from my throat.

"I don't think I'll ever get used to calling you *Pujerak*, you surly bastard," I returned, crossing my arms over my chest as my eyes returned to the ice-covered lands. *Pujerak.* My second-in-command of the horde. The horde of Rath Serok. "And yet here we are. Freezing our *deva* off in the North Lands."

"You should have left me in *Dothik*," Nassik said, a wistful tone in his voice. "I even miss the smell of those piss-covered roads. But at least it was warm."

"*Nik.* You miss the smell of Lakkri," I informed him. "Of the oils she likes to use. In your mind's eye, you see her sliding them over her skin when the weather turns cold. You smell them mingling in your furs. And you can taste them on your tongue. *That* is what you miss."

"And how the *vok* do you know about those oils?" he grumbled.

I laughed, deep and long. Clapping a hand on his shoulder, I regarded the Orala Pass as I said, "Because Lakkri always had a voracious appetite. One no single male could satisfy. Well...at least until me. You ever wonder why she never returned to your furs after she came to mine?"

"*Vok* off," Nassik scoffed.

He knew I said the words in jest.

Well, partly in jest. Back in *Dothik*, back in the network we ran, I didn't know a single male who *hadn't* been between

Lakkri's thighs. The female was beautiful, charming, and she liked sex. I liked that about her.

"Stay behind with the horde," I told him, my voice hardening. "Make sure they are well protected."

Nassik bit at the inside of his cheek. If he was surprised by how fast I changed subjects, he didn't show it. Nassik knew me better than anyone. He was used to it.

"I'll be back within three days if the pass isn't blocked."

"And if they deny you entry to the temple? If they refuse to speak with you?" Nassik asked. "What then?"

Licking my bottom lip, I told him, "Do you not know me at all, *Pujerak*?" I smiled. "It's not like I'm going to *ask*."

"They are still priestesses of Kakkari. And this isn't *Dothik*, Serok," he murmured. Using my family name—my *mother's* name—though he knew my given one. "Are you not worried that the goddess will think it a strike against her?"

"I will leave Kakkari to you, Nassik," I told him, my voice gruff. With a wry smile I didn't feel, I added, "The goddess has long scorned me. So pray for me if you wish to, my brother. If the priestesses are as vicious as the rumors...I think I might even need it."

Chapter 3

After I left *Kalloma's* library, my appetite had gone. Instead of joining the others for the evening meal, I trudged up to my tower, taking the circular set of stairs to the very top of the west wing of the temple.

Kalloma never understood why I'd chosen this place as my little home. There were more comfortable rooms with the *kalliris*. Warmer rooms. Larger rooms. Ones I didn't have to climb to reach.

I told her that the stairs kept my legs strong. I told her that my tower room might be small but it had the best view of the North Lands, even better than her own. I told her that I kept it warm with my fire basin, that I enjoyed the crackling sounds of the fire fuel and the light it gave me to read in the evenings.

I'd feathered my little nest with comforts. White *wrissan* furs I kept clean and plush. Colorful cushions I'd sewed myself. Stone pots lined the ledge of one large window. Inside them were blue ice plants I'd dug up from the forest. They'd been withering in the prolonged cold temperatures this year, so I tended to them myself, setting them outside the sill when they needed the icy air.

A stack of books was next to my bed. Old books that the

kalliris—or *Kalloma*—didn't seem to miss. Books that were of no great importance to Dakkar's history, and so I'd been allowed to keep them.

Kalloma had given me Bekkar's book when I'd left her library. She'd handed it to me wordlessly, staring at me with a pained expression I could still *envision*, as if she knew I needed the distraction of it to comfort me when she could not.

Sighing loudly, I sat down on the edge of my bed, gingerly placing Bekkar's hefty tome next to me. I could inscribe more pages tonight. That should've excited me because I was *so* close to having a copy all my own. I could even *finish* tonight. So why couldn't I focus?

He is coming for you, Kara. And soon.

My heart had frozen with the words.

I didn't know what to think. The fog. The lies. The hordes. *Him.*

What did it all mean?

I was so deep in my thoughts I didn't hear the shuffling from the landing outside my door.

"Kara?" came a familiar voice before the door creaked open on old hinges. Avala stepped inside, frowning when she saw me sitting on my bed. "You weren't at the meal, so I was worried. And why is it so dark in here?"

I stood and went to my fire basin. After piling it with tufts of fire fuel, I watched a flame catch easily. The light was gentle at first, but then the shadows began to disappear across my wall.

"What's wrong?" Avala asked, closing the door behind her. "Is it about what happened in the sanctum? Did the *Seta Kalliri* say anything?"

"She said plenty," I told her, still feeling a prick of disappointment and hurt, especially knowing Avala hadn't told me about the *thesper* messages. "Is Trissa mad at me?"

Avala made a sound in her throat. "She will move past it.

She won't outright say she's mad. But you know that face she makes? That was how her face was at the evening meal."

"If you see her tonight when you meet, tell her I'll mend her dress, all right?" I said.

"What's wrong?" Avala asked again. "Your voice is strange. What did the *Seta Kalliri* say to you?"

Maybe I should go down to the hot baths tonight, I mused silently. The others would be meeting. I would have the entirety of the room to myself. And I could relax and...*process.*

"Kara."

I turned from the wall, biting my lip to keep from crying. My throat already felt tight, my nostrils stinging. "Why didn't you tell me about the *thesper* messages from the hordes?"

Avala blinked. She reared back just a tiny bit, but then I watched as realization spread over her expression. And shame with it.

"Because the *Seta Kalliri* asked me not to."

"All our lives," I began, "we have never lied to each other. We have no secrets. So why this one?"

Belatedly, I realized that that wasn't true. *I* had kept something from Avala, hadn't I? Something only *Kalloma* and I knew.

"You know I cannot go against the *Seta Kalliri*, Kara," Avala started. "You *know* that."

"Tell me about the fog," I said. "*Hanniva.*"

Please.

When Avala hesitated, I added, "She showed me a message from the horde of Rath Kitala. The East Lands have been covered in fog for *months,* and you all knew about it. Yet none of you traveled to see it. None of you responded to the hordes. None of you went to *Dothik* to seek guidance from the *Dothikkar.* Or the *Laseta Kalliri.* I'm trying to understand *why.* I'm trying to understand *what* is going on!"

"We don't know," she said quietly. "We don't know *what* it is. The *Seta Kalliri* most of all. Every waking moment she is not in prayer or with you, she has been in the archives. And in her own library, searching for answers. Many of us have been."

"And I could've helped," I said, going to her. Taking her hands in mine, I said, "I could've been helping you search."

"All I know is that she wanted you to be kept away from it," Avala said quietly. "And for good reason, Kara. The reports from the hordes say it is a destructive force. They say it came from the Dead Mountain. It's driven our beasts from the East Lands. No one has seen a Ghertun for months. And worst of all, if anyone breathes it in, it steals their strength. In some cases, if they do not escape it in time, it takes their lives too."

There was something pressing into my mind, but every time I tried to let that thought take shape, it eluded me.

"They are dying?" I whispered, my eyes widening. A flash of anger wound in my belly. "All the more reason to leave the temple! To go investigate what's really happening. Why did she not go to the hordes when they asked for help?"

"You cannot expect the *Seta Kalliri* to go into the wildlands without protection, can you?" Avala responded. "When we know *nothing* about this fog? Or why it's appeared? They look to us for answers, and we are *trying* to find them! Don't be too hasty to act, Kara. That is not the way of the *kalliri*."

"I'm not a *kalliri*," I responded, narrowing my gaze. My tail flicked against the rug lining the cold stone floor. "Maybe that is why I cannot understand."

Avala bit her lip. "Kara, that's not what I meant. And you know it."

Releasing her hands, I took a step away. Arguing with Avala, taking out my hurt and frustration on her, would lead me nowhere. It would only make me feel worse.

"I need to think," I whispered, my brow furrowing. I walked away from Avala, going to the window. Though it was dark, the moon was rising, twinkling off the blue ice that still covered some of the nearby mountains.

"I'm sorry, Kara," Avala said. "I never wanted to keep it from you. But I felt I had no choice."

"I know," I said quietly. She was a *kalliri*—a priestess of Kakkari. And the High Priestess had specifically given her an order, one she could not break. "I understand."

"Do you forgive me for it?" she asked quietly, the solemn tone in her voice making my shoulders sag.

"Of course I do."

"I have to get down to the sanctum," she said. I heard an apology in the words. "But if you want to talk more later, I can—"

"*Nik*," I said, turning back to her. "You go. I think I'll go down to the baths and then get some sleep."

I'd do no such thing. I'd sneak down to the archives during the meeting. I'd have the grand room to myself for an hour at least.

Avala nodded.

I said, "Tell Trissa I'm sorry. Tell her I'll come get her dress in the morning."

"I will," my friend said. Then she turned to the door. Before she left, however, she asked, "Are you sure you're all right, Kara?"

I forced a small smile. "Of course. I just need some sleep. It's been a long day."

I had no luck in the archives. I spent nearly the entire night with books and words and stories and accounts. It should've been wonderful. Instead, my eyes blurred and stung from the dim lighting. And I was constantly on edge, listening for footsteps since I was not allowed to be in the archives. Not that it had ever stopped me before.

No one came, however, but when I briefly fell asleep in the

middle of reading a passage about an ancient Dakkari village—in a time before the hordes, even—I decided I couldn't risk being found here in the morning.

I replaced every book carefully and slipped back to my tower just as dawn peeked over the mountains of the Orala Pass.

When I slid into my bed and pulled the furs over my face to keep out the dawn light, my mind was stuck on the fog. A destructive force, Avala had said. A disease in the air. Something that poisoned the earth, driving beasts from their homes and keeping the hordes away.

It has happened before, I thought distantly. But I was already asleep.

The thought formed fully in my dreams—the thought that had eluded me all evening. Except that thought mingled with *him.*

In my dream, I saw him rising from the earth. I'd always thought of him like Drukkar, but Drukkar was of the sea. *He* was a god of the earth. I watched as soil and dirt fell away from his body but he emerged perfectly clean. A body that was strong, taut, beautiful, and crafted by the goddess's own hand.

He was as he always was.

Achingly handsome. Infinitely terrifying.

Expansive bronzed flesh met me in the dream, though his skin was not marked with words. He wore scars and plenty of them as he emerged from the earth. Strange eyes. Gold that mingled with red. A knowing smirk curved over full lips, but I had seen that face contorted into several different expressions throughout my life.

Only this time, something was different.

Something was *changed.*

And I realized what it was when I saw gold cuffs flash on his wrists.

Vorakkar cuffs.

The soil that fell from him was diseased. Red soil. It was infected with a plague. *Riddled* with it. Something that had also killed. Something that had *taken* so much—

"Kara," came the voice.

I jolted awake, turning my head to regard the door of my room, blinking quickly.

Kalloma was standing there. I stared at her as my heart thundered in my chest. There was a headache blooming, my forehead was slick with sweat, and my eyes still felt raw from last night. My throat was bone dry.

"The sun is setting," *Kalloma* said, worry in her tone. "Are you unwell?"

"He's a horde king," I croaked, pushing up from the bed, though the room swayed. The words came out in a rush. I needed to get them out before I forgot them. "He's a horde king. And it's happened before—the fog. Though it was not a fog. It was a plague of the earth. *Soil.* The soil was sick. Just as the air is now."

"Kara," *Kalloma* said, coming quickly to the bed, reaching out to cup my cheek. She was looking at me like a specimen again. "Are you certain?"

"*Lysi,*" I breathed, turning to her groggily with aching eyes. "I know how we can stop it."

CHAPTER 4

"Your theory is weak at best, Kara," came the *Niva Kalliri's* voice. The Second Priestess. "There is no evidence that the heartstones actually *worked* in that instance."

Even now, I couldn't shake off the remnants of the dream. *Kalloma* had always told me it was powerful magic. Magic that crossed over from sleep into reality. But I still felt like I was dreaming. My body felt light. Yet there was a heaviness in my head. A strange contrast.

"They did," I argued, standing before the circle of the *kalliris*, where *Kalloma* had brought me once I'd dressed. "The plague was gone. The soil was restored. Life returned. The evidence is there in the book—you just have to see what *isn't* written in ink."

There was murmuring among the priestesses of the temple. We were in the sanctum. All of the priestesses had gathered here. The book in question—the book I remembered—was spread open on a marble stand, not far from the heartstone.

"There is not much even written," the *Niva Kalliri* shot back. "What's a miracle is that you even remember you read it. It was an old time. We do not know what happened. The records of it are sparse, and much of the original account is lost."

"I saw it," I rasped. The voices hushed around the sanctum. I caught sight of Avala, lingering on the edge of my vision. "I saw the soil in my dream. I saw the disease."

"In a *dream*, Kara," another priestess said, emphasizing the word. "Not when you were awake. Besides, your gift is unpredictable at best. You know that."

The words stung. I looked to *Kalloma*, who presided over the circle of priestesses. She was listening, assessing. She had yet to say anything.

I had no voice here. I had no voice among them, no reasonable amount of authority or knowledge. All I had was the *Seta Kalliri's* trust. And now, judging by the look on her face, I wondered if I had even that.

But I would not give up.

"The record says that the *Rivalla Lo'Kilan* were used," I said quietly. I looked to Jrikanna, one of the priestesses in the half circle. An expert in old languages. "What do you think of it?"

"Those words can mean many things," she said after a moment of hesitation. "It could be in reference to the sacred wells in the West. Or it could refer to the high priestesses of old."

"Or it could mean the heartstones," I finished for her, furrowing my brows. "*Rivalla* refers to *the Five*—the five heartstones of Kakkari—does it not?"

She shuffled on her feet. "It could, *lysi*."

I looked back to the high priestesses. Five of them in total, which included my *kalloma*.

"Or it could mean the five priestesses of old figured out a way to rebalance the earth," came the *Niva Kalliri's* hardened voice. "The knowledge is in the archives. I am sure of it. We just need more time to uncover it. But taking the five heartstones and using *all* of them at once is *not* the answer. It's dangerous, impulsive, and it might fuel whatever created this fog instead of eradicating it. We simply cannot take that chance."

A breath whooshed from my lungs. I lifted the end of my tail and brushed through the tuft of hair with my fingers. I didn't know how to explain to them that I was *certain*. This was a certain thing. I felt it in my dream.

But to *act*, there would need to be a majority ruling among the *kalliris*.

It was abundantly clear to me that no one was convinced.

"Then let me go."

My words surprised even me. I blinked, especially when I sensed *Kalloma* freeze.

"*Neffar?*" the *Niva Kalliri* questioned, sniffing. "Go where?"

Determination rose in me, and I filled my lungs with it. "Maybe the answers aren't in the archives. Maybe they are with the Dakkari instead."

"Kara," *Kalloma's* voice cut in, imposing and strong. "Enough."

"The land," I said, pushing my shoulders back. "The land where the disease spread in the records. There is an outpost there now, is there not? And guess what? That outpost has one of Kakkari's heartstones. It is one of two outposts whose *Sorakkar* were entrusted with keeping a heartstone safe."

Sorakkar used to be *Vorakkar*. The most successful of them, who decided to settle in the wildlands, creating small cities and villages of their own, once their time as horde kings had come to an end.

"I told you, we are not using the heartstones, Kara," the *Niva Kalliri* said, a small growl in her tone.

"Let me go," I said again, not looking at the Second Priestess but instead looking at my mother. At *Kalloma*. "Let me go to that *saruk*, that outpost. None of you want to take the risk. That's understandable. But I am not a *kalliri*," I said softly, my throat tightening with the words. "So there is no risk for me in leaving. I will speak to the *Sorakkar* there. I will speak with the Dakkari that live on that land. Memory might fade, lives may end, but stories do not die. If the heartstones were used to restore the land, then the people of that *saruk* will know. And if they tell me that it *was* the five heartstones, I will bring theirs back to you. I will bring it home. To here. To the *orala sa'kilan*. Then you can decide."

Kalloma's gaze was thunderous. She was angry with me, for daring to speak this way among the priestesses. But my heart was racing in my chest. My hands were shaking.

She didn't think the path of the *kalliri* was for me?

Well then, maybe *this* was.

"Do you forget, Kara?" came the *Niva Kalliri's* voice. "Do you forget the vow we made to your blood mother? The vow we made to her that no Dakkari would know of your existence? That no harm would come to you because of it? We have taken many risks to keep you safe. You forget the hatred of the *Dothikkar*. The hatred of the hordes when it comes to the *vekkiri*."

The *vekkiri*. The humans.

And yet *Kalloma* had told me that I was meant to *leave* this place. But perhaps she hadn't told the Second Priestess that.

"I can pass as a Dakkari female," I said, throwing my shoulders back.

Not entirely true. My eyes were human, though their color was a Dakkari gold. My tail was slimmer than a Dakkari female's. I was shorter. I possessed less physical strength. I had five human fingers instead of the Dakkari six. Though my skin was the warm, bronzed color of a Dakkari's, my face held the small brittle bones of a human's...or so I'd been told.

I'd never *seen* a human before, after all.

My home had always been the temple. It was all I'd known. And though I had spied hordesmen from my tower whenever they neared the temple to drop off supplies for us—though those visits had ceased this last year—I'd never seen a male up close. Never spoken to one...except the statue of Drukkar.

And the male in my visions. I'd seen him up close, hadn't I? So close I could count his scars and know that his eyes were a mixture of gold and red, swirling together like a small storm.

Yet was he even *real?*

"Let me go," I said softly again to *Kalloma*. She stepped forward into the circle of the priestesses, breaking the line briefly. "I want to help."

I want to...be enough, I pleaded quietly.

Kalloma's expression was a brittle thing, and I hated that I put that expression on her face. She was still afraid for me. Whatever she thought was coming...it *terrified* her. It was terror that she could not show the others because it would weaken her.

"*Seta Kalliri!*" came the echoing voice, booming down the hallways. "*Seta Kalliri!*"

Gasps broke out among the priestesses, and *Kalloma's* expression shuttered. Closing off, going cold, right before my very eyes as she drew her shoulders back.

"*Seta Kalliri!*"

It was Beyla. Her voice was panicked. And if she dared to shout *Kalloma's* title within the closed sanctum, it must be an emergency. A dire one.

The female who cooked our meals, who kept the temple in tidy order, who cared for us all nearly slipped as she sprinted into the sanctum.

She was wearing her heavy fur cloak, which was still flaked with ice clinging to the shoulders and the hem. There was a basket in her arm, though I saw it was empty. Whatever had been inside it had likely fallen out in her haste.

Beyla was huffing, her chest heaving as she dragged in lungfuls of air. But the warmth of the sanctum made her cough.

"What is it?" *Kalloma* asked, going to Beyla immediately, reaching out a hand to steady the female. "What's happened?"

"A male," Beyla gasped out.

I saw *Kalloma's* hand tighten on Beyla's arm. "A male? Where?"

"I—I was out gathering, and I heard a *pyroki* riding fast. He's coming straight toward the temple," Beyla finally managed to say. "I took the tunnels to get back—to try to warn you."

Kalloma met my gaze. Her lips pressed as I took a step forward.

Beyla continued, "But he's already at our gates, *Seta Kalliri*. He's *here*."

CHAPTER 5

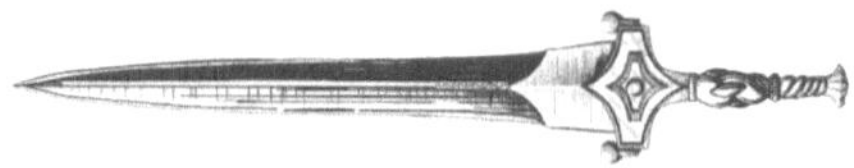

The road to the temple was long. And the path leading to it was nondescript. I would have missed it entirely had I not spied a rocky, ice-covered pillar that struck me as out of place. When I drew closer, I saw words carved into the stone beneath the ice: *Lik Kakkari srimea tei kirtja.*

May Kakkari watch over you.

The pillar itself was small. It blended in with the dark mountain behind it. Had the sun already set, I would not have noticed it. I would have continued traveling down the road of the Orala Pass, but the base of my tail prickled and I somehow knew that *this* was what I sought. My instincts had never led me astray before.

The path next to the pillar was overgrown with ice plants, blue and winding and wild. After a brief moment of deliberation, I steered Syok, my *pyroki,* toward it, his clawed hooves crunching over the rigid plants.

We traveled slowly but only for a brief time. Without realizing it, my hand had strayed to the hilt of my sword as my eyes scanned every shadowed place of the new road.

When we rounded a bend in the path, the priestesses' temple revealed itself.

Even Syok paused as he regarded it.

A breath whooshed out from my lungs and I laughed to myself, the sound reverberating down the small road, which was bracketed by tall mountains on both sides.

I had always envisioned the priestesses' temple to be a modest place. Though I knew they would not live off the land in the way of the hordes, I had not expected *this*.

The temple looked even more grand than that of the *Dothikkar's* palace in *Dothik*. Though it was not gilded in nearly as much gold, I had to crane my neck back to see it in its entirety.

It was constructed from marble, not stone. Unlike the Ghertun's kingdom, the Dead Mountain, the temple was not built from a mountain, and yet it was as tall and wide as one. White and gleaming, it stood proud. The very top was still shimmering gold from the setting sun, but the lower level was shrouded in darkness, cast in shadow from the adjacent mountain. A tall tower—perhaps a watch post—jutted up from the western wing. Another from the eastern side.

It was a fortress. There were shimmering panes of windows on the upper floors. But the lower half of the temple had walls of marble. No weaknesses. No point of entry. A gate stood tall before the temple, thick and impenetrable, and I brought Syok to a halt in front of it.

I wasn't foolish enough to believe that the *kalliris* did not already know I was here. I wondered if they'd open the gates or if they would try to turn me away, just as they had the messages of the hordes.

Scaling the gate would be easy enough. I tracked my gaze along the adjacent mountain and thought I could climb it with little difficulty. But first, I'd try to play nice. Nassik's voice was still heavy in my mind.

They are still priestesses of Kakkari. And this isn't Dothik, Serok.

"I am the *Vorakkar* of Rath Serok," I bellowed out, my voice carrying loudly, lifting over the gate and smashing into the front facade of the temple. "I ask for entry and to speak with the *Seta Kalliri*. As is your duty to Dakkar!"

Underneath me, Syok stomped into the ground. It was still damn cold in the North Lands, though the warm season was upon us. In front of me, my breath fogged silver.

I waited. And waited.

Every moment that passed steeled something in my chest. Were the rumors true? Did the priestesses—and the *Seta Kalliri* —only answer to the calls of the *Dothikkar*? Had they turned their backs on the hordes, just like our king? Our king, who would rather drown himself in wine than deal with the growing threat in the East, the restlessness in his own city, and the threat of the hordes' rising power?

My lips twisted bitterly. And to think I shared his blood. His greedy, murderous, cowardly blood.

"So be it," I growled out, dismounting from Syok, my feet landing with a crunch on the ice-covered ground. "*Okkai,*" I ordered my *pyroki*. *Stay.*

Making sure my sword was in place at my hip, I moved toward the mountain that the wall of the gate jutted from. The gate made a single line across the road. In the back of my mind, I thought that it was a terrible place for a temple, especially if war ever came to the priestesses' door. It was a dead end. There was no where they could run. Armies could batter down the gate. They could flood in like a river.

Just as I began scaling the mountain—the ice nearly freezing my hand off in the process—I heard a *boom.*

Gritting my jaw, I jumped off the mountain wall to stand back. I heard a groaning echo all around me as the gate began to peel back. The entrance slid open. The road was cleared before us, right to the front door of the temple.

There was no one in sight.

"*Jiria,*" I murmured to Syok, taking him by the reins and

leading him on foot through the gate. There was a courtyard beyond, the ground laid with stones, much like the roads of *Dothik*. Syok's hooves made a clattering sound as he treaded over them.

Again, the base of my tail prickled. I was being watched.

When I turned my attention to the heavy, golden door of the temple, I heard a series of locks unlatching and turning from within. Then I watched as it creaked open, leading to yawning darkness.

A tall figure appeared, dressed in the robes of a priestess with a white fur cloak slung over her shoulders to keep the chill away.

The female was much older than me, though time had done nothing to diminish her beauty. Her expression was stern, the look in her eyes cold and calculating. Only priestesses—and the *Dothikkar*—were allowed to meet the eyes of a *Vorakkar* without his permission. And her golden eyes were shooting daggers into my very soul.

She came to a stop at the threshold of the grand door. A large staircase that led up to the temple entrance lay before me. Forty or more tall steps that would likely cause Nassik to tumble over in exhaustion once he reached their peak.

I began to ascend them after patting Syok, never taking my eyes off the priestess.

"I know my duty to Dakkar," came her voice when I was halfway up the steps. "And you know yours, *Vorakkar* of Rath Serok."

At my side, my fists clenched.

"That is why I am here," I growled out, taking the steps more quickly. "To remind you of yours. Because you seem to have forgotten it, *Seta Kalliri*."

The words made her blink. "You cannot speak to me in this manner, *Vorakkar*. Not here."

I grinned. "My apologies. I seem to have missed the lesson

on how to speak with a cowardly priestess *before* I took to the Trials."

That made her gasp. Or perhaps it was a gasp from behind her. Were the other *kalliris* within too?

"Who are you?" the *Seta Kalliri* demanded, narrowing her gaze on me when I finally made it to the top of the steps. Her eyes strayed to my sword, to the manner of my clothes. "You don't look like a horde king. You look like a mercenary."

"Must've missed that lesson too," I said, quirking a brow. "How to look like a *Vorakkar*. How illuminating it must've been."

I was dressed in the manner I'd always known. Thick, worn boots, the soles nearly flat from stomping around *Dothik's* endless roads. Black hide trews. A black tunic that was stretched wide over my chest, though it was soft enough to not irritate the scars on my back that *still* seemed to itch.

My sword was at my hip. A line of daggers on my other. My hair was loose down my back, though it was not adorned with the beads and golden cuffs that *Vorakkar* usually wore.

I flashed my cuffs at her. The wide, hot gold that spanned my wrists. The claiming chains that the *Dothikkar* had placed on me once I completed the Trials, moments before I whispered into his ear that I was the son of Serok. Seeing the blood drain from his face was satisfying enough that I smiled whenever I looked at the cuffs.

"Would you like me to take off my tunic as well?" I asked, my hand lazily resting on the hilt of my sword. "Would you like to see my scars from the *Dothikkar* himself?"

That test of the Trials had been particularly grueling. I hadn't minded the pain. It was the knowledge that *he* was marking me that ate at my soul.

The *Seta Kalliri*, for that was who I assumed she was, tilted her chin up. "What do you seek, *Vorakkar*?"

Good. The last thing I wanted was to undress in this blistering cold. My cock nearly shriveled at the thought.

"Aren't you going to invite me inside?" I asked, giving her a smile. "I've been traveling through the night to reach you."

"You know that no male is allowed to stay within the temple of Kakkari."

"Oh, I'm not staying," I assured her. My voice hardened to steel, "But we will speak. I will not leave until we do."

The *Seta Kalliri* peered at me closely, her jaw set tight. If she clenched it even more, I wondered if the small bones would snap.

She didn't voice her answer, but she stepped back from the door, turning to the side to let me pass.

When I stepped inside the temple, it was like passing into another world. The cold dropped away. Warmth rushed toward my skin, making my flesh tingle. Behind me, the heavy door boomed closed, and then I heard nothing at all.

We were not alone. As I suspected, a line of priestesses stood tall in the middle of the atrium. Four of the *kalliris* stood apart from the others, and I knew that they were a part of the Five. The head priestesses, though the *Seta Kalliri*—and the *Laseta Kalliri* in *Dothik*—reigned over them all.

Above me, I could see to the very top of the temple. A cathedral ceiling. The back walls leading up to it were riddled with windows, allowing the sunset's golden light to flood in, and through them, I could see the wide expanse of the North Lands.

A beautiful, gilded place.

A beautiful, gilded *cage*.

For the priestesses of the North, when they took the vow of Kakkari, were kept away. Apart. It seemed like a lonely, excruciating existence to me. They could never have a family, children of their own. Sex was forbidden. To touch a priestess of Kakkari was to spit on the goddess herself.

Though the *orala sa'kilan*—the name of this temple—was considered the most sacred, as this was where the *Seta Kalliri* and her chosen priestesses resided, it was also the most isolated.

I was used to being around people all the time. Even before I was *Vorakkar*. There were very few moments I was *alone*. Yet here, the endless stretch of silence made my skin itch and my tail flick across the smooth marble floor.

Then came sound.

My head snapped to the right, to a hallway where I heard a swishing of cloth.

Another figure appeared, and I could *feel* the ripple of unease go through the *kalliris*.

Interesting, I thought, narrowing my gaze on the cloaked figure. There was a hood pulled up around her face. A tail peeked out from underneath the heavy cloak. It shielded her body, though she looked short for a Dakkari female. A child?

Nik, that couldn't be right. Priestesses would be cast out from the temple if they lay with a male.

The cloaked figure came to a stop near a column of the atrium. A strange sensation trailed up my spine, like a lover's caress, and it made the scars on my back throb.

Who is she? I wondered. *And why does she shield herself?*

When I turned to regard the *Seta Kalliri,* she was glaring at the figure, her expression thunderous. When she saw me watching, however, a mask slid into place—a mask of cold indifference and of dislike as she peered at me.

"Speak, *Vorakkar* of Rath Serok," the *Seta Kalliri* commanded me. "The sooner you speak, the sooner you leave."

I grinned, slow and languid.

I heard a small intake of air whistle from the cloaked figure.

"Thank you for the warmest of welcomes, *Seta Kalliri.*"

Chapter 6

It was him.

It was him.

In the flesh.

Warm and strong and arrogant and handsome and *real*.

Underneath my cloak, my heart was racing. So loud and fast that I wondered if all the Dakkari in the atrium could hear it. My skin buzzed to life. Heat spread low in my belly, an awareness that shocked me.

When the male—the *Vorakkar* of Rath Serok, as *Kalloma* had addressed him—peered toward me again, I ducked my head so the darkness of my hood would shroud me further. Yet my eyes never left him. They wouldn't dare.

They *feasted* on him, as if starved.

I'd never seen a male before.

Not up close. Not *this* close.

All my life, I'd been kept away from any Dakkari males who entered the temple, usually *darukkars* from hordes bringing us supplies—meat, furs, and other comforts—from the wildlands or from *Dothik*.

From my tower, males had only been tiny little specks on the road.

But this male...this *horde king*...

I knew his face. I knew his body. I knew his voice, even.

That voice was as familiar to me as if I'd heard it all my life —and yet I hadn't. Not once.

His hair was a waterfall of ink down his back, though no adornments threaded through the silky strands. Strong shoulders, almost as wide as the door of the atrium, led to thick, muscled arms. Underneath the black fur pelt, I spied the glint of *Vorakkar* cuffs, seamless and unmarred.

His tunic molded to his chest, intriguing divots and valleys of muscle catching my gaze. Strong, sculpted thighs were encased in tight trews. The glint of a dagger flashed in the light when he walked forward, shrugging off his fur pelt before slinging it over a marble banister that led to the second level of the temple.

Kalloma's lips turned down when they narrowed on his furs, but she said nothing. Though she was the High Priestess of Kakkari, she had to yield to a *Vorakkar*. Only the horde kings and the *Dothikkar* himself held more power than *Kalloma* did.

Judging by the knowing expression on his face, the *Vorakkar* of Rath Serok knew that as well.

It was a face I could sketch from memory alone. Gold and red swirled together in his eyes, a color unlike any I'd ever seen before. The tip of his right ear was pointed, like all Dakkari's, but the tip of his left ear was cut off. Flat and blunt, like a blade had sliced cleanly through it.

He was achingly, unfairly handsome, I thought. He had the regal look of Drukkar, and his high cheekbones looked as solid as the golden statue's. His face was unmarked by scars—except for a single line down his bottom lip. It made him appear like he was always smirking, a haughty, arrogant, knowing expression on his face.

I want to look at him forever, I thought, an ache building in my chest at the realization.

If I showed myself to him, would he recognize me too?

All too soon, he would leave. With a sinking feeling in my chest, I knew that with certainty. Just as I knew I wanted to speak with him. I wanted to *understand* why I'd seen him in the cracks and folds of my gift.

And I wanted to tell him about the heartstones. The *Vorakkar* had a right to know all possibilities in battling the fog. It was not for the priestesses to keep to themselves. Because by the time they *were* as certain as I was, it might be too late.

Kalloma would never allow me to get close to him, however. Not willingly, despite what she'd told me in her library the evening prior.

"Speak, *Vorakkar*," *Kalloma* ordered again, though her tone was infinitely patient. Though I knew she must be fuming inside. "Soon we will need to gather in the sanctum for the evening prayers."

The horde king of Rath Serok's eyes sharpened like a blade. Gone was the charming, though taunting, smile.

"Fifteen," he murmured, his boots thudding heavily over the marble floor as he walked farther into the atrium.

Craning his neck back, he stood in the very center and looked up toward the ceiling. A statue of Kakkari—one of my favorites because she was standing in the sea, in Drukkar's Sea, with waves lapping up her legs—was to his right. When he was finished inspecting the soaring archways, his gaze came speculatively to the statue of the goddess.

He ran his hand over Kakkari's hip, making the line of *kalliris* stiffen as he circled it. There was a slow, predatory grace to his movements, like he was calculating his every step.

And I couldn't take my eyes off him. Not for a single moment. When my vision began to sway, I realized I'd been holding my breath, and I let it out in a *whoosh*, which drew his attention to me again.

Those eyes were so intense and rapt that for a moment, I felt bared before him. Stripped of my cloak and offered up to his eyes. Only for him.

For a moment, I thought he could *see* me.

Then his gaze snapped back to *Kalloma,* and I nearly snagged against the column.

"Am I supposed to know what that means?" the *Seta Kalliri* asked.

"You should, considering that's how many *thespers* the hordes have sent to you in the last few seasons."

That many? I thought, my lips parting in disbelief.

"And would you like to tell me how many you answered?" he asked, lifting his hand from Kakkari to regard the High Priestess. "Would you like to explain to me *why* the *Seta Kalliri* —the High Priestess of the *orala sa'kilan*—could not be bothered to scribble out a few words on a *single* scrap of parchment in all that time? Or would you like to lie and say you never received a single message?"

"The messages were received," *Kalloma* said, her voice hardening. "But I do not appreciate your tone, especially in this temple, in front of my *kalliris.*"

"And we did not appreciate being *left in the dark* as the fog spread over the planet," the *Vorakkar* growled out, making me jump. "You get the *privilege* of being locked away in your sacred temple. You get food delivered to you from the hordes, from *Dothik.* Furs. Trinkets. Fuel. All to make your lives comfortable. All to make this grand place even grander. But do you know what the hordes have battled these last months? The game has left the East Lands, pushing more dangerous beasts into territories they have never before occupied. Outposts have been attacked by *ungira,* by *polkunu.* Lives have been lost. The Dead Mountain is destroyed, an entire race of Ghertun with it. The *Setava Terun* is dead and a coven of *sarkias* with her, who all sacrificed humans and Dakkari alike to try to gain power over the land. All the while, the fog grows. With every passing day. It kills anything in its path, and it is *merciless.*"

The silence was heavy in the atrium. The *Vorakkar* came to a stop in front of *Kalloma*. He towered over her, and she was forced to tilt her head back to meet his eyes.

"You come to blame me for it?" she asked quietly.

"I come to ask *why*," he said. "I'm not an idealistic fool, *Seta Kalliri.* I know you cannot simply wave your hand and make it all go away. But throughout our history, the priestesses of Kakkari have always *fought* for Dakkar. The priestesses of Kakkari did not serve one but *all.* If you did not know how to banish the fog, a simple message to tell us so was all that was needed. Instead, we have wasted time. Time we do not have."

I knew *Kalloma* best. I knew her enough to know that the *Vorakkar* of Rath Serok…surprised her. She couldn't read him. She couldn't figure him out.

And neither could I.

She was looking at him much like how she looked at me sometimes…like I was an ancient tome spread out on her desk that needed to be translated and pieced back together.

"We do not know how to stop the fog, *Vorakkar,*" came *Kalloma's* voice. Rath Serok's face didn't change. He'd already known that, I realized. "But I assure you, we have worked tirelessly in the archives and in prayer to seek the answers you want."

"Then why not tell us so?" he growled, his frustration evident.

It was then I realized why. Why *Kalloma* had kept the messages from me, why she'd kept me in the dark. Why she hadn't responded to the hordes' pleas for help.

Because of…me, I thought, my hand coming up to my mouth in muted disbelief.

Because she'd been trying to find a solution to the fog that didn't include *me.*

She knows, I thought, my tail flicking as anger began to burn in my belly. *She knows how to stop the fog.*

Kalloma just didn't like the solution that she'd found, the solution that Kakkari had given her. And there was only one reason why that would be.

Me.

It was the only thing that made sense. It was the only thing that accounted for her strange words yesterday, for all the lingering expressions of fear and resignation I'd spied on her features these last few months. As if she knew time was running out.

Once, *Kalloma* had told me that she'd never thought she could love someone more than she loved Kakkari. But then she'd found that love in me. *For* me. Her daughter, though she'd never been allowed to have one.

To protect me, she'd turned her back on her duty. To protect me, she'd turned her back on Dakkar.

And if anyone ever found out, she'd be stripped of her title. Banished from the temple, from her life's work and her life's purpose.

Now there was a *Vorakkar* at her door, asking all the right questions that could lead to that discovery. I couldn't allow that to happen.

So give him what he seeks, I thought.

An answer.

"I know how to stop the fog."

The words slipped from my lips before I thought better of it.

A shuddered breath came from *Kalloma,* and I sensed the line of *kalliris* shift with my voice. Avala darted a worried look at me, biting her lip, but I paid her no mind.

The *Vorakkar* of Rath Serok's gaze zeroed in on me once again. He looked past the *Seta Kalliri* and then he stepped around her, as if she were forgotten.

"Tell me, *kalles,*" the horde king commanded, those boots

pounding across the marble as he approached. As he approached *me*. But at least his attention was off *Kalloma*. "Tell me what you know."

With a nervous inhale but with determined hands, I reached up and pushed my hood back from my face. It fell heavy around my shoulders as I revealed myself to him.

"*Nik*," the *Niva Kalliri* bit out.

"Beyla," *Kalloma's* stern voice exclaimed. "Take her to her tower. *Now*."

At the sight of my face, the *Vorakkar* of Rath Serok stopped.

He went deathly still, that gaze widening before it narrowed.

"Who are you?" he rasped, those eyes speculative as they ran over my face before trailing over my cloak-covered body, as if *that* would give him answers. "I— You are…"

The quick-tongued *Vorakkar* at a loss for words?

I ignored his question. My heart felt like it was pounding in my throat. I didn't think I'd ever been so nervous—or excited—in my entire life. My limbs felt weightless with it.

"The heartstones," I said. "The five of them."

"Beyla!" the *Niva Kalliri* ordered.

The temple's keeper came out of nowhere, snagging my wrist, not daring to meet the horde king's eyes as she began to drag me away.

Looking over my shoulder at him, I said, "The *Rivalla Lo'Kilan*. You must use them all."

That golden-red gaze felt like a brand on my very soul, and I held his eyes until I could see them no more.

CHAPTER 7

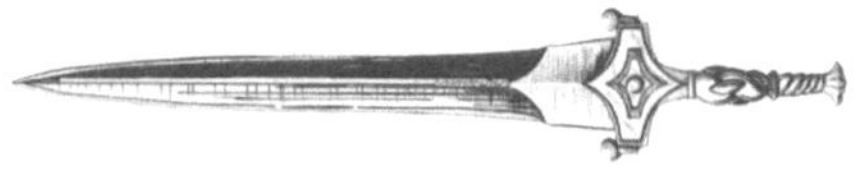

"It seems you have been withholding much more from Dakkar than your help, *Seta Kalliri*."

My eyes were glued to the place down the darkened hallway where the female had disappeared.

A female that had *stunned* me.

A female that had made my tongue twist itself in knots, which was only now loosening.

Who is she? I thought. *And what did she mean about the five heartstones?*

Swallowing hard, shaking off the heaviness in my limbs that had overcome me, I turned to face the High Priestess.

The look on her face could only be described as fear, though she tried to mask it hurriedly. I could almost respect her for it too.

"What is a half-Dakkari, half-*vekkiri* female doing among the priestesses of the *orala sa'kilan*?" I asked, studying her features.

Because there was no questioning that that was what she was. A hybrid female.

And *grown*. She would have had to have been born shortly after the *vekkiri* first settled on Dakkar. Nearly thirty years ago.

And here we had thought the first hybrid child was that of
the *Vorakkar* of Rath Kitala and his human *Morakkari.*

"She is Dakkari," the *Seta Kalliri* said, tilting her chin up.
"She always has been."

Did she take me for a fool?

"Whose daughter is she?" I asked next. "One of yours?"

A gasp rose from the line of the *kalliris.* It was the Second
Priestess, who had a look of fury on her face.

"You dare question our vows to Kakkari? In her own
temple?" she asked me, the words spat out.

"She is my daughter," the *Seta Kalliri* said, her voice loud
and clear, ringing in the vast expanse of the atrium. Did I detect
a hint of pride in her tone? "Though not by blood. My vows
have never been broken."

Despite there being rumors about her and a son from a
highborn family when she'd been a *kalliri* in *Dothik?* Rumors
that had nearly cost her the title of *Seta Kalliri?* Or did her sister
priestesses not know about that?

I grunted, crossing my arms over my chest, though my mind
was still stuck on the female.

"So you have kept her a secret since her birth. Hiding her
away in this frozen temple, knowing the *Dothikkar* will never
care to look. But do you not know that there are others like
her?" I asked. "Other hybrids?"

The *Seta Kalliri* straightened, her eyes snapping to mine.

"*Neffar?*" she asked quietly.

A small laugh rose from my throat.

"I wish to speak with her," I said.

"That is out of the question," the High Priestess said immediately.

"Then what did she mean about the heartstones?"

She said nothing.

"It seems we are at an impasse in negotiation," I said, my
tone soft, seeing the last of the sun's rays vanish on the horizon.

I smiled, flashing my teeth. "And your goddess awaits you in your sanctum."

The *Seta Kalliri* blinked before she swallowed hard. But there was a look in her eye, one that looked like...recognition. It was brief. A small flash of it, and then it was gone. "I've never heard of the line of Serok. Where does your line come from?"

"You may know me from a different line, *Seta Kalliri*. My father's line," I told her, my smile only widening. "Considering you trained in *Dothik*."

I would let her think on those words however she saw fit. She frowned, blinking as if trying to place me.

"But I know the rules of the priestesses," I murmured, inclining my head. "No male is allowed to sleep within the temple, and so I will sleep outside. We still have much to discuss, you and I. Like I said, I am not leaving until I know *everything*. Food and water for my *pyroki* would be appreciated."

"There is a cave nearby that you can sleep in," the *Seta Kalliri* finally said. There was a small relief in her voice, as if she wanted me gone—at least for the night. So she could regroup and make up new stories and lies to keep me at bay. "You and your *pyroki*. I'll send Beyla out with provisions."

"Once she returns from locking your daughter away in her tower," I finished for her.

The *Seta Kalliri's* eyes flashed with anger, but she kept it restrained. "*Lik Kakkari srimea tei kirtja, Vorakkar* of Rath Serok. Have a restful sleep. I am certain I will see you again in the morning, if the frost does not send you scurrying away."

"That is probably what you will pray for tonight, is it not, *Seta Kalliri*?" I murmured gravely as I stepped past her, dragging my fur pelt from its place on the banister. Darkness was descending within the atrium and fast. I turned my back on her, my eyes fastening on the door. "But I have endured much worse than a cave in the North Lands, I assure you."

I had no intention of sleeping outside, but she didn't need to know that.

A flurry of energy rushed past me, and the door opened with a rush, making me pause. But I knew what she was doing. Reminding me of her power. Reminding me of whom I spoke to with such brash disrespect.

"There are humans with your same gifts, *Seta Kalliri*," I said. A small intake of air came from behind me. "So if you think to surprise me with them, it isn't anything I haven't seen before."

With that, I left through the open door. It closed firmly behind me with a resounding *bang*. The icy cold immediately whipped at my cheeks and threaded its fingers through my thick furs.

"*Vok*," I hissed, feeling the cold begin to seep into my bones as I descended the stairs.

Better get used to it, I steeled myself silently.

It would be a long night.

I had a tower to climb, after all.

CHAPTER 8

Kalloma was furious with me. Naturally.

But she wasn't the yelling sort. When she came up to my tower after the evening prayers, it was her quiet disappointment that made discomfort curl and settle in my belly.

"Why would you do that, Kara?" she asked me softly, standing on the threshold of my room, though she didn't step inside it. "You risked not only yourself in doing that but us *all*."

"*Nik*, I was *saving* you," I said, feeling that spark of anger reignite in my belly.

"*Neffar?*" she rasped, her brow furrowing.

"You lied," I whispered, standing from my desk where I'd taken to transcribing Bekkar's book as a means of distraction. "You lied to them all. And I know why."

Kalloma went silent, watching me carefully.

"You knew this whole time how to stop the fog, didn't you? How to help the hordes," I said, desperately wanting it to be false. "And you did nothing."

"You do not know what you speak of," *Kalloma* said. "And speak very carefully from now on, Kara."

"Is it true?" I demanded, facing her, setting my jaw with

determination. "What did you see? What did Kakkari show you that's made you so frightened?"

Kalloma looked out my window, refusing to speak. I waited long moments before I realized that she would not give me an answer.

"Has he left?" I tried instead.

"For the night, *lysi*," *Kalloma* bit out.

But he will be back was what went unspoken.

"It's him," I told her. "It's him that I see. That I've always seen."

Judging by the way her lips pressed together, I assumed she'd figured that out already.

"Knowing that, do you really think that you can keep me from speaking with him?" I asked. "Because he is *here*. And I think deep down, you know that it's already too late for whatever you were trying to prevent."

Kalloma looked as if I'd just slapped her across the face. Her face went pale, and then she closed her eyes, spreading her hand out on my door to keep herself steady.

"You are *my* daughter, Kara," came her ragged voice. "And I have always kept you safe! I have always tried to protect you. Even though it is against my duty, I have always put you *first*."

It was as much of a confession as I would get.

"I don't want to be the reason that the *orala sa'kilan* falls, *Kalloma*," I told her, anguish tearing at my chest. "I don't want to be the reason that *you* fall. Not like this. Never like this."

She took a deep, shuddering breath.

"I'm not a child anymore," I told her. An obvious point, but one I felt she forgot sometimes. "Yet you treat me like one. I'm older than some of the priestesses in this temple, and you have Beyla *drag* me from a room. I may not have experienced everything you have in life, but not because I didn't want to—because you would not *allow* it. You cannot keep me in the dark forever."

Kalloma's shoulders sagged. I could see the exhaustion in the lines of her face. Had she not been sleeping lately?

"Whatever is coming..." I said, gentling my tone as I approached her, winding my arms around her neck to hug her tightly. Her own arms came around me, and I pressed my face into her neck, inhaling that familiar, comforting scent of her skin. "Whatever you have tried to keep from me, I'm not afraid of it. You said it is my purpose. So tell me what it is. Tell me what you saw. Tell me what Kakkari showed you. *Prepare me.*"

Kalloma pulled away from my embrace. Her eyes flickered back and forth between mine, and I saw the raw pain in her gaze. It brought a lump to my throat.

Her voice was a ragged whisper as she told me, "She showed me two paths."

"Tell me."

"She showed me a path that led to your death, Kara. A painful, long death that I feel whenever I try to sleep."

I took a step away, biting my lip as her words sank into my very bones.

It was as I suspected.

"And the other?" I asked.

"The other takes you away from this place forever. Never to return," she said. She smiled, though it was sad. I watched in disbelief as tears welled up in her eyes, but she blinked them back quickly. "And still, that is the path I desperately pray for you to take. The path that Kakkari will guide you toward."

"Paths can be changed," I said quietly. "You know this."

"Perhaps," she said quietly, cupping my cheek with a small smile. From the expression on her face, I knew that she didn't believe it. Whatever Kakkari had shown her...it had shaken her. "Of course."

I'd never given much thought to death. I'd been so consumed with wanting to leave the *orala sa'kilan*—with wanting to see Dakkar, see the hordes, the outposts, *Dothik,*

Drukkar's Sea, Bekkar's campaign trail, the *Trikki*—that death seemed...peripheral.

Now, in a single moment, I was faced with it. Staring right at it.

A raw, aching restlessness rose. In some ways, it was greater than my fear.

I didn't show my terror to *Kalloma*. Not terror that I would die. It was terror that I'd die without experiencing *life*.

"Thank you for telling me," I said softly.

Kalloma regarded me carefully. Likely wondering if I would be all right after hearing about the prospect of a painful, long death. Would anyone be all right after that?

"I must meet with the *Niva Kalliri* now," she told me. "To speak about our...guest. But I will come check on you before I turn in for sleep."

"*Nik*," I said, hoping my tone didn't sound too hasty. "*Nik*, you rest, *Kalloma*. Please try to get some sleep tonight. Put all thoughts of me from your mind, and let your body restore itself."

Her eyes strayed past me, flickering around my small tower. On my desk, her gaze zeroed in on the old, open tome, though I'd been careful with the binding. She saw my pages of parchment and the pot of *kreki* ink next to them.

"You're nearly finished," she commented, seeing the size of the stack. "Finish quickly, *rei kassiri*. Then you will always have a piece of home when you leave."

When you leave.

The words filled me with excitement, trepidation...and agony. Because I could never imagine saying goodbye to *Kalloma*.

She left without another word, and I stood at the threshold of my door, staring down the dark, circular staircase, listening to her retreating steps though I couldn't see her anymore.

When she reached the lower level, I closed the door before

pressing my forehead to the heavy steel. It was cool against my flesh.

A chilly breeze met my back, gently swirling my dress around my ankles. That felt nice too. During my conversation with *Lomma*, I'd felt overheated. I felt terrible going behind her back. But I needed to speak with the horde king, even if I had to sneak out of the temple. *Kalloma* might never allow it, but I needed to explain about the heartstones and—

"I thought she would never leave," came the dark, velvety voice. "I've been freezing my *deva* off out there."

A ragged gasp tore from my throat, and I whirled around.

There, sliding through my open window—which had most certainly been closed—was the horde king of Rath Serok.

CHAPTER 9

Trying to calm my racing heart, and still partly in disbelief, I sputtered, "How did you get up here?"

The *Vorakkar* jumped off my window ledge. I thought that it was a miracle he hadn't knocked off any of my potted ice plants in the process, but he was surprisingly graceful for someone so large.

My tower was the highest peak of the temple. Judging from the ice that he shook from his furs and the way he immediately darted to my flickering fire basin to warm his hands, I'd say he had to have been climbing for *hours*. Probably since he'd left the atrium.

"You *climbed*?" I whispered.

"How else, *saila*?"

I reared back, a hot flush flooding up my neck.

Saila meant *darling*. It was a soft name. Meant for...lovers.

And I liked it entirely too much falling from his lips, even though he seemed to say it flippantly and without care.

Taking a step back, I felt the cool steel of the door press into my back. I was only wearing my nightdress. It was entirely too thin, and I shivered as the cold greeted my spine. I'd wanted *Kalloma* to think I was heading to bed because I'd known she would come up to the tower after the evening prayers. But now I regretted changing my clothes.

The horde king's eyes flashed. His gaze dropped down the length of my body, and I watched his throat bob when it grazed over the hardened peaks of my nipples. A sharp, gruff sound emerged from his lips.

He shouldn't be here, I thought, my heart racing, my cheeks flaming. *If* Kalloma *ever found out…*

"Are you a *kalliri*?" he rasped, those eyes meeting mine.

"Wh-What?"

"Are you a priestess?" he wondered, rounding the fire basin though his hands must still be cold and the ice on his fur pelt was only now beginning to thaw, dripping over my floor. Instead, he was approaching me. "Have you vowed yourself to Kakkari? Because I am having very improper thoughts at this moment, and if you *were* a priestess, well…that would be the gravest disappointment of my entire week, *saila*."

To buy time, I could think of nothing else to say but "Just your entire week?"

He grinned, and I felt the warm slide of it low in my belly. The wide breadth of his shoulders blocked the entirety of my vision. He stepped closer until I couldn't see my bed or my desk or the window through which he'd come.

Only him.

"My entire month," he corrected. "But you should take even a week as the highest of compliments, *saila*, because I've had a *vokking* rough one."

Belatedly, I remembered that looking a horde king in the eyes was forbidden unless he gave his permission. Yet I couldn't look away. It was like I was outside of my body. It didn't feel real. It didn't feel real talking to him in the flesh. For a moment, I thought I had slipped into the cracks of my gift. Had I fallen asleep? Or was I awake? Sometimes, I couldn't be sure.

But he was *here*. Standing in front of me. I could smell him.

He smelled like everything I loved. Old tomes. A crisp breeze from the south. And the raw earthiness of soil as it sifted through my fingers.

That was new. I'd never smelled him before, had I? I knew his face, his voice, but not this. Not until now.

His hand came to rest on the door, caging my head in, swarming me further with his scent. It was all around me. *He* was all around me. Warmth seeped from him, heating me in ways I hadn't thought possible.

Still, I shivered. His smile widened when he saw it.

"Are you a *kalliri*?" he asked again, his voice becoming rougher, deeper.

"*Nik,*" came my answer. "I am not."

His touch came then, as if he'd been waiting for my answer. His strong hand rose and cupped my jaw. I nearly gasped. In the back of my mind, I realized that this was the first time I'd ever spoken to a male. Ever been *touched* by one. Ever been touched like *this*.

I'd thought I would be terrified, trembling where I stood. Instead, I was boldly meeting the eyes of a *Vorakkar*, and instead of shrinking away, I shifted *closer*.

"Then let me look at you, *saila*," Rath Serok rumbled softly.

The pads of his fingers were rough and calloused. Though his touch was gentle, those callouses scraped at my skin, but I didn't mind the sensation. I was wholly focused on his face, on the strange expression that flashed there the longer he studied me.

Because that was what he was doing. I had the feeling he was committing every detail of me to memory. Perhaps because he'd never seen a hybrid before? Or was it that he was trying to place me? Because I was as familiar to him as he was to me?

"Do you know me?" I whispered, the question slipping out before I thought better of it.

His brow furrowed. I almost regretted asking it because his

hand slipped from my jaw, coming instead to rest on the jut of my hip. He held me there, keeping me in place. Afraid I would dart away?

"Should I?" he returned.

His hot palm seeped into the thin dress. A flood of arousal made me dizzy. Despite my lack of experience with males, sexual desire was not hidden among the *kalliris*. Though they were not allowed to lie with another, they believed that there was power and pride in satisfying their own needs. A special connection to one's body, which only strengthened one's bond to Kakkari.

I was no stranger to sexual desire. How many nights had I lain in bed, pretending to be Lessa as I imagined Bekkar between my thighs? The strong warrior king, undone with lust for her? How many times had I pored over accounts of sex, of mating? And the old accounts of enemy hordes taking their mates in the old way? The tradition of the *kassikari*.

Kalloma's library held the best books with those accounts, and I had been reading them since I was old enough to know what sex was.

"Because I know we have not met before," he continued. "I would have remembered you."

Disappointment flooded me, though it made more questions rise.

Even still, I said, "You shouldn't be here."

"And yet here I am," he said, that smirk maddening. I held my breath as he leaned forward briefly, lowering his head so that it hovered just above the column of my neck. Smelling me? His hand on my hip clenched tighter. "What would happen if the *kalliris* found me up here?"

"You would be banished from the temple," I said immediately.

"Then let's make sure they don't find me," he answered easily.

Quick-tongued *Vorakkar*, indeed.

I might've known him, but I didn't really. I knew next to nothing about the male that had me pressed against my door.

"Do you have an answer for everything?" I wondered, meeting his eyes when he pulled back.

"Typically, *lysi*," he murmured. He added, "And if I don't, then I make my own."

Swallowing, I slipped from his grip, ducking under his arm before he could react.

Reaching for the thin furs that were sprawled across my bed, I wrapped them around my shoulders, covering the bare expanse of my arms and the obvious outline of my breasts.

The horde king turned to watch me. His movements were lazy and slow as he leaned against my door, crossing his arms over his chest.

Standing next to the fire basin, I felt heat lap at my side. "It was unnecessary to scale the entirety of the temple walls. I was going to come find you tonight."

He laughed, low and deep. "But I worked so hard to impress you, *saila*. What other male would scale your tower just to catch a glimpse of you again? Besides, we would not have been very warm in that dark, little cave."

I was confused by the words. They almost sounded *mocking*.

"Who are you?" I asked quietly.

His laugh tapered off. He shifted slightly. "The *Vorakkar* of Rath Serok. Who are *you?*"

Which was strange too.

"I've never come across that name in the histories of Dakkar. And horde kings typically come from long ancestral lines, do they not?"

A muscle in his jaw jumped, which I thought was fascinating. When he saw me studying him, however, his lips quirked and the muscle smoothed away.

"I assure you, *saila*, I come from a very long line of kings."

My brow furrowed, hearing that mocking tone again.

"Do you take to studying ancient histories often?" he asked, peering at me. Then he pushed off the door, stepping toward me again, which only served to spike my heartbeat.

"There is not much else to do here except read," I answered him.

"And what of your own line?" he asked, cocking his head to the side when he came to stand in front of me.

I lifted my tail and settled it in my hands. There was a knot in the hair, so I untangled it gently before brushing through it as I deliberated how to answer that. The *Vorakkar* watched all this with intent eyes, and it flustered me when I realized it.

"My mother was human, my father Dakkari," I told him, dropping my tail. "I never knew either one. I was raised here. The *orala sa'kilan* is all I know."

"And you have the *Seta Kalliri* who claims you as her daughter," he finished for me.

"*Lysi,*" I whispered, feeling a wave of guilt settle over me. She'd be furious with me for allowing a male to stay within the temple, especially without her knowing. But it only served to remind me why I'd needed to speak with him in the first place. "We must speak about the fog. About why you're here."

"You mentioned something about heartstones," he said. "Tell me what you meant."

Gone was the lilting, teasing, disarming tone. In its place was a hardened voice. The voice of a *Vorakkar* who expected to be answered. The shift was so abrupt too.

"I believe that the fog has happened before. Or at least a version of it," I told him.

"The other priestesses know this too?"

"They are not convinced," I confessed. "But I know that the *Seta Kalliri* believes me."

"Because she is your mother," he scoffed, looking briefly

from me to look around my tower. His eyes caught on Bekkar's history on my desk.

"*Nik*," I said. "Not because of that."

He moved to my desk and peered down at the book…and then at the stacks of parchment next to it.

When he lifted one, I bit my lip and said, "Please be careful with those."

Those swirling eyes cut to me. A huff left his nostrils, and he gingerly replaced the thin sheet. Parchment had been hard to come by this last year. The last delivery we'd had from *Dothik* had been months ago. Our food stores were dwindling. The crops we grew deep underground were enough to sustain us with proper rationing. Our meat supply was running low too, though messages from the planet's capital assured us that more was on its way to us.

No hordes had journeyed to us in the last year.

As such, I'd taken to scrounging around the temple for parchment scraps. Any I could find. I had enough to finish the book but only just barely.

"How are you so sure?" he asked, crossing his arms over his chest. "What was this fog exactly?"

"It was a famine," I informed him.

"A famine," he repeated. "*Vok, kalles*, I do not think you understand what the fog *is*. What it *does*. It feeds on your strength and kills you when you are weak."

"Just like a famine," I argued, quirking a brow, feeling a small victory when he grumbled under his breath. "It was a plague in the soil. It turned it red and leached all life from it. All over the West. It produced no food during that time. It sickened those that lived near it. Many died."

The *Vorakkar's* uncut ear twitched. "When was this?"

"Two hundred years ago," I said. "Roughly. The actual seasons in the original account are unclear. But I know it was around the *mrok illa*, the shining star. Which last happened—"

"Two hundred years ago," he said softly.

I inclined my head. "The book dates to about that time as well. So that is why I believe it has happened before."

"So why don't the *kalliris*? What makes them doubt?" he questioned. "What makes you so certain that you're right?"

I shifted on my feet, wrapping my furs around me tightly.

There was no getting around it, however. He would never believe me otherwise. He might not even believe me if I told him.

"Because Kakkari showed it to me," I said quietly. "I *saw* it."

CHAPTER 10

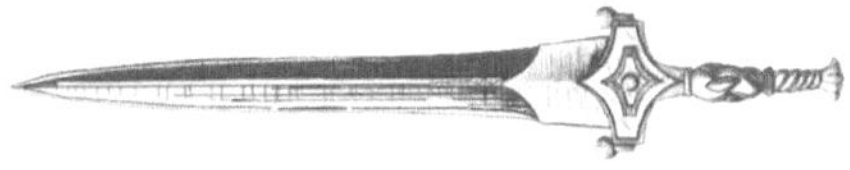

"**W**hat do you mean you *saw it?*" I asked, scowling.

The female stared at my displeased expression, but she didn't seem frightened by it. Instead, she cocked her head to the side, studying it.

I stilled under her perusal.

Who is she? I thought again. Even in that silent question, I felt my frustration.

So many unanswered questions. There had been a hybrid child living in the *orala sa'kilan* for *years*. Did the other *Vorakkar* know? Did the *Dothikkar* know?

Likely not, I realized. The *kalliris* hadn't wanted me to know about her presence. She'd hidden her face from view when she'd come into the atrium. The *Seta Kalliri* had been furious when she'd revealed herself to me.

Why the secrecy? Did the priestesses not know about the human queens on Dakkar?

A lapse of silence settled between us, and I took the time to study her.

Her eyes were gold. A purely Dakkari color, except her eyes had white in them. Like the *vekkiri*. She would be small next to a

Dakkari female, her height and bone structure no doubt that of her mother.

Though...I remembered the outline of her body in her sheath dress. Her breasts had been full, tipped with tight nipples my mouth had watered for. Her hips flared out, wide like a Dakkari's, meant to withstand a Dakkari male's more primal lusts. And her little tail...I didn't know why I was so fascinated by it. But watching her stroke the tuft at the end moments before, I had felt my cock tighten further in my trews.

She was no great Dakkari beauty. That was clear. Her human genetics collided too strangely with the Dakkari ones. Her face was round instead of long. Her cheeks were full, her lips too small, her nose too pointed.

So why couldn't I look away?

Why was my cock beginning to throb in my trews the longer she stared me down?

I smiled, though it was a dark thing and I certainly felt no humor at that particular moment.

The female blinked and seemed shaken enough to finally respond to my question with, "I saw it in a dream."

"A dream," I repeated slowly.

That wiped the smile right off my face. I'd climbed the *vokking* tower for nothing. She didn't have the answers I sought. She was of no use to me.

"*Lysi,*" she said, raising her chin like she was proud of it.

"And last night I dreamed that I was fucking a horde of females, but you don't see that coming true anytime soon," I growled out.

She blanched, shrinking back from me.

"You...you don't believe me?" she asked, the question incredulous, like she hadn't expected that.

Cursing, I looked away from her, back down to the desk. Writing I didn't know how to read. A failing that shamed me. But back in *Dothik*, growing up the way I had...I dealt with

Dakkari. With *people*. Not with words. Instead of learning how to read, I'd chosen to learn the universal tongue. *Language* was more important than ink across a page.

However, I'd never felt more lacking as a horde king than right then. Freezing in the North Lands. My pelt covered in ice. My cock still frustratingly hard. Standing with a hybrid female that told me about her dreams. And looking down at a book that might be the account of the famine she spoke of. But would I know?

Nik.

All the while, the fog in the East Lands grew. The *Vorakkar* of Rath Okkili had been assigned to the territory for the season, but I knew that it would be my turn next. *My* horde that would be at risk next.

Unless I found the answers to stop the fog before then. It was unpredictable. Wild. Every horde was on edge.

"I don't believe you," I told her, in no uncertain terms. "I don't know you, *kalles*. I thought that you knew something the *kalliris* were trying to hide. But I was wrong. I think they are as lost as we all are and are trying to save face."

She glared at me. Her spine straightened.

"If you don't believe me, then how do I know that you have a scar running down your back? Because I saw that in a dream too."

I barked out a laugh. Turning from the desk, I approached her. Her ears were getting red, the very tips of them, in her anger. I found that...eye-catching.

Still, I purred down to her, "Saying I have scars down my back is like saying I wear cuffs around my wrists. They are marks of a *Vorakkar*. Everyone knows this. Even you. Even as sheltered as you are up in this frozen wasteland. But you are no better than the fortune readers on the streets of *Dothik*. At least I can respect them because I know what they want. What they are *hungry* for. Money. Gold. You? I have no idea what you want or how you benefit from telling me these things."

I had stepped into her space. My tone was like a lover's gentle whisper, but the actual words held venom. Lifting my hand to her cheek, I pushed strands of long, black hair away.

"Maybe you *are* trying to help, *saila*," I said, pressing my lips together. She was just a girl. She might only be a handful of years younger than me, but she had no experience beyond these walls, if what she told me was true. "Maybe you think you are."

"I'm not speaking of the *Vorakkar* scars," she hissed, hands at my chest to push me away from her. My palm fell away from her cheek in surprise, and I stumbled back a few steps, my hip catching on the edge of her desk before I righted myself.

At her words, I felt a chill run down my spine.

"I'm speaking of the one that was there *before*," she continued, glaring at me, fire lighting up her eyes. "The one on the right side of your back. That starts under your shoulder blade and ends at the base of your tail."

I froze.

"How do you know about that?" I asked before stalking toward her again, though she turned from me, heading toward the door of her room with angry strides of her own.

"I'm calling for my *kalloma*," she said, grumbling under her breath. "You are not allowed to—"

When she opened the door, I slammed it shut with a firm shove from behind her. She gasped, outraged, but I grabbed her and spun her, pressing her against the door and *keeping* her there.

"I'll scream for the *Seta Kalliri*," she threatened, narrowing her eyes. Her chest was heaving.

"Then do it," I challenged her, knowing she wouldn't. "But before you do, *saila*, I want you to tell me who the *vok* you are and how you know about that scar."

The last test of the Trials was always public. It was possible she'd learned of the scar from someone who'd been present, who'd seen my back *before* the whipping…but the priestesses of the *orala sa'kilan* were sheltered for a reason. If they didn't even know about the human queens on Dakkar, how likely was it that she'd know about one damn scar?

Not very.

She was still glaring at me, and I knew I'd fucked up. I'd misread her, which very rarely happened. I'd been dealing with criminals, with prostitutes, with mercenaries, traders, gamblers, drunks, soldiers, merchants since I could speak.

I could be charming. I could be mean. I could grin as I was slitting someone's throat—mostly figuratively, though that bastard from the Western District a few years ago had deserved it. I could make myself into whoever I needed to be. I'd run the most extensive network right under the *Dothikkar's* nose because I dealt with people *all the* vokking *time*. And in many cases, misreading someone led to death.

So how had I misread *this* female?

This slip of a female who had lived her whole life in this temple reading books all day?

Her chest was heaving wildly.

"Tell me why you're angry."

She gaped at me. "Because I'm trying to *help you* and you treat me with condescension and derision. Are you insane?"

"I'm sorry for that, *kalles*," I said easily, choosing the last word carefully, knowing she wouldn't take too kindly to me if I called her *saila* right now. She'd liked when I'd called her that. But if I uttered it now, she'd likely slap me across the face, *Vorakkar* or not. "I'm sorry. I have had bad experiences with people who claim they possess Kakkari's gifts. All of them were liars."

My words gave her pause. I watched as she blinked.

"You've dreamed of me before," I said, processing the words

and forcing myself to entertain the idea that what she said was *real*. "You've seen the scar before."

Her jaw set and tightened. Then she looked between us, realized that I had pressed my body against hers to keep her from moving. Those golden eyes widened, and she struggled.

"*Kalles*," I growled out, feeling her body wiggle against my cock. Hissing, I said, "*Cease* moving. And talk to me, *lysi*?"

"*Lysi*," she finally bit out, glaring up at me again. It was possible I had a kink for females who hated my guts because I felt my cock only thicken with her rage. How fucked in the head was that? "But it was only a dream, *Vorakkar*, so you cannot possibly have that scar. I must have made it up."

I'd really struck a nerve in thinking she was lying. Or not *lying*, exactly, but not believing her. Mentally, I told myself that I could never do it again or else I tempted her ire.

People had certain tics. Things that were set boundaries, hard lines that most could not cross. This was hers. I would do well to remember it.

"So you have a gift, *kalles*," I said, ignoring her sarcasm. She had a temper. I...liked that. "Tell me about it."

That gave her pause. I wondered why.

When she said nothing, I prompted, "There are others that have Kakkari's gifts. Two human queens of the hordes, for example. The horde king of Rath Drokka. You remember those fortune readers I spoke of in *Dothik*? One of them actually *did* have the gift of foresight, though it was limited to the span of a day. And—"

"*The human queens?*" she whispered, her eyes widening almost comically. I watched her black pupils dilate. She shook her head. "What do you mean?"

Watching her carefully, I told her, "Horde kings have taken humans as their queens. There are five human *Morakkari* now. The majority of them have already given their *Vorakkar* children."

I felt her legs tremble against me, but I pressed her harder into the door to keep her from sliding down it.

"You did not know?" I asked. "You did not know that you were not alone?"

The look she gave me...

Vok.

It twisted my heart, and I thought long ago that *nothing* could made it ache again.

But the look was so wounded. So full of despair. Frustration. Anger.

Longing.

"You are not alone," I told her. "Not in your gifts, nor in the circumstances of your birth. You are the first, *lysi*, but you will never be the last."

"Tell me about them," she pleaded, her eyes hungry for more. "Tell me. *Hanniva.* Please."

"Everything has a price," I murmured, cupping her face in my palm. "I will give you something, and you will give me something. That is how Dakkar operates outside these walls."

She frowned. Genuinely bewildered.

How different we were. Priestesses—and by extension the *orala sa'kilan*—placed no value in money. The hordes were much the same, though they placed value on territories, on tradable goods, on the quality of those goods and the experience of their horde members. *Saruks* too.

But in *Dothik*...

Gold was life.

My life had been nothing but a series of transactions. If I'd learned nothing else, it was that everything could be bartered and bought.

"It is your turn, *saila*," I prompted her gently. "Tell me about the heartstones. I will listen, I promise."

"I already told you," she said, lifting her chin, dislodging it from my grip. "So if that is the way of the world," she repeated, "then you owe me something else before I say anything more."

A low chuckle rose from my throat. I was so very rarely surprised, but she'd surprised me twice this night.

"Very well," I said. "What is your price?"

"If I tell you everything I know?" she asked, swallowing. "Everything I know about the heartstones? Everything Kakkari showed me?"

"*Lysi.*"

It surprised me when her expression turned from fragile to *determined.*

"If I tell you everything," she said, "then I want you to take me with you once you leave. That is my price."

CHAPTER 11

"N*effar?*" the horde king rasped, clearly baffled. "Take you *where?*"

"To eradicate the fog, to restore the East Lands, you will need all five heartstones. I want to go with you to get them. I want to help."

He laughed, and I felt my heart sink in my chest.

"I am not going to anger the *Seta Kalliri* by stealing you away in the middle of the night," he told me, taking a large step away from me. I clutched at the door handle to keep myself from falling. I'd nearly forgotten how close we'd been, how his body had felt pressed against mine. "Besides, I know where all the heartstones are. One is here. Two are in the outposts. Another is in *Dothik*. And the last...well, one of the human *Morakkari* used it. She will tell me where it is. What's to stop me from getting them all without you?"

"Nothing," I said. "Though you won't know what to do with them once you have them all."

He blew out a rough breath. "Two of the *Morakkari* have Kakkari's gifts. They will know if *you* do."

Some of my bravado left me. Suddenly I felt a crushing weight on my chest. Restlessness. Despair.

He will leave, I knew. *He will leave with the heartstone. I will never see him again. And I will be cleaning the dust from Drukkar until my bones are creaking and dry.*

And I will die here, I finished silently.

It was a soft, quiet thought. One filled with certain truth.

I will die here if I do not leave.

And here was a *Vorakkar*, standing in my tower. He infuriated me. He made me desire him. He spoke in riddles, and I wanted to listen to his laugh forever, even though he sometimes laughed in a way that made me want to bury my head in furs and scream.

He had answers to the questions I'd never even thought to ask. About human queens and hybrid children. Beings like *me*. He told me I wasn't alone, and for those brief, glittering, wonderful moments, I *believed* him.

And if he left, he would take that all away from me. Just when I'd discovered it.

I couldn't bear it.

I couldn't *stand* it.

"You must take me with you," I insisted, steeling my spine, hardening my voice.

"Why?"

He was so handsome that it hurt to look at him.

"Because I'm the only one that can use the heartstones," I said.

The lie fell easily from my lips. But when faced with a bleak future, I was desperate. I would say anything to escape it. I wanted to live. And tonight I felt *alive*. I couldn't lose that feeling. Not when I'd just found it.

"Kakkari gave me a gift for a reason. What I saw...she showed *me* for a reason," I continued, licking my lips. "And the *Seta Kalliri* had a similar vision."

Two paths.

One that led to death. The other took me from here forever.

I stilled.

The path to death, however...she'd said it would be long and painful. Was that *here?* Here at the temple? Was that my fate if I stayed?

I latched on to that thought. It must be. *Kalloma* had been mistaken. The death she'd spoken of hadn't been a violent thing. It had been a *silent* thing. A silent, painful, long death right underneath her nose. Because every day I was trapped within these walls, a piece of my soul withered.

If I stayed, I would die.

There is no other way, I thought.

"I must leave," I told him. "The *Seta Kalliri* told me it would be soon. Why else would Kakkari show me you if we were not bound *together* in this?"

That made him hesitate.

"I have seen you all my life," I told him quietly.

His brow furrowed. For a moment, I saw his face. His *true* face. Not the mask he presented to the world, much like *Kalloma's* around the other *kalliris.*

When I saw his true face, I thought that he might *recognize me,* after all.

"I have seen you all *your* life as well," I murmured gently. "We are bound. For reasons that may still be unclear. But I do know that if you leave without me, we will never know why."

At least *that* wasn't a lie.

"So you must take me with you," I finished softly. "*Hanniva.*"

Outside, the wind picked up. Howling against the clear glass. All the while, he never looked away from me.

"And you wish to leave the safety of your temple, to risk your life on the wildlands of Dakkar?" he asked.

More than anything, I thought, wildly. Desperately.

"For people you have never met? For a place you have never seen? Why? Out of the goodness of your own heart? Tell me an *honest* reason. Because I can see straight through lies, *kalles*, and you are not a practiced liar."

My face paled.

He chuckled, low and mocking.

"I think you have no idea what to do with the heartstones once you have them," he said softly. "So I am better off taking my chances alone than risking myself trying to keep you safe."

"I want to live," I whispered.

He cocked his head to the side. "As do I, *saila*."

"*Nik*, I mean...if I stay here, I will die," I said, tears stinging my eyes, the sensation harsh and biting. "Long before I actually do."

His lips pressed together. He went still.

"I want to..." I blew out a breath. I laughed, but it was a wretched sound, huffing from my dry, tight throat. "I've lived my life living *others'* lives, pressed between parchment and ink. I've never left the temple. I want to see Dakkar. I want to see the valleys and the rivers and Drukkar's Sea. I want to see the forests. I want to ride a *pyroki* across the plains like the great Bekkar did. I want to look upon *Dothik* and see the merchant stalls and paved roads and hear the sounds of hundreds of voices. Because all I've known is hushed prayers and quiet hallways and the sound of wind against the ancient walls of this place. I want to *feel* life. I cannot be in this tomb any longer. I cannot. So I'm begging you—take me from this place and let me help you in whatever way I can."

The horde king of Rath Serok stared at me. Those swirling eyes pinned me in place until I felt like I couldn't breathe. Not until he released me.

"I *can* be of use to you. I do have a gift of Kakkari. I didn't lie about that," I added, sniffling. "And when tomorrow comes, when the *kalliris* meet with you again, they will do whatever it takes to make you leave. They don't want to use the heartstones because they think it is too great of a risk. They think it will weaken the temple, the outposts, and *Dothik*. And they are right...it *is* a great risk. But if what you say about the fog is true, nothing will stop it. It will consume the entire planet. And what good would their doubt be then?"

Rath Serok stepped toward me again. I couldn't read him. I had no idea what was going on behind those cold eyes.

His hand was warm when he tilted my chin up. His touch made my lips tingle, and it made hope rise in my breast.

I just wanted a taste of freedom. Of a life that was my own and not anyone else's.

"A word of advice, *saila*," he began, his voice gentle and rasping. "Never reveal your hand before a deal has been made. Because then you will be left with nothing though you still want everything."

A pinch of dread stung my belly.

"*Nik,*" came his purred answer. He smiled, though it didn't quite reach his eyes. "You are a liability out on the wildlands. I will not take you with me. No one in their right mind would."

My shoulders sagged.

My vision blurred over, and I blinked away the tears, turning from him. Ice seemed to freeze my heart. For a moment, I couldn't breathe.

"*Ah, saila,*" he murmured, a gruff tone entering his voice. "Don't do that. I may be a cold bastard, but I still do not like seeing females cry."

Wrapping my arms around my stomach, I avoided his touch when he reached for me and instead looked out the window he'd come in from. The view I'd seen my entire life. Breathtaking. Endless. Beautiful.

And I couldn't stand it.

"They will never let you leave with the heartstone," I told him quietly, though my voice sounded hollow. Wooden. "You'll need to take it. Steal in through the eastern tower after noon tomorrow. The first set of windows will lead you to the sanctum. No one will be in there at that time. The *Seta Kalliri* will be in the archives."

Even out of the corner of my eye, I watched him frown.

"And despite what you think, I have an idea on how to use the heartstones. Using them is easy enough. The hard part is finding those with the power to withstand the energy once it is unleashed. You need strength," I said. My lips twisted bitterly. "Just like the priestesses of old."

"I deny your request, and you help me regardless?" he asked quietly. "You truly do not know how to negotiate, *saila*."

Turning to look at him, I realized I was...disappointed. He was nothing like how I'd envisioned he would be. I'd romanticized him, made him out to be this hero that would solve all my problems. After all these years, I had wanted the story of him to *mean* something.

Now I realized I'd been wrong. Maybe it had meant nothing after all.

So why did looking at him *hurt?*

Wiping away a tear that fell down my cheek, I told him, "Not everything has to be for a price, *Vorakkar*. And if everything in your life has been traded and haggled over and paid for, then I am relieved that *nothing* in mine has been."

For a moment, he looked dumbstruck by the words. Then his expression turned brooding and dark. His tail flicked behind him, hitting the leg of the fire basin, his frown pulling at the thick scar over his bottom lip.

"I'll show you the way out so you don't have to climb down in this cold," I said softly, pulling my furs tighter around my shoulders, though it was the last thing I wanted to do. The bitter part of me thought he *should* climb out the way he'd come. It would serve him right.

Opening my door, I began to descend the stairs, barefoot.

"They are meeting in the sanctum now, so we must be quick. This way," I whispered, catching his eyes and holding them.

He looked at me like…like I'd turned into someone else entirely. Like I had sprouted two tails or even two heads before his very eyes.

After a moment, he followed me quickly—and silently—down the stairs. It was slightly unnerving when I could not even hear his steps behind me, especially for someone so large.

I guided him through the lower-level hallways, keeping my eyes peeled for any *kalliris* that might be milling about beyond the sanctum.

All too soon, we reached the atrium of the temple. The statue of Kakkari glittered in the rising moonlight that came in from the long stretch of windows behind her. Seeing the statue made my heart pang heavily. I could sculpt that statue from clay without referencing it once.

At the door, I untwisted the series of locks one by one. When I pried open the door, just a sliver of a crack that would fit the horde king's girth, I lowered my head so I didn't have to watch him leave.

"*Kalles*," he said, his tone gruff, "you're going to break my heart if you never look at me again."

My gaze lifted, and I frowned. I didn't want him to think I was afraid.

Those golden-and-red eyes were luminous in the darkness.

Something tells me you don't have a heart to break, I couldn't help but think.

He scowled, as if hearing what went unspoken between us.

"Good luck, *Vorakkar*," I whispered, pushing him beyond the threshold of the door. "*Lik Kakkari srimea tei kirtja.*"

May Kakkari watch over you.

He opened his mouth to say something.

And I closed the door in his face before he could utter a single sound.

My vision went blurry with tears. My face scrunched up in silent grief.

Gone. As quickly as he'd come, I thought.

And all I could do was turn back toward my tower.

CHAPTER 12

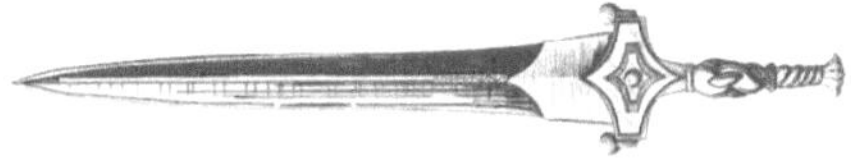

The *kalles* had been right.

At dawn, I'd spoken to the *kalliris* again, stepping into their sun-filled atrium as the *Seta Kalliri* leveled me an indifferent gaze.

My half-Dakkari, half-*vekkiri saila* was nowhere in sight, a fact that made discomfort rise in my chest. The night before, I'd barely slept. Her desperate words had played over and over in my mind. Her glassy, pleading eyes had haunted me whenever I closed my own. Dawn had come much too slowly.

The *kalles* had been right because the *kalliris* had done exactly what she'd said they'd do. Every probing question into the heartstones was met with stony disinterest. They dismissed the possibility that they could be used.

When I told them that the *Dothikkar* would have ultimate say, when I told them that I would need to bring the heartstone to *Dothik* regardless, the *Niva Kalliri*, the Second Priestess, had looked me straight in the eyes and said, "And when the *Dothikkar* himself is on our doorstep requesting the heartstone for Dakkar, we will give it to him. Gladly. But you do not have authority here, and as such, you will not go near it."

Everyone knew the *Dothikkar* had never set foot in the wildlands and likely never would. So her words were meaningless, and yet I could do nothing against them.

The *Seta Kalliri*, the priestess who *did* have authority over the *orala sa'kilan*, had remained quiet. I'd caught glimpses of her throughout the exchange. At times, she looked distant. A lost, vacant look in her eyes. But whenever she noticed me studying her, she blinked and the expression was gone.

We spoke for hours, it seemed. I tracked the sun through the windows. Nassik was expecting me back that evening, though I'd instructed him to take the horde northwest, where we had claimed the territory for the warm season. I was to meet them there, but the journey might take more than a day, depending on when I left the North Lands.

In the end, the discussions had been a waste of time. The priestesses refused to take accountability for their lack of response to our messages. They said that they were working hard to uncover a solution to the fog in the archives, where they spent the majority of their time.

I believed that they *were* trying to help. But it was frustrating that they had let us rot for months out on the wildlands without so much as a message telling us why.

Our discussions ended, rather abruptly, when the *Seta Kalliri* stumbled, nearly collapsing to the ground at the heart of the atrium.

When I tried to offer aid, the *Niva Kalliri* waved me off, helping the High Priestess stand as the other *kalliris* gathered around her.

"You see?" the *Niva Kalliri* accused softly. "She is exhausted. She has worked endlessly in the archives. She barely sleeps. She is trying to help Dakkar, and you come here with your accusations and threats that do nothing but *harm*."

My lips pressed together tight, and I bit my tongue *hard*. Hard enough to draw blood.

"I'm fine, *Niva Kalliri*," came the *Seta Kalliri's* voice. It was soft, though she sounded shaken. "It was just a dizzy spell."

She turned her gaze to me as the *kalliris* began to back away from her after making sure she was strong on her own feet.

"I am sorry, *Vorakkar* of Rath Serok, that we cannot be of more help to you," the *Seta Kalliri* said. And yet I swore I heard a tinge of fear in her voice. "We will send a *thesper* if we find anything of use."

With that, she turned her back. The dismissal was clear, and I watched the other *kalliris* begin to follow suit, trickling out of the atrium until only myself and the *Niva Kalliri* remained.

It wasn't noon yet. I would need to wait before I scaled the eastern tower, but one thing had become clear during my conversation with the priestesses: I was not leaving the temple without that damn heartstone.

"Where is the female?" I asked the *Niva Kalliri*.

She knew which one I spoke of. She clasped her hands behind her back, lifting her chin. "I am not certain. She has many duties within the temple."

"What kind of duties?" I asked, frowning. "Why has she not taken the vow of the priestesses if she remains here?"

I will die here. Long before I actually do.

Last night, those words had been brittle coming from her lips.

"It is the *Seta Kalliri's* choice, and she chose to keep her separated from the path of the *kalliri*," she responded, her lips pressing together as if annoyed she had to answer my questions. "If that is all, *Vorakkar*, I suggest you begin your journey back to your horde. The sun sets early in the North Lands, and I wouldn't want you to travel the Orala Pass when it is dark."

She walked to the door, unlatching the locks methodically. When she held it open, a gust of cold wind blew inside, small icicles skittering along the marble floor before they began to melt in small puddles.

Knowing I would get nothing more from her, I left without another word.

"*Vok,*" I cursed, running a hand through my hair.

Jogging down the steps, I was faced with indecision. A strange feeling in itself, one I was not accustomed to.

"So make a decision," I growled to myself.

Looking over my shoulder, I glanced toward the western tower. Climbing it had taken me hours. I'd nearly frozen my fingers off in the process, and they still felt raw and chafed this morning. The eastern tower was shorter, the first set of windows much lower to the ground. It wouldn't take me long.

I could be in and out of the sanctum before the *kalliris* ever realized anything had been taken.

Smiling wryly to myself, I thought my days as a thief were long gone.

Turning my eyes to the western tower, my smile died.

And I wondered if the heartstone was the only thing I was planning on stealing from the *orala sa'kilan* that day.

Blowing out a breath, I cursed again.

I made a decision.

I would deal with the consequences later.

"Very well," I rasped, remembering her haunted expression last night when I'd denied her. *Crushed her* seemed like a more appropriate description. "Very well, *saila*. But I hope you know what you're getting yourself into when it comes to me."

Jerking awake, I spied a dark flash of movement to my left.

I nearly screamed, but a warm hand clamped down over my mouth. A familiar scent swarmed in my nostrils, and then suddenly, I was staring straight into the *Vorakkar* of Rath Serok's molten eyes.

When he was sure I wouldn't make a sound, he lowered his hand. He was kneeling on my bed, and I was all too aware that my nightdress had ridden up as I slept, revealing my splayed thighs.

Hurriedly, I pushed up, scrambling toward the other edge. "What are you—"

"Get dressed and come with me," he growled softly, his eyes drifting from my bared legs to my face. "Pack lightly."

"Where...where are we—"

"To the West Lands. We have a heartstone to retrieve," he growled impatiently.

Hope burst in my brain, so sudden and quick that it was like sparks going off.

Eyes wide, I breathed, "You're taking me with you? *Now?*"

"*Lysi,*" he growled, his tail flickering behind him like a pendulum. "So hurry before I change my mind."

I scrambled from the bed in the blink of an eye as he straightened. Through my window, I saw the sun was high, nearly at its peak. I'd slept late again, likely because I'd tossed and turned into the early hours of morning.

My window was closed and latched, which meant he'd come to my tower through the door. Had he already scaled the eastern wall?

"The heartstone?" I asked, running to my chest of clothes and unlatching the lid.

"You'll need to guide me to the sanctum," he said. "You were right—they wouldn't let me near it."

Out of the corner of my eye, I watched as he took up a satchel that I used to transport books to and from *Kalloma's* library. He tossed it at me. I didn't have many clothes. I had two pairs of loose trews, one of which I pulled up my legs.

I shoved the other into the satchel, along with some tunics and dresses. I didn't change out of my night shift. Instead, I grabbed my fur pelt and secured it around my shoulders before shoving my feet into boots.

The *Vorakkar* of Rath Serok quirked a brow. Was he impressed? It had taken me less than a minute. Less than a minute to fit my life into that satchel and—

"Wait," I breathed, darting to my desk. I bit my lip, staring at the leaflets of loose papers, ones I'd never had the chance to bind. I hadn't finished the transcription of Bekkar and Lessa's history. The ending wasn't done. But I was out of time.

Carefully, I lifted my unfinished book and nestled it between the stacks of my clothes, keeping the parchment pressed tight so it wouldn't rip. Longingly, I looked at the bound tome that was on my desk. But I could never take it. It belonged in the *orala sa'kilan*.

Dragging one of the loose, blank parchments toward me, I quickly scribbled out a note to *Kalloma*, my heart beginning to pound with dread and realization that I may not get a chance to say goodbye. If she knew I was leaving, she would stop me. She would rip me straight out of the *Vorakkar's* arms if she knew what I was planning to do.

Yet I couldn't leave without saying goodbye.

"*Kalles,*" came the impatient bark from behind me.

Blowing out a shaky breath, with tears beginning to sting my eyes, I wrote:

I'll return to you, Kalloma. Maybe not soon, but I will. Never fear that. Because how can I leave my heart in the North Lands?

I laid the short note on top of Bekkar's history, biting my lip.

Then I nodded, thrumming with determination and excitement and fear and guilt, before turning to the horde and saying, "I'm ready."

The *Vorakkar* of Rath Serok tugged the door open on creaking hinges and gestured for me to move.

We crept down the stairwell and down to the first-floor landing. The sanctum wasn't far from my tower. Making sure no *kalliris* were in view, I led us through two different hallways, my feet traveling a path I'd journeyed thousands of times before.

At the end of the darkened, quiet corridor, I saw the archway that led to the sanctum. We hurried toward it, and then we were *there*. With relief, I saw we were alone. On the opposite side of the circular room, I saw that *Kalloma's* door was firmly shut.

The heartstone sat, unassuming and deceptively quiet, on the pedestal in the center of the sanctum. The colors that usually swirled underneath its surface were calm. During the *kalliris'* prayers, it lit up a bright blue, casting the glow around the entire room—widely for something so small.

I hurried toward it. Did I feel guilty for stealing the heartstone from the very hands that had raised me? A heartstone that they had sworn their lives to protect, to nourish?

Of course I did.

But I also knew that this was more important than my guilt. This was more important than any of us. Than *all* of us.

The horde king pulled a thick cloth from a pocket in his trews, coming to stand next to me at the pedestal. His eyes regarded the silent stone with wariness, his lips pressing in a firm, almost disapproving line.

"You don't trust the heartstone?" I whispered, surprised by the reaction.

A sharp breath huffed from his throat. "*Nik*, I don't trust Kakkari."

I stilled.

Quietly, I said, "That's a loaded remark to say within her temple. Especially from a horde king."

"I trust very few beyond myself. That has never changed."

My brow furrowed. That seemed like a difficult way to live.

"Are you certain about this?" he asked gruffly in the lull of silence.

"About the heartstones?" I asked. "*Lysi.*"

About everything else?

Not so much.

He held the cloth out to me. "Then take it."

Unconsciously, I grabbed the piece of material from his hand, nibbling on my lip when my gaze returned to the heartstone. I'd never touched it before. Not once. *Kalloma* had never allowed it. Because she'd been afraid of what might happen.

"Allow me."

I gasped.

The horde king pivoted, but I noticed that his hand wrapped around my arm before pushing me back. Shielding me?

And there, standing beneath the archway at the threshold of the sanctum, was *Kalloma*.

CHAPTER 14

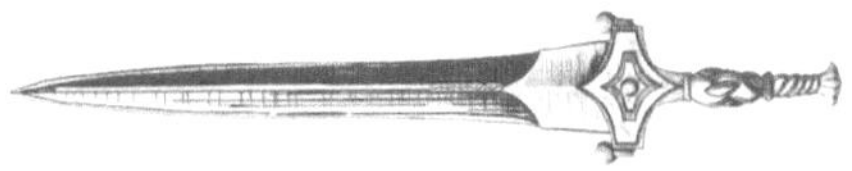

The *Seta Kalliri* had her hands clasped behind her back as she drew near. Hadn't the *kalles* assured me that no priestesses would be near the sanctum during this hour?

"I'm glad to see you recovered, *Seta Kalliri*," I murmured, a muscle in my jaw ticking. If she didn't allow us to leave with the heartstone, it would pose a serious problem.

"Recovered?" the *kalles* asked, a frown in her tone, forgetting that we were in the process of stealing a damn heartstone. She stepped around me to peer at her mother. "What happened?"

The *Seta Kalliri* leveled her with a look that had the *kalles* flushing with shame. But I spied something in the set of the High Priestess's shoulders, in the stricken look around her eyes.

Resignation.

"Do you know why your mother gave you up to us when you were only a baby, *rei kassiri*?" the *Seta Kalliri* asked. *My love,* she'd called her.

"Because she feared the reaction of her villagers," the *kalles* replied quietly.

My fists clenched at my sides. Behind me, I swore I could feel the *heat* of the heartstone. I swore I could feel it begin to throb.

"*Nik*," the *Seta Kalliri* said, stopping in front of her daughter and reaching out to cup her face. "She gave you up because she loved you. She loved you so deeply that even her own grief and pain would not stop her from what she felt she had to do. To love you as best as she could. Even if it killed her."

The *kalles*'s lip quivered, and I felt a sharp ache go through my chest.

Our mothers had that in common, saila, I couldn't help but think, my expression going grim.

"Now I feel like I can finally understand her better," the *Seta Kalliri* continued. "Because this is the last thing I want, and yet I know it must be done. This is the path that I have prayed for. *I know it.* I saw it."

The High Priestess plucked the heartstone from the pedestal...

And then she pressed it into her daughter's hands.

The *kalles* gasped, and a rush of energy filled the sanctum, prickling the base of my neck, a sharp sensation that traveled down my spine. My hand reached for the hilt of my sword on instinct.

Yet all too soon it was over.

With shaking hands, the *kalles* quickly wrapped the heartstone in the cloth, her breath coming in quick gasps. She was shaken.

What had just happened?

The *Seta Kalliri* embraced her. The High Priestess was helping us? After everything she'd done this morning to try to dissuade me?

What had changed?

A sniffle came from the female. Out of the corner of my eye, I saw her nodding at whatever the priestess told her.

"I'll return to you," came the female's quiet promise. "You doubt it, but I do not."

The *Seta Kalliri* smiled, but it was riddled with grief. "I know. I know you will."

Then she pushed away from her daughter, her spine straightening, her expression hardening. The *kalles* ducked her head to hide her tears, but I saw them. I saw her hand deposit the wrapped heartstone into her satchel, tucking it among her precious parchments.

Then the *Seta Kalliri* approached me. Distaste mingled with her determination. She stood close, and for a moment, she simply peered at me. She was incredibly tall for a Dakkari female, and yet I still tilted my head down to meet her eyes.

Then she leaned close. In my ear, she whispered, "Keep her safe, *Vorakkar*. Do not let any harm come to her. I speak this not as her mother but as the *Seta Kalliri*. Kakkari chose her when she was only a child. She has shown me her path, and you will need her to defeat this fog in the East."

"How?" I asked softly, my eyes catching on the *kalles* over the High Priestess's shoulder.

"It will come to you when the time is right," she promised, making my confusion only deepen. These *vokking* priestesses. The whole lot of them always spoke in riddles. "But you must make sure she does *not* use a heartstone before then. And keep her away from *Dothik*. By all means."

My brow knitted together.

"I know who you are, Horde King."

There was a note of mistrust in her voice. She wasn't quite glaring at me, but it was clear that the High Priestess did not care for me. Not one bit.

"I know why you are familiar to me. You look much like him. Your grandfather," she said. "Not so much like your father, however."

Crossing my arms over my chest, I told her, "I gave up all claims to that line."

"Yet that line has not let go of *you*," came her cryptic

response. "You have a path all your own. One laid out from the time of your birth."

"*Neffar?*" I asked, stilling. Her words sparked a memory, one I couldn't *grasp.*

She shook her head, and then her eyes turned to daggers. "One thing is clear to me. She is not a part of *that* path. *Dothik* will swallow her whole. You choose *Dothik,* or you choose her. And I know which choice you will make. So take care, *Vorakkar.* Take care with her. And know that if you ever touch her, if you ever lie with her, she will never be allowed to return here. To her home. To the *orala sa'kilan.* Do not take that away from her."

Realization dawned on me. I understood *exactly* what she was telling me. Only I didn't know if the *Seta Kalliri* was speaking as the High Priestess...or as a mother.

Stepping away, I flashed her a small grin to cover up the strange discomfort that was snapping in my chest.

"You don't have to worry about that, *Seta Kalliri,*" I said quietly, quirking my brow. "I have more pressing concerns outside of bedding would-be priestesses."

Her distaste for me couldn't be made more apparent.

My eyes slid to the *kalles* still standing next to the pedestal. She didn't appear to have heard our conversation. Instead, she appeared deep in thought, her lips parted as she stared down at the marble floor.

"*Saila,*" I called out. It meant *darling.* The *Seta Kalliri's* lips pressed at the soft name I called her daughter. "We need to leave. Now."

The female shuffled forward. Dressed in trews much too large for her and a shift dress that covered them, she looked like a disheveled, bedraggled mess. Her hair was still wild from sleep. The satchel she had slung over her shoulder was tattered and stained, leaflets of parchment poking out from it.

I'd grown up in *Dothik.* And there, appearance was everything. Even if she wasn't a hybrid female, she'd draw attention.

The *kalles* pressed a kiss to her mother's cheek. Her eyes were shimmering, and yet she didn't allow a single tear to fall.

"I'll make you proud" was what the female said. "I promise."

A flash of despair crossed the *Seta Kalliri's* face. "You already do, Kara."

I started at the name.

Kara.

Shaking my head, I thought, *It's just a coincidence. Of course it is.*

Still...

My mother was half-mad with desperation then, I thought. *Nothing she said was true or even made sense.*

"We need to leave," I said, cutting through the silence in the sanctum. "Say your goodbyes, *saila,* if you still wish to come."

Then I turned, knowing she wouldn't be too far behind. It was time to return to my horde and prepare to collect the heartstones.

I got what I came for. More *than what I came for,* I added.

I'd come to the *orala sa'kilan* for answers.

In return, I'd received a heartstone, stinging blisters on my hands from scaling temple walls, a pounding headache, and a damn *female.*

And a warning from the High Priestess herself, I added mentally.

Blowing out a sharp breath, I realized life as a horde king wasn't all that much different from my life in *Dothik.*

From behind me, I heard the *Seta Kalliri* say, "Remember what I said, *Vorakkar.*"

As if I could forget.

"And don't make the same mistakes as your father. Or his father before him."

I froze.

Those words could have a multitude of meanings...and none of them were *good*.

Looking over my shoulder at the *Seta Kalliri*, I saw her embracing her daughter one last time. Kara looked up at her mother with a frown before looking between us.

"I am nothing like them," I growled. "You would do well to remember that."

Chapter 15

It was jarring to have despair and grief mix so thoroughly with excitement and elation.

That was what I felt, however, on the back of a *pyroki*, with icy tendrils of wind whipping through my hair and a horde king at my back.

I wanted to scream out with jubilation. I wanted to tell the *Vorakkar* to take me back, to return me to the familiar quiet of the sanctum. I wanted to cry with relief and victory while I also wanted to sob when I realized I hadn't said goodbye to Avala. To Trissa. To Beyla. To any of the priestesses that I had known my entire life.

"Where is the heartstone, *kalles*?" came the question from behind me, rasped into my ear, a puff of hot breath against the lobe of my rounded ear.

"In my satchel," I replied, peering down at the scales on the back of the *pyroki's* neck, mesmerized. "Will you tell me your *pyroki's* name?"

"That is not for you to know," he said.

I frowned. Were *pyrokis'* names considered as sacred as their masters'? Or perhaps it was just a *Vorakkar's pyroki*.

"Give it to me. Now."

The rhythmic though violent gait of the *pyroki's* run made me fearful to unclasp my hands from the reins. I was seated within the confines of the *Vorakkar's* massive thighs, the strong muscles squeezing around me to keep me from flying off its back. His arms had come around me as well, his fur pelt tickling the back of my neck as I watched his scarred hands expertly maneuver his *pyroki* across thawing ice boulders and fallen mountain rubble.

"When we stop, I will," I told him, my teeth clacking together.

The tendons on the back of his hands flexed. All at once, the *pyroki* came to a halt.

Ringing silence met me. The wind that had been rushing in my ears died down. The sound of the *pyroki's* taloned claws scraping against stone and ice ceased.

Then, before I could blink, the *Vorakkar's* hands were around my waist and he flipped me around to face him. He maneuvered me as easily as he had his *pyroki*, handling and positioning my body swiftly.

Our fronts were nearly pressed together, and he placed my legs over the tops of his thighs, bringing us even closer. My face would have flamed had I not been intrigued by the way his eyes roamed over me.

"Give it to me," came the command again, that molten gaze flicking from my parted lips to my eyes.

It was obvious he didn't trust me. Then again, he'd told me he trusted very few.

Swinging my satchel around, I settled the bulk of it in the small pool of space between our splayed thighs.

"Do you think I'll run off with it?" I challenged.

His expression never changed. "*Nik.* I know you won't. But that satchel looks like it'll unravel any moment, and if we lose a heartstone, we are *vokked*."

"This satchel has served me well, I'll have you know," I

informed him. Nevertheless, I dug my hand into it, searching for the small cloth that I'd wrapped the heartstone in. My palm closed around it. Hurriedly, I plucked it out and thrust it at him.

In the sanctum, I'd touched it with my bare flesh. I shuddered, remembering the flood of voices in my ear with the simple contact. It had been similar to what I heard during the priestesses' prayers...only amplified by a thousand. It was not something I was keen to hear again, to *feel* again. Perhaps it was better if the horde king took possession of it.

The *Vorakkar* looked at me carefully, taking the small cloth-covered stone from my grip before tucking it into a pocket in his tunic.

Distracted, I looked away, tilting my gaze up at the majestic mountains that framed him. A thought occurred to me right then.

"This is the farthest I've ever been from the temple."

"And you will journey much farther from here, *saila*," came his response. His eyes began to glitter, a familiar smile stretching across his face. "Are you frightened? I can still turn around, you know. You can be back in your own bed tonight."

"*Nik*," I said hurriedly, swallowing the panic that rose at his suggestion. "*Nik.*"

His eyes narrowed.

Licking my lips, I asked, "Why did you change your mind?"

He grunted. Then I felt the *pyroki* begin to trot again. Though it was slow, I suddenly felt off-balance, like I'd fall with the jarring movement.

One strong, unyielding arm kept me in place, fastening around my back, his palm spreading wide over my spine.

His touch made me feel off-balance too. Just in an entirely different way. But I liked that he held me, I liked that he kept me from falling.

"I'm not in the habit of disappointing females," he replied, flashing me a slow, languid grin that I felt deep in my core.

I blinked.

Then his expression sobered. "And I know what it is like, *kalles*…to want something so deeply that you are willing to sacrifice everything for it."

My tail twitched at the words.

"And what was that for you?" I asked, my tone a little breathless.

I found I was desperate to know. A whole world had been opened up to me. And I wanted to know *everything* about it. I wanted to know everything that books could not teach me, starting with *him*.

"That is also not for you to know," he growled, but his tone was lilting enough that the words didn't bite as hard as they might've.

The rocking trot of his *pyroki* caused me to sway. Every motion brought me closer to him before I retreated. Our legs slid against one another's. When I moved my bag, I felt the *Vorakkar* stiffen as my body slid into the empty space left by the satchel.

"You said everything had a price," I reminded him, swallowing hard, feeling the tip of my tail curl when my leg slid farther along his thigh. "What is yours? For this? For taking me from the *orala sa'kilan*?"

His nostrils flared. His gaze lowered, fastening on my lips as he watched them form the words. I felt hot. Arousal was rising in my belly and the hard press of his body was not helping matters.

"What I want remains to be seen," he answered, his voice a rough, velvety tumble. "But when I decide, you will know, *saila*."

His body was unyielding. And masculine, unlike anything I'd ever seen or experienced. Like a statue, I thought.

Like Drukkar.

"Did you know that Drukkar was born in the sea?" I asked,

filling the sudden silence with the quick question. My throat felt tight. My skin felt hot. "And that when he was grown, he burst from it on a wave? A powerful wave, higher than the tallest peak in the North Lands. And that when Kakkari first saw him, a tremble went through the earth because she was enthralled with his beauty and power?"

The dark little pinpricks of his pupils dilated, and I wondered what that meant. I wondered what he was thinking.

"*Nik*, I did not," he told me, though his tone sounded clipped. "Why do you tell me this?"

"Because you remind me of him. Of Drukkar."

A sharp bark of laughter emerged from his throat. My gut told me...I'd angered him. Or made him uncomfortable, and yet I didn't know why. Was it not a compliment to be compared to a god?

"And do you think of yourself as Kakkari in this story?"

I gasped. "*Nik*, I would never compare myself to—"

Then, before I could say anything, he had me flipped forward again, settled on his *pyroki* the proper way, and I blinked at the Orala Pass laid before us. A clear road that had been frozen over just a week ago. Now a steady trickle of water ran down the road like a stream.

"Let me make one thing clear to you, *saila*," he purred in my ear, his arms coming around me again to take control of the reins. "I am a *Vorakkar*. I am here only because I have a duty to Dakkar. *You* are here because I think I can *use you*. And when I am done using you, then that will be the end of it."

My fingers pressed into the back of the *pyroki's* long neck. The black-scaled beast beneath me quickened its pace.

"So keep your romantic stories and notions to yourself," he finished. "I am not like Drukkar. In fact, by the end of this, I guarantee that you will hate me."

"I don't hate anyone," I murmured, my throat strangely

tight as embarrassment drowned me. "I cannot fathom hating anyone."

A mocking chuckle met my ears.

"Only because you've never been beyond the temple," he informed me. "Give it time, *kalles*. You might hate me by the time night comes."

Chapter 16

"We will rest here for the night," I informed Kara, bringing Syok to a halt at the end of the Orala Pass. Our pace, at first, had been punishing. I'd hoped to leave the area by nightfall, but I'd noticed Kara stiffening and shifting on Syok's back as the afternoon had dragged on.

It was her first time on a *pyroki*. She wasn't used to riding one, and as such, it would be painful for her. So I'd slowed the pace, giving up my hope of reaching my horde tomorrow. Not for the first time, I was regretting bringing her along. She would only slow me down when time was already not on our side.

"Are you hungry?" I grunted when she slid off Syok's back.

She flashed a quick look up at me. "*Lysi.*"

I went to the travel sack that was attached to Syok's side. "I'll get a fire going in the basin, and then we can eat." Thrusting a water skin at her, I said, "Drink first."

She took it from me, though I found her attention was already elsewhere. Her eyes had begun to wander. It was dark, but the moon was nearly full, illuminating the small clearing we'd found.

"Where are we?" she asked. She'd barely said anything to

me after our conversation earlier. Not that I'd minded. It was better if she knew my intentions from the start.

Still, I found that my mood was dark.

"We are nearing the end of the Orala Pass," I told her, jerking the small fire basin out of the sack along with chunks of fire fuel and a starter. I couldn't shield the grumpiness in my tone, though she didn't seem to notice. "We can make it to the border of the West Lands tomorrow if we rise early."

I'd chosen this spot because I'd spied a small cave to our right, set into the rock face. The mountains of the Orala Pass still towered over both sides of us, but they had begun to slope down and flatten off, forming rocky hills with accessible ledges.

The cave was small. It couldn't even really be considered a cave. It was more like an alcove, a recess in the mountain that would shield the majority of the biting night winds and keep our fire from dying out.

It would have to do for the night, though I eyed the *kalles*'s furs warily. She'd already been shivering by the time we stopped. The night would only grow colder.

But she hadn't complained. Not once. Not about riding the *pyroki* or about her hunger or about the frigid temperature.

Guilt bit at me. Was it because I snapped at her?

I kneeled in the alcove, setting up the fire basin quickly. The fire fuel clunked against the metal, and I struck the starter swiftly.

Fire bloomed. The heat flicked across my skin.

"*Kalles*, come get warm," I ordered over my shoulder. My ears twitched when I heard silence from behind me, and I rose quickly, turning and scanning the empty clearing. "*Kalles?*"

Vok.

She had disappeared.

Abandoning the fire, I strode forward, my tail flicking in irritation and frustration. Where had she gone? The Orala Pass might be safe this time of year, but that didn't mean dangerous beasts wouldn't wander in, especially if the fog was pushing them beyond their natural territories.

I heard an echoing gasp, but I couldn't pinpoint the direction.

"Kara!" I yelled out, using the name I didn't think I'd been meant to hear, as my heartbeat began to thunder. Why had she gasped? Was she in danger—

"I'm here."

A dark tumble of hair popped out from a corner of an elevated ledge, her golden eyes reflecting in the moonlight. A small bite of relief went through me though irritation rose.

"You shouldn't wander off," I snapped, eyeing her position, wondering how she'd maneuvered up the ledge so quickly. "Come down from there."

She shook her head. There was excitement in her voice as she said, "*Nik*, I wanted to see the view. You should come up here. It's *beautiful*."

Though my heart was still thundering, I couldn't bring myself to dampen her exuberance. It was her first time beyond the temple. It was natural she would want to explore.

"Is it?" I asked.

"*Lysi*," she said, and with that, her figure disappeared from view. It didn't seem like she cared if I followed her or not.

Patting Syok on the rump, I murmured, "*Okkai.*"

Stay.

Then I leaped up onto a nearby boulder so that I could jump up onto the ledge. From there, I leaped over a small crack in the mountain's face to land on the weathered, steep incline.

At the very top of the rocky hill, I spied Kara, her back to me, her night shift whipping around her booted ankles.

Behind her was a backdrop of a starry sky, inky and endless. As I began to climb the slope, she regarded me over her shoulder, hearing my approach. Her eyes were glittering with wonder and joy. Seeming to forget the strained tension that had settled between us that day, she flashed me a small, secretive smile.

A dizzying rush of *familiarity* made me stumble.

The world hushed as I froze, as I caught a tendril of a memory, though it danced away from my grip the moment I thought I had it secured. *Nik*, not a memory. More like a *knowing*. The back of my neck prickled and a shiver raced down my spine.

Brow furrowing, I shook my head, dismissing the sensation, but I never gave up Kara's eyes.

Blowing out a harsh breath, I continued up the incline until I stood next to her, until the expanse of Dakkar was laid before us, cloaked in darkness. Well, at least the expanse of the North Lands.

She saw beauty. All I saw was the distance we still needed to travel.

"Isn't it wonderful?" she asked me, shooting me that secretive smile again. This time, it only served to thicken my cock in my trews, unexpected and irritating.

The smile was filled with such innocent and simple contentment that I marveled at it. I didn't think I'd ever seen someone so *unafraid* of revealing their emotions so openly, unless it was to deceive or trick.

Vok, *you are a jaded bastard, are you not, Serok?* I asked myself wryly.

"What's so beautiful about it?" I wondered, jerking my gaze away to scan the horizon to try to see what she saw. "You have a much better view from the window of your tower."

She grumbled a bit under her breath, making my lips quirk involuntarily.

"*Lysi*, but that is a view farther north. The view to the south from the temple is blocked by mountains," she said, a note of exasperation in her tone. Throwing her arms out to gesture toward the expanse, she said, "I've never seen *this*. It is entirely new to me. And I'll never see this for the first time ever again. It's only now. In this moment. That's what's so beautiful about it."

I jolted at the surprising sentiment, turning to stare at her.

When she caught me, she seemed embarrassed though her chin lifted.

Our gazes locked and held. A tendril of hair whipped across her cheek with a sudden breeze, and she tucked it behind her rounded, humanlike ears. My skin began to prickle again. I swore I could hear her heartbeat beginning to quicken.

Then she jerked her head forward, breaking the prolonged, charged contact. She even took a step away from me for good measure, and I let out a soft, chuffing exhale.

"Which way is *Dothik*?" she asked, breaking the sudden silence. "I'm a little turned around out here."

My eyes fastened on the place on the horizon. Like a beacon calling me *home*. A jolt of longing went through me. My tail flicked across the ground, sweeping a rock away that clattered down the incline of the ledge. For a brief moment, I allowed my selfishness to overtake me. I allowed myself to want *Dothik* again. The familiar roads, the familiar faces, the familiar *need* in my chest.

The scars on my back pulled as I shifted, reminding me what I was *now*.

Coming up behind her, I took her by her shoulders, ignoring the way she jumped at my touch. I shifted her body and then crouched, raising my arm to an invisible speck in the distance. Our faces were pressed close, and I felt her hesitation as I said, "There."

"The place that is below Bekkar's constellation?" she asked. "His sword?"

My gaze flitted upward before an amused grin stole over my features. I backed away from her. "That's not his sword, *saila*."

"Then what is it?" she asked, sounding genuinely bewildered.

I rolled my neck, straightening to my full height. "That's his cock."

A choking sound left her throat.

"It is not!" she argued, rounding on me with wide eyes and alluring flushed cheeks. "That is his great sword, the one that *created* his kingdom of *Dothik*." She whirled, pointing into the night sky. "You see? The brightest star is the pointed tip. You follow it up to the hilt."

I laughed, low and long. "Call it a sword if you wish, *kalles*. Everyone in *Dothik* always called it Bekkar's *kakkiva*. And that hilt, as you call it, is not a hilt. It's his *deva* and then his *dakke*."

The cock-and-balls constellation. And it was fitting that it hung over *Dothik* during this time of year.

She gaped, and my laugh grew.

"Bekkar's sword," I repeated, shaking my head. "*Lysi*, it is a sword. Just not the one you think. What is it that they taught you in the *orala sa'kilan*?"

With that, I began my descent.

A moment later, I heard her cry of protest and heard the shuffle of her feet coming after me.

"I'll have you know that I have studied star maps *extensively*. I know every myth and legend in these skies and the stories behind them," she growled.

I froze.

I didn't know why but that little growl *did it for me*.

Rounding on her, I felt my own *deva* tighten below me and my own *kakkiva* thicken.

Growl at me again, saila, I wanted to purr. And when I saw her glaring at me, I nearly groaned out loud.

I pointed above our heads. "What's this one, then, *saila*? Tell me."

She swallowed and then tilted her head back, exposing the

smooth, soft column of her throat. I had the wildest urge to lean forward and bite her there.

Her jaw set. She met my gaze and answered, without hesitation, "Tanniva's hand. The Dakkari priestess who brought peace to *Dothik* during the first uprising."

I grinned. "You think *that's* a hand? Tanniva might have been a priestess once, but she left the temple to become the mistress of the third *Dothikkar*. Bekkar's own grandson."

A strangled sound left her lips. "That's—that's not true!"

"*Lysi*, it is," I told her, quirking a brow. "And you want to know how she brought peace to *Dothik*? Because as the king was seated deep between her thighs, she was whispering into his ear to open trade negotiations with the enemy hordes."

The muted disbelief on her face made amused satisfaction bloom in my chest.

For a moment, I seemed to have stunned her.

"She was a priestess!" she finally protested. "She did not leave the temple for...for *sex*."

I shook my head, blowing out a rough breath. "She didn't leave the temple for sex, *saila*. Though if she did, no Dakkari in their right mind could blame her."

Her brow furrowed, a flush running up her neck that I found entirely too enticing. I imagined my tongue tracing up the column, wondering if she was hot there from the rush of blood beneath her skin.

"Then *why?*"

"Power. What else?" I answered gruffly. "With the king at her beck and call, she could control whatever and whoever she wanted."

"Surely he wouldn't have been swayed that much," she argued, crossing her arms over her chest when a shiver made her tremble. "He was the *Dothikkar*! And she wasn't even his queen."

"Never underestimate the power of sex, *saila*," I purred,

watching that flush only deepen. I chuckled. She shivered again, looking irritated but also...intrigued by the words. "For it has built kingdoms and has also caused many to fall. And not just on Dakkar. Throughout our universe."

She sobered at the words, though there was still a hint of a glare in her expression. Her chin tipped up again to regard the constellation above us, and I smirked when I saw her lips press together.

"Not everything can be learned from books," I said to her. "Especially from books in the *orala sa'kilan*. Those records are so ancient, I'm surprised they don't crumble as soon as you touch them."

Her brow furrowed. She looked down at her feet for a brief moment, debating something in her mind. I found myself wanting to know *exactly* what she was thinking. I found myself wanting to know *exactly* how her mind worked.

"Fine," she finally clipped, raising her gaze. "Not everything can be learned from books. And I may have been wrong about Tanniva. There was some evidence in the translations that she left the temple after all. But," she began, before pointing directly behind her, "*that* is Bekkar's great sword. I refuse to believe any differently."

My chest swelled with amusement, even as I recognized this was another boundary for her, a line that couldn't be crossed. So, she admired Bekkar, did she? Looked up to the great king?

Licking my lips, I inclined my head. In a grave, chastised tone, I said, "Of course, *saila*. That is most certainly his sword. I was very mistaken."

Her chin lifted. The set of her shoulders seemed pleased with the answer.

"Good. I'm glad that's been settled," she said, throwing me a victorious smile that made my cock pulse. Then whatever she saw in my face made her expression die. She frowned. "What are you thinking right now to look at me like that?"

My tail flicked. My claws curled into my palms.

She seemed genuinely baffled.

Trust me, saila, *you don't want to know what I'm thinking,* I thought to myself. *It would send you running back toward the temple.*

On second thought, maybe that was exactly what *should* happen. It would certainly save me a lot of headaches.

Yet I couldn't make the words come. No matter how much I wanted to scare her.

Gruffly, I said, "Nothing. Come. I already started the fire. You need to eat and then get some rest."

As do I, I thought. It would be a long journey to the West Lands tomorrow.

"You said my name," came her gentle voice when we began to descend the ledge's peak together. "When you were calling for me."

I grunted.

"Isn't it only fair I know yours?" she asked.

I stopped.

Turning to her, I said, "You forget I am a *Vorakkar, kalles*. It is not my problem if the *Seta Kalliri* was reckless with your own given name."

"At the temple, there is not so much weight given to names," she informed me. "You truly believe given names hold power? I've never much understood the need for secrecy. Because what are names compared to Kakkari's greatness?"

A sharp huff left my nostrils.

"You may call me Serok if you do not wish to *properly* address me as *Vorakkar*," I told her, hoping that would be the end of it. But she'd grown up in the temple. She didn't know what she was asking was mildly insulting. "You are not of my horde, so what do I care if you do or do not?"

I had a feeling that if I heard my given name from her lips, if she gave me that secretive smile that made my tail tingle as she said it, I might do *anything* she asked of me. So *lysi*, I damn well believed that given names held power. Especially when wielded by maddening females who growled at me when speaking of ancient constellations.

"Serok," she said, looking up at me with large, golden eyes.

I swallowed. My tail still tingled.

Vok.

"Come," I bit out. "*Now.* No more talk of names or *Dothik* or stars. I need to eat and then sleep. And so do you."

"*Lysi*, Serok," she said, her tone positively *dulcet*.

Vok *me*, I thought, mentally groaning, feeling my cock throb in my trews.

This was going to be the longest journey of my life.

CHAPTER 17

The moment that Serok slowed the *pyroki*, I took in a deep breath, a barrage of questions already poised on my tongue.

The horde king bit out an impatient sigh, as if he was mentally preparing himself for whatever onslaught of questions I would bombard him with.

"In *Dothik*," I began, my body swaying with the *pyroki's* slowed movement instead of the jarring, teeth-clattering motions of its sprint, "how is money used? Do you use actual gold? Is it coins, like how it was during Bekkar's rule? I've always wondered."

Serok's grumbled murmur made me think he was praying to Kakkari for patience, a goddess I was certain he did not even worship.

I turned in my seat so I could look him in the eyes, swinging my legs sideways so they dangled near the travel sack. My foot hit it, and I heard a dull *clang*, the fire basin shifting.

"Coins," he finally told me, sighing again. He wouldn't meet my eyes, and there was a perturbed frown on his face as he scanned the horizon.

We had left the Orala Pass when the sun hung high in the

sky. Though we had left at dawn, it still had taken us the better part of the day. I wondered if Serok was tired. He didn't quite look it, but I didn't think he'd slept last night. He'd given me his fur pelt as a blanket—though I had protested as guilt swamped my belly—but every time I'd woken throughout the night, I found him regarding the fire, his back against the cave wall, a knee drawn up.

If he'd noticed me watching him, he hadn't commented. He hadn't even looked at me. He'd seemed so lost in thought as he watched the flames flicker that a part of me *ached* to know what it was he was brooding over so intensely.

"Coins of gold," he continued, his shoulders sagging in defeat when he finally met my gaze. In the bright sunlight, his eyes were even more stunning. "Their size dictates their value. Though there are some old coins—from Bekkar's rule, even— that have higher value than any of the new ones."

Coins from Bekkar's time? Little pieces of history?

"Do you have any?" I wondered, breathless.

"Hordes have no need for currency," he informed me, dodging the question.

"But you lived in *Dothik*," I said, my tone soft but pointed. "Didn't you?"

He cut me a sharp look. "And why would you think that?"

"Because your accent sounds like my *kalloma's*," I told him. "And she was born and raised in *Dothik*. She came from the *Dothikkar's* own temple there. There is a subtle difference between the *Dothik* accent and that of those that were raised in a horde or even in the outposts. I've studied the way the other priestesses speak, and they don't sound like you."

I must've surprised him because he laughed. Rich and husky—it made me want to shiver.

"And your clothing," I said.

He looked down at it, frowning. "What about it?"

"Messengers from *Dothik* have come over the years, bringing us caravans of supplies."

"So have horde kings," he pointed out. "And I thought your *Seta Kalliri* kept you hidden away during all visits to the temple."

"*Lysi,*" I said, shifting in my spot uncomfortably. "But I watched from my tower and listened through the railings on the upper floors when they came to the atrium. And your clothing resembles the *Dothik* way of dress. The horde kings that came to the temple...they never had a belt of daggers or boots not lined in fur. Your boots make no sound, you know. *Kalloma* would call them thieving boots."

His head cocked down to me. "So you assume I am from *Dothik* because of my *boots?*"

"And the way you speak," I reminded him.

He huffed out a sharp exhale. Exasperated? He shook his head, his eyes flitting back toward the landscape around us. And while I wanted to absorb every little bit of scenery I could outside of the temple...strangely enough, I couldn't look away from *him*.

"*Nik,*" he said. Confused, I looked up at him questioningly, especially when he flashed me a dark grin. "I do not have any coins from Bekkar's rule."

"So you have no coins from *Dothik*? None that I can see?"

He sighed. Then he leaned back in his seat. His trews had a multitude of small pockets, the material soft from wear and time. Then he dug out something small and gold, which flashed when it hit the sunlight just right.

When he handed it to me, it was shockingly warm from his body heat. The coin was heavier than I expected for its size, and I peered down at it, my heart throbbing with excitement.

The front was stamped with a swirling pattern, though there were no words. The back held the image of a male. A face. Strong and regal, though the etched lines were sloppy. The edges of the coin were rough and straight, not perfectly rounded, but looked like they'd been cut by a blade.

"Is this the *Dothikkar*?" I asked, tilting the coin so that it caught the sunlight again, letting me study the detail more clearly. I squinted at the words on the back. "What does it say here? The gold is worn."

"What does it matter what it says?" he asked, frowning when I pressed the coin toward him. He didn't look at it and waved my hand away. "It's a coin."

I peered closer. Two letters were worn, but I could guess what they spelled.

"*For the glory of Dothik.* Interesting."

Dothik and not *Dakkar*. Because only the capital used money like this? Even the outposts relied on a trading and bartering system, probably because they were once hordes, because it was what they knew.

"And this is the *Dothikkar*?" I repeated because he hadn't answered me.

"*Lysi,*" he grunted. "That is the *Dothikkar.*"

I jerked my gaze up from the coin, stilling. There was a strained tone in his voice as he said the words.

"You don't like him?" I guessed.

His gaze cut to mine. For a moment, I had the strangest feeling that he would tell me something *honest,* something actually *real.* But then he grinned and the moment faded away.

"Does anyone?" he questioned. "Besides his advisors because the *Dothikkar* pays them with his gold?"

Glancing back down at the coin, I brushed my thumb over the flattened surface. It was so worn. I thought it must be very old, but it couldn't be if it had the face of the current *Dothikkar* on its surface.

"Is this the only one you have?"

"*Lysi.*"

"Why?"

He inhaled a sharp breath. "What do you mean *why?*"

"Were you wealthy in *Dothik*? If you come from a line of horde kings, I would assume you were. And if you were wealthy, why do you have only *this* coin? Where are the others?"

His eyes rolled to the heavens above us, as if asking Kakkari herself for patience. Or perhaps Drukkar, though the god was not known for his restraint.

"It is rude to ask that, *kalles*," he informed me, his clipped words matter of fact.

"Is it?" I asked, biting my lip. "Why?"

"Because wealth is hard to come by in *Dothik*," he answered me, though his words were oddly patient. "It is insulting if you assume that it is easy."

Oh.

"I'm sorry," I said, feeling a sinking in my gut. "I didn't mean to offend you. I just wanted to see other coins."

"Well, I only have the one, so you will be disappointed," he told me. He jerked his chin toward my legs. "Turn around. You've had enough of a break. Time to pick up our pace again."

Looking back down at the coin one last time, I thought over his words. There was so much I didn't know. And he was right. There was so much that books hadn't taught me—or *Kalloma* or any of the other priestesses.

I handed him the coin, and he returned it to his pocket swiftly.

"Will you take me with you to *Dothik*?" I asked before I turned.

His eyes came to me.

"One of the heartstones is at the *Dothikkar's* temple."

Like he needed the reminder.

Yet...we hadn't spoken about what would happen next. I was assuming that he would bring me to the western outpost— the *saruk* of Rath Hidri—because we'd spoken about the plague there. That was the direction we were heading, after all, though I knew his horde was also there.

But after that?

What would happen?

"You will only slow me down," he informed me. The words stung, though I knew he hadn't meant to hurt me. "I need to travel quickly to collect all the heartstones. Though I am hoping the other *Vorakkar* will help with the task. At least with two of them."

"You don't have to take breaks for me," I said quickly, breathless. "We can ride all day and night. I can handle it."

Behind him, I saw his tail flick.

"Taking you to *Dothik* is a risk that has no reward," he told me next. "Your appearance would only draw attention to us. So *nik*. You can stay behind in my horde if you wish."

I felt determination rise in me.

"You have to bring me to *Dothik*," I informed him. "I can wear a cloak and hood if I need to."

"During the warm season in *Dothik*?" he laughed. "You'll draw even more eyes that way."

Frustration rose in me. "You have to bring me."

"Why?" he growled. "Give me one good reason."

"I can give you one *very* good reason," I informed him. "Because *Kalloma* knows the *Laseta Kalliri* there. The High Priestess of *Dothik*. She told me to give her a message, and she will let us *take* the heartstone."

Serok stilled. He even brought his *pyroki* to a stop.

Narrowing his eyes on me, he said, "You lie."

I lifted my chin. "I'm not lying. She told me that the *Laseta Kalliri* is still loyal to her, that she will respect her wishes if I give her the message. That's what she told me in the *sa'kilan* after she gave me the heartstone. That's what she whispered to me."

"And what is the message?" he asked.

"Like I would tell you," I rasped, eyes widening. "I'm not *that* foolish."

"*Vok! Kalles,*" he started, anger building right before my very eyes. "This is not a *game*. This is not a—"

He broke off, jerking his face away from me, trying to get hold of his temper.

"There is a very real danger on Dakkar," he finally said. His voice was significantly softer though his tone was still grim. "You are playing with everyone's fates in your search for freedom and adventure."

I sobered. And yet...

"You wouldn't even know where to start if it weren't for me," I told him.

He glared at me.

"A fact that your mother and your beloved priestesses will answer for once the fog has been eradicated," he said. Then, without waiting for me, he grasped my waist and turned me forward himself. Great, we were back to fighting again. *Wonderful.* "And their day of judgment will come when all of Dakkar realizes that. All of Dakkar will witness their treachery."

Disbelief and fear shot through me.

"Is that a threat?" I asked quietly.

"It is the *truth*," he purred in my ear. I stiffened in my seat, staring at the hilly landscape before us. The earth was wet, as if it had just rained, or perhaps it was from the frost thawing. "I will not take you to *Dothik*."

"We'll see about that."

We didn't speak for the rest of the afternoon.

Even when he slowed his *pyroki*—something he'd been doing on and off all day—to allow me a brief reprieve. If he expected me to unleash a wave of questions on him after what he'd said to me, then he was sorely mistaken. I'd never been one to hold a grudge, but his threat had really grated on me.

It was nearing nightfall when he slowed the *pyroki* once more. I held back my wince when we slowed, not wanting him to think I couldn't handle the extended travel. But I couldn't feel anything below my waist that wasn't burning and prickling pain. It hadn't been this bad yesterday. I was frightened of what I would find when I inspected myself down there on the next stop. *If* we were even planning to stop.

Not like I would ask. I was thirsty, ravenously hungry, tired, and in pain. But he wouldn't hear a peep from me about it.

"Are you going to speak to me again, *saila*?" he pondered, his lips close to my ear.

It was always loud when he was pushing his *pyroki* hard. My bones felt like they were grinding together. The rushing wind always roared past. The clatter of hooves and the scraping of talons echoed in my ears.

Had I thought that racing across the wildlands on the back of a *pyroki* would be *fun?*

The first few moments had been fun. Then everything had started to ache.

When Serok had gentled the *pyroki's* pace, it became incredibly quiet. Which made his voice in my ear all the more surprising.

"Are you going to be mad at me all of tonight?" he wondered when I didn't answer.

"I'm not mad at you," I informed him.

Even to my own ears, I sounded mad.

His soft laughter made my neck prickle. His hand came to rest on my waist, and I nearly forgot to breathe when I felt the wide expanse of his palm seep into the material of my dress.

"None of that, *saila,*" he told me, his tone oddly gentle. "I do not like being ignored and frozen out. And it is not good to leave so much anger pent up. Tell me."

Swallowing, I said quietly, "You threatened my *kalloma*. You threatened the priestesses of the *orala sa'kilan*. My family."

He blew out a rough breath. The last tendril of sunlight disappeared along the horizon. The sky was a beautiful vision of purples and greens and gold, and yet...I couldn't even find it in myself to enjoy it.

"How would you feel if I threatened yours?"

"Every moment we delay threatens them," he told me, but his words were quiet, not biting. "Do you see that?"

Back to this again.

"I didn't ask you to stop your *pyroki*," I pointed out. "I will stay right here until we get to wherever we need to go. You have my word."

His hand moved. It slid from my waist, and I gasped out

loud, the sound strangled and surprised, when his fingers pressed against my inner thighs. Not over my sex but *around* it.

And I hissed out a painful wince, one I couldn't contain, jumping in my seat.

His touch stung and burned, and I felt tears blur my vision. It felt like my inner thighs were on fire. My buttocks were numb. I couldn't even feel my tail. Or my feet, for that matter.

Without another word, Serok led his *pyroki* to a nearby hill. The mountains of the North Lands were giving way to grass-covered knolls the farther we traveled west. I knew that the horde king had wanted to cross the border by nightfall. Had we? Or was that just another disappointment to him, another milestone he hadn't reached with me in tow?

I bit my lip.

Maybe...maybe he was right.

Maybe I was only a burden, just like I was at the temple.

And if the fog was as terrible as he claimed, I could understand his frustration.

Was I being too selfish?

My shoulders sagged.

Maybe it was the pain or my tiredness or the stinging realization that I might not ever be enough to see this task through, but I started to cry.

It was gentle at first. A few drops dripping down my cheeks.

But once they unleashed, I couldn't stop the tidal wave of emotion that followed.

His exhale lifted the back of my hair. "Kara..."

A choked sob tore from my throat. Great, now I was *really* crying. And once I started crying, I could rarely stop. Not when I felt like *this*. This crushing disappointment and feeling of helplessness.

Serok brought his *pyroki* to a stop and slid off his back. I refused to look him in the eye. Avala had always told me I was an ugly crier. My face got all splotchy, and the skin below my eyes swelled. Looking at him would only make me cry harder, and I probably already looked ugly in his eyes. How could I not be when he was likely used to having a plethora of Dakkari beauties at his beck and call? And me...I was so *different*. So *other*.

"Kara," he called out, reaching out for my hand. "Slide off. I'll catch you."

His words only made me cry harder. "*Nik!*"

"Why not?" he asked.

"We are no-not stopping tonight!" I exclaimed, wiping my arm over my cheek. "I told you I'd ride all night, and I meant it!"

"You are in no position to ride all night," he told me, his tone infinitely patient yet firm, and I *hated it*. "You're hurt. You have *pyroki* burn between your thighs, and we need to get some *uudun* on it. It will only get worse if you don't rest."

"I don't care," I sniffed.

Serok took a deep breath. "What is this really about?" When I didn't answer him, he said, "Kara, look at me. *Now*."

Jumping a bit at the tone, my gaze flickered down to him. He was standing next to his *pyroki*, looking up at me expectantly. For the first time, I realized that he was likely only a handful of years older than me, and yet...he seemed like he'd lived a thousand lifetimes, at least compared to me.

With that realization came resentment. And I felt so ashamed for it that I wanted to shield my face again.

"Don't look at m-me," I cried out, absentmindedly stroking the *pyroki's* neck. "Just go away and le-let me cry for a bit."

His lips quirked. Just slightly. But enough for me to notice, and I leveled him a pitiful glare, even as fresh tears pooled down my cheeks.

"*Saila*," he said, sobering quickly. "I'm not going to leave. Now tell me why you're crying."

My shoulders sagged. "Because."

"Because why?"

Why was he being so nice and patient right *now* when he'd been such a jerk earlier this afternoon?

"Because I'm tired," I answered, sniffling, petting the *pyroki* to help calm me down.

Serok's gaze flicked to my fingers and then back to me.

"That's not why," he told me. "Try again."

My brow furrowed, and I frowned. Through a watery gaze, I told him, "*Fine.* Because I can't feel anything except pain below my hips. I'm hungry. I'm thirsty. I want to sleep for a *million* years. And I'm mad at you because you're *right.*"

Serok was polite enough to keep his expression neutral. "Tell me more about that last part, *saila.*"

A sob tore up my throat. I tilted my head back, looking up at the darkening sky above us. Still too bright to make out the constellations, but a few stars were beginning to twinkle. I focused on those stars, my gaze zeroing in on them, as I focused on my breathing.

"Because I *am* a burden!" I burst out, and it *vokking killed* me to admit it. Serok's nostrils flared. I cried harder. "I-I don't know anything beyond my life in the temple. My life was so structured there. I had a routine. Every day. I thought being out here would be exciting and wonderful and exhilarating. And it is all those things, but it's also incredibly *frightening.* Because out here, I have no purpose. There is no routine, no floors to polish, no statues or ancient weapons to dust, no books to pore over. I left it all behind. For the first time in my life, I have no idea what tomorrow will bring."

The words surprised me. But once I started I couldn't stop, even though my lips were trembling and my heart was beating incredibly fast.

"And you were right! I'm selfish. I'm so incredibly selfish. I thought I could help. I thought I could help stop the fog...to prove myself. I really did. But how can I help you when I know nothing? How can I be of use when I...when even my own *kalloma* didn't believe I could do this? I'm only here because I gave her no choice but to agree."

I swung my gaze back to Serok, who was looking at me with a strange expression I couldn't read.

"And even though you're right in saying she shouldn't have kept the information about the heartstones from you...she was doing it to protect *me*. Knowing she could be stripped of her title, knowing she could be shamed, all because of *me*...I can't bear the thought. I can't bear the thought that it will be *me* that ruins *her*. That ruins them *all*. Just like the *Niva Kalliri* has always said."

The tears came quick and hard as my words dried up. My body was shuddering with the sobs, and I couldn't even bring myself to be embarrassed that a *horde king* was witnessing this breakdown.

What he must think about me... I thought silently.

I was showing him how weak I truly was. I had hoped to be a little farther from the North Lands—at least out of the territory—before he discovered what a mistake he'd made in bringing me along. Would he turn his *pyroki* around? Would he make a mad dash for the *orala sa'kilan* with me in tow and deposit me back on the steps of the temple like I was a cursed thing?

It was a trigger for me...the knowledge that I wasn't *enough*. It had been my whole life. That was why I'd started to cry. That was what brought this on, though I strongly suspected it was coupled with the exhausting day on the back of a *pyroki*.

Serok didn't say one word. Not for a long time. He waited until my tears died down and my hiccupping sobs tapered off. He waited until I took a deep breath and gazed out at the now-dark sky.

As I stared straight forward, I felt a sense of calm descend. My impromptu crying session released some of the tension that had been building throughout the afternoon.

I felt better. Now all that remained was my mortification and my body's aches, pains, and needs.

Serok didn't ask this time. He reached up, fastened his hands around my waist like I was a child, and pulled me off his *pyroki*. He set me down in front of him but kept a firm grip around my waist. I was thankful for it because it felt like I was stepping on needles and *everything hurt*.

To distract myself, to avoid his eyes, I petted the *pyroki*, stroking my hand down her—his?—snout. It seemed to like the attention and pressed more deeply into me, eyelids fluttering over glowing red eyes.

"I'm sorry," I whispered quietly. Then taking a deep breath, I looked up at the horde king, whose face was as familiar as my own. He was watching me, but I didn't know what he was thinking. "*Kalloma*'s message for the *Laseta Kalliri* is...*you will find the answer in the heart of Dothik.*"

Serok went curiously still. "She told you those exact words?"

I nodded. "*Lysi.* Do they mean something to you?" I asked quietly, sniffling.

He went quiet. Those eyes flickered.

"You really don't know how to negotiate for what you want, *saila*," he finally said. He didn't seem uncomfortable at seeing me break down in front of him. He acted like this happened regularly. Like females came crying to him all the time. And for all I knew, maybe they did.

I shook my head, feeling a bit of a headache bloom. "No bargains. This is the right thing to do. You were right. It's not about me, and I was being selfish."

His hand moved.

I swallowed when his warm palm came to settle against my cheek. His hand was so large that his clawed fingers scraped against my scalp behind my ears and his touch even extended down my jaw.

My petting became a bit more frantic on his *pyroki* as restless energy rose inside me. I wasn't used to being touched like this. I wasn't used to being studied like this.

"I never said you were a burden."

Softly, I said, "You didn't have to."

A chuffing exhale came from him. "Do you know the story of Bekkar and the horde of Jina?"

"*Lysi*," I whispered, my mind flashing to the excerpt in Bekkar's tome.

"And what happened?"

His thumb began to stroke the length of my cheekbone. It made it hard to focus.

"Bekkar was just beginning his campaign across the West," I recited. "Jina's horde lay in his way. But he was outnumbered against Jina's *darukkars*, who were far more skilled and experienced than Bekkar's own."

"And what did he do?" Serok asked, his voice a velvety grumble.

"He knew he could not defeat them," I said, brow furrowing, wondering what the point of this was. Because Bekkar...

Then my lips parted. I looked at Serok.

"Bekkar surrendered. He walked into the horde alone and lay his sword on the ground before the *Vorakkar*," I said. "The *Vorakkar* of Rath Jina could have killed him right there. Bekkar was weaponless. Defenseless. He told his own warriors to stay beyond the horde's territory so they would not be harmed."

"Do you think that was easy for Bekkar to do?" Serok asked.

"Of course not," I said immediately. For someone like Bekkar, it would have been excruciating. For another male to hold his life in his hands.

"Yet Bekkar knew that he was nothing without the *Vorakkar* of Rath Jina," Serok told me. "To Jina, Bekkar was a burden on the threshold of his territory, a weight in his mind, a pinch in his side because he was a threat to his people. But that changed when Bekkar lay down his sword before him. Without Jina, without their respect for one another, the kingdom would have never been formed, *lysi*? So you admire Bekkar, *saila*. But it is not Bekkar that *I* admire."

"You admire Jina," I said quietly, my mind working, processing the words. "You...you see the people that *made* Bekkar great. Not the greatness itself."

I...*liked* that. Not once had I ever thought of *Jina* as the hero. But Serok did. It was like seeing a story—one I'd read over a hundred times—in a whole new light.

He inclined his head. "It was Jina who made the choice. It was Jina who showed mercy that day. Only because of *him* did Bekkar become the *Seta Dothikkar*. Without Jina, there would be no Bekkar. There would be no *Dothik*. The kingdom would not exist."

The *pyroki* nudged my hand, and I realized that I'd stopped petting its snout. Chastised, I resumed my movements, and the beast made a pleased sound, the taloned hooves clomping into the grass.

"Bekkar followed his instincts that day. So did Jina," Serok continued. "You may call it Kakkari's guiding hand. You may see it as Kakkari's influence. But I felt it when you asked me to take you from the temple. *I* made that decision. You are here because of that instinct. Or because of Kakkari. However you wish to view it."

My lips parted in wonder.

"You asked why I changed my mind, and that is why," he finished. "It was *instinct*. *Why* I felt it remains to be seen. But the path will reveal itself. As it is always meant to."

The path.

Serok took his hand away from my cheek, and cold air rushed in. He went to his *pyroki's* side and began to dig around in the travel sack, bringing out the fire basin, fuel, and a little pot of *uudun* salve, green and thick in its jar.

"I cannot promise to take you to *Dothik* with me. In fact, your *kalloma* specifically asked me not to," he said suddenly, his tone firm.

My brow furrowed. She had?

"But I do promise to take you to my horde and then bring you to the western *saruk* to retrieve that heartstone. After that..."

"You will follow your instincts," I finished for him. It was a relief to hear it spoken out loud. His plan for me. Because at least now I knew what to expect.

I knew what tomorrow would bring.

His gaze lingered on me. "*Lysi.* They have never led me astray before."

Taking in a deep breath, I leaned my cheek against the *pyroki's* snout. I didn't feel nearly as tired as I'd been before. The needle pricks in my feet had faded. I could feel my tail again as it hovered over soft grass. Even the burning between my thighs had lessened. I just needed time to calm down, to regroup.

Out of the corner of my eye, I watched Serok as he began to set up our makeshift camp. Not for the first time, I wondered about him. I wondered about what his life had been before. How had he become a *Vorakkar*? Did he have a family? A...wife? A lover?

A strange sensation burned in my belly at the thought. One I didn't like, and so I pushed it from my mind.

The *pyroki* nuzzled my hair, and sharp teeth nibbled through the strands. The sensation tickled, and I couldn't help the grin that stole over my face, the small giggle that followed. I'd always thought of *pyrokis* as fearsome, dangerous beasts.

This one just liked petting and cuddling.

"You'll make me jealous of my own *pyroki, saila,*" came Serok's dark voice, though there was a hint of amusement in his tone. "Syok knows a pretty female when he sees one. He's a relentless beast."

My face flushed, a little ball of pleasure blooming in my chest, even as surprise made me blink.

Syok.

He'd...told me his *pyroki's* name?

At least now I knew it *was* a male.

"Syok," I whispered, ignoring that Serok had just called me *pretty*. I dismissed those words immediately, thinking it likely that he just wanted to make me feel better after my crying session.

The fire crackled to life, the horde king making quick work of it.

"Come," he called out. "You need to put *uudun* on the burn."

Sighing, I turned and limped across the clearing. Serok shrugged off his fur pelt though there was a chill in the air, revealing his tight tunic, sculpted muscles, and brawny arms.

I swallowed, watching as he spread it on the ground next to the fire. For me?

"You should wear your furs, Serok," I told him. "It's cold and—"

My breath hitched, my gaze zeroing in on his tunic when he turned. The left pocket, which his furs had covered until now.

His brow raised when he saw me staring intently. A slow smile curved over his lips. "*Saila*, if you'd like me to take off my tunic too, I am nothing but generous."

I nearly choked at his arrogance, but it wasn't what caught my attention.

"The heartstone," I rasped. "It's *glowing*."

CHAPTER 19

"N*effar?*" I asked, frowning. Then I looked down to the pocket of my tunic I'd placed it in.

Fittingly, the heartstone was right over my heart and it was, indeed, glowing. Blue diffused light spread from my pocket, and I dug out the small stone slowly.

When I unwrapped the cloth, Kara shuffled forward. "Careful," she said, biting her lip in apparent nervousness.

Her eyes were still red from crying, but I felt a pulse of warmth and awareness when she neared. Affection? Why? Because I'd always had a soft spot for distressed females?

Likely so, I grumbled silently. I couldn't help myself, it seemed. I hadn't liked watching her cry. Seeing her shoulders sag and hearing her voice wobble had made restless discomfort rise.

"Why do you think it's glowing?" came her bewildered question, watching as I peeled back the cloth to reveal the stone.

"I don't know," I returned. "*You're* the one who grew up in the *orala sa'kilan.*"

Whereas I'd grown up in the slums of *Dothik.*

The *Vorakkar* of Rath Tuviri and I had that in common. But

123

where Tuviri had only seen desperation and hopelessness, I'd seen *opportunity*. He'd only wanted to leave his world behind. I'd built mine up around me so high that no one would *dare* touch me.

"*Lysi*, I know," she said, a hard, annoyed edge in her tone, and I nearly grinned hearing it. At least she wasn't crying anymore. I'd take her ire over her tears any day. "But it only ever glowed during the *kalliris'* prayers."

"Well...are you praying right now?" I wondered, cocking my brow.

"Do I look like I'm praying right now?" she returned, meeting my eyes and holding them.

I scratched at my jaw as my trews tightened. Just like her little growl last night, her sass was unexpected and refreshing... and it was making my *deva* heavy.

"You know," I started, "I could have you bound and imprisoned in my horde for looking me in the eyes without my permission."

Her pupils dilated. For a moment, she reared back.

In a light tone, I added, "Just thought you should know."

Kara blinked wildly.

Serves her right for her sass, I thought, hiding my smirk.

"I am the *Seta Kalliri's* daughter," she shot back a moment later. This time, she took *me* by surprise. "I think I can look you in the eyes if I wish to."

I threw my head back and laughed. This moment felt surreal. Her face was glowing blue from Kakkari's heartstone. She was giving me a hard time about chastising her after I'd watched her cry and sob on the back of my *pyroki*.

Maybe she will be fine in Dothik after all, I couldn't help but think. She had some teeth on her, some *bite*. She would need it if I decided to bring her to the capital.

Kara bit her lip, looking a little surprised by her own

bravado. But then her chin lifted and I watched as she owned it, like she'd always meant to say that. I approved.

Clearing her throat, she glanced back down at the heartstone.

The heartstone of the *orala sa'kilan* was rumored to be the most powerful on Dakkar. The priestesses would feel the loss of it. Wherever a heartstone was, prosperity always followed, power always followed. The heartstone in *Dothik* was rumored to be embedded in Bekkar's own sword once, paving the way for his great campaign, though something about that tale had always given me pause.

For something so powerful, it looked small in my palm. A smooth stone, the surface unblemished. Inside, colors swirled.

Like the fog, I couldn't help but think. The colors moved like a breeze cutting through the fog. Except instead of red, the heartstone was blue.

When it wasn't glowing, it was a dark gray. Unremarkable. Just a rock trod over on a long journey. Forgotten and useless. It made me wonder how they'd even been discovered in the first place.

Kara's hand reached out, hesitating. Reacting on instinct, I closed the cloth, wrapping it tight.

"What are you doing?"

She swallowed. "I touched it in the *sa'kilan. Kalloma* pressed it into my hand, and I swore I heard voices. *Millions* of them. I was just thinking I should learn what they are saying."

"*Nik,*" I growled out, thinking how dangerous the heart-stones were. Especially if she had a gift. Because only those with Kakkari's gifts could unleash a heartstone's power. "That is out of the question."

"Why?"

"Because the last heartstone that was used likely *created* the fog in the East Lands," I told her.

Her lips parted. "But you said a human *Morakkari* used it. You didn't say it caused the fog!"

"We do not know for certain. The heartstone was used under the Dead Mountain. Shortly after, the fog appeared. I do not think it's a coincidence."

"She used it at the Dead Mountain?" she asked, her jaw hanging open. "But why?"

"The Ghertun threatened the life of her horde king," I informed her gruffly. "They were trying to kill him, and instead, she killed them all."

Kara sobered. Her gaze flickered to the heartstone. "Do you...do you think the *Seta Kalliri* knew this?"

My lips pressed together. Though the heartstone was still glowing and we had no idea *why*, I tucked it back in my pocket. We wouldn't find the answers tonight.

"*Lysi*, she was informed by *thesper*," I told her.

Her shoulders sagged again. "What else has she kept from me?" came the soft question.

I didn't know how to answer that. Kara had said she'd kept the heartstones a secret to keep *her* safe...and I wondered what she'd meant by that. I wondered if it had anything to do with what the *Seta Kalliri* whispered into my ear in the *sa'kilan*.

"Sit," I ordered her. Then I tossed her the pot of *uudun* salve. "Put that on. The faster you heal, the easier tomorrow will be."

She shook her head but did as I told her, sinking down onto the furs I'd laid out for her. "Why would it be glowing?" she whispered, though I got the sense it was more to herself. I watched her eyes flicker and dart around, like she was running through a catalog of information in her mind. "It doesn't make sense."

"Think on it tomorrow," I advised her. "With a fresh mind, after a good night's rest. There is nothing that can be done tonight, so why worry about it?"

I sank down next to her after I retrieved our rations. The sides of our legs touched and pressed together. She froze, and I snorted.

After being between my thighs and in my arms all day on Syok, was she really going to be shy about my proximity now? I didn't want to sit on the wet ground, and neither did she.

"*Uudun,*" I reminded her, digging in the bag before procuring dried chunks of *wrissan* meat and thick slices of *kuveri* bread. *Vok,* I was hungry. "Then we can eat."

"But I'll need to take off my trews," she said.

"*Lysi,*" I said, looking over at her and raising a brow.

"Then you'll be able to see my *melir,* and you might want to mate with me."

I nearly choked on the bite of crumbly *kuveri* bread I took. Coughing, I pounded at my chest with the side of my fist before taking a swig of water from the skin.

Then I laughed, despite my near-death experience.

"Are you *vokking* with me?" I asked, turning my wide smile on her. I coughed again. "Truly?"

"If I show you my *melir,* you'll want to mate. Isn't that how all males are?" she asked. That was when I saw the genuine confusion on her face. The flush of her cheeks.

I blew out a breath.

All right, maybe she isn't ready for Dothik, I amended silently.

"Where did you hear that?" I wondered. "Wait, let me guess. From your *kalloma?*"

The word was a strange mash-up of *kalliri* and *lomma.* I guessed what it meant and thought the title was charming.

"Well, *nik,*" she said. "From Avala. And Trissa."

"Two of the *kalliris?*" I guessed. At her nod, I shook my head. "*Vok.* I cannot imagine…"

"Imagine what?" she wanted to know.

"Growing up in a temple," I told her. I blew out a rough

breath. "I hate to break it to you, *saila*, but I have seen plenty of *melirs* in my lifetime. Yours will not be life changing to the point where I *need* to 'mate with you,' as you call it."

She frowned. "And what do you call it?"

"Fucking," I offered helpfully, tearing into the *kuveri* bread again. "*Vokking.*"

She blinked rapidly. I noticed she did that when she was caught off guard or embarrassed or both.

"So...if you see my *melir*, you won't demand a mating?" she asked.

Like...she needed to be absolutely *certain*.

Vok me, I thought, groaning.

It took everything in me not to laugh, but then I remembered. The *Seta Kalliri* had warned me that if I lay with Kara... then she would never be welcomed back to the temple.

But wasn't this another level of control the *kalliris* had over her? Though she was not a priestess, she was still not allowed to take a male? Not allowed to explore sex?

The depressing reality of that made me sober. Truthfully, I pitied her.

"*Nik*, Kara," I said, meeting her eyes. "That's not how it works. It is more complicated than that."

She reared back before she shifted her gaze to the fire. A thoughtful expression passed over her face. "In what way?"

Scratching at the edge of my jaw, I debated how to answer her innocent question. On one hand, I *really* didn't want to teach her those things. On the other, no one else was going to tell her.

"I've read a lot about mating," she offered quietly. I cleared my throat, shifting on my furs. "All the accounts in the books I could find."

My lips quirked. *Vok*, if I was stuck in the priestesses' temple, I would do the same.

But I'd have to learn how to read first, I grumbled silently.

"But they were never very detailed."

I snorted. I would bet they were, indeed, very dry accounts.

"It always seemed as though the female simply approached a male and it was a certain thing."

"Because more times than not, it is," I informed her.

"But you said—"

"There is seduction, *saila*," I said, cutting her off. "A very careful building of desire is what leads to mating. A knowing look, a bold touch, a few whispered words to arouse the interest. You have to *want* to fuck someone."

"So..." She trailed off, a high-toned pitch in her voice. "You don't *want* to mate with me?"

Was that *hurt* I heard in her voice?

Vok, I couldn't win either way.

Very carefully, I avoided meeting her eyes though I felt hers pinned on me. I could feel her frown. Tilting my head back to peer at the sky, my gaze very appropriately landed on Bekkar's cock and balls.

"I didn't say that," I said quietly. Then, hurriedly, I added, "But you have to understand that simply seeing your *melir* is not going to change anything. Not tonight."

She seemed to perk up at the words, and I nearly groaned.

This female was going to be the death of me.

"I see," she said, but I wondered if she truly did. This was not a conversation I'd expected to have tonight...or *ever*. But it only highlighted how different we were. How different our lives were. I heard a rustle of clothing and watched as she began to unlace her trews. "Thank you for explaining."

Swallowing, I turned my gaze away and stood. "I'm going to go take a piss."

She wrinkled her nose at the crude words but was too focused on the laces to look at me. I didn't wait. I rounded the back of the grass-covered hill, blowing out a deep breath when I had the privacy. I did my business but then decided to wait a moment more.

Staring up at the night sky, I thought over her words and shook my head. But it didn't stop an amused, disbelieving grin from stealing over my features.

Kara was something else. That was certain.

And the temple had done her a grave disservice.

Peering down at my tunic pocket, I saw the heartstone wasn't glowing anymore. Whatever it was...perhaps it had been a fluke. Or maybe Kara had influenced it in some way without realizing it. She'd been crying. We knew the heartstones fed off pain, thanks to the *Morakkari* of Rath Rowin. Could it also feed off emotional pain?

Discomfort swam in my belly. I didn't like keeping the heartstone so near, but it was necessary.

After another moment, I decided to return, thinking I'd given her enough time to slick on the *uudun*.

When I rounded the hill, however, I froze.

I was *not* prepared to see her with the hem of her dress tucked under her chin, her trews still off, and her thighs splayed wide open. The pot of *uudun* was perched precariously on her knee as she smoothed the salve over her chafed inner thighs.

Swallowing, I couldn't help it when my gaze zeroed in on her cunt. A purely male instinct, my gaze was drawn to it like a *vokking* magnet.

She had her legs spread in a way where the bottoms of her feet were touching and her knees made sharp angles. As such, I spied the deep pink of her *melir* parted for my gaze. She was completely hairless, which surprised me. Then again, I'd heard about the hygiene rituals of the priestesses, and I wondered if Kara followed them as well.

And despite what I'd told her, I felt my body react to the

mere enticing sight. My cock thickened, blood rushing so fast it made me lightheaded. My *deva* grew heavy, beginning to pulse.

Then I felt like the lowest of bastards because I'd assured her that that wouldn't happen.

When Kara saw me return, she blinked, the hem of her dress dropping into her lap, covering her cunt. A relief. I blew out a breath and returned to the furs, sitting next to her like nothing was out of the ordinary.

When in reality, I was aching and hard and trying to hide the tenting of my trews from her gaze.

"Are you hungry?" I asked. *Vok*, my voice sounded dark and husky. Clearing my throat, I added, "The *kuveri* is a bit dried out, but it'll do until we reach the horde tomorrow."

"You think we'll reach them tomorrow?" she asked, surprised. Excitement lit up her voice, and I relaxed a little, watching as she began to shimmy her trews back up her legs. When they were secured, she capped the pot of *uudun* and said, "*Kakkira vor*—it already feels better."

"*Lysi*," I said in regard to her first question, taking the *uudun* from her and pocketing it. "Though it depends how far my *pujerak* took them. I'll need to start looking for tracks in the afternoon."

"I've always wondered what a horde is like," she told me, plucking a slice of *kuveri* bread from my grip when I offered it to her before happily munching on it.

"You'll see for yourself."

We ate in silence, the crackling of the fire the only sound that sizzled between us. When we were done and we'd both had our fill of water, I watched as she tugged her own satchel toward herself, lifting it into her lap before rummaging inside it.

When she lifted out her precious stack of parchment, I thought of how impractical such a thing was out in the wild-lands of Dakkar. A strong gust of wind could rip it to shreds in mere moments. But then my chest warmed as I watched her thumb through the pages carefully, as if they were sheets of solid gold.

"What is that anyway?" I asked, leaning back on my elbow, stretching my booted feet—my *thieving* boots, as she'd called them—toward the fire.

She flashed me a look. That secretive smile was back—my cock pulsed in reaction. "The history of Bekkar."

I barked out a laugh before grinning and lying down, using a mound of grass as a pillow, though it was a little damp. I threaded my hands to cradle my head.

The stars were laid out before me. My gaze flitted from one to another, making up constellations in my mind, seeing different ones than the ones that were sketched in tomes.

"You really have a thing for Bekkar."

It was strange to think he was my ancestor. It was strange to think I had any claims to that line, even if the *Dothikkar* had attempted to sever them.

As if on cue, the tip of my thumb pressed to my sliced-off ear, tracing the remaining flat cartilage.

"I'm looking for the passage about Jina," she told me quietly. "I'd like to read it again. Because now I can read it with a fresh perspective. Through new eyes." She glanced at me, her expression a little shy. "Through *yours*."

My heart gave a solid little thump at the gentle sentiment, and I briefly rubbed the skin over it, my fingers hitting the heartstone.

"Read it to me," I murmured. "Will you?"

She smiled.

And that smile damn near *killed* me.

Beautiful in her simple joy.

I'd never seen anything like it.

While I'd never been struck breathless by a female in my life, this half-human, half-Dakkari temple girl was…surprising.

"Really?" she asked, hopeful.

Clearing my throat, I nodded.

"Of course," I said, shaken from that smile, though I hid it with my own smirk. "How else will I understand why you're so taken with Bekkar? A male likes to study his competition after all."

CHAPTER 20

"That didn't happen."

I sucked in a breath, simmering. "It's been confirmed by two different texts in the archives. I researched it myself!"

We were back to bickering. It had begun last night, truthfully, after I'd read pages of Bekkar's history to him. The sniping had bled into the morning and afternoon.

Serok was infuriating.

"I don't care what your dusty tomes say," he retorted, his tone patient and absolutely maddening. "Mirak was not a *Vorakkar*, not even briefly. He was Bekkar's *prikri*, his lead advisor in *Dothik,* because he was loyal during the campaign across the West Lands. Bekkar did not 'recruit' him from his own horde because he never *had* a horde."

I focused on breathing in through my nostrils.

"Then let me ask you this," I began, "in the description of Mirak, it said his wrists bore golden cuffs. *Vorakkar* cuffs. How do you explain that?"

Serok snorted from behind me, his arms tightening. "Horde kings didn't even wear cuffs during that time. It was the third

Dothikkar that began slapping them on *Vorakkar's* wrists. And you want to know why?"

My lips pressed together. "Enlighten me."

"Because the third *Dothikkar* was an insecure, weak male who never should have been king in the first place. *That* is the problem with bloodlines."

I frowned, turning in my seat to meet his eyes. He looked unflustered. Calm, cool, and collected, whereas I was certain my cheeks were burning with frustration and my hair was a tousled mess from running my hands through it too many times.

"But...you said Tanniva was his mistress, didn't you? That the third *Dothikkar* brought peace to Dakkar. I've read his history. Despite his rocky beginning on the throne, the capital flourished under his rule. You can't deny that."

Serok blinked, long and slow, as he swayed on the back of his *pyroki*. Our pace was much gentler today than it'd been yesterday. I knew it was for my sake.

"The trade wars," Serok told me, as if that would answer all of my questions.

"*Lysi?* And?"

"Who were they against?"

"The hordes of the wildlands," I answered, as if it were obvious.

"Who were angry that *Dothik* was limiting their freedoms. Suddenly you have a great kingdom rising in the West Lands, one that goes against everything the hordes knew, everything they believed in. Bekkar's campaign stretched far and wide. He was a friend of the hordes because he was a horde king himself. But then his sons took rule and they started wanting things that could only be found in the wildlands. So what happened?"

A tendril of my anger seeped out from me. "*Dothik* started demanding those things from the hordes. Furs. Spices. Crops. Meat. They paid them."

Realization went through me.

"But...but the hordes have no need for money. For coins," I finished. Serok inclined his head. "So *Dothik* had nothing of value to offer the hordes. They were self-sufficient already."

"The hordes began to refuse *Dothik's* wishes. Which led to uprisings. Which led to the trade wars. *Dothik* sent out armies, and hordes sent out *darukkars* to defend their territories. And all of this was happening under the third *Dothikkar's* rule."

I nodded.

"It went on for years," he added. "And then Tanniva, a revered priestess from *Dothik's* temple, slipped into the *Dothikkar's* bed."

"But what did she say?" I asked hurriedly. "How did she fix it?"

"By offering the hordes what they needed, even if they didn't realize it yet," he told me. "Dakkari steel. Weapons. *People*, new members that would grow the hordes. Gold instead of coins for their markings. More efficient tanning racks. Tools to dig out wells and crops. Softer silks for their females. So a new system of trading and bartering was put into place. The same system that continues even now."

I nodded again, but then I looked at him suspiciously. "We were speaking of *Vorakkar* cuffs. And about Mirak."

He grinned. "I haven't forgotten."

"Then make your point, *Vorakkar*."

His brows rose. Belatedly, I realized it was probably disrespectful to speak to him in such a way.

"*Hanniva*," I added. *Please*.

His low chuckle warmed my belly.

"Throughout the third *Dothikkar's* rule, the hordes became more and more dependent on the goods coming from *Dothik*. Finally, war began to break out among the hordes, fighting over those goods. And those hordes asked *Dothik* for more weapons, for aid. So suddenly *Dothik* was in the position of power. Not the hordes," Serok said, frowning.

A chill went up my spine. I had read something about the trade wars, but the text hadn't been detailed. The history of that time was condensed, mere scribbles across a page, and I marveled that one of the most important events of our history —one that forever changed the future of the hordes and *Dothik* —had been glossed over so hastily.

What else has been scrubbed from the books? I couldn't help but wonder.

"*Dothik* decided that they would only give aid to the hordes that bent their knee to them," Serok said, his tone gruff. "As a symbol of loyalty to the capital and to the *Dothikkar*, it was decided that the *Vorakkar* would wear the cuffs. The ones that agreed were the victorious hordes in that war because they had finer weapons, more warriors. And then over time, it was decided that the *Dothikkar* would choose all future horde kings. The old way of the hordes slowly vanished. They were small kingdoms in their own right. Now they are kingdoms that belong to whatever *Dothikkar* is in power."

"Even yours?" I couldn't help but ask softly. I heard something in his voice. Strained tension. Muted disgust.

"Especially mine," came the soft words. My brow lowered. Serok smirked, and his brooding expression was gone. "So you see, *saila*? Mirak could not have worn *Vorakkar* cuffs during Bekkar's rule. Perhaps he was simply fond of adornments."

My shoulders sagged. "It doesn't mean he wasn't a *Vorakkar* before," I grumbled.

A chuckle of disbelief went through Serok. "After all of that, you still don't believe me?"

I eyed him. "How do you know all this anyway? Did you study in *Dothik*? I've heard they have an institution for scholars there."

"I'm no scholar." His gaze slid from me. "My *lomma* was fond of *Dothik's* history and had a very extensive education beginning when she was a mere child. She took it upon herself to educate me, should I ever have need of it."

"Is she in *Dothik* now? Or did you bring her to your horde?" I asked, curious about any tidbit of information I could glean about this male. He fascinated me. I couldn't figure him out.

"Neither. She's dead," he said, his tone deceptively conversational.

I squirmed on Syok's back. "I—I'm sorry. I didn't mean to..."

"I know, *saila*," he said, flashing me another smile that made me relax. He didn't seem entirely grief-stricken at the mention of his mother, which made me wonder what type of relationship he'd had with her.

Was it like Avala's? Avala's mother had sent her to the priestesses when she was only a young girl. She hardly knew her. Avala didn't know if she was alive or dead.

Or was it like my relationship with *Kalloma*? Where it had been difficult to unwrap my arms from around her when we left the *orala sa'kilan*? Where I missed her so deeply it ached?

A strained silence fell between us. Or perhaps it just felt strained to me. Serok didn't seem all that bothered. His expression was neutral, and his eyes darted along the horizon. I faced forward, feeling a little awkward simply staring at him when we weren't speaking.

Clearing my throat, thinking it would cut some of the tension, I asked, "Well, do you at least agree with the book's account of Jina?"

"*Lysi,*" he murmured. "Something it actually got right."

I sighed.

"Your complaints don't diminish my love for that book, you know," I informed him. "It's my favorite out of all that I've read."

"Why?" he wondered, guiding Syok up a grassy incline. We had crossed the alleged border into the West Lands earlier this morning, an anti-climactic event that Serok only informed me of hours later when I asked. "What do you find so intriguing about it?"

"The excitement of it. The adventure of it," I told him. I sighed loftily. "His love for Lessa. You talk of how it was people who made Bekkar great. If that's true, then it was Lessa who made him the greatest of all."

Serok grunted.

I looked at him over my shoulder. "No biting remarks about the first queen of *Dothik*? No stories of how she was actually a conniving spy sent by her father's horde to take the throne?"

His chuckle was low and languid. I listened to it, the base of my tail tingling in pleasure. His laugh made me feel, briefly, like I was floating. The discomfort of Syok underneath me was forgotten. The crick in my neck from constantly turning to look at him disappeared.

"Lessa was a great queen," he told me. "Befitting of the first —and arguably only—great king."

I grinned. "Something we finally agree on."

Serok shook his head, murmuring under his breath, his red-and-gold eyes flashing with mirth in the high afternoon sun.

"I think you're wrong about one thing though," I told him.

"*Hanniva,*" he murmured, his tone teasing. Repeating the words I'd said to him, he ordered, "Enlighten me."

"I don't think the hordes belong to the *Dothikkar,*" I said. "Hordes are powerful. There is a reason they still exist after hundreds and hundreds of years. And *Vorakkar are* kings. So how can one king rule them all? That would be a dangerous thing."

Sometimes it was easy to forget he *was* a horde king. He was everything I'd thought one would be: Battle bred. Intimidating. Handsome. Strong. Frightening.

And yet...I found it easy to talk to him. Even when we'd bickered throughout the morning and afternoon, he was never malicious. His smiles came easily, his laugh even more so. I didn't feel *unsafe* with him. Quite the opposite, actually.

"If the *Dothikkar* calls us to the capital, we must go. Like a *pyroki* yielding to its master," he told me. "One day it may change. But for now, the *Dothikkar's* influence stretches wide. All the *Vorakkar* know it, even if they do not want to admit it."

"How would you like it to be?" I asked, curious at his reply. "If you gave up your horde and somehow became the *Dothikkar*, how would you like it to be?"

His expression was a strange thing as I asked the innocent question. A brief flash of what I thought was *rage* caught me off guard. His lips pressed together tightly. Then he went quiet.

He...looked as serious as I'd ever seen him.

He said, "I would build *Dothik* back up. I would ensure that we were not as reliant on the hordes so that the hordes do not feel as though they are reliant on *Dothik*. It is a strained relationship already. Deeper ties would wreck it completely and send us spinning into war. We are in a time of peace, despite the fog in the East Lands. Dakkari have not warred with one another in quite some time, focusing all our efforts on the Ghertun. Now they are gone. Soon we will begin to turn on one another again. There is already unrest in the capital. I would do everything to soothe it before it spilled beyond the city walls. I would want to open up the seas again. I would want to negotiate with the outposts and their *Sorakkar* to create a working relationship with the capital. I would let the people choose their horde kings. That decision should not belong with one male alone."

My mouth went dry just listening to him. He'd obviously spent a lot of time thinking about this.

It looked as if he wanted to say more...but then he caught himself.

He shifted. His expression changed. I watched as a small

smile spread. "And if I were *Dothikkar*, I sure as hell wouldn't make the *Vorakkar* wear these damn cuffs."

Turning to face forward, I looked down in front of me. The gold of those cuffs flashed in the sunlight. I couldn't help but touch them, running my finger down the smooth, hot metal.

Serok went still behind me. I watched as the veins in the back of his hand flexed, his knuckles going white.

"Do they hurt?" I wondered softly.

"If I said they did, would you kiss them to make me feel better?" he teased, though his voice sounded guttural and dark.

I swallowed, feeling his words spiral down my body, pooling in my core. I imagined it: Brushing my lips over his skin. Feeling his warmth seep into me.

But then I realized what he was doing. Deflecting.

Frowning, I opened my mouth to ask him why, but then my ears twitched.

Serok seemed to hear what I did because his hand immediately lifted from the reins to wrap around my waist, pulling me more fully into him.

I would have been flustered had I not frozen up.

"What is that?" I whispered, trying to determine the direction of the vibration, swinging my head wildly.

The earth began to shake. A low rumbling that started small but then grew in intensity.

My teeth began to clatter.

There was little warning when a black mass rolled over the hill, directly next to us. Like a wave that spilled over the land. Coming straight toward us.

"*Vok*," Serok cursed before his *pyroki* kicked into motion. My head jerked back and hit Serok's chest with the sudden sprinting speed. "*Bveri!*"

CHAPTER 21

B *veri?*

My eyes went wide when I realized it wasn't a strange black mass but rather a *herd*. A herd of *bveri*, prized for their meat and fur. Hundreds of massive beasts began pouring over the hill, running at top speeds, their weight vibrating the earth.

And we were right in their path.

"*Draki*," Serok growled. *Faster*. Beneath us, Syok's pace increased. My bones seemed to echo. I gritted my teeth when he landed particularly hard, and I felt like my backside would be bruised come morning.

If we make it to morning, I realized.

"Serok," I breathed, my eyes trying to find where the herd ended. There just seemed to be more and more rippling down the hill. I could hardly hear my own voice over the sound.

"I know," came his growl. "We need to get behind that hill."

I spied what he did. A hill that was half stone. It looked like the steep mound had been sliced neatly in half, revealing the rocky structure on the smoothed side. It made me wonder if all these hills were made of stone.

Regardless, the *bveri* wouldn't be able to climb it, for the incline dropped steeply. If we reached the hill, we'd be protected by the rocky face as the herd passed.

It didn't change the fact that we were riding perpendicular to a massive herd hurtling toward us in an unbreakable line. If they hit us, we'd be toppled off Syok and trampled in a single moment.

This can't be happening, I thought, my breath heaving from me, adrenaline rushing through my veins.

But that was why being out on the wildlands was so dangerous, why *Kalloma* had been so loath to let me leave. It was unpredictable. Deadly. The moment you dropped your guard...you could be struck down in a single moment.

The herd was so close I could smell them. A cloying, intense musk that nearly made me gag. I tightened my thighs on Syok's back, though Serok kept me pinned against him, leaning over my back to keep my secure. Even Serok's tail wrapped around mine, and I took comfort in the small gesture.

Gritting my teeth, I saw we were nearly there! My head swiveled from the herd to the rocky hill and then back again.

"We'll make it!" I gasped out.

I had to believe that.

I could see the red of the *bveri's* eyes. Then I squeezed my own shut briefly, counting down the seconds.

A moment later, we burst across the invisible line that meant *safety*. That meant *protection*.

The clattering of hooves rumbled behind us. Serok wheeled Syok around, and I watched as hundreds of *bveri* went streaming past the rocky hill. Not paying any attention to us at all, continuing on their way.

My heart was thundering in my throat. The stench was unbelievable. I tried to swallow the saliva pooling in my mouth but couldn't. I felt like I couldn't catch my breath at all.

"Is...is Syok okay?" I asked when my tongue untied. The *pyroki* was restless underneath us, continuing to wheel around, as if to make a break for it. But Serok kept pulling on his reins, keeping us in place.

"He's fine," came his rumbled, gruff voice. "Are you?"

Slowly, Serok straightened, no longer hovering over my back to keep me down. I rose too, but my eyes never left the herd. More and more came. What I thought was hundreds at first was likely more than a thousand.

"So many," I whispered in disbelief, bringing my forearm up to cover my nose.

Serok blew out a rough breath. His tail was still wrapped around mine, entwined.

"*Bveri* breed quickly and grow fast," he informed me. "In the last year, the hordes have not kept their numbers in check as they should."

Because of the fog, I guessed.

"This is not their normal migration path," he continued. "Now that the days and nights are warming, they are heading toward the North Lands. But they usually head up from the eastern border. The fog must've pushed them west."

I focused on the gentle lull of his voice, spoken directly in my ear, letting it calm me. His palm was spread wide on my waist. Despite the near-death experience, I felt comforted.

I nodded, though I still watched the migration wide-eyed. Studying the beasts I'd only ever read about and seen drawn in books.

They were shaggy, brawny beasts. I knew the hordes used their dense black fur as insulation for their *volikis* and for the colder frost months. They stomped around on four legs, as thick as the columns in the atrium of the temple. Curved horns protruded from their heads, and I shuddered to think that we'd nearly been speared by them.

Dangerous beasts.

And the hordes hunted them regularly. A brave, frightening mission, I thought.

Finally, the majority of the *bveri* seemed to pass us by, leaving only a few stragglers that raced to catch up with the rest of the herd. I lowered my arm from my nose. Slowly, the earth stopped shaking. The low rumbling sound slowly began to fade away until we heard nothing at all.

"It's a rare sight, you know. The *bveri* migration," Serok told me. "I've never seen it before either."

A hysterical laugh bubbled up from me. I turned to look over my shoulder at him. "That's because those that have seen it probably don't live to tell the tale."

Though he wasn't grinning, I heard the amusement in his voice, "Likely so. But we did."

I blew out a shaky breath, holding his eyes. "*Lysi*, we did."

His palm reached out to cup my face. And whether it was nerves or the last tendrils of adrenaline or just because he touched me, I felt my heartbeat quicken and my belly flutter. A sensation I wasn't familiar with but *liked*.

"Are you sure you're okay?" he asked, his voice serious. "Because the *Seta Kalliri* would cut off my *deva* if you were harmed."

Some of my excitement faded. Was he only concerned about that? That he'd be cursed by *Kalloma* if something happened to me?

"I'm fine," I assured him, patting Syok's neck beneath me.

Serok nudged Syok into motion. But instead of continuing in the direction we were heading, the horde king steered Syok around the hill.

"Where are we going?" I asked.

"To watch."

Understanding hit me when we started ascending the hill we'd been hiding behind. It was steep. It would give us a good view of the hilly valley. When we reached the top, I could still see the black mass of *bveri* heading north. Dust kicked up around them, sending a gritty plume into the sky.

Studying the migration, a sinking feeling settled in the pit of my gut, even though it mingled with my awe.

"What is it?" Serok asked quietly from behind me. As if he sensed something was wrong.

"I'll never see this again," I told him softly.

"You may, *saila*," he said, and I heard the frown in his voice. "You don't know that for certain."

But I do, I thought, watching the herd move, a solid mass that seemed to eat up the West Lands with ease. Traveling more quickly than a *pyroki* could ever hope to.

I gave him a soft smile over my shoulder. "I promised *Kalloma* I would return to the *orala sa'kilan* after this. And I meant it."

After this.

Whatever *this* was.

I would return. It was all I'd ever known. All the people I loved were there—a small, strange family that I'd known all my life.

So it was wonderful and frightening and thrilling to be away, to be sitting on the back of a *pyroki*, watching a *bveri* migration with a horde king whose grin made my tail curl. But I knew there would be an end to it. Maybe not soon but eventually.

And I'm determined to see and experience as much as I can before I return, I thought quietly to myself. *Because these memories will have to sustain me for the rest of my life.*

We watched the migration until the herd disappeared from view entirely, the rolling hills eventually sloping down. In the distance, I could faintly make out the tipped mountain peaks of the Orala Pass.

Suddenly Serok murmured something under his breath. When I turned to look at him, he was peering intently to our left, leaning forward.

"What is it?" I asked, before fastening my gaze on whatever it was he saw.

My lips parted. I straightened on Syok, my fingers gripping the thick, muscled column of his neck.

In the distance, nestled in a valley surrounded by hills and forests, I spied an encampment. A thin wisp of smoke had begun to rise in the sky. Even from here, I could see the bustle of activity.

Serok met my eyes.

"My horde."

Chapter 22

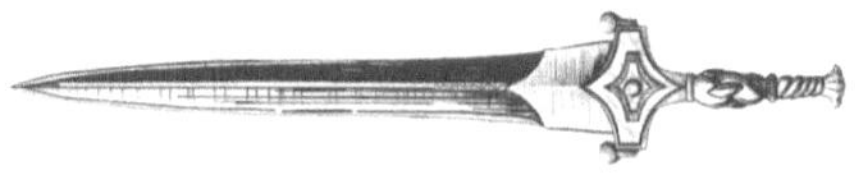

Kara kept squirming on Syok's back, which only served to rock her backside perilously close to my groin.

"Will you stop moving?" I rasped in her ear, keeping my *pyroki's* pace gentle for her. And partly for me. If her movements combined with the hard, rocking gait of Syok's full-speed sprint, I'd be unleashing in my trews, making them slick and sticky with my come. It had been much too long since I'd last had the company of a female. Between the East Lands and moving territories with my horde, there'd been no time to sleep, much less fuck.

"I'm excited," she said over her shoulder, her tone a tantalizing mixture of a defensive growl and a gleeful exclamation. That growl made my cock thicken even more, and I clenched Syok's reins tighter. "I've never seen a horde before. Only ones drawn in books. And the stories, of course. Can we go faster?"

My blown-out breath ruffled her hair. Truthfully, I hadn't given much thought to how I would explain her presence to my horde. Briefly, I debated asking her to cover her face with her cloak hood, at least until I spoke with Nassik. A half-Dakkari, half-human female—a *grown* female—would spark questions and interest and...perhaps even discomfort. Tensions were already high within the horde after the long journey to the West Lands.

And the hordes were angry with the priestesses, thinking they'd turned their backs on us all. What would bringing Kara into the midst spark, considering she was the *Seta Kalliri's* daughter?

"Tell no one about your relationship with your *kalloma*," I murmured in her ear, not responding to her request. "*Lysi?*"

"Why?" Judging by her tone of voice, I could tell she was frowning.

"Because the hordes feel betrayed by the priestesses. I do not want any taking out their frustrations on you."

She went quiet. Her excited squirming had stopped. "You think they would do that?"

"*Nik*. But I like to be prepared for any possible outcome. I think it is safer if you say you are a ward of the priestesses."

"But I am," she said softly, sounding lost and uncertain.

My hand grazed her forearm, and she reached her fingers out to touch mine. As if she needed the comfort and small contact.

My chest did that aching thing again. My heart squeezing until it felt like I couldn't breathe.

"I'm not ashamed of the *Seta Kalliri*, despite how she's handled this," she informed me. "And I won't hide who I am just because you think it might be easier. I'm not afraid of your horde."

A tendril of guilt mixed with my anger. "This is the first time you've ever been beyond the temple, Kara. The rules are different, and people can be cruel. Ruthless, even. I'm trying to protect you. I promised your *kalloma* that I would protect you."

She turned around to look at me with a sunny smile, completely at odds with the hurt I'd heard in her voice. However, even I recognized the determination in her eyes, the calculated certainty as she declared, "I won't bring it up voluntarily. But if someone asks—which they likely will—I will not lie."

I broke out in a series of harsh, whispered curses and rolled my neck, which suddenly went as stiff as my aching cock.

Vok, what was it about this maddening female? It took a lot to stoke my temper. It took a lot to lead me away from my tight control.

"Are there baths?" she wondered, turning back around in her seat, changing the subject entirely. "I haven't bathed since that little stream we came across, and the water was practically frozen over."

I stiffened. The sarcastic retort was out of my lips before I could stop it. "You think the hordes don't bathe? You think we wrestle around in the dirt and muck and go to our furs stinking of *pyroki* shit every night?"

She leveled me a look over her shoulder I could only describe as *prim*. "Of course not."

Before I could say anything more, the distant rumbling of a *pyroki* met my ears. We'd descended into the valley already, but it had taken us the better part of the afternoon to reach the horde from where the *bveri* migration had been. A small clearing among the trees of the forest opened up a road to us. That road would lead us to the clearing where I'd seen my horde.

Nassik was riding out on his *pyroki* to greet us, his brows furrowed in rapt confusion, a frown on his expressive features. Kara stilled when she saw him. I heard her breath hitch.

My *pujerak*, my second-in-command, met my gaze when he drew near before they flickered to Kara. He looked over her, fastening on her eyes, her hair, and the bulk of her cloak. His eyes stilled on her tail, widening slightly, before they flicked up to me.

"What is this, Serok?"

Seemingly unconsciously, a growl rose in my throat and my

hand went from Syok's reins to wrap around Kara's waist, pulling her back into me. Her spine stiffened at the sudden contact, but then I felt her relax into me, as if she was used to my touch.

My head swam. But one thing was certain, I did *not* enjoy watching Nassik run his eyes over her, even if the gaze was more assessing than in interest.

I released Kara's waist a moment later when I realized what I'd done—when the confounded look on Nassik's face reached me and my *pujerak*'s jaw went slack.

"Serok, what the *vok*?"

"Sorry, my friend," I murmured, shaking off the strange wave of possession that had coursed through me so suddenly. I'd never felt anything like it before. I had never been one to be *jealous*.

What had just happened?

I met Nassik's gaze. Our *pyrokis* didn't like one another, and Syok stomped his clawed talons into the ground, rumbling out a sound of warning when Nassik's drew too near.

"*Pyroth!*" I growled out to Syok, tugging on his reins as Kara's hand drifted down to Syok's neck. Her touch seemed to calm the beast more than my sharp command.

"The markings on your *pyroki* are very beautiful," came her voice, addressing my *pujerak* despite the sudden tension between us. "Blessed markings, are they not?"

Nassik blinked at her voice, dumbfounded by her words. His gaze went to his *pyroki's* flank. The birth markings along the *pyroki's* side were a swirled pattern. If you looked at it sideways, they were indeed the mark of the goddess, but I had never noticed before.

"I suppose so. The lucky bastard," Nassik said, recovering quickly before flashing her a smile, one that I knew had charmed half the females back in *Dothik*. Kara swayed a little before me, and I nearly growled again. His gaze came to me.

"*Vok,* we send you to the *orala sa'kilan* to speak with the priestesses and you come back with a pretty female. You haven't changed one bit, have you, Serok?"

He'd meant the words in jest, but Kara stiffened immediately, her spine straightening so tight before me that I swore I heard the bones snap.

I licked my lips and urged Syok into a gentle walk. Nassik came up beside me, though a respectful distance from my *pyroki*, the temperamental beast who snapped its jaws at the other *pyroki* before Kara patted his head.

"Who are you?" Kara asked, seeming to brush off whatever had overcome her.

Nassik raised a brow. His gaze came to me and then he said, "His *pujerak.*"

Her breath hitched in excitement. "You are?"

Nassik looked at her strangely. Trying to get a read on her? "*Lysi.* Does that impress you, *kalles?*"

Kara laughed. Nassik grinned. And I bit the inside of my cheek.

Cutting off their conversation, I asked Nassik, "How was the journey? There is a *bveri* migration an afternoon's ride from here. Do you think the hunters have rested enough?"

Kara's laugh died. "You would go hunt them?"

"We need to eat," I said tightly. "That is the way of the horde. And our supplies are low after the journey to the West Lands."

Kara went quiet as Nassik responded, "*Lysi.* I can have them sent out by the evening if you wish."

I nodded. "Do it. It's an opportunity we cannot waste."

Nassik's questioning gaze returned to the female perched in front of me, his brows raised in a stern look I recognized immediately.

Blowing out a sharp breath through my nostrils, I told him, "Later."

He inclined his head. "We are in the process of setting up the *volikis*. The *pyroki* enclosure and the *bikkus'* kitchen have been set up. The common baths are still being filled, but we located a well nearby from a previous encampment."

Kara squirmed in front of me.

"She would like a bath," I told Nassik, feeling a tendril of amusement curl in my belly despite the tension between us.

"Your *voliki* has been set up already," Nassik informed me. "Would you like me to send the bathing tub there?"

I swallowed. "There is not another *voliki* ready for her?"

Kara stilled, listening to our conversation.

"She can take one of the families' *volikis* perhaps," Nassik said. "We will have more up by tonight, but the entire horde has been up since dawn. We have another full day ahead, perhaps longer if you send out the hunting party."

"I don't want to take a family's *voliki*," Kara's gentle voice came. She turned to look at me. "Can't I sleep with you?"

I reminded myself that she was too naive to understand what message that would send rippling across my horde. I reminded myself that she'd been sleeping next to me on our journey—well, *she'd* been sleeping, *I'd* been watching the fire so she was warm—and that she would see no issue with it now that we'd arrived back at my horde.

Nassik cleared his throat, though I thought it was a well-concealed laugh. My mood darkened a little, my mind flashing to the High Priestess's warning.

Take care with her. And know that if you ever touch her, if you ever lie with her, she will never be allowed to return here. To her home. To the orala sa'kilan. *Do not take that away from her.*

That was what the most powerful and respected priestess on our planet had said to me before we left.

But I had tasted the fear that had tinged those words. Her fear had swirled over and coated my tongue in the most delicious way. And I wondered why the *Seta Kalliri* was so concerned that I, a bastard-born son raised in the streets of *Dothik*, would lie with her daughter.

Did she think me such an animal that I didn't have control over my own needs?

My jaw snapped at the thought. The *Seta Kalliri* was highborn, no doubt. Born and raised to a wealthy family in *Dothik*, blessed from a young age, who had never wanted for anything. Of course she would see me beneath her, even though I was a horde king now.

A spark of dangerous desire lit up my blood.

"Very well," I rasped. Turning my gaze to Nassik, I inclined my head. "Have her bath sent to my *voliki*. It will only be for a few nights regardless."

Nassik frowned. "Why?"

"We need to leave for the *saruk* of Rath Hidri."

"So soon?" My *pujerak's* eyes widened as he leaned toward me. "The priestesses gave you their answer?"

I nearly snorted.

"*Nik*, but she did," I told him, wrapping my hand around Kara's wrist. "And the High Priestess corroborated her theory when she was cornered."

"She was *not* cornered," Kara argued, throwing me a frown over her shoulder, loath for me to speak of her mother in such a way.

"What do you call it, then, *saila*?" I purred to her, my fingers stroking the inside of her wrist. She scoffed quietly and turned back around.

Nassik had more questions perched on the tip of his tongue as he watched us closely. But I would tell him everything—and in detail—when we were alone. Unlike the other hordes, I chose to take no council from the elders. It was just him and me. Like when we were young.

The path opened before us. The horde was surrounded by trees, which would not have been my first choice. Not with the reports of rabid *polkunu*, though, admittedly, they had been toward the South Lands.

The South Lands.

"How many *thespers* do we have right now?"

"Two," Nassik answered. "I sent one to *Dothik* because our steel supplies are low."

I continued to stroke my fingers over Kara's inner wrist, being careful not to cut her skin with my claws. She shifted on the *pyroki*, her tail flicking against my booted ankle. I heard her hard swallow, and I wanted to grin.

"Serok?"

Nassik was studying me with interest.

"*Dothik* will not come to our aid," I told him.

There was one thing I'd kept from him. One thing I'd kept to myself.

I'd never told him what I'd said to the *Dothikkar* after my Trials were completed, after he'd acknowledged my victory and my claim to all of *Dothik*. I'd never told him what I'd whispered in his ear. I'd never told him how satisfying it was to watch the blood drain from his face, his jovial, smug expression turning to one of horror right before my very eyes.

As such, the *Dothikkar* would never acknowledge me as a horde king. He'd already sent out one assassin for me in the wildlands—one I'd dispatched quickly and silently before anyone in my horde found out. And it wouldn't be the last time he tried to kill me. It hadn't even been the first. It was why I slept with my sword at my side and a dagger under my cushions. It was why I trusted very few.

Because I'd already survived assassination attempts. One had cost me my mother. Would I survive another? And if I did, what would be the price?

Kara winced, the sound breaking through my dark thoughts.

When I looked down, I saw a line of dark red blood well up

from a shallow cut across her wrist. I stiffened, seeing the human-colored blood, knowing I'd been the cause.

"I'm sorry, *saila*," I rasped down to her, feeling my chest tug with anger and concern. I'd cut her with my claw.

She shook her head and used her dress to blot at the blood. "It's all right."

When I met Nassik's eyes, I felt a surge of discomfort. His gaze went to Kara, narrowing on her.

"I need to send the remaining *thespers* to the *Vorakkar* of Rath Drokka and Rath Okkili," I told him, replacing Kara's hand with my own to stop the bleeding myself. I'd bandage the wound once we reached the horde. "We will need their help in the East Lands."

"You really know how to stop the fog?" Nassik asked, his voice guttural.

"It's our best hope" was what I told him.

Just then, we rounded a bend in the road and the horde came into view.

The familiar stirrings of dread rolled in my gut.

It will take time, I reminded myself. *It's been less than a year. Less than a year on the wildlands.*

Yet I still couldn't shake the feeling that I didn't belong. That I was meant to be *home*, in *Dothik*.

Instead, I was in the West Lands. A king in my own right, even though another throne would've been my birthright.

Home.

This was my home now. I needed to remember that.

CHAPTER 23

"Does it hurt?" Serok asked, kneeling before me where I was perched on his bed.

I bit my lip, watching him wind the soft cloth bandage around the cut carefully. He acted as if he'd taken a huge chunk of my flesh off. In reality, the cut would be gone in a day, maybe two. I healed slower than full-blood Dakkari, I'd come to realize. But I figured I still healed faster than humans.

"Terribly," I told him. His lips pressed, and I couldn't help but giggle. At my laugh, he looked up at me, those swirling eyes narrowing on me when he realized I was jesting. "Serok, I'm fine. I clean the temple every day. You know there is an ancient weapons vault, right? We even have Bekkar's sword. You know, the one from the constellation."

I hoped my teasing would at least break him out of the foul, brooding mood he'd been in ever since we reached his horde.

"You have his cock in the temple?" he asked next. "Because that's the only *sword* in the night sky, I assure you. How would the great Bekkar like it, knowing the *kalliris* cut his cock from him after death and it now hangs in a dark vault in the frigid North Lands? Do you have his *deva* too? Does your *kalloma* use it to hold her ink for her parchments?"

Rolling my eyes, I pushed at his strong, warm shoulder when he was finished securing the bandage.

"Bekkar was buried fully intact, I'll have you know," I informed him, sniffing. "But I have cut myself on his sword. Twice actually." The first had been across my hand. I showed him the second, baring my shoulder. A long scar ran down the back of it. I'd accidentally stumbled back into the blade one day, years ago. "It's still sharp. After all this time."

Serok went quiet, but he continued to kneel before me. Even though he was kneeling, I still had to raise my eyes to meet his.

"You truly have his sword?" he asked, something odd in his tone I couldn't place, as he reached forward to run the pad of his calloused finger down the scar.

"*Lysi,*" I told him, my tone climbing higher as I suppressed a pleasurable shiver. "I polish it every week."

A piece of our history. And I was the keeper of it.

Perhaps...perhaps what I did in the *orala sa'kilan was* important. Perhaps I'd just been thinking about it all wrong. I'd wanted adventure, hadn't I? Instead, I was the keeper of things that had had great adventures of their own.

Serok's gaze was dizzying. The rushing started in my ears as I focused on his finger smoothing over the scar. Then his touch lowered, tracing the line of my arm until it met the thick bandages he'd just wrapped around the tiny, tiny cut.

The desire I felt wasn't surprising. He was a handsome male, even more handsome than his already handsome *pujerak*. Being in both of the males' presence had been...overwhelming. And still, I wanted to look at Serok.

I'd been wanting to ask him something ever since our conversation last night, and yet I didn't know how to bring it up. It seemed like such a ridiculous thing to ask too, in the midst of the chaos in the East Lands, in the midst of the long journey we had ahead of us.

But it still remained that I wanted to experience everything

I'd ever dreamed of before I returned home. Back to the North Lands and *Kalloma* and the quiet of the temple.

Biting my lip with uncertainty, I was reminded of his *pujerak's* words. The words that had filled me with potent jealousy, something I'd only ever felt before when I was left out of important meetings in the temple or when Avala and Trissa giggled over a shared memory that I was not a part of.

"Your *pujerak* said you come home with females all the time," I started, unsure how to broach the subject, my own inexperience with males never more apparent than right then. "Do you make that a habit?"

"He was speaking of *Dothik*," he told me, cocking his head to the side, suddenly *very* interested in me, his gaze sharpening. Then he grinned, and I was a little relieved to see it. It made my belly flutter with nerves and excitement. It lightened his face even though it always looked a tad mocking. "Did you feel something ache when you heard that, *saila*? Is that why you're asking me now?"

His tone made my spine straighten. Were all males this maddening? His *pujerak* seemed friendly enough, if not a little wary of me. And as we rode through his horde, I'd caught the eyes of all sorts of males, tall and short, old and young. And the females too.

It had been overwhelming. I'd never seen so many Dakkari in my entire life. I was glad when it was just the two of us again, though I still itched to explore the horde.

Small steps, I told myself. One step at a time to get what I wanted.

"Did you not want me to sleep in your *voliki* because you think we might mate?" I asked him, ignoring his suggestion that I'd been jealous.

He stilled. I blinked up at him, holding my breath as I waited for his answer.

"This conversation again?" he asked gently, his voice smooth and languid, and I wanted to wrap it around myself.

"Do you...do you think that we will mate eventually?" I asked next, my heartbeat in my throat. I was determined. He was a handsome male that I liked looking at. He made hot desire pool low in my belly whenever he laughed or grinned or teased. Even when I was angry with him, he could still make me *want* him, which didn't make much sense to me. But I didn't question it.

"Is that what you want?" he asked. My lips parted at the question, and his dark, rough voice drifted over my tongue before threading down my throat.

I sucked in a soft breath.

"I want to feel what it's like," I told him, raising my chin. "I want to know what it's like before I go back."

His jaw was like a sharpened blade, glinting in the evening light that trickled down the venting hole at the top of his *voliki*. This whole place smelled of him. Like frosted leaves on the ice plants on my windowsill and rich soil. Parchment and ink. I wondered if I could bottle his scent in a little vial so I could take it with me wherever I went, so I could take it back with me to the *orala sa'kilan*.

"*Nik,*" he told me.

The word made me rock back. I frowned, not understanding.

I watched as he rose from the floor, covered in a soft tapestry of spun gold and indigo threads. "*Nik?* But why?"

I was too shocked to be mortified. That would come later, I supposed.

He was...*angry?*

"If you're looking for a quick and easy fuck, I'm sure one of my *darukkars* would be more than happy to oblige. Or maybe my *pujerak*," he told me. He flashed me a cutting smile. "You liked him, did you not?"

"I like you too, though not right now," I informed him, standing from the bed with a huff. I felt something burning in my chest. "Why won't you?"

"Why won't I...what? Fuck you?" he asked, cocking his head to the side.

My face burned. "Can you not say it like that? It sounds... crass."

"But fucking is exactly what it would be," he pointed out, his voice raising. "I'm sorry if it offends your little ears, *rullari*, but if you're looking for soft furs and gentle lovemaking like in your precious books, it won't be with me."

I glared at him. He'd called me *rullari*. It was a version of *princess*, though it was more commonly attached to *rukkari*, which meant *horde princess*.

He'd said it mockingly, naturally.

"And what would it be like with you?" I snapped back, feeling my temper rise. I'd never realized I'd *had* such a quick temper. Not until *him*.

He grinned, though it was feral and sharp. "Oh, *rullari*. You'd be on your hands and knees as I fed my cock into you from behind. My hand would be at your throat. Your knees would be scraped raw. I would bite your neck. I would draw your blood. And I would be *merciless*."

My breath left me.

My belly quivered.

I...liked that? *Wanted* that?

It sounded violent and rough and nothing like how I'd envisioned mating would be.

Yet I couldn't deny the intrigue that burst through me or the way my knees trembled. Between my thighs, heat throbbed, making me ache.

"All right," I whispered eagerly because I didn't trust my voice. "Let's do that."

Serok's nostrils flared. The tension between us was so thick it felt like the air was congealed.

For one breathless moment, I thought he might actually give in to my demands—though when I'd broached the subject, I hadn't meant to have sex *now*. Just...in the distant future before I returned to the North Lands.

But he took a step toward me, fire in his eyes. His scent seemed to bloom stronger, and I sucked it in deeply, greedily. I trembled, waiting.

Then a short huff burst from his nostrils. His full lips quirked up, and disappointment crashed in my belly because I recognized that look.

He would give me a flippant comment that would defuse the situation. And then he would pivot toward a new topic of conversation, no doubt hoping I'd forget about the entire thing. He'd done it often enough. Bobbing and weaving when a thread of conversation didn't suit him.

"Now that I know what you prefer in the furs, I'm kicking myself for not climbing your tower sooner, *saila*," he purred, though there was a sharp edge to his glinting words.

I blinked.

Then the hide flaps of his *voliki's* entrance pushed back, two Dakkari males entering with a washing tub. Judging by their struggle, it looked completely filled already. Their eyes widened on me after they greeted their *Vorakkar*. One almost stumbled over the rug and would've tipped over the tub had he not caught his footing.

"Put it there," Serok commanded, a hint of an impatient growl in his tone. He was sure in a mood. I thought...I thought he might *want* to have sex with me. He'd hinted at wanting to, just last night, hadn't he? Or had I read his words wrong? That... seemed more likely by the second.

The Dakkari males left, and I watched them go.

"Should I call one of them back for you?" came Serok's

rough voice. Angry again. When I met his eyes, he quirked a brow at me though his jaw was set tight. "Perhaps one of them can help you bathe."

That was when a thought occurred to me.

Perhaps it was *he* who felt something ache when he thought of me with other males.

"Are you jealous?" I asked, bewildered, though I felt strangely *light* with the realization. My eyes widened. "You are! That's why you've been so moody since your *pujerak* found us on the road."

"Moody? I'm not moody," he scoffed, jabbing a finger at me. "Don't get that bandage wet."

Then he stalked from the *voliki* before I could say anything more, murmuring something under his breath I couldn't make out.

As I watched him go, I realized he never denied the jealousy.

I let out a laugh of disbelief, my belly fluttering, my skin tingling. Suddenly alone but feeling oddly giddy. Like I'd just successfully broken into *Kalloma's* office to steal my prize of a book for the night.

"Moody," I decided, shaking my head, my eyes turning to the bath with steam curling off its surface.

My hands went to my cloak, pushing it from my shoulders. The drag of the furs made me shiver. Heat still bloomed between my thighs from Serok's very specific declaration of how we'd mate.

It had been nearly a week since I'd pleasured myself. For all my inexperience with males, I knew my own body perfectly. And there was something about bathing—the warm water, the drag of a cloth across my skin—that made it my preferred time to touch myself.

So after I stripped off the rest of my clothing and climbed in the bathing tub, I sighed in contentment. The water was wonderfully hot. My inner thighs stung from riding Syok for the last few days, but the pain quickly melted away.

And when my fingers trailed to the throbbing between my thighs, I bit my lip and imagined the scene that Serok so generously gave me.

Mere moments later when I came, an explosion of sweet ecstasy that made my tail curl, it was to the imaginings of the sharp bite of Serok's teeth at my neck.

Chapter 24

Nassik was peering at me with a hard look he'd worn ever since he was a child.

"Don't look at me like that," I said to him, running a hand over my jaw, my tone low and even.

He spread his hands over the table, his palms flat, the six fingers on each spaced wide.

"How do you know they're not lying?" Nassik asked, his gaze lowering to rest on the heartstone. Gray and dull, it lay in the nest of the cloth on the table. "Such power in such a small thing."

"The *Seta Kalliri* let us leave with it, didn't she?" I asked. "That should be proof enough."

Nassik met my gaze. "And the female?"

Averting my gaze, I peered around the *voliki*. My council *voliki*, though my council only consisted of Nassik and myself. If Bakkia had accepted a place in my horde, he would be here as well. But he'd decided to remain behind in *Dothik*, reasoning that his presence would do me more good in the capital than out here on the wildlands. Begrudgingly, I knew he was right.

The *voliki* was smaller than my own. Sparse and bare, it held only the circular table we stood around, maps of Dakkar, of

165

Dothik, and stray parchments littering it. I'd help Nassik finish setting it up now that we'd arrived at the horde. I'd lugged in the table myself while he sent for food.

"The female is..." I trailed off, not knowing how to explain why I'd brought her. Instead, I told him a half-truth. "The *Seta Kalliri* told me that she was necessary."

"To stop the fog?" Nassik asked, incredulous. "*Vok*, she's just a temple girl."

Who claims she's dreamt of me all her life, I couldn't help but think. A shiver raced up my spine. I detested magic in all forms. It was unpredictable. Kakkari's gifts were unpredictable. The fog was evidence of that.

"She's stronger than she looks," I informed him. "And she's smart. We can use her."

Nassik seemed interested in the defensive thread in my tone, plucking it out with ease. "Don't tell me you have a soft spot for her, Serok. Especially if she's as useful as you claim. And I don't mean in your furs."

"She's a temple girl," I growled. "Protected by the *Seta Kalliri* herself. You think I would risk the High Priestess's ire just to fuck her?"

Nassik didn't relax. If anything, more tension shot through his shoulders. "You think she is yours. Don't think I have forgotten your reaction earlier."

"I told you I was sorry for that," I told him, my gaze flickering down to the heartstone. "It was...frustration, maybe. The journey took longer than expected to reach the horde. She got *pyroki* burn, and I didn't want to hurt her."

Nassik sighed, the sound heavy, filling the *voliki*. Then silence descended between us. I knew what he was thinking.

"She's truly never left the *orala sa'kilan*? And her first experience away is with *you*?" Nassik shook his head, flashing me a sharp smile. "Poor female."

"*Vok* off," I growled. Then I gave him a rueful grin. "She's half in love with me already."

Nassik laughed, dragging a small scrap of parchment toward him. "What messages do you want to send out?"

I sobered, staring down at the blank sheet, watching Nassik drag an ink pot toward himself. The golden pen shaft—made in *Dothik*, naturally—soaked up the ink, a drop bulging from its end.

Nassik's father had taught him to read and write before the male had died. It was something I'd always been envious of, but something that my friend never used against me. Rather, he used it *for* me.

"Rath Okkili first," I told him. "Tell him I spoke with the *Seta Kalliri*. Tell him about the plan. We need all five heartstones, and we have a better chance of getting the one in his father's possession if he asks for it himself. Write to Rath Drokka with the same. He knows where the last heartstone is. He needs to retrieve it."

The sound of the quill's tip scratching across the parchment grated in my ears. I watched Nassik's hand, memorizing the swirling lines, the graceful flourish. I didn't speak as he wrote. My jaw grew tighter and tighter the longer he wrote.

When he was done, I was relieved. I took the parchment when he held it out for me and quickly rolled one, tying it tight, as he did the same with the other.

"So we'll have three heartstones," Nassik said. "And you will go to the *saruk* of Rath Hidri to retrieve the fourth. As for the fifth..."

I inclined my head in affirmation. "*Dothik*."

Nassik's eyes glowed. I saw the longing on his face because I was certain it matched my own.

"And you will leave me behind when you go," he guessed. "Bastard."

I grinned. "I'll give Lakkri your regards."

He grumbled under his breath. Then he commented, "You can't mean to take the temple girl. Tell me you're not."

Kara's words—rather, the words of the *Seta Kalliri*—flowed through me.

You will find the answer in the heart of Dothik.

A chill had nearly frozen me in place, hearing those words tumble from her lips. Because the message wasn't *in the heart of Dothik.*

It was *in the Heart of Dothik.*

The Heart was a place, a specific location in the capital.

And that subtle change meant everything.

"I haven't decided yet," I grunted. "But if I run into trouble at the temple, she might be useful. Getting her into *Dothik*, however…"

"We can send a message to Bakkia. To Kalik. To prepare for your arrival, to alert the others. Getting her in shouldn't be a problem, especially if you take the south tunnels. It's when she's in the city that you should worry."

"I know," I said softly. "Regardless, I think you should keep the heartstone here. Just in case we run into trouble after the *saruk.*"

Nassik went quiet. His tail flicked behind him. "We can use it, you know."

My lips pressed. My fists clenched at my sides.

"*Nik,*" came my soft whisper.

"Heartstones are power," Nassik murmured, lowering his voice. "We can use it to—"

"I said *nik,*" I growled, leveling him a stern glare, and he wisely bit his tongue. "There won't be a *Dothik*, there won't be a *throne* to take if the fog continues to spread. We stick to *this* plan. Put those thoughts out of your mind."

Nassik inclined his head. "*Lysi, Vorakkar.*"

With narrowed eyes, I told him, "You remember what we agreed? Before we left *Dothik*?"

Nassik's jaw clenched. I knew his opinions. He didn't need to tell me what a mistake he thought I was making.

"*Lysi,*" he bit out.

"Remind me."

His nostrils flared. "That the throne was not yours. Not yet at least."

"The *Dothikkar* is like the serpent monster in the ancient stories. He will swallow his own tail and then eat himself up with his greed," I told him.

"And *Dothik* might fall when that happens," Nassik growled.

"Then let it," I told him. "We will make our own kingdom. We will make our own way. *That* is what we agreed."

"There is already a kingdom for the taking. *Yours.* I'm just asking you to *take it,*" Nassik said. "Don't turn your back on *your* city."

How many times had we had this conversation? How many ways had he pleaded with me? What he didn't understand was that I would rather burn the *Dothikkar's* palace to the ground before I ever stepped inside it.

That was the extent of my own hatred.

Until I shook it, I would not be the right choice for *Dothik.*

"*Enough,*" I told him. He recognized the tone of my voice, for he quieted immediately, stepping back from the table to give me space.

He bit out a rough breath, calming. After a tense silence, he asked, "When will you leave for the *saruk*? It should only be a two-day ride from here. If you take the temple girl, likely longer."

My eyes went to the map on the table. I saw where Nassik had marked our position. Then, unwillingly, my gaze trailed to *Dothik.* The distance was not far. Perhaps four or five days of travel. The *saruk*, my horde, and the capital were all in the West Lands, but this region was vast. We were more north, closer to the Orala Pass, whereas *Dothik* was closer to the South Lands. And the *saruk* of Rath Hidri was between us, though it veered toward the western coast. Three days to *Dothik* from the *saruk*, if I took Kara with me.

"I will rest tomorrow and then leave the next day at first light," I informed my *pujerak*. "I need the sleep. And I want to make sure the horde is settled and finish building the *volikis*. I will likely barter for some crops from the *Sorakkar* of Rath Hidri. Their farms offer them plenty. We need the food and we have furs to spare, so I'll take a bundle of those with me."

Nassik nodded. "I'll have them prepared. I sent out the hunters when you were with the temple girl. We will have fresh *bveri* meat soon if they can catch up with them."

"Good," I said, finally feeling the pull of weariness. I handed him the rolled-up parchment. "Send the messages out tonight."

He nodded. I gathered up the heartstone, careful not to touch it, and I turned toward the entrance flap of the council *voliki*. On the threshold, I hesitated.

Over my shoulder, I looked at Nassik and said, "*Kakkira vor.*"

My friend blinked, though understanding seeped through his gaze.

"You know I could have done none of this without you," I told him.

He chuffed. Then gave me a crooked, smug smile, the previous tension between us forgotten. For now.

"I know," Nassik said.

I hesitated again. I hadn't dragged in the fire basin yet, so the darkness continued to grow with nightfall in the *voliki*.

"I haven't forgotten what we've always worked toward," I told him. "Remember that. I would never forget. I would never forget the sacrifices we've made. Sacrifices we've *all* made. Bakkia. Errana. Kalik. Bodin."

The last name was a soft murmur, and Nassik's jaw clenched.

Guilt swarmed me, as it often did. His death hadn't been my fault, and yet it had. Because I'd been the leader. Bodin had put his trust in me. And I'd failed him.

His death had been the beginning of the end. The reason I'd chosen to enter the Trials in the first place. Because if my place wasn't in *Dothik*, if every answer I sought was met with another torment, another setback, then I would make my own path. I didn't want anyone else dying for me. Not again.

"I know, Serok," came Nassik's words. "But Bodin knew the risks. He believed in what we were fighting for. He wanted *you* on the throne. Because he believed in *you*. The question is—and has always been—the *exact same*. Is Dakkar better off with your father as king? Or would Dakkar be better off with *you?* I know my answer. Bodin knew his."

My shoulders went tight.

Nassik added quietly, "I'm just now realizing that you may have lost faith in your own answer. And I damn well hope you find it again, Serok. For all our sakes. Or else it will all be for nothing."

When I woke, I was surprised to see it was to soft blue light. I felt frozen. My body felt heavy. My mind murky.

I'd seen him again.

In my dream.

Even now, I struggled to disentangle myself from it, as I always did.

The image of him had been clear and crisp. The same sinful grin and mischief-filled eyes he had in the daylight. Only now in the dreams, I could smell him. I knew what his scent was like because I was wrapped in it now. It muddled my brain and made a shiver race down my spine.

The dream had been a mere moment of a vision. Something Kakkari wanted me to see? I'd seen Serok, standing next to a massive column of gleaming white, craning his head up to look at something toward the sky.

At his side, he'd carried Bekkar's sword. Polished and sharp, just as I'd left it in the *orala sa'kilan's* vault. A heartstone had been gleaming, set perfectly in the hilt. Though it had been *white*, not blue.

Taking in a sudden, deep breath, I felt my limbs loosen. I

dragged in lungfuls of air, greedy for it. As I caught my breath, I decided to push the image from my mind. Sometimes the things I saw didn't make sense. They *felt* like dreams—strange and thick—rather than visions, like the *Seta Kalliri* insisted they were. Truthfully, I hadn't had a full vision in years. I much preferred the dreams because they weren't painful. They didn't make me feel like I'd been hollowed out.

Perhaps this one *had* truly been a dream. We'd been speaking of Bekkar's sword, after all. That conversation had simply slipped into the realm between reality and sleep and manifested there.

At least, I dismissed it as a dream until I realized the blue light in the *voliki* wasn't morning light at all, as I'd originally assumed. It was coming from a nearby chest, from the seam where the lid met the base.

The heartstone, I knew, recognizing the color of that glow.

Then, all at once, the light vanished. The chest's seam went dark. The *voliki* was, briefly, plunged into darkness, until tendrils of gentle light floated down the venting hole at the top of the domed tent.

It *was* morning. Just before dawn.

Next to me, Serok slept.

I turned on my side to look at him. I'd never seen him sleeping before, not once during our entire journey. He hadn't returned last night when I was awake, though admittedly, I'd fallen asleep shortly after my bath, the exhaustion from the day claiming me quickly. I'd climbed into his furs and made a little nest there, wondering if he would mind it or not.

I thought he might.

And so, at the last moment, I *had* crawled down to sleep on the floor. I'd curled a spare fur around me, soft and smelling of him, and I'd fallen asleep next to the comfortable, warm bed.

With my belly fluttering, I realized he must have scooped me up from the floor and placed me beside him.

I studied him as he slept, my eyes tracing the strong structure of his face. The sharp cheekbones, the wide, angled jaw. I counted his scars and noticed that the tip of his unsliced ear would twitch every now and again in sleep, which I thought was darling.

There was a warm ball of affection winding up in my chest. Even I knew that was bad news. He was a horde king. Even in my naivete and inexperience with males, I knew I had no business longing for one. He was not—and would never be—mine.

Quietly, I shifted from the bed, tiptoeing toward my boots where I'd left them next to the bathing tub. There was a small pile of my clothes there, clothes I needed to wash before our journey to the *saruk*. My night shift—the one I'd worn to sleep before Serok had snuck into my tower. My trews—the insides of which were stained in blood from my chafed thighs. I plucked my fur cloak from the pile and wrapped it around my shoulders, my stomach rumbling.

I hadn't eaten the night before. I was ravenously hungry, and I was itching to explore the horde.

I stopped to rummage in my satchel, pulling out a fresh pair of trews. After my bath last night, I'd gone shamelessly snooping through his *voliki*. I'd stolen one of Serok's tunics I'd found in a chest, clean and big enough to hang down to my knees. Perfect for sleeping since I didn't like my legs encased. I was a restless sleeper, the furs always slung around haphazardly when I woke.

I knotted his tunic and tucked the excess material into my trews. Just as I was about to sneak out through the entrance, his deep, husky voice came from the bed.

"Where do you think you're going this early?"

Biting my lip, I suppressed the shiver I felt building up at the base of my tail. His voice felt like it was scratching inside my head. I felt it reverberate and echo down my throat, rattle in my chest, before it pooled *low* and *hot*.

Turning, I approached where he slept until I stood within arm's reach. That voice pulled at me, drawing me to him like a magnet.

"I'm hungry," I told him softly, eyes greedily eating at him. I could tell he wore no tunic though the furs were drawn up to his broad, golden shoulders. Underneath his blanket, I saw the outline of one of his legs, cocked to the side, the pose relaxed. And then I saw a rigid bulge that had me sucking in a soft breath.

Serok grunted before bringing a hand up. He wiped it down his face, scrubbing at the hard line of his jaw, blinking the sleep away from his eyes.

"Did I wake you?" I asked in a whisper, forcing my gaze away from the tantalizing bulge. Was it terribly rude to ask to see his cock? I was immensely curious, and yet something told me Serok wouldn't appreciate the question.

Or he might give you that mind-numbing grin and give you what you want, I couldn't help but think, suddenly remembering the fantasy of sharp teeth at my throat, feeling my knees tremble a bit.

He could do either.

That was the thing about Serok.

I simply didn't know *what* he would do.

"If you so much as shift, I wake," he told me. His voice was fascinating. It sounded twice as deep as it usually did. I wanted him to talk to me forever in that voice. "I've always been that way."

"I'm sorry," I told him, thinking I must've kept him awake all night with my twitching and squirming. "Nothing can wake me. I didn't even hear you last night."

A small grin curled over his lips, making my heart pound. "I know."

Then he was up, throwing the furs off his body and standing from the bed. The sight of his bare chest nearly made me sway, the heat I felt between my thighs shooting up to my face. My ears went hot, and I rubbed at them unconsciously.

Serok—the arrogant, handsome bastard—likely knew exactly what I was thinking because that sleepy grin only widened. He looked down at me with a knowing expression, though my eyes were glued to his chest.

He looked *warm*. Like if I were to press my face between the slabs of his pectorals, my cheeks would burn. He was all tanned, dark golden flesh, and there was a lot of it. I was surprised that he looked larger without his tunic and furs on. Then again, the material had hidden the thick ropes of muscle that ran over his shoulders, his arms, leading down to a wide chest and a tight abdomen.

Again, I was faced with the realization that he resembled Drukkar.

He had the body of a god.

The difference was that when I looked upon Drukkar's statue in the *orala sa'kilan*—when I ran a soft cloth over the gilded strength and pressed and scrubbed to make him gleam —I never felt lightheaded. Weightless. The only thing keeping me grounded was the heavy pulsing between my thighs.

Suddenly, I wished for another bath. The warm water, the rough scratch of cloth over my flesh. My body tingled with the wanting.

"*Kara*," came his voice, gruff and husky. His grin had faded. His nostrils flared. Scenting me? "Enough."

With disappointment, I saw he was wearing trews, though they were a lighter color than the ones he'd worn on the journey—the color of cream. When he saw me peering at the heavy bulge, he made a sound that resembled a groan, low and deep and choked.

My lips parted as I watched the bulge pulse and throb.

"Kara."

The sharp bite of his words had me meeting his eyes in a daze.

Serok glared. And yet I had the sensation that he didn't know what to say. At a loss for words?

My feet brought me closer. Serok tensed, the cords his arms tightening and thickening.

Fascinating.

I walked around him, my knees brushing the furs of the bed, the furs that had draped over his body.

Serok continued to stare forward as my eyes met the wreckage of his back. *So many,* I thought, feeling a prick of anger. I thought back to our conversation about the *Vorakkar* cuffs. The whipping marks were just another pronouncement of the hordes' service to *Dothik,* when I thought it should be the other way around.

Biting my lip, I traced the *Vorakkar* scars with my gaze though I only sought one scar in particular. There was a part of me that wondered if I'd made it up entirely. If everything was a coincidence. If I'd been *wrong.*

With a quiet burst of acceptance in my chest, I took a deep breath when I found what I sought.

The horde king sucked in a sharp inhale when I touched the scar. Long and jagged, it looked like it had been made with a dull sword. The edges of the scar had healed poorly and had been stretched as he'd grown. It stood out from all the rest, though its appearance was dulled by the plethora of scar tissue on his back.

I traced the line of it with the pad of my fingertip. His back rippled under my touch. His tail flicked against my leg. I swore I saw him shiver. The scar started beneath his shoulder blade and ended underneath the band of his trews. My hand lingered there. His scent seemed to bloom around me, heating the air.

The scar was exactly how I'd known it would be. Every jagged edge. Every raised and flattened surface.

"There was a part of me that thought I'd made you up," I whispered, my eyes suddenly filling with tears. I was confused. Aroused. Determined to understand *why*. "That maybe *Kalloma* was wrong. That what I saw was not Kakkari's influence but something else."

Serok didn't say anything.

Then he turned, and my hand fell away from the waistband of his trews. When I looked up to his face, I saw his lips press at the sight of my watery tears.

"*Nik*, Kara. None of that," he murmured, his voice losing the sharp bite of before. I thought that perhaps I'd made him nervous. Maybe that was why his tone had gone hard.

Shaking my head, I blinked back my tears. I heard the sound of my blood rushing in my ears.

"The heartstone was glowing when I woke up," I told him, pointing to the chest. "And before you ask, *nik*, I was not praying."

His lips quirked, but I saw the concern in his eyes at the announcement. "It was?"

"I wish I could speak to *Kalloma*. Maybe she would know why it is glowing away from the *orala sa'kilan*," I told him, my gaze dropping to his chest again, feeling the strangest urge to lean into him. He looked so strong. So unlike the lithe, graceful, quiet females I'd grown up around. I thought it a shame that males were not allowed to stay within the temple.

"Perhaps we will find more answers in the *saruk*," Serok told me.

I nodded. When my head tilted down, I saw a patch of wetness at the front of his trews. Was that...

My tail curled.

"Can I see?"

The words were out of my mouth before I could stop them.

Serok went dangerously still.

My gaze flashed up to his. "*Hanniva?*"

He groaned. When I tilted my face back down to his cock, I saw a fresh bloom of wetness slick the material.

"*Nik,*" he growled, stepping away from me, giving me his back as he turned to the chest where I'd stolen one of his tunics. "You may not *see.*"

"Why not?" I demanded. "Are you aroused right now? You must be."

A choking sound left his throat, and then he was laughing, though it sounded strained and tight to my ears.

"You will be the death of me, *rullari.* You know that?"

My eyes lingered on his scar until he pulled a fresh tunic over his front. It was white in color, the material soft and spun. Of the same make as the one I'd stolen.

His hands began to unlace his trews, and then he stilled, turning to level me a narrowed gaze.

"Turn around."

"*Neffar?*" I asked, my eyes straying to the undone laces, eager. I frowned. "Why?"

"Because I need to change my trews and I do not want you to latch yourself onto me once you see my ass."

I gaped. Then I laughed, a bright giggle that filled the *voliki.* A sound rumbled in his chest in response, a growl and a purr.

"I won't," I assured him.

His lips pursed. "I am not so certain. Look how you acted seeing my chest. You practically went into heat right before my very eyes."

That cut my laugh short, embarrassment making my ears heat. Then I glared, my spine straightening. "So did you," I accused, dropping my gaze to the wet spot on his trews meaningfully.

My gaze lingered, and I bit my lip, curiosity prickling the back of my neck.

"You see!" he exclaimed. "*Vokking* hell. You're doing it now. I changed my mind. Go wait outside. I cannot trust you not to look even if you do turn around."

Rolling my eyes, I stalked to the entrance of the *voliki*.

Despite his edged words, I thought he was...amused. He seemed to be in good spirits this morning, though I wondered how long it would be before we began to argue again.

Well...I suppose we already are, I thought, as a smile tugged at my lips.

"You're ridiculous, you know," I shot over my shoulder. "You're really going to make me wait outside?"

"Absolutely," he said, those molten eyes swirling with barely concealed mirth. "Get out, *saila*."

I huffed. With one last look at the front of his trews, I sighed in disappointment and then ducked under the entrance flap.

And immediately forgot my disappointment as my eyes took in the sight before me.

Something *new*.

Dawn was just breaking, the sky turning a soft, muted pink and purple. The horde was camped in a clearing of a forest. Towering, ancient trees bracketed the borders like old guardians. The air was crisp and clean. At this time of morning in the North Lands, the air would sting my lungs. But when I inhaled, it felt soothing. Refreshing.

Already the early morning was warmer than any temperature I'd ever felt at the *orala sa'kilan*. It was the warm season, I knew, but I'd never really understood what that meant. Not until I shrugged off my furs from around my shoulders and stood in just my tunic and trews.

Before me, the horde was quiet. Half of the *volikis* were up, I saw. The other half were in varying stages of building. I saw tucked-up fur rolls on the ground, sleeping Dakkari snoring loudly as fires roared in basins close by. Smoke rose from one of the largest domed tents, the scent of meat on the soft breeze making my stomach grumble with impatience.

On the northern end, I saw a *pyroki* enclosure, dark masses of dozens and dozens of sleeping beasts. There was a Dakkari female milling around the enclosure, her hair pulled away from her face.

To the south, I saw another enclosure being built, though I couldn't guess its purpose. Some Dakkari were up, I noticed, quietly rousing from their sleep, stoking fires or stretching.

Excitement rose. I wanted to see it all. I wanted to learn everything I could.

Behind me, Serok ducked under the *voliki* flap and joined me. The trews he'd pulled on were a light brown color. His boots—his *thieving* boots—were laced tightly.

"Is that mine?" he asked, raising his brow at my tunic—his tunic—as he took my furs from my hands. He tossed them back inside the *voliki,* and I heard the weight of them thud onto the ground.

Sheepishly, I smiled. "I may have snooped last night. And it was so soft. The softest tunic I've ever felt. I couldn't help myself."

He bit out a sigh and then shook his head. "And you call me the thief?"

"Because of your boots?" I asked, my gaze going to them. "Well, *lysi,* and because you broke into my tower. *Twice.* Or did you forget that part?"

He chuckled.

"Come, *rullari,*" he murmured. "Let's find you food before you go snooping inside anyone else's *voliki*. We have a long day ahead. And I intend to put you to work."

CHAPTER 26

"Everything hurts," I whispered, my cheek pressed to the plush rug. Then I flopped over, grinning. "I wouldn't trade it for anything."

Serok snorted from his place at the low table. Steaming plates of braised meat, roasted roots, creamy broths, and thick, pillowy slices of *kuveri* bread were laid out before him.

"Come eat, *rullari*. Replenish your strength," Serok said, his voice low. It was the first time we'd spoken all day, though I'd caught long glimpses of him often. As the sun set, he'd found me at the training grounds, helping a few *darukkars*—who were endlessly charming and friendly—slot in the last of the fence rungs.

My arms felt wiggly, but I managed to crawl over to the table, much to the amusement of Serok. The horde king pushed over a small bowl of broth. I was ravenous. I hadn't eaten since the afternoon. A few *bikkus* had brought over a tray for me alone and peppered me with questions about the priestesses, the North Lands, who my parents were, how I'd ended up at the *orala sa'kilan*, and my relationship with their *Vorakkar*.

I'd encountered similar conversations throughout the entire day. The questions didn't strike me as malicious, simply curious, and so I answered them all. Though about my relationship with Serok, I'd simply told them that I was helping him find the heartstones. And I'd left it at that.

One thing was clear to me, however. Every Dakkari male and female—and child, even—I'd spoken to throughout the long day had all been immensely relieved when I mentioned the heartstones. Just seeing some of their tension drain from their faces and shoulders and a light mirth take its place made me realize what an incredible disservice *Kalloma* had done to these people. Even if she'd been protecting me, even if she'd been trying to find another solution, it had given her no right to keep the hordes—and all of Dakkar—in the dark.

I could understand Serok's frustration with her, with them all. Even still, every time a stray, biting comment was said about the priestesses, my spine stiffened. I didn't like it, even if *Kalloma* had been wrong.

Still, it didn't diminish the kindness I'd found among his horde. I'd expected wariness. I'd expected mistrust.

And while there had been pointed questions about my age and my birth parents, I hadn't encountered one malicious word.

After years and years of the priestesses keeping me shielded in the temple—it was incredibly jarring.

Serok's horde didn't *care* that I was a hybrid. Or at least, they were too polite to say anything about it to my face.

"Kara," Serok's voice cut through my thoughts. When I fastened my gaze on him, he asked, "Are you going to fall asleep at the table?"

"*Nik,*" I said, straightening. "I'm starving. Are all hordes like yours?"

He shrugged, taking a healthy swallow of something from a golden goblet. "I am only the *Vorakkar* of my own horde. How should I know? Besides, you already know I grew up in *Dothik,* not in a horde."

"So you admit it," I shot at him, grinning triumphantly.

Seeing him again after not speaking to him for hours filled my belly with fluttering. I'd spent every waking moment with him for days until we reached the horde. Now I felt like I'd been starved for him.

He grumbled something under his breath, but I watched the way his eyes shone. "Impossible female."

"Everyone was very nice to me," I told him.

"Did you expect them to string you up and roast you over a spit?" he asked.

"*Nik*, of course not. But..." I trailed off, sighing. As I collected my thoughts, I took a sip from the broth bowl. Rich, silky soup slid over my tongue, and I nearly moaned at how good it tasted. "*Kalloma* always feared that I would be shunned. She always feared violence. Uprising."

"Because a Dakkari male lay with a human female?" he asked.

When he put it like that...

"My father loved my mother, you know," I told him. "That was what my mother told *Kalloma*."

Serok paused. "Do you know what happened to them?"

Despair bloomed in my chest. Perhaps their story was why I'd had fear too, not just *Kalloma* and the other priestesses.

"My father was a *darukkar* of a horde. I'm not certain which one," I told him. "When the humans first settled on Dakkar, one of the villages posted up close to his horde. There was a lot of tension between the two groups. But because of it, my parents met. Fell in love. My mother got pregnant." I sighed. "They knew that they could not be together unless they left. Everything was so new then. Most of the Dakkari hated the humans. Hated them encroaching on their territories. And the humans hated the Dakkari for their violence. There was no other way except to leave."

"And did they?" Serok asked, golden-and-red eyes swirling at me over the rim of his goblet.

"*Lysi*," I said. "They were gone almost a week. And then their rations ran out and my father had to hunt for them. On this hunt…he got injured. Terribly injured. A few days later, he succumbed to his wounds. And my mother was alone. On the wildlands. Pregnant with me."

A gruff sound chuffed from his throat. "I'm sorry, *saila*."

I shrugged my shoulder. It felt strange to speak of them. Because I didn't know them. Didn't know what they looked like, how their fingers felt smoothing over my cheek or brushing through my hair, what their voices sounded like.

Well, nik, *sometimes I hear her voice in my sleep,* I thought. My mother's voice.

"She had no choice but to return to her village. But as she grew heavier and heavier, the accusations started coming from her villagers. I…I cannot imagine what they said to her. And when she had me, she said the villagers tried to kill me while she slept. She realized she could not stay."

His brow furrowed. "But how did she reach the *orala sa'k-ilan*? Or even know how to reach it? That journey is treacherous, especially for a human without a *pyroki*."

I gave him a small, sad smile. "Even *Kalloma* could not answer that. Though she has her theories. My mother told her that she didn't remember the journey at all."

Serok leaned back, his brow furrowing. "Impossible."

"*Kalloma* believes it was Kakkari. The goddess brought her to the *orala sa'kilan*. *Kalloma* said my mother was in perfect health when she arrived at the gates with me. She was grieving but unharmed. She was warm, despite her lack of suitable clothing for the North Lands. She looked well fed though lost. Depressed. She couldn't explain it, except for Kakkari."

Serok blinked. His nostrils flared.

"That was how I came to be at the temple," I told him.

"And what happened to your mother?" he asked quietly.

"*Kalloma* always told me she left. She gave me to the priest-esses, and then she simply *left*."

His eyes flickered back and forth between mine. "But you don't believe that?"

I swallowed. I plucked some meat off the plate and chewed on it thoughtfully before I answered, "It never made sense to me why she would leave. If her village turned their backs on her, she had nowhere else to go. The priestesses would've taken her in. I know they would have." I sighed, feeling a moroseness rise in my chest at the thought. I looked at Serok and said, "I—I don't like talking about it."

"Then let us speak of something else," he said easily.

I gave him a small smile of relief. "*Kakkira vor.*"

"You worked hard today," he murmured, leaning forward to take a slice of his beloved *kuveri* bread. "You'll feel it in the morning, however. And we leave for the *saruk* at dawn."

"So soon?" I asked, blinking. "But there are still more *volikis* to build."

The horde, however, looked entirely different than how it had looked this morning. Transformed. The common baths were filled. The training grounds were sectioned off, the fence nearly done. Close to a hundred *volikis* had popped up throughout the day.

The horde had been a chaotic bustle of activity and noise, and I'd loved every moment of it. It was disappointing that I would have to leave so soon—especially since I enjoyed the company of so many people—but I understood why it was necessary.

"Only a few," Serok informed me. "But you can stay behind at the horde if you wish."

"*Nik,*" I said quickly.

He quirked his brow. "You wish to return to the horde after the *saruk*?"

My eyes narrowed. His tone was deceptively light.

"*Nik*," I said. "I wish to go to *Dothik*. With you."

He blew out a breath. He went quiet, and then he said, "The hordes are used to humans. But the *Dothikkar* does not know what has been happening on the wildlands. We keep him in the dark for a reason."

"You're speaking of the human settlement? And of the humans that live among the hordes?"

I'd learned that a human *saruk* was being built in the South Lands, a joint effort by humans and Dakkari alike. I'd been amazed at the prospect, feeling an incredible restlessness to *see* it. There was so much happening beyond the *orala sa'kilan*. More than once today, I'd felt a moroseness that one day I would have to leave this exciting part of the world behind.

"*Lysi*," he told me. "But make no mistake, *saila*, it is not that way in *Dothik*. Most there have never seen a human in their entire lives. If you expect kindness in the capital, you will not find it."

"I still want to go."

He licked his bottom lip, and the flash of his tongue made my belly tighten. I reached for my own goblet, suddenly parched. Thinking it was water, I nearly choked at the tart, bitter flavor.

I realized what it was. "Is this *wine?*"

"*Lysi*," he murmured.

"It's terrible," I said, frowning into its content. "How disappointing."

He chuckled and watched as I took another sip. I made a face but begrudgingly admitted that it went down a bit smoother.

"Hmm," I murmured, cocking my head. "Actually, it leaves a very pleasant taste."

"Oh, really?" he murmured, leaning forward. My mouth went dry again when his gaze dropped to my lips, and he watched as I licked a drop of wine from them.

The way he was suddenly looking at me...

It made my ears flame.

"Are you...are you going into heat right now, Serok?" I asked pointedly.

He nearly choked.

"*Rullari*, you will *know* if I'm going into heat. You won't need to ask" was his response.

I blinked, frowning.

He shook his head, smiling.

Changing the subject, I asked, "So we really are leaving at dawn tomorrow?"

He sobered. "*Lysi.*"

"And do you have a plan for when we get to the *saruk*?" I asked. "Are you simply going to ask the *Sorakkar* of Rath Hidri for the heartstone that he swore to the previous *Dothikkar* he would protect at all costs?"

Serok leaned back against the tall, stabilizing pole that ran up the center of his *voliki*.

"*Lysi,*" he said, his tone all arrogance. "He cannot deny a *Vorakkar*. That is what I am, is it not?"

That and so much more, I couldn't help but think.

"Can I send a *thesper*?" I asked, another thought crossing my mind. "To the *orala sa'kilan*? I wanted to ask the *Seta Kalliri* about the heartstone. I think it would be helpful."

"I already sent out the two *thespers* we have," he informed me. "But perhaps the *Sorakkar* will allow you use of one of his once we reach the outpost."

I nodded.

He finished eating more quickly than I did and then stood from the low table, towering over me. "I have to go meet with my *pujerak*. I'll have a bath sent in, *lysi*? Then get some sleep."

"In your bed?" I couldn't help but ask. He stilled, that heated gaze pinning me in place. "I tried to be polite last night. I fell asleep on the floor. I figured I should ask."

I hadn't brought up the fact that he'd brought me to his bed until now. The knowledge hung between us, thick and tight in the air.

"*Lysi,*" he murmured. "In my bed."

A pulse went through my loins, and I squeezed my thighs together at the gruffness in his voice.

"But do not cling to me as you did last night," he said, jabbing a finger at me. "You trapped my tail between your thighs and kneed me in the *deva* more than once."

I gaped.

"I did not cling to you!" I exclaimed. My face flamed. "Or the other things!"

He threw me a smug smirk. "You did, *rullari*. Now that you've seen my naked chest, I'm afraid you might not be able to keep your hands to yourself."

A strangled sound left my throat. I knew he was only teasing but...still!

"Maybe you won't!" I shot back, embarrassed...and a little aroused.

He chuckled and went to the entrance of the *voliki*.

"I have self-control, Kara," he purred. "Do you?"

Between my thighs, I felt a rushing, hot throb of heat.

My bath *could not* come soon enough.

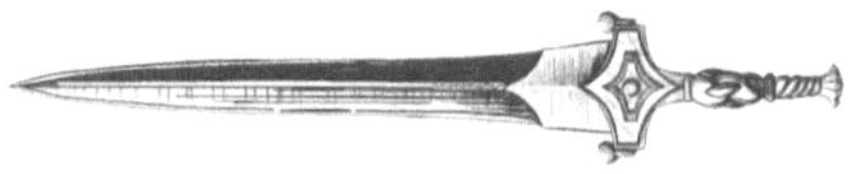

CHAPTER 27

"I don't want to talk about it," I growled, my hackles rising at the smug expression that I just *knew* was on her face.

"I didn't say anything."

The tone of her voice was *vokking prim*. The tone of voice that made me want to flip her onto her hands and knees and work her cunt until she could only scream. Only then would I be satisfied.

"I just find it amusing," she added after a hefty silence sank between us, "that you were all high and mighty about *me* clinging to *you*. And what do I wake up to?"

I grumbled under my breath. Beneath us, Syok was still shaking off the deep sleep I'd woken him from. He didn't seem pleased to be awake this early, but he had perked up at the sight of Kara, who cooed softly to him as we made our way through the silent encampment. Now we were out on the road leading out of the forest, and the maddening female *would not* let it go.

"A *Vorakkar*-sized blanket draped over me," she finished. "That's what."

I focused on breathing through my nostrils.

There's no way I'll make it to Dothik with her, I realized, furthering my resolve to return to the horde after we reached the *saruk* of Rath Hidri.

Mostly because I feared I wouldn't be able to keep my hands off her.

Not only because she didn't hide her arousal from me—the little thing was endlessly horny, but who could blame her after being locked away in the *orala sa'kilan* all her life?

It was also because I was beginning to doubt my *own* self-control around her.

"And did you like it?" I murmured into her twitching ear. Because if she was going to tease, then I would tease right back. "Did you like waking to me over you? Did you feel something ache, *saila?*"

Her breath hitched. "When will we mate? I'd like to know."

A laugh and a groan tumbled from my throat. The *Seta Kalliri's* warning sounded more and more mocking every waking moment I spent with Kara.

"I told you," I rasped. "We will not."

Disappointment and restless dread mingled in my belly at the pronouncement. I wasn't such a bastard that I would steal Kara's only means of safety, her only family, her only true home, would I? If I lay with her, she would not be welcomed back to the *orala sa'kilan.*

Only if they find out, a treacherous little voice in my head whispered. *How would they know unless Kara told them?*

My fists clenched on Syok's reins.

I could hear the bewilderment in her tone. "*Nik,* you never said we *wouldn't.*"

"Get used to it, *saila,*" I told her gruffly. "It is for your own good. So let me play the honorable horde king, *lysi?* Don't tempt me."

I could almost *hear* the way her eyes narrowed. As we journeyed farther from the horde, I kicked up Syok's pace. Not a full sprint but one that made Kara's head bounce in front of me. One that made her buttocks move between my legs.

Vok.

Why hadn't I given her her own damn *pyroki*?

Well...mostly because I couldn't teach her how to ride one properly in such a short time.

Partly because I was a selfish bastard who liked to tempt *myself.*

"How many lovers have you taken?"

The question was out of her mouth, her tone innocent though it was mingled with frustration. Similar to the little growl she'd given me after we left the *orala sa'kilan*, the growl that made my cock cut into the laces of my trews.

"You do not need to know," I told her.

"I'm curious," she argued.

"Remember when we spoke of things that are considered rude to ask?" I murmured. "This is one of those things."

"Why?"

I sighed. "How many lovers have *you* had?"

I could hear her frown. "You know I've had none. Unless you mean myself?"

My brow quirked in interest, my spine straightening, bringing my abdomen in close proximity with her back. "Oh, really? Tell me more."

You shouldn't be doing this, I thought. *Just let it go.*

She squirmed when she looked over her shoulder at me, our faces entirely too close together. Instead of rearing back, I held her gaze.

Such lovely eyes. I watched them flicker to my lips before she looked at the tip of my nose. Her gaze went a little soft, making my heart thunder in my chest. *Vok,* why was she *looking* at me like this? When my self-control was already perilously thin?

"Knowing one's body only brings one closer to Kakkari," she

told me, though it felt like a recitation. "She is the goddess of life, after all. Pleasure brings a body to life. Pleasure is a celebration of her."

"So you have pleasured yourself, *rullari*?" I rasped. "To please Kakkari?"

The tips of her ears went red. I wanted to lean forward to bite them. My jaw actually snapped down with the *need*.

"*Nik*, to please myself," she told me quietly. She wiggled again, and I swallowed. If I dipped my fingers beneath the waistband of her trews and sunk my hand between those thighs, I knew that I'd find her wet and slick right now. The knowledge made my heart pound in my jugular, hot and violent.

"If the priestesses believe that, then why are they forbidden to lie with males?" I asked. "Especially when it is said that when Kakkari and Drukkar come together, a powerful storm unleashes over Dakkar, bringing with it new life and prosperity? And during the warm season, when Drukkar rises from the sea? There are storms every other day."

My words were a tease. I didn't believe the old legends. I'd never been a worshipper at Kakkari's temple in *Dothik*, though my mother had often left her tributes, had often prayed to the goddess to watch over me.

"Because the priestesses are the extensions of Kakkari *before* Drukkar," Kara told me. I straightened, interested in what the *kalliris* had taught her. "Kakkari was more powerful before Drukkar came."

I snorted.

"It's true. The priestesses believe that Drukkar tempered her power, that he restrained her, that he softened her. Perhaps it was necessary," she said softly. "But the priestesses serve her and only her. They are receptors in this mortal world, outlets of her power that even Drukkar could never reach. It is why so many of the *kalliris* are blessed with Kakkari's gifts."

I pressed my lips together. Was this why the *Seta Kalliri* told me to stay away from Kara? Because she had a gift of Kakkari? Because the priestesses believed that those with the gift were extensions of Kakkari—the *old* Kakkari, untainted by Drukkar—and as such were to be protected?

It was ridiculous.

I told her so.

And when I did, Kara stiffened, her nostrils flaring.

I had half a mind to fuck Kara right then, to shove the *Seta Kalliri's* threats right back into her face so she could see that nothing catastrophic would happen at the stroke of my cock. The world wouldn't end. Kara would survive. Life would go on.

"We are already fighting," she informed me. She turned in her seat, hanging over the side so she could see behind me. "I can still see the horde. That didn't last long."

A surprised bark left my throat, and I nudged her forward before she fell off Syok's back.

"Whatever you believe," she continued, her voice softening, "that is what you believe. Whatever the *kalliris* believe, that is what they believe. Who is to say what is right and what is wrong?"

"And what do you believe?" I asked quietly.

Her gaze met mine over my shoulder. "I believe that I have not taken the vow of the *kalliri*. I believe that I would like to experience what it is like to lie with a male before I return to the North Lands. I believe that I would like it to be you. And I believe that you dodged my question and distracted me until I nearly forgot it."

A thread of awe shot down my spine. This female was...I'd never truly encountered any female like her, had I? In all my years? Of all the people I'd met?

"What question?" I rasped, her eyes scrambling my mind until I felt like a haze surrounded me.

"How many lovers have you taken? I don't care if it's rude. I'm very curious."

A sharp exhale left my nostrils.

"Many" was what I told her.

She frowned. "Many?"

The expression on her face was so adorable that it made my teeth ache from the sweetness. It looked like she didn't know whether to be insanely curious—the urge to rapid-fire questions toward me was in the opening and closing of her soft lips —or insanely jealous.

I chuckled. I nearly kissed her. Nearly nibbled on those plush lips and stroked her tongue with my own. I wanted to taste her. I wanted to see her blinking, wondrous expression when I pulled away.

But I knew that would be a very, very bad idea. Because once I kissed her, I didn't know if I could stop. The last thing I needed right now was this distraction of a female.

What a beautiful distraction she is, I thought.

"In *Dothik*, I took many lovers," I told her. "Though I wouldn't call them lovers. That implies longevity."

"And...and what about in your horde?" she asked.

My hands clenched on the reins again. "I have taken none in my horde."

A fact that was biting me in the ass now. When this temple girl was making my cock so hard I couldn't think straight.

She blinked rapidly, processing the information.

"None?" she asked. "But why? How long have you been a *Vorakkar*? Or do you mean you go to *Dothik* when you...when you feel urges?"

"Urges?" I asked gruffly, narrowly keeping my lips from twitching.

"*Lysi,*" she said. "Surely you have them."

Oh, I have them, saila, I couldn't help but groan silently.

Especially for half-human, half-Dakkari females with sharp tongues and innocent eyes.

"Enough," I told her, cutting off the thread of conversation even as I brushed my fingers across the back of her hand where it rested next to the reins. "We need to pick up speed. Tell me when you need a rest."

But I didn't wait for her to respond as I urged Syok into a full sprint. Maybe it was cowardly—or maybe I just didn't need my cock to get any harder. Nassik would send a *thesper* to the *saruk* of Rath Hidri once he heard back from Rath Drokka and Rath Okkili.

We needed to reach the western outpost quickly.

And questions about *urges* would only delay us, especially when they made me want to bend Kara over the next boulder we came across.

Keep your damn distance, I growled at myself. *And keep your damn cock in your trews.*

CHAPTER 28

When we stopped for the night, I was incredibly grateful. While I had spread on *uudun* salve between my thighs before we left the horde and padded my trews with a spare tunic, I was still stiff and sore when Serok pulled me off Syok's back.

"All right?" he murmured, his voice scratchy and gruff from the constant wind whipping our faces as we rode across the wildlands.

I blinked up at him and flashed him a small smile. "*Lysi.*"

I didn't think I chafed this time, at least. When he released me, I bent over with a small groan, reaching for my boots as I stretched the backs of my legs. Serok pulled out a familiar basin and got to work setting up our camp.

There was a small cave in the rock face. The West Lands, I found, were riddled with rocky structures that were half-covered in soft, brightly colored green grass, tall stalks of it that felt like strands of hair.

This particular rocky structure sloped up like an incline, creating a sharp cliff at the very top, grassy wisps swaying in the breeze. At the bottom of it was a cave. It would block the wind for the night, and it was surprisingly roomy. Even Serok could stretch out and be completely protected.

"Can I help with anything?" I asked him once my legs no longer felt like they'd give out from underneath me.

Serok dug around in the satchel. He tossed me a heavy brown brick, and I flashed him a triumphant grin when I caught it successfully. His lips twitched, and then he jerked his head to Syok.

"Feed him, will you, *saila*?" he said. "He'll be hungry."

"Are you hungry?" I cooed softly, stepping up to Syok, who stomped the ground with his taloned claws, making a chuffing sound in the back of his throat. I chuckled and pressed my face to the side of Syok's snout. "Of course you are. You worked so hard today."

I heard Serok clear his throat as I let his *pyroki* begin to chomp on the brown brick. When I looked over at the horde king, I stilled, seeing him peering at me with an expression that made my tail curl.

"What is it?" I asked him.

He only swallowed and then shook his head, turning his attention back toward the basin. A moment later, a fire roared to life, casting the hard planes of his face into both shadow and light.

From underneath my lashes, I admired him, nearly letting out a wistful sigh.

"What is it?" he asked from a distance, turning my question around on me.

"You're so handsome is all," I found myself telling him honestly. There was no harm in it, was there? The male had to know he was handsome.

His teeth flashed in the golden light. His eyes glittered with his grin, making my heart pulse. "You are very good for my ego, *rullari*. Maybe I will keep you around."

My brows rose. "Maybe if I compliment you enough, you'll take me to *Dothik.*"

He chuckled, low and dark. Then he said, softly, "Maybe."

I tamped down the hope that started fluttering in my breast. I was wearing him down. I knew it. Just like I did with *Kalloma.*

"Your ears also twitch while you sleep, which I think is *very* cute," I informed him. "And you talk too."

Serok's gaze was pinned to me as he rose from his crouch. He'd made the fire outside of the cave, likely so it wouldn't fill with smoke as we slept.

"And what is it that I say?" he wanted to know. I stilled at his tone. The back of my neck seemed to prickle with warning as I hesitated.

"I couldn't make it out entirely," I told him, frowning. "A name, maybe? Brodin? Bodin?"

Serok's jaw shifted. And just like that, I felt his mood change.

He didn't say anything to me. He simply crouched again, adding more fuel to the fire until it burned higher and brighter than necessary. Then he rose again, full of restless energy that struck me as carefully—and perhaps barely—contained.

"I'm going to take a piss," he informed me gruffly. I blinked at the words and nodded, watching as he stalked around the rocky structure, disappearing from view.

Overhead, the constellations shone. I plucked out the Staff of Batevik, my eyes tracing the bright stars. I wondered if Serok would try to tell me it was *not* a staff. *Likely,* I thought.

Serok didn't return for a while, and I fidgeted, huddling closer to Syok when the breeze picked up. I regretted mentioning him speaking in his sleep. The revelation had soured his mood, and I didn't know why. But I wanted to. I wanted to know everything about him.

Finally, Serok reappeared. His expression was noticeably

lighter as I approached. When I touched his forearm, just above the warmth of his *Vorakkar* cuff, he stilled.

"I didn't mean to upset you," I told him softly. "You know, when we argue, it's not supposed to *hurt*. If I upset you, then you should tell me why. Isn't that what you want me to do with you? Like when I was crying."

Serok's gaze was narrowed on me. "You didn't upset me."

"*Lysi,*" I replied, "I did."

"It was not you, *saila,*" he informed me, his tone gentling. His other hand came to rest on mine, on his forearm. He grasped my hand, giving it a squeeze.

"Who is Brodin? Or was it Bodin?" I asked.

His lips pressed. "No one. Leave it, Kara."

His tone was sharp, and he dropped my hand quickly as if it burned him. Stung, I watched as he finished setting up our camp for the night. He shrugged off his furs, crouching to spread them out in the cave for us. He added more fuel to the fire before digging around in his satchel again.

Hesitantly, I stepped forward as he pulled out a fresh water skin and a wrapped bundle of food.

"Don't you think it's strange?" I asked softly, standing over the fire basin, crossing my arms over my chest.

"What is?" he asked, flashing me a look that told me to tread carefully.

"That we've spent all this time together and yet I don't know anything about you? Except for the fact that you lived in *Dothik,* where you apparently had many lovers, that your mother had an extensive education, and that you are horde king," I continued. "And you know a lot about *me*. Is that by design? Or should I learn to keep my mouth shut and not speak so much? I'd like to know before we go to the *saruk*."

There was surprise mingled with frustration on Serok's face.

"You won't even tell me your given name," I added. "Though maybe that's not so surprising. Maybe all the Dakkari outside of the *orala sa'kilan* are equally private and incredibly frustrating to befriend."

"And is that what you're trying to do, *saila*?" he asked quietly. "*Befriend* me?"

His tone told me just how laughable he found that, and... that hurt.

I could count on two fingers how many friends I had in this world: Avala and Trissa. *Kalloma*...I didn't consider her a friend. She was my *mother*. The one being I loved most in this entire world. The one being that I trusted would always be there for me, who would give up everything to keep me safe.

The other priestesses in the temple...they were not so much friends as distant family. I'd grown up with them. They were kind to me, humored me when we spoke, and I knew they cared for me. But they kept their distance. Perhaps because of what I was—a hybrid female—or perhaps because of the *Seta Kalliri* herself.

But Avala and Trissa—especially Avala—were my two friends, who had never tiptoed around me like the others.

Talking with them was easy. Laughter came quickly.

It was like that with Serok too, though he also made me want to scream and pull at my hair and bite his neck and huddle close to his chest, all at the same time. Was that normal? I wasn't certain.

"Do you not want to be friends?" I asked quietly, nibbling on my lip when I felt it begin to tremble. "Would it be so terrible if we were?"

I *thought* that we were friends. But maybe I was mistaken.

A deep sound rose from his throat. For a moment, he hung his head, rubbing at his neck before he scrubbed at his jaw. His brows knit together as he regarded me across the flames of the fire basin.

When I shivered, he swallowed hard and he sat back against the wall of the sloping rocky structure.

"Come here."

Two words that sent a prickle racing down my spine. My feet moved without me realizing it. When I stood before him, uncertain, with my tail flicking dangerously close to the fire, he tugged me down. I gasped, but then he huddled me into his side, one arm wrapped around my shoulders, heat seeping into me. Hesitantly, I rested my cheek on the strong ball of his shoulder, unyielding and rigid.

A position that was similar to how I'd woken that morning, though Serok's entire front had been plastered to my back from behind and his arm had been draped over my hips. I still tingled when I remembered the soft puff of his breath rustling in my hair.

I waited for him to speak, peering up at the side of his face, which was so close to mine. His opposite knee drew up. The hand that wasn't wrapped around my shoulders came up to rub at his eyes.

He was silent until he said, "Bodin was a friend in *Dothik*. A loyal friend, one of the best I could ever hope for. One I'd known since I was a child. And he died." My blood turned to ice in my veins. "He died a terrible death, one I have a lot of guilt and anger over, even to this day."

His hand clenched around my shoulder, tight like his voice, and I didn't dare breathe.

"So I do not like to speak of it, and I very rarely do," he told me, turning his eyes down to mine, his lips edged in a dark frown. "Except in my sleep apparently."

I knew better than to question him about *how* Bodin died. I feared that I didn't want to know. Was living in *Dothik* very dangerous? Was there more to Serok's fears over me accompanying him to the capital?

"I'm sorry," I whispered because I didn't know what else to say. I had very little experience with death. One of the elder priestesses had died at the *orala sa'kilan* when I was younger.

Jani. That had been my only real brush with it, but I still remembered the *silence* during her funeral. The lack of *everything*. Of emotion. Of sadness. Of the celebration of her life. It had felt empty. I had been the only one to cry because Jani had always combed through my hair and given me kind words when I spoke with her.

"You should not *want* to be my friend, Kara," he said. "It is better if you are not. It is better if you return to the North Lands after the *saruk*. It is better if you never see me again after this."

"*Nik*," I said quickly, his words creating a sudden sense of panic that raced through my blood, spiking my heart. And it wasn't just because he was trying to send me away after the *saruk*. It was that I would never *see* him again. He knew it. I knew it. "*Nik*, I don't want that."

Serok's sigh ruffled my hair. The fire popped in the basin, and I heard a chunk of the fire fuel spring against the metal.

"I like when you do *not* keep your mouth shut," came his voice, bringing us back to what I'd said earlier. "I like that I know exactly what you're thinking—because I grew up around people who did everything they could to *hide* what they were thinking, people who played games, who lied as they smiled, who plotted and stole to get exactly what they wanted. People like me. But not you. You are everything that I am not. Everything good."

A flutter in my chest made me push at my breastbone. "*Lysi?*"

"*Lysi,*" he murmured, his voice warming, making my insides feel like they were sliding. "And I like when we argue. I like that you're unafraid to tell me exactly what you feel. Never change that, Kara. Never think that you need to. Because it is a rare thing in this world." Softly, he added, "*You* are a rare thing in this world."

I wanted to bottle his words and take them with me everywhere.

"You should remember that the next time I try to be a *vokking* prick to you," he informed me. "Because I'm a moody bastard, and you would be right to remind me of that."

"All right," I whispered. "I will."

The edges of his mouth tugged up. His face went soft as his eyes roved around mine, and it took me a moment to realize I was smiling back at him.

When those molten eyes dropped to my lips, my lungs squeezed. I had read about kissing. It always...*intrigued* me.

But instead of leaning into him, I moved back, dropping my eyes with a rueful smile. I was beginning to think that my wanting to have sex with him—and being outspoken about it—was not something that was appropriate. I was beginning to feel like it made him uncomfortable. He always brushed away my words with a teasing grin and a flippant comment...but what if he was only trying to spare my feelings?

So, I shouldn't press anymore, I decided. If we were to be friends, then that was what we would be. And while I embraced my friends—talked and laughed with them—I certainly didn't try to kiss them or try to have sex with them.

Sighing, I shifted away, savoring the feeling of being in his arms, his warmth, his scent before I sat upright. His hand slid away from my shoulder. He was watching me carefully.

"Arik."

My brow furrowed. "*Neffar?*"

He lifted one shoulder, drawing up his other knee so he could clasp his arms around them. The tip of his tail was lying over my ankle, and my toes twitched in my boots.

"You wanted my given name, did you not?" he asked. My breath hitched, and I straightened in surprise. "It is Arik."

My eyes went wide, but I told myself to *relax*. His lips twitched when I smoothed my fingers through my own tail, as if he knew exactly what I was doing.

"Arik," I murmured, tasting his name on my tongue.

The horde king stilled. His nostrils flared.

"Arik of Rath Serok," I said softly, meeting his eyes, which seemed to light on *fire*. But I couldn't be certain if it was the reflection of the fire in the basin…or something else. Something else entirely.

Whatever it was, I felt it reverberate through me. It zinged through my body. It made my scalp prickle and desire pinch tight between my thighs. It made me aware of him in a way I'd never been before.

I swore I could *hear* his heartbeat.

I swore I could hear the slide of his skin against his clothes when he shifted.

Every part of me was in tune with him.

The oddest thing of all was that it felt *right*. It felt *good*.

His voice was a guttural croak when he said, "*Lysi*, Kara."

I took in a deep breath, letting the cooling night air fill my lungs.

"Well, Arik," I murmured, going to my knees before I stood. "I was going to read for a little while. It will help me sleep."

"You brought your book again?" he grunted, watching as I rustled through my travel sack. "I thought you left it back at my *voliki*."

"Where I go, the book goes," I informed him. "You know that."

Arik shook his head. Whatever spell that had come between us seemed to be broken. Or at least, not as intense. His shoulders loosened. He licked his bottom lip, which tightened my belly, but I stayed silent about it.

"Read to me again," came his voice. "Will you?"

I smiled. My hand closed around the loose sheets of parchment, and I carefully extracted them. I regretted that I hadn't had time to finish transcribing it. Or bind it. But I was still grateful I had the majority of it.

"Of course. I'll read you the excerpt of Bekkar's battle with the enemy horde of Rath Orkan." I slid him an assessing look. "What else would we argue over all day tomorrow? You'll probably say that the *Vorakkar* of Rath Orkan was right to try to assassinate Bekkar."

His brow slid up with arrogance. "He *was*."

I sighed, hiding my delighted laugh.

"So it begins," I told him.

CHAPTER 29

Kara squeezed my wrist, her hand only large enough to wrap partially around it. I slowed Syok to a gentle trot, thinking she needed to relieve herself again or that she was thirsty.

"*Lysi?*" I murmured, my eyes stinging from the ride. Wind was a constant factor in the West Lands. Riding a *pyroki* at full speed ensured they were dry and itchy whenever we rested.

"There's a lake!" she exclaimed, excitement coloring her voice, which had begun to feel tired and worn once the sun had started to dip in the sky. "Is that what it is? Oh, I've never seen one before!"

I felt my lips quirk as I dragged my gaze toward where she was pointing. I'd seen it but hadn't thought to stop for her. There were many lakes dotting the West Lands, some so small they could be considered ponds, while others stretched so wide they could be mistaken for Drukkar's Sea.

The one she was referring to was a decent size. I could see the banks of it, wrapping around in a haphazard circle.

Kara turned in her seat, swinging her other leg over Syok so they both dangled over his side. I should've expected her question before she asked, "Can we go? I'm dying for a bath!"

I hesitated, assessing the sun in the sky. The distance wasn't too far. We still had an hour or two of daylight left, hours I would have rather spent chipping away at the stretch of land that still lay between us and the *saruk*.

"Please, Arik," she murmured, her eyes wide. "*Hanniva.*"

Then I sighed. Already I regretted giving her my name. Because she could wield it against me and make me do whatever she wished, including stopping at lakes for her precious baths. I'd been right—Kara was meticulous about hygiene, and a day or two without bathing began to sour her mood steadily. The female liked to be clean.

"Very well," I said, giving in. When she gave a little squeal of delight, I grunted, pleased by the sound—but I would never let that slip. We'd been up since dawn. We'd been riding hard all day with very few breaks. Kara deserved a longer rest.

I led Syok down a different path. We were up on an incline and would need to trek back up the valley once we finished. A dense forest of trees surrounded the back half of the lake. Grassy knolls lay between us and the nearest shore of it.

"We should leave before sundown," I told her when we reached the flat bank littered with stones, my gaze tracking to the towering forest in the distance.

"You don't want to camp here for the night?" she asked, her voice wistful as she looked over the smooth water of the lake. "Imagine how the moonlight reflects on this! How magical it would be. Like something out of my books."

I snorted, feeling my chest warm at her...fanciful imaginings.

"*Nik,*" I murmured. "There is nothing magical about being stalked and hunted by the multitude of hungry beasts that will come here to drink at dusk."

That silenced her. "Really? They come here? How do you know?"

"This is the only lake we've seen. There are more farther

inland, but this will be a drinking hole for this territory. The water looks clear."

I reached up for Kara's waist once I slid off Syok. She was biting her lip, her hands skimming over my forearms to steady herself as I tugged her down.

"Maybe we shouldn't stop, then," she murmured, her concerned gaze tracking up to me when I set her on her feet. My hands lingered on her waist, however. I stayed closer than I needed to. "If you think it's dangerous."

"It will be fine until sundown," I assured her, feeling a wiggle of guilt at making her worry when she'd been so excited. "Do you not trust me to protect you, *saila*? I *am* a *Vorakkar*, you know. Or have you forgotten?" I teased. I patted my sword and the line of my daggers at my hip. "Why else would I carry all these if not to protect you?"

The tips of her ears went red, and I chuckled.

"Maybe you just like to *look* frightening," she pointed out, stepping past me, making my laugh only deepen.

There was a series of large boulders that dotted the lake's shore. Kara stepped toward one, bringing her travel sack with her. I watched her, studying her, as her hands went to her fur pelt and she draped it over the nearest blackened rock.

She'd been different today.

I couldn't quite put my finger on *why,* but I'd thought more than once that she was holding herself back. There were moments in the conversations we'd had where I'd been deliber-ately teasing her, eager to hear her thoughts. Her responses had been perched on the edge of her tongue—I'd seen them glit-tering in those pretty eyes—and for some reason, she'd swal-lowed them back down.

"It's safe to bathe in, right?" she called out from the boulder, going to the lapping lake's edge and peering inside. She looked over her shoulder at me next. "No lake creature will come up and snag me?"

"Lake creature?" I repeated, approaching. "What exactly have you read in those books of yours?"

"So it's safe?" she asked, cocking her head to the side. She crouched down, gingerly touching the water with her pointer finger. She grinned. "It's warm!"

After realizing that, she didn't seem to *need* my assurances. Her hands went to the hem of her tunic, and she had begun tugging it up—my body stiffening, in more ways than one— before she froze.

"Are you—are you bathing too?" she asked, the question innocent. Yet the sudden huskiness in her voice had my cock throbbing.

"Might as well," I rasped. "We are still a couple days away from the *saruk*. We might not get another opportunity."

She nodded, but she'd gone back to nibbling her lip, thinking intently about something. "Then you should go bathe over there," she told me, pointing to a distant shore. "And I'll be over here."

Case in point. The Kara I knew yesterday—the one who'd impatiently asked *when* we would be mating, as if it was a certain thing—was not the Kara in front of me today. This was a prime opportunity for her to get what she wanted. Me, naked and aroused at the sight of her. Her, naked and aroused at the sight of me.

Hell, we would be halfway to fucking, all the groundwork laid.

And now she was acting as if the mere thought of me naked worried her. Like she had changed her mind about wanting to experience a male before she returned to the North Lands.

Perhaps she had changed her mind.

"Do we need to have another talk about how just seeing your *melir* does not mean—"

"I know," she snapped out, a tantalizing flush steadily spreading up her neck now. "If anything, I would think you would be worried about *me*. You're the one who made me wait outside your *voliki* when you were simply changing your trews."

I couldn't help but think, *And why did I have to change my trews, you little—*

"Do what you like," she said suddenly, shrugging one shoulder up. Her hands went to her tunic again. "But I will be getting my bath."

With a dry mouth, I watched as she tugged up her tunic, baring the expanse of her smooth back to me. She tossed the material—*my own damn tunic*—onto the boulder with her fur pelt and then began to toe off her boots. When her fingers fumbled with the laces of her trews, I resolutely turned my back, watching as Syok trotted up the lake to drink. I heard the swish of hide join the rest of her clothes and then the telltale signs of sloshing water as she stepped into the lake.

She sucked in a breath. Alarmed, I turned. Growling, I asked, "What is it?"

Then I swallowed hard at the sight of her. She was faced away from me, but her backside was bared. All smooth, warm skin. Wide hips and a perfect, round ass I wanted to grip, her small tail jutting from the base of her spine, the tip hovering over the clear water.

Dark, black spots peppered her back at random intervals, and I studied them, wanting to trace them with my tongue as I simultaneously wondered if they were human markings.

The dark waterfall of her hair hung down, her ankles disappearing under the surface of the water as she strode forward, determined. Then her calves disappeared. Then the end of her tail.

She let out a little squeal on her next step—and then suddenly plunged all the way in, her head dropping below the water. *Gone.*

"Kara!"

Alarmed, I sprinted for the edge, throwing off my sword and

my belt of daggers. Water squelched in my boots as I launched myself forward. The icy surface of the lake hit me like a wall as I dove down. I spied her kicking legs and thrashing arms, and I gripped her waist tight, catching a flash of her breasts as I tugged.

The lake was deceptively deep, but all I felt was relief when I pulled her back up to the surface. As she sputtered and coughed and wiped the wet strands of hair away from her eyes.

"I d-didn't expect it to-to drop off like that!" she exclaimed with a rattled cough, squeezing her eyes closed. The water was salty. It stung, especially since our eyes were already dry from the wind. "And it's c-cold! But it felt warm!"

"Are you all right?" I growled, my heart still thumping as I kicked my legs below us to keep us afloat.

"*Lysi,*" she breathed, unconsciously clinging to my shoulders as my palms wrapped tight around her naked waist. The pebbled scrape of her nipples dragged across my chest.

Vok.

She began to laugh, the sound clear and beautiful, and I huffed when I felt my cock respond in my trews, cutting into the laces.

"I'm glad you found that amusing because I did not," I growled. My boots were soaked. My clothes too. I had a naked, tantalizing female in my arms, one I was *not* supposed to be touching, and my balls had been aching for *days*. Frustration was running high.

Kara sobered. Then her eyes widened as she finally seemed to realize the position we were in. When she released me with a gasp, disentangling her limbs from around me, she immediately began to sink, and I snagged her again, another spike of fear funneling through me.

"What are you doing?" I shouted.

"I—I don't know how to swim."

"So you think it's a good idea to *let go of me?*"

Kara blinked at my harsh tone.

My nostrils flared as I continued to tread water. Then I took in a deep, steadying breath, trying to calm the racing of my heart. I hadn't thought the lake would be this deep. I hadn't thought the drop-off would be so dramatic, so sudden. This wasn't her fault, and I shouldn't be taking my fear out on her.

"All right," I murmured, making an effort to calm my voice. "You don't need to know how to swim. You just need to know how to keep your head above the water, *lysi*?"

She nodded, her teeth beginning to chatter. "How?"

"Watch my legs below the water," I told her. She did as I told her. I watched the way her hair spread across the surface of the water, counting the seconds until she surfaced again. She wiped the water from her eyes, her face scrunching up in an adorable expression as she blinked the salt away. "Try it, *saila*. Hold on to me."

Her legs kicked against mine as she tried to emulate what she'd seen. It took her a little while, but eventually she fell into a smooth rhythm, grinning up at me in triumph.

"Like this?" she asked.

When I let go of her, she squealed, briefly forgetting to keep her legs moving as she went under again.

When I snagged her, I felt a trickle of amusement as she sputtered. "You need to keep treading water when I let you go," I said slowly.

"Obviously!" she snapped, squinting, looking like a ruffled, wet, cranky *privixi,* and it made me laugh in her face. "You didn't warn me."

A curl of amusement and alarming affection warmed my belly. "Try it, Kara."

"All right," she said, giving me a grave nod that had my lips twitching. "I'm ready. Let me go."

I shook my head, hiding my grin, and did as she asked. Her hands thrashed at the surface of the water briefly in her panic, but she managed to stay afloat. Below the water, I watched her legs swirl, settling into a steady rhythm. Resolutely, I avoided looking at anything else.

"There you go," I murmured, meeting her eyes. "Good."

She gave me a shy smile that had my cock pulsing, even in this cold water. Then she gave me a sheepish look as she took in my wet hair. "I'm sorry you got your clothes wet for me. I'll tend the fire tonight so I can make sure they dry by morning."

I grunted, leading her back to the edge where the lake had dropped off. It was a steep incline, and the ledge was a perfect height for sitting, though rocks dug into my ass. "Don't worry about it. I have others. Guess I got a bath *and* the opportunity to wash my clothes. And a scare," I added.

"I didn't scare you," she said, though her voice was tinged in uncertainty as she sat and gave her legs a rest. She huffed out a long breath, settling onto the ledge, the lake's surface lapping at her delicate collarbone. "Did I?"

"For a moment, I thought maybe there *was* a lake creature," I admitted.

She laughed, but it sounded a little winded. Wrapping her arms around her front to cover her breasts, she peered down into the depths of the lake and shuddered. "Now I keep thinking something will grab my ankle and pull me down."

"*Kakkira vor.* Thank you for a fear I never knew I had, *saila*," I grumbled, dragging my leg back from the edge.

She threw me that sheepish smile again. Then she bit her lip. "Oh, I forgot my soap in my satchel."

I shook my head and then stood. "You mean *my* soap. That you stole."

"*Borrowed.*"

"You cannot borrow soap. You *use* soap. It's not like you can give it back."

She huffed out a breath from behind me as I strode toward

the shore. "Impossible male," I thought she muttered under her breath, making me smirk.

When I found the rattling vial of soap granules, I turned back to her, only to catch her watching me, her head tilted to the side. My smile widened, especially after hearing her surprised gasp. The wet clothes clung to my body, no doubt leaving nothing to her imagination. Those eyes were still glued to me, blinking endlessly.

"Would you like me to undress, Kara?" I murmured, narrowing my gaze on her, already toeing off my sodden *thieving* boots. "For your obvious curiosity?"

I expected her to immediately say *lysi*. With eagerness and certainty of what she wanted. And right now? She wanted to see me. She wanted to see my body bared for her and only for her.

Instead, she swallowed. She shrugged her bare shoulder and then turned forward quickly. "If you wish to."

Narrowing my eyes on her back, frowning, my hands went to the laces of my trews and I tugged at them. I saw the tip of her ear twitch when the wet slap of hide landed on the lake's shore. Almost imperceptibly, her head turned, as if she couldn't help it.

I saw the tip of her nose come into view when my wet tunic joined my trews. And there I was, standing as naked as the day I was born, on the shores of a lake in the West Lands, and I was just *daring* this temple girl to turn around. To take what she wanted. To take what she'd asked me for.

When she did, her lips parted.

Her eyes glided over my body, and I swore I could *feel* them like a touch, a caress. I nearly groaned. My cock bobbed against my abdomen, and when her gaze settled there, blinking those widened, heated eyes, I strode forward, hardly able to stay still.

Her mouth opened as if to speak, a question perched on the

edge of her tongue. One that, up until recently, I would've guessed would be *Are we going to mate now?*

And *vok*, did that imagined question *heat* my blood.

This is wrong to do, I couldn't help but think. Because I still had no intention of taking her the way I wanted.

I could imagine fucking her in every position I knew. I could imagine the sounds she'd make as I was sheathed deep inside her. I could imagine the taste of her, how her hips would jerk as I laved at her clit. I could imagine her wide eyes looking up at me as her mouth was stuffed full of my cock.

But it wasn't like I would *act* on any of those instincts. I wouldn't do that to her. I was beginning to care for this female—more than I probably should and certainly more than I'd expected to. To lie with her would take more from her than I thought she was prepared to give.

However, it wouldn't stop me from winding her up, I realized as my ankles swished through the cool water. It wouldn't stop me from teasing her, from making her wet and needful, from making her *want me*. Maybe I was a bastard for doing it, but it was only fair, I thought. It was only fair considering I spent the majority of the day with a cock so hard I could use it as a *vokking* weapon. If I suffered, she would suffer too.

I could *feel* her gaze on my cock. When I stopped in front of her, I let her look her fill. She made an unconscious mewing sound in the back of her throat as those wide eyes ran up the sides of my cock. It twitched under her gaze, and it was that mewing sound that made a dab of pre-come push from my tip and begin to roll down my thickened shaft.

And *that* was when I realized I'd taken it too far.

I handed her the jar of black soap granules that she'd taken from a chest in my *voliki*. She'd likely found it while she was snooping through my things—and she called *me* the thief.

She took it from my offered palm wordlessly, and then I sunk down next to her, sucking in a sharp breath when the cold water met the heat of my arousal, a contrasting sensation that only made me *harder*.

This has backfired spectacularly in my face, I thought, silently groaning.

But maybe I'd just wanted to shake the truth out of her. She'd purposefully avoided my flirting and teasing today. I wanted to know *why*. I wanted to know what had changed.

My voice was dark and gruff when I asked her, "No requests, *saila*?"

"Requests?" she asked, like she was in a daze.

I grinned.

CHAPTER 30

Was it possible for your heart to beat so fast that it simply *exploded?* I wondered, unable to tear my gaze away from the massive *appendage* jutting up from between Arik's thighs.

"Requests?" I murmured, my blood rushing in my ears. His grin only served to triple my heartbeat.

Thud, thud, thud, thud, thud.

When I felt my heartbeat between my legs, I squeezed them tight under the water, shifting.

He's your friend, I reminded myself, looking away from the rounded, darkened head of his cock where it bobbed *above* the water. It looked so hard that it looked painful.

I'd done so well all day. I hadn't made one inappropriate comment, or at least I hadn't thought so. But this...

My mouth was dry. I could barely swallow, and for a moment, I deliberated scooping up some lake water to soothe my parched tongue but then thought better of it.

"At any other moment, you'd have asked to touch me already," he pointed out, his voice deep and gruff.

I went a little dizzy, the constant, violent throbbing of my clit a terrible distraction.

Bath, my mind screamed. With trembling hands, I fumbled with the stopper on the vial. It came undone with a loud *pop,* and a few granules shot out, sinking into the lake.

Next to me, Arik leaned back on both his hands, his pose deceitfully relaxed. The hard lines of his chest were even more on display. The scars I had the strangest urge to *lick.* And as my eyes ran down, I realized the position pushed the smooth, rounded tip of his cock even farther out of the water.

My belly bottomed out. Unconsciously, my hand seemed to reach for him before I snatched it back with a gasp.

Serok's eyes went even hotter. A deep rumble of a growl threaded up his throat.

"Do you want to touch me, *saila?*" he murmured. I gaped at him, my nipples so hard they were painful as he ran the pad of his thumb lazily over the tip of his cock. I watched as it twitched, and the harsh breath that escaped him at the small contact made a whimper escape me.

Desperately, I tipped the vial into a shaking hand, spilling out more granules than necessary. Furiously, I rubbed my palms together, lathering the soap before slapping at my exposed arms and shoulders. Scrubbing. Watching him.

Biting my lip, I resisted the urge to plunge my fingers between my thighs. I didn't think it would take much. One moment, maybe two, a single stiffened stroke against my clit, and then I'd feel sweet relief from this madness.

That was how aroused I was. How much watching him, *wanting* him made me feel.

When I thought of experiencing sex for the first time, all I could imagine was Arik. I wanted it to be with him. Only him.

"*Hanniva,*" came my whispered plea, my soapy hands forgotten.

I'd tried so damn hard to be good all day. But this was...this was too much.

His jaw tightened, a little muscle beginning to pulse there, in time with the pulsing between my thighs.

I didn't remember who reached for who exactly.

All I remembered was a sudden flash of movement and then Arik was pulling me toward him. His expression was dark, *needful*, I thought. I lost sight of it when he pulled me between his thighs. Like how I'd been all day as we traveled on Syok, his hard, unyielding chest at my back.

"*Ahhh!*" I cried out when I felt the strong delve of his fingers between my legs.

"*Vok,*" he breathed into my ear, angling his head down so he could run his nose through my wet hair. "You're so hot here you'd burn me right up, *rei saila.*"

My eyes were unseeing as the pads of his calloused fingers stroked and rolled my clit. A touch that was not my own. Rough and demanding and utterly *perfect.*

His low chuckle made the first pulsing of my orgasm come. "So sensitive," he murmured when my hips bucked up. "You need this so much, don't you, Kara? You need my touch and my cock and my words in your ear. Could I make you come just talking to you, I wonder?"

"*Lysi,*" I breathed, sparks bursting in my vision, my back arching so much that the top of my head met the middle of his chest. I was bowed over, and I looked up at his face in a daze, my lips parted in disbelief at the strength of my orgasm.

His expression was tight as he watched me. His fingers never let up between my thighs as my body jerked, a mewing sound leaving my throat as his gaze wandered down the line of my body, lingering on my tipped-up breasts jutting from the water, darkening on his fingers at my *melir* before snapping back to my face. Like he didn't know where to look. Like he wanted to look at it all.

"*Leika,*" he praised, his voice soft. *Beautiful,* he said. I felt that praise tingle and stroke and pet and linger. It was perfect.

"*Oh,*" I whispered, my eyes widening when I felt myself come again, so close on the heels of the first. Something that had never happened before, but my cries carried over the surface of the lake, echoing in the valley of the West Lands. "*Arik!*"

My eyes never left his, and I saw a feral expression come over his features at the sound of his name.

"*Lysi,*" he hissed. "Know who you belong to, Kara. Know who this cunt belongs to."

His words unleashed a fresh wave of pleasure, pulsing and endless. My hips bucked, and I chased it for as long as I possibly could.

I felt his cock bob against my spine. His touch became too much as my pleasure began to wane, and I squirmed, my legs thrashing, until he finally relented. Then I was sitting up, turning, going to my wobbly knees between his thighs though the rocks dug into them painfully.

Arik growled, sucking in a harsh breath when I gripped his cock. His head lolled around his shoulders, his gaze dragging over my bared breasts though he didn't move to touch me or kiss me there.

My lips parted in awe. His cock was so big that my hand didn't wrap around it fully. He was so unbelievably *hot* under the cool water that he nearly seared me. And so incredibly hard. Harder than the boulders that lined the shore or the rocks that dug into my knees.

I knew nothing about pleasuring a male. But my touch was greedy, and I traced my fingers over him, memorizing the intriguing, thick veins and the velvety steel of his flesh. His *dakke,* that tantalizing bump at the base of his shaft, was hard and throbbing when I skimmed my pointer finger over it.

All the while, Arik groaned and harsh whispered curses left his throat in a constant stream. His hips rocked underneath my touch, creating rippling waves on the otherwise calm surface of the lake.

Finally, one of his hands gripped around mine. He'd grown greedy with his own need, and he showed me how to touch him wordlessly, how hard to squeeze him, how to run my palm up and down his shaft in quick strokes, focusing on the swell under his tip.

"Just like that," he croaked in that delicious voice. "*Perfect*, Kara."

When he released my hand, he blew out a long breath, the muscles of his thighs tight around me.

"*Ahhh, vok, lysi.* Make me come, *saila*. Make me come," he whispered to me, his words awed and gruff and dark and tight. When I squeezed at the crown, making a tight circle with my fingers around him, his abdomen sucked in and his hips jerked. "*There. Vok,* I'm going to come so hard for you! *Vok, vok, vok!*"

Biting my lip, I watched as he came apart completely. At the same time, I felt my own body *snap*. A pinch came from deep inside my *melir,* and in disbelief, I felt his orgasm trigger a small one of my own. Unstimulated and completely unexpected, I moaned and rocked, my breasts swaying as his molten, half-lidded gaze pinned me in place.

"Again, *saila?*" he croaked as my fist tightened on him.

"*Arik!*"

All the muscles in his chest seemed to tense before growing in size. Deep, ragged groans tore from his throat, and I watched a violent pulse of seed arch from his tip, bathing his heaving abdomen. More and more came in seemingly endless amounts while he jerked against me. Hot come bathed the side of my hand, and in a daze, I continued to stroke him, watching, *wanting.*

When he could take no more, he stilled my hand, his hard swallow loud in the sudden quiet. All I could hear was the rapid pound of my heart and his ragged breaths.

Reaching forward, I smoothed my thumb through a little pool of come that had settled into the ridges of his abdomen. Hot and thick and silky. Arik stilled, the heaviness of his gaze darkening, and he snatched my hand away, squeezing lightly as if in warning.

Before I knew it, he splashed his chest with water, washing away all evidence of it as I sat between his thighs, shivering.

I didn't trust my voice. I didn't even know what to say. All I knew was that I was ridiculously happy. Pleased. Triumphant. *Satisfied*, even though it was on the tip of my tongue to ask him if we could do it all over again.

That had been...*wonderful*.

A shy grin spread over my face as I watched him. His expression hadn't changed, but I noticed that he had stilled considerably. His tail, which had twitched with his orgasm, was straightened. His thighs were hovering around me, but he'd widened them so they didn't touch my skin.

Next to me, the vial of soap granules bobbed on the lake's surface. Arik's gaze seized on it and he snatched it, pushing it into my hands.

When those eyes slid over my shoulder to look out over the expanse of the calm lake, I frowned.

"Finish bathing, Kara," came his guttural, husky voice. A voice that had rasped wicked things to me just moments before. Wicked things that made my toes curl and my belly flutter. "We should leave soon."

Confused, I watched as he stood, leaving me kneeling in the rocky shallows.

That was *not* what I'd expected.

At all.

I'd expected that signature grin, maybe a teasing comment or two, but I certainly hadn't expected to feel a hollowness begin to spread in my belly at the sight of his scarred, bared back walking away from me.

"Arik?" I called out, bewildered.

He paused. I saw his shoulders rise and fall with a deep breath.

I eyed the sharpness of his jaw when he turned his face toward me. His gaze flittered across my expression, taking in my frown, my furrowed brows, my limp hand with the vial of soap.

"What's wrong?" I asked softly, trying to understand.

His eyes flashed and steeled. In a soft voice, softer than I expected, he told me, "That shouldn't have happened, Kara. I took it too far. For that, I'm sorry, *lysi?*"

"*Neffar?*" I asked in disbelief, reeling.

"It cannot happen again."

The words were clipped. Strong.

Final.

I sat, shivering in the cold water, processing his words, feeling the heat and pleasure and contentment begin to wither inside me.

He was *sorry?*

His shame was easy enough to recognize, and the knowledge made a snap of incredible hurt and anger rise in my breast. He was ashamed of what had just happened between us? Because...*why?*

Unless...

Unless...

Unless he finds me lacking. Unless he doesn't think I'm enough for him. Unless he doesn't think me worthy of a Vorakkar's *touch,* that treacherous voice whispered in my head. A voice I hadn't really heard since I left the *orala sa'kilan.*

But here it was now. Making me doubt. Making me *burn.*

Swallowing, I moved without really thinking. I finished bathing. I even washed my hair, tipping my head back underneath the cold water as tears stung in my eyes.

How would I ever face him now? I wondered. How would I

ever look him in the eyes now, knowing what he truly thought of me?

When I surfaced from the water, I took in a shuddering breath, still feeling the heat of his hand between my thighs.

Serok was dressed already, I saw. In clean, dry clothes. His back was to me as he rummaged in the satchel at Syok's side. I darted up to the shore swiftly, feeling a pinch in my belly when I saw he'd left a dry cloth for me to use. I ran it over my body, absorbing most of the moisture, before I pulled on fresh clothes from my satchel. My last pair of clean trews and a baggy tunic that did *not* belong to Serok, thank the goddess. I stuffed my feet into my boots and ran my fingers through my wet hair, attempting to comb it out before I plaited it.

I was procrastinating. Buying time before I had to face him.

And when my time ran out, I approached Syok, keeping my chin high though all I wanted was for the earth to swallow me up.

"Are you ready?" came his soft question. There was an edge to his voice that hadn't been there before. I felt the intensity of his gaze flicker around my face.

Looking at the notch at the base of his throat, I said, "*Lysi.*"

That shouldn't have happened, Kara, he'd told me.

That was all we said to one another for the rest of the night.

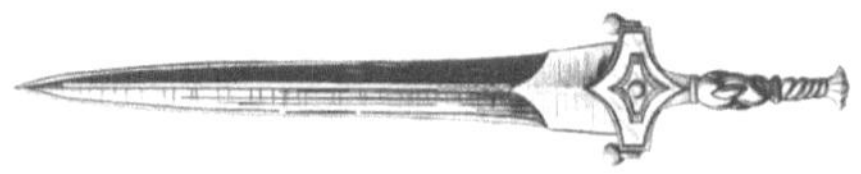

The *Sorakkar* of Rath Hidri was wary and weary. An aging male, well on in his years, with hair so long that the end of the plait nearly brushed his ankles.

I couldn't help but stare at the obvious indentations around his wrists. The skin was still two different colors, the flesh slightly compressed around the bone. Where his *Vorakkar* cuffs had been. Years after being cut off, they still showed.

Looking down at my own, I pressed my lips together, straightening, perching my hand on the hilt of my sword though it was more in comfort than because I felt threatened.

Across the dim, quiet room sat Kara.

Hands cupped in her lap, she was sitting in a chair that the *Sorakkar* had pulled forward for her as he studied her exposed features intently. Our arrival had caused quite the stir, but I didn't feel any hostility toward my half-human, half-Dakkari companion. If I had, we would have left already.

The *Sorakkar's* gaze held softness for the female, but when those yellow eyes flitted to me, they narrowed. His tail twitched every single time he met my eyes. His shoulders tensed.

There was always tension between *Vorakkar*. There was

always tension between *Vorakkar* and *Sorakkar* as well. But something in my gut told me this was different.

He doesn't want us here, I knew.

What I really wanted to know was *why*.

Throughout the pleasantries we'd exchanged as he'd guided us to this dim, depressing room—where his council still met, he'd informed me—I got the impression that he was restless. That he was rushing the conversation along.

"We come for one thing and one thing only, *Sorakkar*," I informed him, watching his fingers curl over the back of the chair he was standing behind.

Saruks were strange. A strange mixing of a horde's simple lifestyle coupled with the luxuries of *Dothik*. The chairs, for example. In a horde, meals were taken on the ground, on cushions. To remain nearest to the earth, to feel it vibrating under you.

This chamber, for another. It was built of stone. It had doors and stairs and windows, things I hadn't seen since I left the capital city. There were no domed hide *volikis* here, no entrance flaps that rippled and snapped in the wind. The wind met this stone structure and whistled around it.

It made nostalgia and longing course through me. My home in *Dothik*—the one I'd made for myself and the company I kept —was one of the tallest structures in the Southern District. Wide and imposing, it was a solid stronghold of weaving hallways and hidden rooms.

"And what is that, *Vorakkar*?" Hidri asked me, frowning, his gaze flitting to Kara once more before returning to mine. His tail twitched.

"Two things," came Kara's voice, cutting through the sudden tension. I felt a knot in my chest release at the sound of it. I'd barely heard her voice in the last two days, and it soothed the restless energy that had been building inside me since the lake. "Well, three things, truthfully, if you would be so kind."

If her voice was like a balm, the small smile that lifted the edges of her lips was like sinking into a hot bath after a long day.

At my sides, my fists clenched, and I swallowed hard, narrowly keeping my feet from moving toward her. I'd missed her voice and her smile and her eyes. The tension between us had been tortuous since the lake, and I knew I was being a coward. It wasn't like me to let something fester for so long.

Tonight, I thought.

Tonight we would talk.

"And what are they, *kalles*?" the *Sorakkar* asked, seemingly eager to do her bidding.

Perhaps it wasn't just me, then, I mused, even as I felt a stirring of jealousy bite at me. Which was ridiculous. Perhaps I wasn't the only one that wanted to give her anything she wanted.

"Firstly, accommodations for the night," she said softly, holding the *Sorakkar's* gaze. "We have been traveling for four days, and I confess that I've been dreaming of a bed."

I bit the inside of my cheek.

"Of course, *leikavi*," Hidri said. *Small, beautiful one,* he'd called her. She beamed at the term of endearment, which only made the aging *Sorakkar*—who was very happy with his wife, or so I'd heard—even more eager to hear what she said next. "You will have your bed and a hot meal and a bath. What else?"

So much for trying to get rid of us so quickly, I couldn't help but think.

Or maybe he was just trying to get of *me.*

"I am interested in speaking with someone," Kara began, "who might have heard about the famine that spread over these lands nearly two hundred years ago."

The *Sorakkar* actually recoiled in his surprise, blinking. "The famine? Two hundred years ago?"

"*Lysi,*" she murmured, inclining her head. Briefly, her eyes came to mine, and I wanted to pin them to me. I wanted to hold them to me...but all too soon, they refocused on Hidri. "Of course, no one would be alive today who'd experienced it, but I was hoping that perhaps a descendant of someone who *had* was living in your *saruk*. You are the great-grandson of the *Vorakkar* who made this outpost, are you not? And even though you were once a great *Vorakkar* of your own time"—Hidri's lips twitched at her praise—"you returned to your home, to your roots. Many stay close to their roots. That is what I'm relying on."

Had I really thought that she would flounder outside the walls of the *orala sa'kilan*? I stared at this female—who asked me strange, uncomfortable questions, who spoke to me honestly, who didn't hide what she was feeling or thinking—and tried to match her to *this* female. The one who sat perched in her chair like it was a throne. Who looked at the *Sorakkar* with a small, charming smile and wide, knowing eyes, who could make him do anything for her.

For a moment, I frowned. For a moment, I wondered if *this* was the gift she'd spoken of before. Not her visions from Kakkari, but perhaps she wielded a different power entirely.

"Many remember the famine, *kalles*," Hidri told her, his wavering voice grave. "It is not something that is easily forgotten. Not in this part of the West Lands."

"So you remember your great-grandfather's stories of it?" Kara asked eagerly, leaning forward in her chair. At his nod, she asked, "Was the soil...did the soil turn red? With dark veins like roots that spread through it?"

The *Sorakkar* blinked, his lips parting briefly. "How do you know that? Where did you hear it from?"

She settled back in her chair. Again, her eyes met mine. She held them for a moment longer before they dropped to her lap.

"I saw it," came her gentle voice. Not one to lie. Not Kara. Even as my hand tightened on the hilt of my sword, as my eyes narrowed on the *Sorakkar* to see how he'd react. "Kakkari showed it to me. I saw the veins leaching the soil of its life. *Drinking* it away. They only grew and grew. Spreading across the West right under everyone's feet."

The *Sorakkar* reached out a hand to steady himself on the table in the center of the room.

"You...you possess a blessing of Kakkari?" he asked her.

"*Lysi,*" she said. "I believe so. And so does the *Seta Kalliri* in the *orala sa'kilan.* She sent me here because she believes that you can help banish the fog that spreads in the East."

Hidri's eyes came to mine, but I only stared at Kara.

Perhaps...she could lie. For she knew very well that her *kalloma* would never have sent her here. What was she doing?

Securing the heartstone, I realized a moment later.

Had she sensed the same unease within the *Sorakkar*? Had she sensed that if we simply asked for the precious stone that his family had dedicated themselves to protect, he would turn us away with a curse and without a backward glance?

Vorakkar or not, I knew that the *saruks* only needed to obey the direct orders of the *Dothikkar.* He didn't have to give us the heartstone.

I was impressed. I was almost *proud* as I watched the *Sorakkar* of Rath Hidri blink at her in astonishment.

"The *Seta Kalliri?*" he asked softly. "She has sent you here? To my *saruk?*"

"*Lysi,*" Kara said, her chin lifting subtly. "I am her ward. She took me in when I was a child and raised me as her own. And she believes that the fog that currently plagues the East Lands once happened *here* in the West. On your land. On your ancestors' land. Only in a different form. But she believes it is the same and that it can be defeated once more."

"The heartstone," Hidri said next, swallowing. Then his expression became pained. "*Kalles,* you know I cannot simply *give* it to you. It would be against every oath I have taken to protect it. An oath I made to the *orala sa'kilan,* even."

"So you know how the *kalliris* defeated the famine," she murmured. "With the heartstones."

Hidri inclined his head. "*Lysi.*"

"Why did you not share this with the *Vorakkar*?" I asked, no longer keeping silent as I watched Kara weave him up in her own little spell. "If you knew that the heartstones helped save the West, did you not think they could do the same in the East?"

His eyes narrowed on me, and I felt the chill wash over his features at my accusation. "I heard from the *Vorakkar* of Rath Kitala himself that the hordes believe a heartstone *created* this mess to begin with. Why would I suggest using *more* heartstones to stop it? I did not think the fog and the famine were related in any way."

"I understand," Kara cut in, throwing me a stern look that had me swallowing a growl. She looked back the *Sorakkar.* "Of course you would not know. Even the *Seta Kalliri* had her doubts in the beginning. Until Kakkari showed her the true path."

The *Sorakkar* was mollified by her words, though it was evident that he did not care for me. He angled his back in such a way that cut me from the conversation, turning only to give Kara his full attention.

"Even still, unless I have direct word from the *Seta Kalliri* or the *Dothikkar,* I cannot give you the heartstone."

Kara stared at him. Behind her serene smile, I saw her mind working. I was fascinated by this new creature, could hardly keep my gaze off her.

Though that's been true since the North Lands, I couldn't help but think.

"We're not asking you to give it to us," she murmured.

I cut her a sharp look, even as the *Sorakkar's* shoulders

relaxed a fraction, imperceptible in his relief. He didn't want to disappoint her either, it seemed.

"But the *Vorakkar* of Rath Serok and I," she continued, "were tasked with collecting the heartstones. All five. We are in possession of three. There is yours. And we journey to *Dothik* soon for the last."

I held in my sharp sigh. She assumed she would be coming with me to *Dothik* still? After what happened at the lake?

She's ensuring that she does, I realized, *the little sneak.*

"You have three of them already?" the *Sorakkar* breathed.

"*Lysi.* In possession of the *Vorakkar*. So you do not have to *give* the heartstone to us. I know you take your oath seriously, and the *kalliris* were right to entrust one to you and your line before you," she informed him. What was she doing? "We just ask that you journey to the East Lands when you are called upon. You must bring the heartstone. And all five will be used together once more."

I stared at Kara, the tuft of my tail hovering above the ground, held still as I processed her words.

This was...the right move, I realized begrudgingly.

She'd read the *Sorakkar* with ease. She'd realized he wouldn't part with something so valuable for nothing. She'd played to his pride, had allowed him the honor of aiding Dakkar in a way that did not trample his oath.

"That is all we ask," she murmured.

And he would come, I knew. I saw it in the way his spine straightened. His weariness seemed to disappear. It looked as if he'd been reinvigorated with purpose.

"I will," he vowed, inclining his head toward the hybrid female still perched in the chair. She had windswept hair and tired eyes. The bridge of her nose was reddened from the sun and streaked with dust. She hadn't bathed for two days, since the lake. Her clothes were dirtied. And I knew how much that bothered her.

Yet I'd never thought her more beautiful than when she gave the *Sorakkar* a pleased smile, sitting in her throne of a chair.

Kara, your queen.

The chosen, curious thing.

Who will make you a king.

My blood drained from my face, and I flattened my hand to the stone wall behind me, my nostrils flaring.

My mother's lilting song rang in my ears, a song I hadn't heard in years, and yet...it came clear and strong. A strong *memory*. I'd thought it a coincidence when I heard Kara's name in the temple.

Now?

I wasn't so sure.

I'd dismissed my mother's songs and sayings as symptoms of her...of her *anger*. Of her delusions. Of her quiet plots that had begun when the *Dothikkar* turned his back on her.

"*Vorakkar?*" came Kara's voice, cutting through my own shaken disbelief.

When my eyes met her, I felt the world swirl and tilt. She was looking at me with a frown, as was the *Sorakkar* of Rath Hidri, though his eyes were assessing, seeking weakness. I realized I'd stumbled back against the wall.

I straightened, the scrape of my sword cutting through the quiet room.

"Those accommodations," I murmured to the *Sorakkar*, shaking away the song's melody though I could still hear the words like a taunting whisper. "We would like them now."

We would revisit this conversation tomorrow. After a full night's rest. If the *Sorakkar* thought he could get rid of me so swiftly, he would be in for a rude surprise. I excelled at overstaying my welcome, especially if it got me what I wanted.

"Of course," the *Sorakkar* said coolly, his lips pursed. "I will have a *soliki* prepared for you, *Vorakkar*."

Then he turned to Kara. "I have another *soliki* in mind for you. It is very comfortable. And has a wonderful view of—"

"*Nik,*" I cut through the conversation, even as Kara's gaze snapped to mine. "She stays with me."

An uncomfortable silence descended, and I felt the throb of Kara's sudden anger. I'd felt it bubbling for the past couple days, truthfully. Like a simmering pot about to boil over.

"That *soliki* sounds wonderful, *kakkira vor,*" she told the *Sorakkar,* giving him a sunny smile. "The *Vorakkar* can sleep wherever he pleases, but I will have my own bed."

In no uncertain terms, she dismissed me. In no uncertain terms, she drew a line between us.

I had a feeling that Hidri could barely conceal his snicker. "Follow me, then, *kalles.* And in the morning, you can speak with my wife. Her entire family grew up in these lands. She can tell you everything you wish to know about the famine, *lysi?*"

Kara ignored my presence as she fell into step beside the *Vorakkar,* making for the door that would lead to the *saruk's* main road.

"That would be most appreciated," she told him.

I snagged her wrist when she got close, though my touch was gentle and my thumb began to stroke the underside of her wrist immediately. "We need to talk."

She pulled away from my grip as if I'd burned her. When she met my eyes, she said, "It can wait until the morning. Sleep well, *Vorakkar.*"

The door closed behind her.

CHAPTER 32

My fingers slid down the handle of the gold brush. The intricate carvings on it were beautifully detailed, depicting a kind of flower I'd never seen before.

Such luxuries in the *saruk*. My brush was not something I'd packed when I left the temple in a hurry, something I found myself regretting often. But even my brush had never been a fraction as fine as this one.

Picking it up, I smoothed it through my wet hair, sighing happily. *Kalloma* had often brushed my hair when I was younger. It brought me comfort even though I found my heart squeezing with missing her as I slowly worked through the tangles.

The *soliki* reminded me of my tower. Made of stone, quiet, sturdy, stable. Even the floor beneath my bare feet felt familiar. In a room down the small hallway was the bath, where I'd soaked until the water turned cool. I'd scrubbed away the journey, scrubbed away Arik's touch from between my legs—though my own fingers had begun to stroke there—and scrubbed away the frustration and hurt until my skin was raw and not a single speck of dirt could have survived.

I sighed, turning my attention to the mirror. Its edge was

gilded, and I stared at my appearance as I brushed my hair. My skin was darker from the sun—slightly burned in some places. The tops of my cheekbones were raw from the wind. But my golden eyes sparkled in the fire's light.

I was in the West Lands.

I was in a *saruk*.

I'd experienced so much since I left the North. And it only whetted my appetite for *more*.

In the mirror, I saw the door open behind me.

There was nothing to warn me of his presence, though I'd had my suspicions that he'd come. And in his arrogance, he never thought to knock. He simply walked through the door and closed it behind him like he had every right to do so.

And so he does, I thought. He was a *Vorakkar*. He could damn well do what he pleased, even in a *saruk*.

In the mirror, our eyes met. He'd bathed too. He was dressed in a fresh tunic and trews whereas I had dressed in the silk shift that was left for me. The *Sorakkar* of Rath Hidri was a gracious host. He'd had a chest of supplies—including this brush—brought in. The dress, and two others for the daytime, had been within it as well.

Arik's nostrils flared, and I saw his gaze drop down the length of my backside. The dress was cream in color and shimmered in the golden light. It was similar to what the *kalliris* wore during their evening prayers, I thought. Wearing it made me feel like I'd borrowed it from Avala or Trissa. It made me feel connected to them in some small way.

"I'm tired," I told him, returning my gaze to my own in the mirror. It dropped to the strands of my hair, and I continued to brush. "I told you we could speak in the morning."

"I've put this off for too long," came his voice. I was pleased with myself when I suppressed my shiver. His voice was low and quiet and deep. Intimate, even. He never spoke to others the way he spoke to me. Especially when we were alone. "I cannot another night."

"Put this off," I repeated softly, feeling annoyance burn in my chest at the way he'd phrased the comment. "If it is so aggravating to you, *Vorakkar*, please know that there is no need to speak about anything. You don't need to put anything off, for there is nothing to discuss."

His growl signaled him stepping toward me. "Kara."

My eyes snapped to his in the mirror. I really *didn't* want to talk about the lake. Every time I closed my eyes, I saw him lounging on the lake's ledge at his leisure, those dark eyes pinned to me, a teasing, wicked grin on his face. *That* was the Arik I wanted. Not the one that had come after.

I couldn't escape the memory. I would think about it for the rest of my life. But now it was sullied with embarrassment and dizzying mortification that made me want to curl up. I couldn't think about the pleasure without thinking about the *shame*.

And he'd taken that from me. He'd taken an exciting, *good*, tail-curling experience and turned it into something that I felt I should be ashamed of.

Suddenly, I wanted him to know that. I felt it rising in me, *needing* to get out.

"Why did you do it?" I asked him, knowing he wouldn't let this go, though he was perfectly happy *not* speaking about it until it suited him. "I was trying to...to keep my distance. But when I tried, you pushed harder. I'm trying to understand *why*."

"Is that what you were doing?" he asked. "Trying to keep your distance? What made you suddenly decide to do that?"

I rounded on him with round eyes. Was he serious? "Because you made it perfectly clear that you had no interest in sex with me!"

The thing about *solikis* was that we could fight and no one would overhear. Our voices slammed into the stone and didn't leave, unlike in a horde, unlike in a *voliki*.

He huffed out a sharp breath that sounded *mocking*.

I recoiled, biting my lip. "I was trying to be your friend," I finished softly, swallowing hard. "I was trying to be respectful, and you didn't even allow me that."

I walked away from the mirror, though I didn't really have any idea where to go. Only my feet were restless. I felt that little ball of hurt begin to expand and grow. The outside world beyond the temple was...confusing. It was strange and mean and duplicitous but also exciting and wonderful.

Everything that Arik was, I realized.

When I passed him, his hand flashed out and he caught my wrist, pulling me toward him. The brush clattered from my grip in surprise as my brows furrowed when I felt him drag me closer. Until our bodies were pressed together and I felt...I felt how hard he was, pressing into my soft belly through the silk. I felt his strength, the sudden tension that was buzzing through him before zipping into me.

"You don't think I want you?" came his soft rasp. But he was glaring at me, his expression furious. "Are you *vokking* joking? When all I can see is you?"

My eyes went round, and before I could process those words, Arik was cursing. There was a flurry of movement.

Then his lips were on mine.

Shocked, I could only stare at him as he glared at me, his brows furrowed. His lips were surprisingly soft and warm. My spine tingled as they began to move against mine, angry and hard ...but hungry.

Ever so slightly, Arik began to soften.

On a deep pull of my bottom lip, a gruff sound left this throat and his eyes closed. Mine did too. His hands slid around my waist, large and strong and hot, and then moved down my back, gripping my hips, holding me to him so tight it was almost painful.

My tail twitched when his lips moved against mine...and

then I began to respond to him, my heart skipping and sputtering in my chest. I gasped, my hands moving to his shoulders when I felt my legs tremble and my core begin to warm.

So...this was kissing.

And it's pleasing, I thought, eager. It took a little while for me to match his guiding rhythm, but when I did, he groaned, his grip tightening on me. He tasted of heat and wine. His scent made me dizzy. His tongue stroked and delved, making my head spin.

The kiss deepened. I could *feel* it growing hungrier. I could feel it growing punishing and needful and rough.

"*Vok*, Kara," came his deep rasp. He was so hard I felt his cock begin to pulse against me, a cock I'd stroked and studied and admired only a couple days ago.

A shuddered sigh escaped my throat, and he stole my breath. Maybe this was his answer. Maybe he'd just needed time to think it over. Maybe he would give me what I wanted.

My hands drifted down his shoulders, skimming along the wide berth of his chest. I wanted him. Even in my anger, I wanted him. How was that possible?

A strangled growl left his throat when my hands settled on the thick heat of his cock. I cupped the outline of him through his trews, squeezing, and then—

Arik tore himself away.

One moment he was as close as he could possibly be. The next, he was putting space between us as cool air rushed in where he'd been.

He was huffing, panting. So was I. With kiss-stung lips, I watched as he ran a hand over his jaw, scrubbing over a scar there. His eyes were wild. His shoulders rose and lowered with heavy breaths.

I simply stood there. My skin was tingling. My fingers were still curled from how they'd wrapped around his cock. The taste of him was on my tongue. I wanted to kiss him again, but I also never wanted to touch him again. Two feelings that were completely at odds with one another.

Strangled disappointment crashed over me. I felt like I was sinking into the lake again, thrashing my legs, desperately trying to surface.

He was doing it *again*.

And like a fool, I'd let him.

Strangely, I wasn't as furious about it as I thought I'd be. Instead, acceptance slid into me, quelling the disappointment with realization.

"I know what I want, but you don't know what you want, Arik," I said softly, bending down to pick up my brush with trembling fingers. Still, my voice was strong. For that I was proud. When I straightened, I met his gaze. "Until you do, I'm not doing this anymore. We can still be friends, but just...just don't touch me anymore, *lysi*? It's not fair. You're not being fair to me."

His eyes closed tightly at my declaration. Before my eyes, I watched as he struggled to gain control over himself, something I didn't think he showed anyone. I watched as he pulled himself together, piece by piece, straightening imperceptibly to his full height, smoothing the lines over his features, running a hand down his face once as if to reset his expression.

"Let's just forget about the lake," I said quietly, wiping the back of my hand across my lips. "Let's just forget about *this*. You may *want me* like you say but, for whatever reason, not enough to change your mind. This will be easier for us both. And I promise I won't touch you either. I won't."

His swallow was audible. When he finally met my eyes across the room, they looked more red than swirled. A shiver raced down my spine at the sight of them. For a moment, he looked like someone else entirely, someone who looked familiar, though I couldn't quite place who.

"And what of your desire to be with a male before you

return to the temple?" came his roughened voice. He might have schooled his expression into impassiveness, but he couldn't change his voice.

I hesitated. Turning from him, I went to the chest that was sitting on the table, where it'd been when I arrived. Replacing the brush carefully, I murmured, "I will return to the North Lands when I'm ready to. For thirty years, the *orala sa'kilan* was all I knew. I'm in no rush to return, though I know that I will eventually."

"That doesn't answer my question."

A burn of anger sparked in my chest.

"It means that I have the time to find another male," I told him, facing him. "Someone who wants what I want."

The words were a trigger, and Arik of Rath Serok suddenly loomed before me, his expression no longer indifferent but *furious*.

Nik, not furious, I realized, swallowing.

Jealous.

Which only confused me more as I clutched my hands on the table behind me. Arik pressed me into it, the edge against my spine, until his arms were bracketed around me.

"You think so, *saila*?" he purred. He wasn't touching me, I realized. Not at all. Doing what I asked of him, but it was still entirely *too much*. "If you think I'll let that happen, then you truly have no idea who you're dealing with. Who you're trying to provoke."

My brow furrowed, and I scowled. "I'm not provoking you, Serok."

I swore I caught a small flinch at the sound of his name— his family name, his horde's name, but not *his* name.

"I'm not provoking you at all," I told him softly, meeting his eyes. "But you can't give me what I want. That's a *fact*."

His jaw tightened, and it only made his expression all the more fierce.

"I even *understand*. You have a duty to your horde. To Dakkar. To the oath you took as a *Vorakkar*. The last thing you need is for someone to distract you," I said, a sinking sensation in my belly when I realized something. "To make even more demands of you. Especially with the fog looming in the East."

Had I been doing that without realizing it? Pressuring him toward something he would rather not give? He might *want* me—the evidence pressed against me earlier was illuminating enough—but it didn't mean he wanted to act on it.

With the exception of the lake, I couldn't help but think.

But his anger was still written on his face. If anything, my words seemed to infuriate him more.

"If you think to control me with jealousy, I will not take kindly to it," he hissed, glaring at me. "Other females have tried before, and they *never* got what they wanted. So don't even try it, Kara. I'm warning you now."

What other females?

I shouldn't have said anything, I thought, blowing out a small breath.

"You have nothing to worry about," I assured him. Something flashed through his eyes. He blinked, calming briefly. Trying to read me? "I'm not trying to do anything, much less control you."

That was the truth.

Sex isn't the most important thing right now, I chastised myself silently. The fog and the heartstones were, however. We would deal with *that* before I turned my attentions to anything else. That was how it should've been from the very beginning.

I'd just gotten a little caught up in Arik. In the surprising, alarming, deep attraction I had toward him.

But no more, I decided resolutely. We had a task to finish. Laid out before us. *That* was what was important.

Quickly, I ducked under his arm to escape him and then went to the door. I was tired. I wanted sleep.

When I opened the door for him, I felt a warm breeze rush in, rustling my dress around my ankles. The warm season was upon us. It felt so wonderful. The deeper we'd traveled inland, the warmer it had become. I wondered if the *Sorakkar* of Rath Hidri would let me live in his *saruk* for a brief time once the fog was gone. I thought I'd enjoy living here for a spell before returning to the temple.

Maybe…maybe I could even split my time between the two places. Maybe that would be an option available to me. A way for me to be with *Kalloma* and the *kalliris*, while also having my own freedom.

"I'll speak with the *Arakkari* tomorrow," I said, distracted by the hopeful, dizzying thought. The *Arakkari* was the queen of the *saruk*. When I refocused on him, I felt…*in control*. I actually felt much better now than I did when Arik first entered. His palms were still flattened on the table as he turned his head to regard me, his brow furrowed, darkening his eyes. He watched me. I said, "But I'd like to sleep now. So you'll need to leave."

His nostrils flared. Slowly, I watched as he pushed up from the table, straightening. His boots were a whisper across the stone floor as he approached.

"You're breaking my heart, *saila*," he murmured, and I blinked, frowning, surprised by the words. "Ever since the North Lands, we've never slept apart. Have you realized that?"

Ah.

Now I wasn't so surprised.

Arik was deflecting.

This was his offhand comment, the one meant to disarm me, to rattle me.

"You lived your entire life without me sleeping next to you," I replied, looking into his eyes. I saw his pupils dilate before contracting on me. "I trust that your heart will survive it."

Because you don't have a heart to break, I thought. Hadn't I thought that before? Back at the *orala sa'kilan*? Perhaps I should've listened to my own instincts when it came to Arik.

Nik. He did have a heart. He just had a thick Dakkari-steel wall around it. I wondered why. Because of his friend? The one in *Dothik* he'd told me about?

Or was it more?

A rough breath escaped his lips. Looking up at his handsome face, a fierce longing went through me, but it was met with disappointment. He wasn't mine. He never had been. Soon, simply looking at him would stop making me ache. *Soon.*

Not soon enough though.

"Good night, *Vorakkar*," I said firmly.

Then I nudged him out the door before he could say another word.

And this time, I locked the latch behind him.

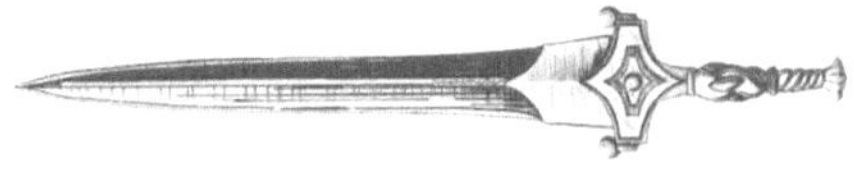

"You're looking for Ojak?" the *mrikro* asked, keeping his gaze pinned to the notch of my throne, not meeting my eyes.

"*Lysi*," I said, crossing my arms over my chest. "I'd ask your *Sorakkar*, but I cannot seem to find him this morning."

"He's..." The *mrikro* trailed off but then shrugged, his gaze darting to the line of the forest that the *saruk* lay next to. This was the woodland area of the West Lands. Lakes and forests littered this place. "Ojak should be working with the *darukkars*. You'll find him over there."

He gestured to the northern end of the *saruk*, and I inclined my head in a nod. "*Kakkira vor.*"

When I turned, I heard a quick, chuffing sound from his throat, as if he meant to speak but stopped himself at the last moment. Looking over my shoulder at him, I quirked a brow. "*Lysi?*"

The *mrikro* met my gaze briefly in his embarrassment. "Are you...are you..."

He stopped. His swallow was audible.

Then he said, "For the glory of Dakkar."

My nostrils flared, and I watched as he scuttled away, back into the *pyroki* enclosure. The *saruks* didn't have as many *pyrokis* as the hordes did. There was no need to keep so many creatures. Still, it was a high-ranking job in a *saruk*, caring for the beasts that allowed the strength of the hordes to continue.

For the glory of Dakkar.

Not *for the glory of Dothik.*

Ojak's influence had obviously begun to take root. The *mrikro* knew who I was.

I didn't know how to feel about that. Kara's words returned to me from last night. *I know what I want, but you do not know what you want, Arik.*

She'd never been more right about anything. Once, I thought I knew what I wanted. I had felt my hatred propel me toward action. I had felt that drive settle deep in my bones and *burn* there.

Once, I wanted to tear the whole of *Dothik* down. Then I wanted to remake it. But most importantly, I wanted the *Dothikkar* gone from the throne. For years, I had planned to assassinate him myself. We had constructed plan after plan, all viable though risky.

And then, one day, I woke up and told myself *enough*. I had worn my hatred and my anger and my grief for so long that I realized it had begun to rival my mother's. *That* I never wanted to happen.

But I had many relying on me. I had many *believing* in me. Who had given their lives to see one thing and one thing only.

Me. On the throne in *Dothik.*

Now, as I watched a *mrikro* shovel *pyroki* shit into a corner, it hit me square in the chest how far I'd strayed from that end goal.

Even Nassik had been surprised when I announced I was entering the Trials. Nassik, who knew me best. Who'd known me almost my entire life. Who knew me longer than my own mother, even.

My feet carried me toward the northern end of the *saruk*. Males, females, and children alike literally stopped in their tracks when they saw me near. Staring, though when I looked at them, their gazes darted away. Save for a few of the bolder females, who kept my gaze not long enough for it to be considered disrespectful but long enough for me to see their interest.

An impatient huff whistled through my nostrils. Since when had the attentions of beautiful females begun to irritate me?

Never. Not until Kara.

The ringing of swords alerted me to the fact that I neared the training grounds. And I saw Ojak almost immediately, a genuine grin sliding over my face as I listened to him shouting at one of the younger *darukkars*, critiquing his form.

"If you don't move your damn feet, I'll cut them off you!" he shouted, the words hostile though his tone was almost...bored.

He was standing at the fence, his arms leaning against the rails. As he was distracted by the *darukkars*, his eyes quickly darting as they ran through their practice spar, I sidled up next to him.

His head turned, his gaze catching on my tunic before he dismissed me, thinking me a member of the *saruk*. Then he did a double take.

When his gaze connected with mine, I grinned at him. "Still using the same threats, I see? I seem to remember you saying you'd cut off my arm if I didn't wield my sword at the correct height."

A boisterous laugh bellowed from his wide chest. "Serok."

His hard embrace was familiar. The responding fist pound against my back was comforting.

"I heard a *Vorakkar* had come in the night," he said in my ear. When he pulled back he was smiling, his eyes crinkling with the expression. "I did not think it was you."

"I thought so," I told him. "Because if you had, I'm certain you would've been banging on my door while I tried to sleep."

"Bekkar's sword," he breathed, pulling back to look at me. We were quiet for a moment as we regarded one another, a comfortable familiarity spreading between us even though it had been nearly two years since we'd seen one another. "I cannot believe you're standing in front of me right now. I—I cannot believe that you're *here*. But why are you here?"

"The heartstones. They believe they can be used to stop the fog in the East."

Ojak nodded thoughtfully, blinking as he processed the information. His head turned, and he scowled at the two young *darukkars*, likely training for a future in a horde, and yelled, "Did I tell you to stop?"

Immediately, the two males began sparring once more, though their movements seemed stiff and I caught their gazes tracking to me every now and again behind Ojak's back.

"How's Wreika?" I asked. "And your daughters?"

The reason Ojak had left *Dothik* in the first place. There were some that viewed his leaving as a betrayal, but I knew better. He hadn't needed my blessing to leave, but he had *wanted* it. His wife's health was abysmal in the capital. When she fell pregnant with their second child, Ojak had feared that her strength would fail her.

And so, he'd brought her back to her roots, back to this *saruk*. Ojak was *Dothik* born and bred. But not the female he'd fallen in love with.

"Well," he told me. "Very well. Her cough went away. She is strong here, as if she is connected to this land, like so many wildlanders are. And we are happy. Life is...different. Different but good."

I inclined my head. I knew the guilt Ojak had carried with him from *Dothik*. I hadn't wanted him to bear it. But after Bodin, he had always felt partially responsible for his death.

Adding that onto his decision to leave the capital, he'd been... changed.

"I'm glad to hear it, my friend."

His gaze went behind me, scanning the clearing. "I heard the *Vorakkar* came with a female."

Swallowing, I told him, "She is with the *Arakkari*." The image of her in her night shift from last night returned to me. So achingly lovely that I'd felt something crack in my chest. At his pointed look, I chuckled, scrubbing a hand at the back of my neck, and said, "She is...well, she's the daughter of a *kalliri*. The *Seta Kalliri*."

"*Vok*," Ojak said slowly. "I heard she was a hybrid female. Human and Dakkari. Did the *Seta Kalliri* really—"

I laughed. "*Nik.* Her mother brought her to the temple seeking safety for her when she was an infant. She was raised there. The *Seta Kalliri* raised her as her own."

Ojak pinned me with a thoughtful look. "You never went about things easily, did you, Serok?"

I sobered at the words. Ojak had always been annoyingly perceptive. It was what had made him a good spy, even though he never blended into crowds as well as Kalik or Vala.

"You are good here?" I asked him pointedly. "Do you need anything? Tell me, and it's yours."

He smiled, but it didn't quite reach his eyes. "There is no use for gold here. You know that, Serok. We have everything we need."

I nodded.

"But *kakkira vor* for the offer," he continued. "I know I can come to you if I do ever need anything."

Satisfied, I reached out to squeeze his shoulder, tight and unyielding under my palm. "Or Wreika. Or your daughters," I added.

"Is there anything *you* need?" he asked, crossing his arms over his chest.

My gaze slid to the line of the forest.

"I spoke to the *Sorakkar* last night," I murmured to him quietly. He shifted, tilting his head in a way that exposed his ear toward me. Something that had never changed when we talked like this. "I got the impression that he didn't want *me* here specifically. Does he know who I am?"

"He's heard the rumors, no doubt," Ojak said. "There are those within the *saruk* that know your name and who you are. But the *Sorakkar*...he is of the old way of the *Vorakkar*. He values strength and loyalty." He tipped his head toward me. "As do you."

"He wants me gone," I informed him. "Though he took a liking to my female."

I regretted the slip of tongue almost immediately. *My female. Vok.*

Ojak raised his brow but wisely didn't comment on it. Though I caught the pleased smirk that threatened to break over his expression.

Then the smirk died slowly. His feet shifted toward me ever so slightly.

"He has a deal with the Killup."

That was not what I expected him to say.

"*Neffar?*"

The Killup?

"He is expecting them back any moment and would rather not have you find out. That's my best guess. He thinks all the *Vorakkar* are still loyal to the *Dothikkar*. If only he knew."

"Expecting them back from *where*?"

"A hunt," Ojak told me.

As if on cue, I heard a long, rumbling howl echo in the distance. My heart froze in my chest, stopping me cold, and I could only think of Kara. I knew she was out beyond the *saruk's* borders, close to the forest with the *Arakkari*.

"*Jrikkia*," I murmured, disbelief shooting through me. In my mind's eye, I saw snapping, bloody teeth and glittering eyes. "Is the *Sorakkar* out of his mind?"

"It's all right, Serok. They are—"

Kara.

I took off in a sprint without hearing another word.

CHAPTER 34

"What was that?" I asked the *Arakkari*, frowning, the sound chilling and frightening as it echoed through the trees.

The sound had been a combination of a howl and a growl, as if it had been roared to the sky. I was crouching over the earth where I had been running my fingers through the soil, thinking that it might trigger a crack in my vision. I could feel the soil buzzing with life though, not death. And Kakkari's answer was silent, the cool earth sifting through my fingers as I slowly stood.

The *Arakkari* shifted next to me, throwing me a careful look. The queen of the *saruk* was one of the most beautiful Dakkari females I'd ever seen. Everything I'd thought a queen should be. Regal and poised. Gentle but unyielding. She'd answered my endless questions with patience. She'd made me feel welcome, safe.

Right now, however, she was shuffling on her feet.

"The *Vorakkar* you came with," she said quietly. "Does he have loyalties to *Dothik*? I know he was the last horde king to withstand the Trials."

He was?

My brows furrowed. "*Lysi*, he lived in *Dothik*, but he's a horde king now. Why would that matter?"

"I meant, does he have loyalties to the *Dothikkar*?" she asked, just as another howl shot up in the sky.

My breath hitched, my heart beginning to thunder in my chest. It was coming from the forest right next to us. And whatever it was, it was coming closer.

"Perhaps we should return to the *saruk*," I said to the *Arakkari* quickly. "I don't think—"

Even the hairs on my tail rose when I heard the growl coming from the line of the forest.

I gasped and whirled, scanning the darkened, shadowy spaces between the trees.

"*Arakkari*, we should leave," I whispered, my heart feeling like it was clogged in my throat. "This doesn't feel right."

"It's just the *jrikkia*," she said, something resigned in her tone. "The *sarl*. They will not harm you unless their masters order them to."

The *jrikkia*? Why did that name sound so familiar? And yet I couldn't place it within all the research I'd done about Dakkar's creatures.

Just then, I spied the glowing orbs from the darkness. I wouldn't have seen the blackened eyes at all but they caught on the shaft of light that speared through the dense trees, and I suddenly realized that we were being watched.

I must've let out a squeak of fear, the eeriness of it making me stumble back. The *Arakkari* caught my wrist.

"Hold still, *kassiri*," she told me. *Love*, she called me gently. "Don't run. Don't show fear."

"Kara!" came a familiar booming voice, one that made me relax in relief. When I darted a quick look over my shoulder, I saw Arik running toward me, a burly, unfamiliar Dakkari male a good length behind him. The *Vorakkar's* expression was drawn tight, fury and tension lining his face. "Get back!"

A mass of black fur catapulted beyond the line of the forest, sunlight hitting its bulk, illuminating the beast in a way that made it seem all the more terrifying. Its weight shook the ground when it landed. Two more followed, flanking the largest of the beasts. The alpha?

Arik's scent hit me, signaling his presence to me as I looked at the *jrikkia* with wide eyes. The largest one was bigger than Syok, with sharpened claws that dug into the earth as if prepared to leap toward us. Claws that could shred us to bits in mere moments, if the blood-slicked teeth didn't tear us apart first.

Arik pushed me back, one palm on my abdomen, spread wide across my front as if he needed to reassure himself I was there. The other hand unsheathed his sword. Gleaming and sharp. The gold of the hilt looked new even though the handles on his daggers looked worn down to the very blade.

My heart was beating faster than it had at the lake. Fear for Arik suddenly took hold, and I wrapped my hand around the belt at his waist where he tucked his daggers, using it like an anchor to secure me to him. His palm on my belly flexed, but the arm that held his sword at the ready was unwavering.

"Serok," came the heaving, panting voice of the unfamiliar Dakkari male. In a rush, he said, "Don't. They won't hurt her. They belong to the Killup."

The Killup? I thought, my breath hitching.

Arik's head turned to the side briefly as if he heard something familiar in the male's voice. His tone was clipped when he asked, "You are certain?"

"On my life," the Dakkari male wheezed. "*Vok*, don't make me run like that again! I tried to tell you."

I didn't know what was happening. Or who this male was.

But whoever he was...Arik must've trusted him because a moment later, his arm lowered just as the *jrikkia* snarled. I tensed and made a squeaking sound of alarm, but Arik stepped in front of me, always keeping me behind him.

"It's all right, *saila*," he murmured. His face was turned to the side, so I saw his jaw moving, but he never took his eyes off the *jrikkia*, watching its every move. The hand on his sword twitched. "If he says they won't hurt you, then they won't."

What I heard in his voice made my body soften. Some of the tension released from my shoulders. I managed to swallow past the thick lump in my throat. Arik trusted this male. And I trusted Arik. At least when it came to my safety. I trusted him when he said he would keep me safe.

He'd put himself between the *jrikkia* and me, after all. He'd done it without hesitating.

A sharp whistling sound cut through the sudden silence, and immediately the largest *jrikkia* straightened. The growling in its throat ceased. Behind it, the other two relaxed.

A male appeared but not from behind the *jrikkia*. There was a road west of where we were, cutting through the trees. The male bit out something in a language I'd never heard, and the *jrikkia* bounded toward him, booming the earth in their wake.

As the male drew closer, more appeared behind him. Long spears were perched against their shoulders, blades tucked into straps at their thighs. They moved silently. Quickly. Another *jrikkia* appeared, but this one was harnessed to a cart, the wheels creaking behind him as he stalked closer.

Killup, I thought with parted lips.

They were tall beings. Unlike the sheer bulk of Dakkari males, the Killup were leanly muscled though still imposing in their obvious strength. They had gray skin, all in varying shades of it—some darker, some lighter—and their eyes were black, glassy orbs. At their necks, I saw slitted gills.

I swallowed. I didn't know much about the Killup, but I had read that their gills could emit a toxic poison if they felt threatened. If Dakkari—or humans—were susceptible to it, I didn't know for certain.

Still, as they drew closer and closer, I couldn't help but be intrigued. I thought they were a beautiful race, their features composed of sharp angles, revealing their symmetry. I found them immensely pleasing to look at...despite their *jrikkia* nearly stopping my heart in my chest.

The wagon, harnessed to one of the *jrikkia*, was loaded with...

Wrissan, I thought, my eyes widening. Two thick beasts had been hefted into the back of it, and the *jrikkia* didn't seem fatigued by their bulk in the slightest.

These were hunters.

Yet...hunting was forbidden to the Killup and to the *vekkiri,* agreements made with *Dothik* when both races were offered refuge on Dakkar. Right?

Even the Dakkari that lived in the outposts and in the hordes. Unless they were given the title of *hunter,* they were forbidden to take life.

Behind me, I heard heavy footsteps approach as the Killup drew nearer and nearer. They were a group of ten, I counted. One male was obviously in charge. I didn't know how I knew that, but there was a male that was in the center of the pack. I had the strangest feeling that the other Killup males were moving *around* him. As if to shield him.

I heard the *Sorakkar's* voice break out. He'd been the one to join the growing group, and when I looked over my shoulder, I saw he'd stopped at his queen's side. I saw his hand curl around her hip, drawing her close. I didn't miss the assessing stare the *Sorakkar* of Rath Hidri threw Arik's way, especially when the *Vorakkar* turned to regard him, a brow quirked, his expression darkened.

"Care to explain, *Sorakkar?*" came Arik's words. They were light, almost conversational. But I knew better.

The *Sorakkar* hesitated. We were a small group now. Myself, Arik, the *Arakkari*, the *Sorakkar*, and the other Dakkari male who my traveling companion obviously knew.

And then the pack of Killup strode up to us, the impact of so many people in one area overwhelming. Their four *jrikkia*, however, stayed behind them, prowling along the edge of the forest restlessly. Their presence still made me nervous, and I eyed them even as my gaze flitted to Arik, the *Sorakkar*, and the Killup. Too many things to look at at once.

"Two of your *wrissan*," came a Killup's voice. I started at it. Soft and raspy, I felt it drag across my skin like a touch. Almost like how Arik's voice affected me. "As promised."

My hand was still wrapped around his belt. At the Killup's voice, Arik pushed me farther back.

"*Kakkira vor*, Erul," the *Sorakkar's* strained voice sounded.

"Tell me now," Arik ordered softly, stepping back so he could keep his eyes on both the *Sorakkar* and the Killup. But then his gaze snapped to the other Dakkari male. "Ojak."

I started at the given name, but the command in Arik's voice was unmistakable.

Ojak flitted a quick look at the *Sorakkar* but then his arms crossed over his chest. "They are friends of the *saruk, Vorakkar*," Ojak told him.

"And the hunting?" Arik asked, his eyes focusing on the two dead *wrissan* in the back of their wagon. "And the *jrikkia*, so close to the *saruk*?"

"The *sarl* obey our commands," came the Killup's voice again. *Sarl* must be what the Killup called their *jrikkia*. The one who spoke was the one I assumed was their leader. The Killup stepped forward, the one that the *Sorakkar* had addressed as Erul. "They would not disobey us, just as your own *pyroki* would not disobey you. If they are well trained."

Arik stiffened at the slight barb, but he turned his grin to the Killup, as alarming as it was meant to *disarm*.

"That's what worries me. My *pyroki* can sometimes have a mind of his own. A stubborn streak I don't quite have the heart to break."

The *Sorakkar's* gruff sigh sounded, and he stepped forward. "The Killup and our *saruk* have had an arrangement for quite some time, *Vorakkar*. One that mutually benefits us."

"And this was why you wanted me to leave so quickly," Arik said.

If the *Sorakkar* was surprised that Arik had picked up on that, he didn't show it. "We know you have loyalties to *Dothik*. If the *Dothikkar* knew of this arrangement, he would likely seek to punish us. I could not take that chance."

Ojak's voice was considerably *affronted* as he claimed, "The *Vorakkar* of Rath Serok does not have allegiances to the *Dothikkar*."

Speaking for him? How was it that these two knew each other exactly?

"*Nik?*" the *Sorakkar* asked, his tone pricking my interest. Hidri speared Arik with a long look. "Are you not his son? Of his own blood, of his own line?"

The world seemed to tilt beneath my feet, and my legs nearly gave way underneath me. "*Neffar?*" I breathed. Then I laughed, but it sounded too loud even to my own ears. "He is not the *Dothikkar's* son. He is…"

The *Sorakkar* turned his assessing gaze to me as I trailed off. Then I rounded on Arik, needing to see his face.

"You're not his son," I said softly, my brows furrowing, though the statement came out more like a question.

I struggled to understand. He'd mockingly told me he'd come from a long line of kings, hadn't he? But surely he'd just been joking. I thought it strange that his horde's name, Serok, was not in the histories of Dakkar. I hadn't remembered coming across it in all the books I'd read. I'd shrugged it off, however, thinking he was the first of his line to complete the Trials, an impressive feat in itself.

Arik's gaze held mine. I forgot about the Killup. I forgot about the *Arakkari* and the *Sorakkar*. Arik's friend. The *jrikkia*.

"I am his son, *saila*," came his soft confession. "His bastard. But of his blood nonetheless."

I reeled back. My mind froze.

"But...but that would make you..."

Next in line for the throne.

CHAPTER 35

In my cowardice, I found that I tried to avoid Arik for the rest of the evening.

There were too many jumbled emotions and thoughts after the revelation that had come to light. I'd stayed away from my temporary *soliki*, knowing he'd likely try to come find me there. If I happened to catch sight of him, I would dart the other way. I took my meal with a group of females who were sitting by a fire, chatting away. They were happy to have me join them, and their barrage of questions about my life in the North Lands and about me were a welcome distraction. I purposefully avoided speaking about Arik, however, if the conversation ever strayed toward the *Vorakkar*.

They were as curious about him as they were about me, giggling over how handsome he was while discomfort burned in my belly.

But now it was nightfall and growing dark. I would have to face him eventually, especially given the way I'd walked away from him after his confession earlier. I was embarrassed. Mortified. I couldn't help but feel a sliver of betrayal.

How he must have been laughing at me, I thought, my fists clenching at my sides.

Me, a half-human, half-Dakkari female who'd been raised in a temple. Him, the next *vokking* king of Dakkar. No wonder he didn't want to be with me. I couldn't be more beneath his status. Hell, I'd been way beneath his status even when I thought him a *Vorakkar*.

Like always when it came to Arik, I had more questions than I had answers.

I was growing weary of it.

So why did he kiss me last night? I couldn't help but wonder, running my fingers over my lips.

Unconsciously, I weaved in and out of the roads that lined the *saruk*. There was a cobbled main stone road that ran through the middle. But there were also compact alleys between the *solikis,* and I found myself discovering them all in my procrastination.

Doing so, however, I unwittingly stumbled across the Killup.

I froze when I saw them. I gasped when I heard the growling of the nearest *jrikkia*, startled by my sudden presence.

A soft order slithered from the Killup's leader, who I recognized. Erul. The *jrikkia* immediately quieted, lowering its head to lay it back down over its massive, clawed paws. Its eyes closed, deeming me a non-threat, apparently.

"I'm sorry," I said quietly in Dakkari. I knew the universal tongue too but didn't know if the Killup spoke it. "I didn't mean to disturb your evening. Or your...*jrikkia.*"

There were only three Killup seated around a fire basin instead of the ten I'd seen earlier. Platters of food were being passed around between them. The *wrissan* that they'd hunted.

Nik, there were four Killup, but the last was a short distance away. And he had his arms wrapped around a Dakkari female I remembered seeing earlier. One who worked in the crop fields when I'd gone to see them with the *Arakkari*.

"You are not disturbing us," came Erul's voice, those black

eyes pinned to me. Beneath them, I saw a thin gray film and could make out where his pupils were tracking. When he blinked, his eyes closed from left to right.

I hesitated. I was curious about the Killup, wanted to speak to them, but the *jrikkia* still made me nervous. I eyed the massive beast closest to Erul, and I heard something that sounded like a laugh come from his throat. Husky and rasping.

"He will not harm you."

"Because you won't allow it?"

"He is bonded to me," came Erul's voice, and I watched as he stood from his place by the fire. "He wants what I want."

That was curious, and I cocked my head to regard the Killup male. He towered over me. I thought he was probably the same height as Arik.

"Who are you?" he wanted to know, peering down at me. "You have been a topic of conversation among us this evening. For I know you do not live in the *saruk*. I would have noticed you before."

Something about the way he said the words made the tips of my ears heat.

"*Nik*, I am not from the *saruk*," I said, shuffling on my feet.

I'd learned from the group of females I'd eaten with that the Killup had come to the *saruk* often over the years. They had a hunting agreement with the *Sorakkar*. The *Sorakkar* shielded the Killup from any hordes that happened upon them and offered his *darukkars'* protection. And the Killup were given free rein to hunt within the *saruk's* territory. They would then share whatever beasts they took down, enough to keep both the Killup's people and the *saruk* fed for a couple months at least. It was a regular occurrence.

Regular enough to create bonds, I couldn't help but think, my gaze fastening on the Killup-Dakkari couple in the distance. The Killup's head was bent low enough that I saw him murmuring into the female's ear, her small giggle sounding. Her hands weaved up the lithe strength of his chest.

"You are from the North Lands," he finished for me.

My eyes snapped back up to Erul. I tucked stray strands of hair behind my ear. "You've been asking about me."

A slow blink. He stepped closer. "Perhaps."

A smile tugged on my lips. "You are their leader."

His head cocked. "Have *you* been asking about *me?*"

"*Nik*, I guessed," I told him. "Though I know of your arrangement with the *Sorakkar*."

"Ah," he murmured. His hands rose. They were strong and veined and calloused. A hunter's hands. I was fascinated by the way his gray skin seemed to diffuse the light from the fire. "Would you like to touch him?"

I swallowed, my gaze flitting away from his hands. "Who?"

"My *sarl*," he said, gesturing to the *jrikkia*.

My throat went tight. "Oh, I do not think that's…"

I trailed off, biting my lip. But then I asked myself when I would *ever* get to pet a Killup's *jrikkia* again. I wondered if its fur was really as tough and wiry as it looked.

"All right," I said quickly before I could talk myself out of it. "If you're sure he won't—"

"He won't," came the Killup's definitive answer. And I didn't know why I trusted what he said, but I did.

I was surprised when he took my hand. His gray skin was cool and surprisingly velvety to the touch. Not hot and rough like Arik's hands. He pulled me forward gently. When I looked back to the fire pit, I saw that the other two Killup had disappeared.

"Oh, where did they go?" I asked.

"To sleep, no doubt. Our hunt was long," Erul replied, stepping in front of his *jrikkia*.

"Do you sleep in the *solikis*?" I asked next, seeing no encampment for the Killup nearby.

"Yes," Erul said. "The *Sorakkar* is always generous in his welcome."

I'd found the same, I thought. Though perhaps Arik felt differently.

Just thinking about him brought a dull thud in my breast, but I tried to shrug it off, focusing my attention on the snoring creature in front of me. Oddly enough, I had the suspicion that he wasn't sleeping at all.

"Kyel," came Erul's voice. Immediately the *jrikkia*—or rather, the *sarl*—opened his eyes, his snoring ceasing. So similar to his master's eyes that it was almost eerie.

Then, slowly, Erul brought my hand down to the *sarl's* head and then his cool touch retreated. I gasped at the softness of Kyel's fur. It was the softest thing I'd ever felt, even though its appearance looked coarse and rough. So soft it was like running my hand through warm water.

"You see?" Erul rasped, seemingly pleased as I hesitantly stroked through the *sarl's* fur.

In response, the *sarl* pressed his head up toward my touch. I grinned, losing my fear entirely, which was perhaps foolish. But Kyel's chest had begun to rumble in an uneven purr, and I couldn't resist scratching at his head.

"What does it mean that he's bonded to you?" I asked, curious.

"It means that Kyel and I came into the world at the same moment," he informed me. "His life force is entwined with mine."

"Do all Killup have a bonded *sarl*?"

"No. We all revere the *sarl*, but a bonded pairing is much different than a *sarl* raised for hunting," he told me with a soft quirk of his thin lips. "Kyel is the reason I am the leader of our clan. Only clan leaders are blessed with a bonded *sarl* at birth."

So like the *Vorakkar*, he was a king to his people in his own way.

"How many clan leaders are there on Dakkar?" I couldn't help but ask. Softly, I added, "I know very little about your race. Even less about the Killup who live here."

"Three clans," he told me. "But on our home planet, there were once hundreds."

"And do you all live together?" I wondered. I could only imagine the tensions that would arise if all the hordes lived together as one. I wondered if it was similar with the Killup.

"No, we do not," the Killup answered me with an unreadable tone. He was close enough that his arm brushed my shoulder. "Though we all live in the North Lands now. We journey to the West Lands when we need to hunt again."

"You live in the North?" I gasped out. I wondered if *Kalloma* knew. "Where the temple is?"

"We stay far from the temple," he told me. "In a place where we are undisturbed. We once lived in the East but left not long ago."

"Because of the fog?" I asked, sobering.

"Because of the Ghertun," he informed me. "We left before the fog ever came to be."

Behind me, I felt a familiar presence prickling the back of my neck, and my heart began to thunder in my chest. I didn't know how I knew he was drawing near, but I did.

The Killup held my eyes, however. There was an expression on his face as he peered down at me, one of interest and intrigue.

"You never told me who you were, female," he murmured.

Blinking, I opened my lips just as Arik's voice cut through the air between us like a blade.

"*Saila*, get away from the *jrikkia*," came his dark voice. I swore I heard a tendril of fear in that voice. "*Now*."

Erul's expression twisted slightly at the *Vorakkar's* interruption. His lips tightened briefly, the circular, nearly transparent irises darting to the entrance of the clearing.

Then he straightened and, if anything, stepped closer to me, just as the horde king strode forward.

I felt Arik's hot touch on my wrist. Familiar.

"It's fine, *Vorakkar*," I said, briefly meeting Arik's eyes before dropping them. I couldn't fake a smile if I tried, so instead, I continued to frown. Just looking at him made me ache.

The *sarl* began to growl once more. Only this time Erul didn't stop him. The Killup's face was impassive as he watched the two of us, his black eyes darting, studying.

But then I spied the distaste on Erul's expression when his gaze locked on Arik. The two males didn't like each other. Like beasts fighting over a territory, I thought, they wouldn't back down.

Arik's scent slammed into me as he pulled me away from the *sarl*. Like it was trained, my body reacted on instinct to that scent, a shiver of anticipation running down my spine. My belly tightened with longing. With need.

Stop, I pleaded silently. *Enough.*

But Arik controlled me even when he was not aware of it.

Something came over the Killup. Suddenly, he went stock still. I watched the gills on the side of his neck fan out briefly and the flatness of his nose twitch. His head tilted back, exposing the front of his neck, though he kept his eyes pinned to me. He seemed to grow taller before my very eyes.

It was...an *intense* look. One that made me freeze. One that made Arik huff out a whispered curse under his breath.

"Would you like to mate, female?"

For a moment, I thought I hadn't heard him correctly.

"*Neffar?*"

"Would you like to go mate?" Erul asked simply again, his voice deepening. So husky it bordered on a growl. "You are throwing out your scent very strongly. It is impossible to ignore."

My ears flamed, but I continued to watch Erul, shocked. Arik's grip at my wrist tightened, and he tugged me back.

"She is not yours to claim, Killup," came his snarl.

Erul's intense gaze snapped to the *Vorakkar*. "My apologies. I did not realize she was spoken for. I do not scent you on her. Nor do I see any claiming marks."

Claiming marks?

Arik stiffened. Out of the corner of my eye, I watched his shoulders bunch tight. The tension in the clearing was so thick that I could suffocate on it.

This Killup...would mate with me?

This was how I'd thought it would be, wasn't it? Straight forward, no questions, no guessing. He was offering to give me what I wanted, wasn't he? Arik had made it clear that we would not have sex. And while I'd been disappointed—and hurt and embarrassed—I'd told myself to move on. I wanted to experience intimacy and touch. I'd gone thirty years without it, and I didn't want to wait anymore.

Was I extremely disappointed and a little heartbroken that it wouldn't be with Arik? Who I had deep attraction toward, who I actually *liked*, who made my belly flutter with anticipation and want and anger and frustration and excitement?

Absolutely.

But I refused to wait for him to change his mind, if he ever would. I'd told him what I wanted. He was unwilling to give it to me.

This Killup, however, was.

"I am not his," I told Erul softly.

"Kara," came Arik's tight growl in my ear. "*Enough.*"

Erul's expression didn't change, but I got the impression he was pleased with my answer.

"When a Killup female is aroused, it is the male's responsibility to satisfy her," came his words, as surprising as they were intriguing. His gaze cut to Arik. This time, he *did* smirk—as much as a Killup could with their slim lips. "You are obviously not doing your duty for this one, so I was offering to do it for you."

I gasped when Arik lunged.

The movement was quick. Shockingly fast.

"Stop," I cried out, watching as Arik reared back his fist, as the Killup's eyes narrowed and seemed to shine with malice. "Stop!"

A rough growl burst from the *Vorakkar*. I actually saw his arm shake from the discipline it took him *not* to strike the Killup across the face. When I saw Erul's gills flare, even more panic spiraled in my chest.

"Stop," I breathed, though my words were truthfully directed toward both of them. I'd had a feeling that Erul had been purposefully goading Arik. But what I hadn't expected had been for Arik to respond to those barbs so swiftly and without his usual restraint.

His jealousy was palpable, and for a moment, I felt shame. Shame because I'd *wanted* to make him jealous. For a moment, it had felt *good*.

But not anymore. I was shaken by the raw ferocity I'd seen flash across Arik's face, and suddenly, I just wanted to be in my bed. Alone. I just wanted to think. *Kalloma* always preached self-reflection.

And tonight, I'd have a lot of self-reflecting to do. Like why I'd found it so satisfying to make Arik lose control, if only briefly.

Because it means he does give a damn about me, I thought next. *And that's a powerful feeling.*

Arik's arm dropped, but there was no denying the rage on his features when he whirled on me. His eyes were glowing in the darkness. The lines of his face were drawn and tight, the firm muscle in his jaw jumping with irritation.

"Do what you wish. Fuck him if you like," he rasped to me.

Even I could see the way the entirety of his body rebelled at those words, how he had to force them from his throat. "But you don't think you're mine? How *vokking* wrong you are, *saila*."

Then he snagged the back of my neck with his wide, hot palm. The one that had been squeezed into a fist moments prior.

His lips crashed down onto mine. A surprised breath whistled through my nostrils as he gave me his punishing kiss. It was rough and demanding, and it made my nipples tighten beneath my dress and my head swirl with his scent, touch, and taste.

It was over much too soon, and when he pulled back, I swayed on my feet, dizzy. Then he did something entirely unexpected. His head dropped. His lips grazed the side of my neck.

And then he *bit down*.

A flood of confusing, alarming arousal made me whimper as I felt his teeth tighten against my flesh. I gasped into his hair. My eyes were wide with astonishment and *need*.

Then he released me, and I nearly collapsed onto the ground when I stumbled. With a growl, the *Vorakkar* stalked away, and I watched him go, my fingers coming to the bite mark he'd left on my neck, running the pads of my fingers over the imprint of his teeth.

When my shocked gaze returned to Erul, I saw his expression was dark. His eyes were locked onto my neck, and I suddenly realized *what* Arik had been doing.

Erul had accused him of not marking me as his.

Well, Arik just *did*.

And he hadn't been subtle about it. Not in the least.

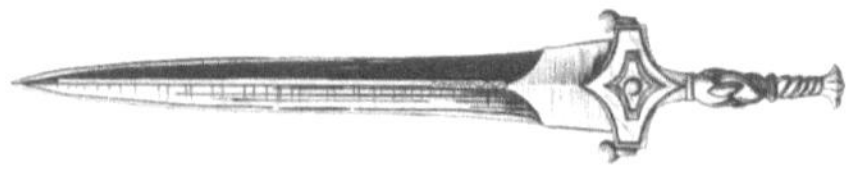

For a brief moment, I debated *not* going to her *soliki* this night.

Very brief, admittedly.

I'd been honest when I told her I didn't take kindly to threats. If a female made demands of me in the past, if they wanted more than I could give them, I'd cut them loose *immediately*. I hadn't had the time or the energy for games, for jealous lovers. In the end, I'd grin at them and weave them up tight in a discussion where it seemed like it was *them* ending the relationship. It was easier that way. No scorned females left in my wake. Because a single scorned female was almost as dangerous as an army of *darukkars*.

Only, as I thought of Kara and that damn Killup...I knew that I'd never actually been *jealous* before. Not like this. And certainly not over a *female*.

Because now I knew what it looked like...

Another male's desire for Kara. The way his eyes darkened for her. The way his breath quickened for her.

And it *vokking* ate me up inside.

Knowing another male was *ravenous* for *my* female.

A female I hadn't claimed. A female I'd barely even touched.

I was utterly trapped in a strange, peculiar position. On one hand, the *Seta Kalliri's* threats were a constant whisper in my ear. On the other, Kara had made it clear to me that she would make her own decisions. She wanted sex. She would get it. With or without me. Considering there were a multitude of males in the *saruk* that would likely jump at the chance to be with her, it was only a matter of time before she got what she wanted.

And I couldn't allow that to happen. If my jealousy told me anything, it was that I would never *allow* another male to touch what was *mine*.

The Killup was wrong.

I had claimed Kara.

I just hadn't known it yet.

Stalking up the steps to the door of her *soliki*, I reached for the handle and tugged it down. Only to find it locked.

Did she turn to the Killup after I left? Had she been with him already? Had she sighed as his hands had run over her and gasped into his kiss, as she had mine?

Rage like nothing I'd ever felt built up in my chest at the thought. It was a mindless sort of rage. Unparalleled and dangerous. I had always prided myself on keeping a level head. I might *play* angry if the anger suited my needs. But I had never been driven toward it with such ease.

With a gritted jaw, I broke the lock easily, snapping it in two when I barreled into the room. I slammed it shut behind me when I saw Kara, in much the same position as I'd found her the previous night.

Brushing her long, beautiful hair before the mirror. In the same silk shift dress she'd worn the night before. As if my control wasn't already perilously close to snapping.

It had been over an hour since I left her. She was freshly washed, her warm skin still reddened from her bath.

Immediately, I threw off my sword, slinging it into an empty chair that sat in the front room. Her bedroom was down the hall, but the front room was where the meals were taken, where a family gathered after the day. A high table was laden with a small tray of treats for her, a goblet of wine sitting half-full.

The fire in the basin was burning steadily, and when Kara stepped in front of it, I saw the outline of her form. All lush curves that I wanted to palm roughly, gripping and squeezing her to me.

Next, I unwrapped the belt of my daggers so they wouldn't cut her. They joined my sword, slung over the back of the chair closest to the door.

Even as I glared at her, my shoulders heaved in anticipation of having her in my arms.

"What did you think of the Killup?" I asked her roughly, snagging the brush from her hand and tossing it onto the table behind me. My gaze dropped down the line of her body, snagging on her tightened nipples that made my mouth water. "Did he make you come as hard as I made you come?"

The breath she sucked in whistled between us.

"Didn't think so," I purred down to her after her lengthy silence. "Because *no one* would be able to make you come like I did. Remember that, *saila*, the next time you make me jealous."

"So you're admitting it?" she asked, staring up at me with round eyes. "You are jealous?"

"*Lysi*," I hissed, my patience snapping. "I'm *vokking* jealous. Does that make you happy? Is that what you wanted to hear?"

She blinked and then bit down on her lip. "*Lysi*," she whispered. Then she looked thoughtful. "And *nik*. I don't know."

My jaw pulsed. Maddening female.

"Tell me," I said, my eyes fastening on her neck. My bite was still there. It would likely bruise, and I couldn't bring myself to feel terribly about that. It had filled me with satisfaction to mark her. A *rightness*. I'd never had such instincts for a female before. It made me feel like I was losing my mind while something unknown also slotted into place.

"Tell you what?" she asked quietly, her brow furrowed.

"If you fucked the Killup or not," I growled.

"Of course not," she told me quietly, her eyes fastened to mine. "You really think that I would have?"

A knot in my chest loosened considerably.

"He is handsome. And attractive," she murmured, making that knot begin to tighten again. "But I didn't feel desire for him. Not...not like..."

Not like the desire I feel for you was what went unspoken between us. I saw it in her eyes. She didn't need to say the words for me to hear them, loud and clear.

Right then, I made my decision. Just like the decision I'd made to take her from the *orala sa'kilan*. It happened in a split second.

"I'm tired of fighting you," I informed her gruffly. "I was trying to be an honorable male. I was trying to do the right thing. For once in my damn life, I was trying to be *good*. For you."

Her brow furrowed. "What are you talking about?"

"Take off your dress."

Her eyes went comically wide. "*Neffar?*"

"Take off your damn dress," I repeated. "I'm not waiting anymore. Neither are you."

Kara processed what I was saying rather quickly.

"*Nik,*" she said quickly, suddenly nervous as she began to back away from me until her back hit the small table where her precious mirror was perched.

"*Nik?*" I growled, going after her.

"You'll...you'll regret it like you did at the lake. You'll turn away from me again."

Another knot formed in my chest. "*Nik.* I won't."

Because I was going into this fully committed this time, not driven purely by lust. I'd made my choice. I was done fighting her. I was done denying us both what we truly wanted.

I would deal with the consequences later. We both would.

"Take off your dress," I ordered her again, steeling my jaw.

"*Nik*, you don't want this, Arik. You—"

My hand whistled out, and I ripped the material clean off her body. Her jaw dropped as a pleased rumble vibrated through my chest at the sight of her.

She damn near brought me to my knees.

"Look at how pretty you are, *rullari*," I murmured. Dragging her into my arms, I flipped her around until her back was to my front so she could see herself in the mirror. "You like to admire yourself in the mirror, Kara? You *vokking* should."

A gasp whistled from her throat as my hand trailed down the front of her body, and her eyes tracked it in the mirror. I kept my claws short—as I always had in *Dothik*—and I teased the blunt edge of one against her pebbled nipple.

A moan burst from her throat, and her back arched. Then she wiggled against my groin, desperate sounds falling from her lips.

"Arik, you don't want this," she whispered, even as she thrust her chest forward into my hand. "You don't—"

I laughed, low and dark, in her ear. "I've wanted you since I first saw you, Kara. Don't tell me what you think I want because you have *no vokking idea*."

Her cry echoed in the *soliki* when I pinched her hard nipple before flicking it with my thumb.

"Mmm, does that feel good, *saila*?"

She squirmed, and I didn't want to wait anymore. I swept her up into my arms. The next moment, her back hit the table where the tray of food clattered. The impact tipped over the goblet of wine, and the sound of it spilling to the floor made Kara's eyes widen.

She opened those red lips to say something, but I didn't give her the chance.

Before she could speak, I dropped to my knees, pushed her thighs wide.

Then I buried my face in her cunt.

Her pleasured cry was loud enough to satisfy me as the taste of her, sweet and heady like the spilled wine, burst on my tongue, making me groan. Making me even more ravenous for her, which I didn't think was possible.

"A-Arik?" she asked when she caught her breath. "What are you *doing*?"

"Isn't it obvious, *saila*?" I asked, pulling back briefly to meet her eyes before lapping at her slick slit. "Licking your pretty cunt. Something I enjoy quite a lot. So get used to it if you're going to be with me."

CHAPTER 37

"Arik!" I cried out, my back arching and sweating. The table was hard and unyielding beneath me. As was the maddening *Vorakkar* between my legs, steadily driving me to madness. "*H-Hanniva!*"

"Mmm, I like when you beg me, Kara," came his dark rasp. A hot swirl of his tongue came next, and I could *feel* the edge of my orgasm right there. I was on the cusp. "It makes my cock even harder."

And he wouldn't let me fall over it, I thought, frustrated and more aroused than I thought I'd ever been.

I was in a strange state of disbelief and need. The air seemed to rush around me, thick and hot, but when I looked at Arik, it was like the world seemed to slow. There was a part of me that thought this was a dream.

And if it was, then I was going to enjoy it. I was going to enjoy every moment of it before it disappeared forever.

My hands clenched in his hair. Every lap and teasing suckle against my clit had me sobbing with need. Arik *would* love this. He *would* love to tease me within an inch of shattering to pieces. This was punishment. Punishment for making him jealous. The most sublime punishment I could think of.

I tugged at his hair, creating a responding rumble in his throat.

He told me he enjoyed this? That I should get used to this?

Gladly, I thought, nearly sobbing with the pleasure.

If only he would allow me to *have it.*

"Beg me more," he ordered. "Beg me to make you come, *rei saila.*"

My darling, he said.

In the end, I didn't *need* to beg.

Because he had me so overstimulated that it was his *words* that set me off, not the lap of his tongue.

The pleasure burst in my belly, and a keening cry released from my throat.

"*Vok,*" he growled from between my legs, and then he suckled hard at my clit, making a flash of white explode in my vision, dots pricking it, as my orgasm crashed down *hard.*

I thrashed and squirmed, my nipples so hard they *hurt,* and dimly, I recognized that Arik had to hold me down. That he bracketed an arm around my waist to keep me from falling off the table completely. That his mouth never left my sex, that his tongue never let up on my clit.

"*Lysi, Arik!*" I cried out.

After long moments, I slumped back down on the table, the waves of intense pleasure finally receding.

As I caught my ragged breaths and wiped a hand over my sweaty brow, I watched Arik rise from the floor, his hands going to the laces of his trews. He tore at them as he eyed me, as that dark, feral gaze ran over my body until it fastened between my legs.

He stepped up to the edge of the table. He didn't undress. He simply shoved his trews down until his massive, hard cock sprang forward, bobbing against me.

I gasped. If anything, my orgasm had done nothing to satisfy me. It only made my need for him *worse.* My gaze ran over his cock, memorizing every inch of it like I had at the lake. So familiar, and yet I wanted to know him even *more*.

His groan was quiet. "*Vok, saila*, I can *feel* your gaze on it."

Biting my lip, I watched as he laid the weight of his cock between my legs. I jerked, a sharp huff escaping my lips as he grinned wickedly. It was so *hot* it nearly scalded me.

"Is this what you want?" he murmured down to me, lowering himself over me. Dizzy, I watched as his tongue swirled over my belly before he licked a line up my body. I felt every rasping inch of it. And when it lapped at one of my nipples, I whimpered, arching into his mouth. "So *vokking* sensitive."

Then he sucked my breast into his mouth, and I felt every tugging pull as if he was sucking on my clit again. Between my thighs, I felt his cock jerk and twitch. Something hot pooled onto my lower belly, and when Arik released my breast with a *pop*, I saw the tip of his cock was slick and shiny with the beginnings of his seed.

"*Hanniva*," I begged quietly again. "I want you. I want you so much it *hurts*, Arik."

"Where does it hurt?" he murmured, reaching down to run his fingers between my legs. "Here?"

"*Everywhere.*"

His chuckle was dark. "Good."

I wiggled against his cock, savoring the weight of it against me. In none of the books and accounts I'd read about sex had there ever been a warning of this *need* rushing through me. This single-minded determination toward pleasure. I wanted Arik. I wanted him more than I'd wanted anything in my entire life. Even more than I'd wanted to leave the *orala sa'kilan*.

The realization was humbling and dizzying.

"*Hanniva*," I whispered to him, tilting my head up toward him. He knew what I wanted, and he groaned, dropping his head to meet me. His lips were demanding. His kiss made another burst of arousal tingle deep.

I can love him, came the quiet thought. *I can love him so easily.*

And I didn't even know what that kind of love felt like. I'd never experienced it before. But I felt it now. I felt it in his lips. I felt it in his touch.

Arik shifted his hips, and I felt the wide, hot press of his hardened cock at my *melir*. His shuddered hiss escaped his throat as he pumped his hips forward. The *stretch* of him made my eyes widen.

And just when I thought I couldn't take any more, he pulled out and slid inside even deeper. He stretched me so wide it burned. But he took his time. He took his time with me.

"Good?" he huffed out. When my eyes flew to his, I saw his jaw was tight, but it was the expression of wonderment that had me nodding my head.

"*Lysi,*" I murmured, even when I felt a sharp pinch of pain as he pressed and pressed and pressed. "*Oh goddess,*" I whispered, closing my eyes.

"*Vok,*" came his low groan, and I felt the final snap of his hips. I gasped, my walls spasming around him, pain mixing with pleasure.

He held there until the pain slowly began to melt away and I started to squirm against him.

Then he pulled out before entering me again. This time, I moaned, feeling the delicious slide of him. It made tingles burst at the base of my tail, which flicked restlessly.

"You take me so well, *saila*. Like you were made for me," he growled against my neck, brushing his lips over the bite mark he'd given me earlier in the evening.

Because I was, came the stray, delirious thought. *And you were made for me.*

Nothing felt as right as that thought.

"*Arik,*" I whispered, tight and low.

"*Lysi*, I know," he said. "I'll give you everything you want, *rullari*. I promise. My impatient, greedy, lovely little female."

A gasp tore from my throat when he withdrew and then thrust back into me, hard and quick. He did it again. And again. Each time more exquisite than the last.

"How could I not give you everything you want?" he growled, his swirling, molten eyes meeting mine. One of his palms came to cup the back of my head so that it was cradled. "Especially when you look at me with those beautiful eyes. I couldn't even say *nik* to you from the beginning, when I hardly knew you."

My lips parted, the tips of my ears hot, my cheeks hot. My whole body was hot. Where we were joined, it felt like a forge. Remaking me. Remaking us. Hammering and hammering and hammering until we were both made new.

Right then, I didn't think about the fact that I'd avoided him for most of the day. I didn't think about the consequences of this. I only wanted him. I only wanted the Arik I'd come to know, who teased me about constellations and argued with me about the stories in Bekkar's book. Whose smile lit me on fire and whose laugh made me see stars.

And this Arik?

The one between my thighs, who whispered wicked things into my ear—about how good my cunt felt, how well I was taking him, how I was going to make him come so hard—this Arik made me lose control completely.

His pace quickened. The table began to screech backward across the stone floor, scraping and raw. But Arik didn't care. He became a male possessed between my thighs, his dark gaze pinned to me, his hands stroking down my body, petting my breasts, my throat, my clit. Then it was his tongue, laving over my washed skin. It was what I craved. I craved his scent all over me. I wanted to smell him as I drifted off to sleep, and I wanted to smell him first thing in the morning.

"*More,*" I demanded, the voice that emerged from my throat unrecognizable. A stranger. It was husky and low. Powerful. "Now!"

"You want me to make you come, *saila*?" he purred, though his brows were drawn tight with his own effort to keep his control. "Are you going to come on my cock? Is that what you want?"

"*Lysi!*"

The table slammed into the wall, and Arik's grip on my thighs tightened. He wrapped them around his waist. The delicious scrape of his clothes against my bare skin felt wicked. Wrong. And yet so right.

The tray of food clattered to the floor as Arik's thrusts became rougher, swifter. I paid it no mind. A knot was unravelling deep inside me. Every teeth-rattling, toe-curling thrust helped loosen it a little more.

And when the very last piece came undone, I was held suspended for a brief moment of time. A moment where my breath hitched and my wild eyes fastened on Arik, whose forehead was gleaming in the firelight with his exertion and determination.

"Let me see you fall" was what he told me. A hushed murmur. Those knowing eyes almost *dared* me.

A choked cry filled the *soliki*. But it wasn't mine. It was Arik's as he felt me clenching and tightening around him as my orgasm nearly blinded me in its intensity.

"*Vok*, Kara!" he cursed, his hips beginning to piston, so fast that they were a blur. "*Lysi, lysi, lysi!* I'm going to come! *Ahhh*, take it from me! Take it all."

I felt the burst of his seed, foreign and curious, hot and punishing. The lashes of his come coated my walls as I squeezed and thrashed underneath him.

"Going to mark me too, *rullari*?" he groaned, and it took me a moment to realize I'd turned my head to bite his wrist, just above his *Vorakkar* cuffs. "*Vok, lysi.* I want those teeth on me. Harder!"

The pleasure seemed never-ending. It came, wave after wave, breaking me down, bit by bit.

And when it finally receded, I gasped as if coming up for air.

Then the tears came, quick and fast. I was thankful that Arik's face was pressed between my breasts, that his rapid pants were huffing into my skin, that he didn't see the tear that rolled down my temple.

I laughed. Then realized my mistake when Arik looked up. I felt him tense and freeze when he saw me crying.

"Kara," he murmured, his voice torn and ragged. "Did I—"

"*Nik, nik,*" I whispered, still feeling my body clench and pulse around him. He was still inside me, and I found that immensely comforting. "You didn't hurt me."

I knew what he feared.

"It was just *so* good that you made me *cry,*" I told him, wiping at my wet temple where the tears had rolled. I blinked the rest back as a small chuckle escaped my throat again. "How will I ever handle your already enormous ego now?"

Arik's head dropped back between my breasts, and I felt his amused huff press into my skin. Then his lips brushed there before they traced the underside of my right breast.

"Don't cry, *rei saila,*" he pleaded softly, his eyes fastening on mine even as he rubbed his lips over my peaked nipple. My breath hitched. He groaned when he felt me tighten around his cock. "You know I don't like it when you cry. Even when it's because I fucked you *too* good."

I groaned, pushing at his shoulder. "Impossible male."

I could feel the way Arik sobered. A part of me feared that I'd lose him again. That he'd pull away from me, tell me that he shouldn't have done that, that it had been a mistake. Just like at the lake. My heart was suddenly thundering with that very possibility.

If he did that, I didn't know if I could forgive him for it. I didn't know if I could handle it again. Not after *this*.

"Did I hurt you?" he asked instead.

"*Nik,*" I told him, even though I thought I'd be sore. "Do you...do you regret it?"

A breath whistled through his nostrils, and he frowned. "Never."

A wave of relief pulsed through me.

"But you may come to regret it," he murmured softly, almost to himself.

It was my turn to frown. "Why?"

He shook his head. "Later. For now, I'd like to bathe. Then fuck you again. Then sleep."

A flurry of anticipation fluttered in my belly.

"That's quite the plan."

He grunted, and I bit my lip as he slowly eased his cock from inside me. I felt a gush of wetness drip down my thighs.

"*Vok,* I made a mess of you," he murmured. But there was a delighted wickedness in that tone that made my heart begin to pound. He *liked* that.

Acting on instinct, I opened my thighs wider for him, hearing the need in his voice.

"Mmm, good female," he whispered, his praise making another tight knot bunch low in my belly. "Let me see you. Just like that."

I bit my lip when he slicked his thumb through my folds. I was still sensitive, but his touch sent sparks shooting through my limbs.

"Arik," I pleaded softly.

His jaw ticked. Then he was peeling off his tunic before shoving his trews down. *Finally* undressing.

"*Vok* a bath," he growled. "I need you again. *Now.*"

CHAPTER 38

It was late into the night, but I had energy as if I'd just slept for *years*.

I was sated—for now—and sore. I was in Arik's arms, listening to the steady thump of his heart, thinking that nothing had ever felt so good.

Had I really thought I could be with anyone else? Had I really thought that I could find another male, one that would even come *close* to what I felt for Arik?

It seemed foolish now. Maybe that was why he'd been so upset. Because he'd found the notion as ludicrous as I was finding it now.

"You're not tired?" came his rumbling voice as his fingertips slid down my arm, grazing it back and forth, stroking me while I arched into his touch.

There was a part of me that feared sleep. To lose this moment. Because when I woke, I didn't know what I would find. Would our bubble burst? The quiet understanding that I'd felt grow between us?

I didn't want the outside world to rush back in. Selfishly, I didn't want to think about the fog. About the heartstones. I didn't want to think about discovering that Arik was actually the *Dothikkar's* son. I didn't want to think about what that meant. About what it meant for *us*.

But I would have to.

"Are you?" I asked softly, turning to meet his eyes.

"You've kept me awake for days," he informed me. "So *lysi*, I am."

He hadn't slept because we'd been...on edge with one another?

I swallowed down my guilt and said, "Then sleep. I'll watch over you now."

His low chuckle made a soft smile cross my features, one he watched with lazy eyes.

"I find that I can't. Even though I want to," he told me.

"Why?" I asked.

"Because we left things between us unresolved. I hate the feeling of it. I cannot sleep, knowing what I will wake to."

A feeling of dismay crashed down. I didn't want to talk about this now. But Arik seemingly did. What if we fought again? What if this hazy, warm spell was broken between us? Like a perfect glass ball bursting on the ground, shattering into a million pieces?

"What do you want to talk about?" I questioned softly, turning in his arms, as if to remind him that I was naked and relaxed next to him. That he had the furs of my bed drawn up around us. That he wouldn't be returning to his own *soliki* this night...unless we argued again. "And can I distract you away from it?"

"*Nik*, you cannot," he informed me. I grinned when I heard the uncertainty in his voice, however. He groaned. "Female, cease. Have mercy."

"All right," I whispered. Then I sighed, my gaze flitting away to rest on the notch of his throat.

Arik was silent for a long while, so long that I felt hope rise in me. I felt hope that he might decide *not* to talk about anything tonight.

Then he said, "There's something you should know. Something you should've known before I ever touched you. But I was so out of my mind for you. And now all I feel is regret about it."

It felt like a dagger to the chest. I struggled to sit up, even as his arms tightened around me. "You...you regret what we did?"

But he'd said...

"*Nik*," he said, his brows furrowing. "But I fear I took something away from you, something you were not ready to give."

"Enough with the riddles, Arik, and tell me," I ordered.

His breath huffed from him, and then he said, "Before we left the *orala sa'kilan*, your *kalloma* told me never to touch you. Never to lie with you. She told me that if I did, you would never be able to return to the temple. That the *kalliris* would not accept you back."

Whatever I expected...it hadn't been *that*.

My brows furrowed. I leaned against the wall where the bed was perched and hugged my knees to my chest. "*Neffar?*"

Realization hit me over the head.

"That's...that's why you didn't want...why you turned away from me at the lake?" I asked.

Arik ran a hand down his face. "*Lysi.*"

He told me that it shouldn't have happened.

This was why.

Now his words from earlier made sense.

"You said you were trying to be an honorable male. That you were trying to be *good*. For me."

His quiet inhale sounded. "*Lysi*," he said.

A sharp ache had me rubbing my fingers against my chest. I didn't know why *Kalloma* would tell him that. Unless she just wanted to keep him away from me. For whatever reason.

"I'm not a priestess, Arik," I said quietly. "I never took and will never take the vow."

"Your *kalloma* said that—"

"She might've said that, *lysi*," I said quietly. "But she's wrong. She has her reasons, I'm certain. She always does. But she lied to you."

His nostrils flared, as if he had never considered the possibility of the *Seta Kalliri* actually *lying* to a *Vorakkar*.

"Me lying with you," I started, reaching out to trace my fingers across the wide berth of his chest, catching on scars I wanted to know the stories of, "will not affect my standing with the *kalliris*. I assure you."

"You are certain?"

"Even if I wasn't, does it matter now?" I asked, looking pointedly between our naked bodies in bed. Arik caught my hand and brought it up to press to his lips. "I made my choice."

And it was always going to be you, I added silently.

He'd pushed me away, not because he didn't want me...but because he'd been trying to *protect* me. The knowledge only made me soften toward him more.

A long silence stretched between us, Arik's eyes on my own.

"Kara," he said, his voice breaking through the silence moments later.

"*Lysi?*"

"In the morning," he started, a tense expression flitting across his face even as his lips smoothed over my hand once more, as if to soften his words, "I want us to go to the *mokkira's soliki*. I would like you to be taking *kana* while we are together."

I didn't know how the words made me feel, but I was suddenly very aware of the fact that Arik had released his seed into me multiple times tonight.

"Right," I whispered, unsure how to feel about the disappointment that pressed against my breast, though it was mingled with the knowledge that Arik was being sensible. And embarrassment that I hadn't thought of it before.

Still, I couldn't help but ask, "You don't...you don't want children?"

My face flamed when his gaze cut to me, his mouth pressing into a firm line.

"Kara," came his warning.

"I didn't mean for it to sound like that," I said quickly. "I'm just curious."

Arik blew out a long sigh.

Then came his words, soft but certain.

"I don't want bastards."

And just like that, his words reminded me of everything I'd been trying to avoid. This was what I'd been afraid of. For the outside world to come crashing around our ears while we were still warm and safe and tucked against one another. Was there a dimension in this universe that could envelope us, just like this, until I was ready to leave his arms? Could I fold us among the pages of one of my books and slide us into a shelf where we would be undisturbed?

I almost laughed at the ridiculousness of the thought. But was it so bad that I wanted to be selfish? That I wanted Arik all to myself, if only for a little while?

"Because you are one," I whispered, finishing the sentence for him. A bastard son of the *Dothikkar* himself. I took in a deep breath. "Why didn't you tell me who you were?"

Arik's pose was deceptively relaxed. He was a magnificent male. All broad, golden planes and strength that I wanted to bite.

"Because it doesn't matter."

I gaped at him. I was sitting up, and when I straightened, the furs fell away from my breasts, Arik's gaze catching on them. He went to his side, leaning on his elbow, as his other hand reached out to stroke the underside of my right one.

Swallowing, I pushed his hand away because I knew what he was doing. Another of his distractions, his deflections.

"You're the *Dothikkar's* son, Arik," I said, my breath coming quickly. "How can you say that does not *matter*?"

His nostrils flared. "I'm his *bastard*. Of which he's had many. I'm the only fortunate one to actually survive his assassination attempts. Or perhaps the unfortunate one. Who can really be certain?"

"The…" I trailed off. "The assassination attempts?"

Arik gave me a smile, dark and cutting and glittering. "You have this idealistic vision of who you think the *Dothikkar* is, just like your *kalloma*. You think he is like Bekkar, don't you? Heroic, strong, a good leader who only wants what's best for his people and his planet?"

I was already shaking my head, feeling a prick of anger ignite in my chest when I heard his flippant tone.

"Stop," I whispered. Then I grabbed the side of his face and pressed my lips to his, hard and long. Against his lips, I said, "I know what you're doing. Don't try to start a fight with me. I only want to understand."

After a moment, a deep sigh whistled from Arik, funneling between my lips, and he pulled away. He turned onto his back, staring up at the stone ceiling of the *soliki*.

His voice was considerably softer when he said, "The *Dothikkar*—the male who helped create me, *lysi*, but who I would never consider a father—is a greedy, spineless, glutto-nous king who only wants to ensure he remains in power until the end of his days. He doesn't care what happens to Dakkar once he dies. I have it on good authority that he's dying already, but will he ever name an heir? *Nik.* Because he wants to be the last king of Dakkar. He wants his name to live on in memory, though he has done nothing to boast of such greatness. He's never stepped foot on the wildlands. He's never met with the *Sorakkar* in their *saruks* or the *Vorakkar* at their hordes to try to strengthen their ties with *Dothik*. He only wants to make them dependent on *Dothik* so they cannot pull away."

I had the strangest feeling that there was so much more to Arik's words than I could possibly understand. I'd never felt more out of my depth than I did right then. All the books and words scrawled across a page could do nothing to prepare me for this.

And there were so many questions rolling around in my mind that I didn't even know where to *start*. Or even how to ask them.

"But if what you say is true," I murmured, "if the *Dothikkar* is dying and he had all his other children killed...then that leaves only you, Arik. *You* are his heir."

His grin returned, though I didn't find it quite as cutting as the one before. "And he—or his council—would never recognize me as such before he died. To them, I'm a *duvna* off the streets. Who became a *Vorakkar*, if only to prove that I could."

"*Nik*, I don't think that's why you did it," I murmured, frowning. "I don't think you would be that spiteful."

"Then maybe you don't know me at all, *saila*," he purred, his voice a soft rasp.

But I wouldn't let him retreat. Especially when he moved to slide from the bed. I moved quickly, pushing him onto his back and scrambling over him to straddle his hips. Keeping him pinned to the furs.

His gaze darkened as those beautiful eyes roved over me. I wouldn't let him retreat from this, however. He'd wanted me to tell him what was wrong when I sat on the back of Syok, crying. I would demand nothing less from him.

My palms spread over his chest, and I felt the solid thumping of his heart as it increased its pace. My hair was a dark curtain around us as I stared down at him. Behind me, I felt his tented arousal press against my backside, and I couldn't help but flick my tail over the outline of his legs.

"Why did you do it?" I asked. I was proud of myself when

my tone was soft but unyielding. I wouldn't let him retreat. Not again. "Was it your idea? Or was it another's?"

Arik's body was buzzing with relentless energy. His brow cocked, and he smirked. "Lift off a little so I can move the furs down. How can you expect me to fuck you like this when my cock is trapped?"

"Arik."

His neck tilted back. Whatever he heard in my voice, it made him laugh. But it was a huffing, soft sort of laugh, and I didn't sense any derision in it.

Then he went quiet. I saw the decisions playing over his face, as fascinating as they were curious.

"Nassik didn't want me to enter the Trials. Very few did," he finally told me, his voice a sharp bark, as if I were pulling these words straight from his lungs with a string.

"Nassik?"

"My *pujerak*," he growled.

My eyes widened in realization. In my mind, I conjured the handsome male, who'd ridden out to meet us when we'd approached Arik's horde.

"But he has been more like a brother to me. I've known him nearly my entire life. Even he couldn't understand why I entered the Trials, so how would I expect *you* to?"

"Why don't you try explaining it to me?"

"Because as much as I love *Dothik*, the place was beginning to make me feel sick," came the rushed words, tumbling from his mouth. He glared up at me, even as his hands came to clench at my hips, keeping me in place. "You want to know why I keep that coin with me? The one I showed you? Because it was my first. The first one I ever made for myself, the first one that created this empire, *my empire*, right in the *Dothikkar's* streets."

My brow furrowed, hearing the sudden passion in his voice.

"In *Dothik*, I did everything you could possibly think of, Kara. I dealt with merchants, negotiating trade agreements in exchange for protection during their transports. If a prostitute came to me with the name of a male who had beat her, I'd track him down and give it back to him tenfold. Why? Because her brothel was under my protection, which they *paid for* in gold. I employed street children with no mothers or fathers, who kept an eye on the ground for me, who could slip into places unnoticed and unseen, who funneled back information, information I could use. I knew every shopkeeper and every tradesman in my district, every beggar and every drunk, every family and every orphan. And there are other networks just like mine, in the other districts of *Dothik*. Unseen, perhaps even unnoticed by the guards who patrol the city, but they are there. I've killed, Kara. I've been a mercenary, as have others in my employ.

"And that first coin? I got it because I stole a sack of *lobbas* roots from the *Dothikkar's* own cart, a crop from one of the hordes, in exchange for Dakkari steel. And I sold that sack to an innkeeper who needed the roots for his stews. I was five at the time. So you were right about my *thieving* boots, *saila*. Because I've been a thief since I was young enough to know what stealing was."

I was breathing hard as I stared down at Arik's seemingly impassive expression. There was a maelstrom in his eyes, swirling and angry.

"What do you think of me now, *rullari*?" he asked, his hand tightening on my hip, pressing me down into the outline of his cock as his own hips shifted. "To know that a thief, a murderer, a bastard child of the worst *Dothikkar* in our history was between these pretty thighs tonight? Maybe it is *you* who has regrets now. Hmm? Tell me what you think of me now."

His eyes dared me as I bit my lip. "I'm thinking I never really knew you at all."

His eyes closed. Perhaps he'd expected that answer. Perhaps it even *relieved* him in some way.

Those eyes didn't open when I pushed off of him. Maybe he

expected me to turn away from him. Maybe he expected me to turn away in disgust and fear, and maybe that was what he was hoping for.

Those molten eyes *did* snap open, however, when I pushed the furs down between us.

His breath hitched when I moved back and let his cock jut up from between my legs, the heat of it pressing against my sensitive folds. The length of it seared me.

"I'm coming to realize that I'm not easily frightened," I informed him. "And even the things that I thought I would fear turn out to be completely harmless."

Like the *sarl*.

Like Arik.

Arik grunted, even as his hips shifted, letting the length of him drag against my slick sex. "Is that what you think I am, *saila? Harmless?*"

He gave me that signature grin. A warning. A tease. I was certain it had disarmed many, many beings in the past. But I knew better.

"*Nik*," I breathed, rolling my hips because it felt *good*. Arik groaned. "I think you are the most dangerous thing on this planet next to the East Lands. Yet all I want to do is lie next to you. All I want to do is argue with you about constellations and ancient battles. And *this*. I want to do this too."

"Then you're a fool, Kara," he said softly. "To let me get this close to you."

I smiled down at him, and his nostrils flared at the sight of it. He didn't wait anymore. When I shifted my hips, he guided his cock to my entrance and thrust up, *hard*. Making us both moan as my spine tingled.

"Then I'll be the fool," I told him, leaning over him, letting my tightened nipples drag over his chest as my lips met his. "I'll be the fool if it means I can have *you*."

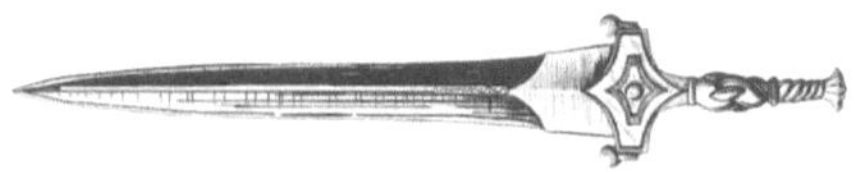

CHAPTER 39

"It must be taken daily," the *mokkira* told Kara. "Steep a sprig of it in your tea every morning or every evening. No need to take it twice in one day, unless you like the taste. Though most do not."

The *mokkira's* gaze flitted to me briefly. He was an older male, his back beginning to hunch, no doubt from his time spent over his workbench, grinding herbs and roots and brewing his tonics and medicines.

"*Kakkira vor,*" my newest lover murmured, taking the satchel from the *mokkira's* outstretched palm. Kara chanced a look over her shoulder at me, and I felt my heart speed in response. She looked...well fucked, truthfully. And so *vokking* beautiful it made me ache. I'd watched from the bed as she brushed her hair this morning, plaiting it into a neat braid, but the flushed glow on her cheeks, her reddened lips from my kiss, and the mark on her neck told everyone exactly what they needed to know.

That she was mine. That she was mine alone.

At least until she couldn't be anymore.

We'd seen the Killup male this morning as we walked toward the *mokkira's soliki*. I'd kept my eyes fastened on his as he took in Kara's appearance. When those eyes came to me, he inclined his head, as if to say *Very well, you've made your point, Vorakkar.*

Then he'd turned away without another glance, and I'd felt smug, my jealousy quenched, as we walked through the *saruk*, my hand pressed to the small of her back as we walked side by side.

Thinking about last night—and the early hours of this morning—had me suppressing a pleasurable shiver. Kara had been passionate and eager. I didn't think I'd ever had a female in my bed quite like her, who smiled and laughed as much as she gasped and groaned.

And the pleasure?

Vok, the pleasure.

I didn't think I'd ever come so hard in my life as when I filled her to the brim, over and over again. Pleasure so intense that it bordered on pain as it squeezed mercilessly at my *deva*, making me twitch and pulse and groan.

Undone at the hands of an inexperienced female. What were the odds?

But it was Kara. It was *her* that did this to me.

I nearly grinned in the *mokkira's soliki*. I had half a mind to order the older male to leave, if only so I could take her again over the table that was a perfect height for my hips. I could smell myself on her. I'd made sure to cover her in my scent, and I hadn't allowed her to bathe this morning. With our scents mingling together, I felt deep masculine satisfaction reverberate through me every time my nostrils flared.

In the back of my mind, I knew this should make me wary. I knew that my lingering fascination for Kara would not end well. I knew it would only be a distraction, a distraction that I didn't need.

Yet I was a selfish bastard. I wanted her. I wanted her so bad it hurt, a thought that mirrored words she'd said to me last night.

And I couldn't not think of the way she'd reacted after I gave her a brief glimpse of my life in *Dothik*. She'd reacted in a way that lit my blood on fire, while also…surprising me.

Sex was easy to come by in *Dothik*. The females in my district knew me. They knew who I was. They knew what I did. For some, it was actually an incentive to invite me to their beds, a turn-on. Because I was the one in control. I was the one with the power.

Females in my horde were different, though I had taken no lovers since I'd been a *Vorakkar*. They didn't just want sex. They wanted to be a queen. A *Morakkari*. Most had vied for the position since they'd been young. They wanted power too. It was easier not to get involved with any of them, even though some nights my balls had been so heavy and tight they felt like they'd burst.

But I had restraint. I had control. When it came to sex, I'd always been able to think clearly about it, weighing the options, the consequences, if any, and the upsides.

Not with Kara though, I thought, unable to take my eyes off the female who was currently smiling shyly at the *mokkira* as he instructed her on how to prepare the *kana*.

Not with Kara. Everything in me warned about getting involved with her. Not only because of the *Seta Kalliri's* threats, not only because my new lover was inexperienced and I didn't want her to get too attached, but also because I knew that being with me would only bring her *harm*.

The *Dothikkar* still wanted me dead. I'd deceived him for years. I'd made him think his assassins had been successful, that I'd been dead all this time. But I'd revealed my hand at the end of the Trials, waving his failings right in his face as I looked him *deep* in the eyes.

He'd sent an assassin for me during my first season out on

the wildlands. The male had posed as a messenger from *Dothik*...until he'd tried to slit my throat in my sleep.

I'd been tempted to send his head back in a parcel straight to the *Dothikkar*. Perhaps the old Arik would've. I would've relished imagining the expression on his face when he first opened it.

But I was a *Vorakkar* now. I couldn't afford to make spiteful decisions because it was my horde that would be punished.

And if the *Dothikkar* ever learned of my attachment to Kara, to this female who took me by surprise at every turn, he would come after her too.

I couldn't allow that to happen.

This female had wiggled under my skin in the short time we'd traveled together. I'd been right in my fear that she could make me do anything for her. She'd gotten her way at every turn. Sex had been my last line of defense against her, and given last night, she'd shattered me completely.

I had nothing left against her.

What else would she demand of me?

Later, after we left the *mokkira's soliki*, as we walked through the *saruk*, I told her, "We should leave soon."

She'd been smiling at a group of children who had all stopped their chasing to gawk at us passing. When she'd asked me last night if I wanted children, I'd been wary that she'd already gotten too attached to me. That now that we'd had sex, she would assume that our relationship was just that...a relationship. A partnership.

But as I watched her smile at the gaggle of small children, there was a part of me that couldn't help but think about what she'd look like heavy with *my* child. A primal part of me *purred* in satisfaction at the surprisingly arousing image.

Kara turned her attention back to me at my comment. "All right."

"No arguments?" I asked softly. "You seem to like it here."

"We've done what we came to do," she answered, catching my gaze. "There is no reason to stay."

"You learned all you could from the *Arakkari*?" I questioned. We'd spoken about it briefly this morning, but then I'd become quickly distracted by her dressing. And then *undressing*.

"There was one thing she told me that I found curious. Something I'd never encountered in my books," she said, her mouth pinching into a little frown that made me want to kiss it off her features. She looked up at me. "She said her great-grandmother believed that a member of the *saruk* created the famine."

"*Neffar?*" I asked, drawing my brows together. "How?"

"I don't think it's a coincidence that a *saruk* in possession of a heartstone finds that a famine is spreading beneath their very feet," Kara said.

I sobered. "You think this *saruk* member used the heartstone here? For what purpose?" I asked.

"The *Arakkari* didn't know when I asked her," Kara said. "But she said this member was a young female. A gifted one, no doubt, in order to use a heartstone. But I think your fellow *Vorakkar* are right. I think the *Morakkari* of Rath Drokka unleashed more than she bargained for under the Dead Mountain. There is something odd about the balance of the heartstones. As if when one is used, it makes all the others more powerful. But when that power climbs too high, a price needs to be paid. I'm certain *Kalloma* would have more thoughts or theories on it."

The *Vorakkar* of Rath Rowin had said something similar, hadn't he?

That the power the heartstone unleashed had changed everything. It tilted Dakkar off-balance, and the fog was Kakkari's way of seeking harmony once more. Bringing the world back into a stable state.

Truthfully, it didn't quite make sense to me. Especially

considering that all five heartstones had needed to be used at once to end the famine that plagued these lands all those years ago. How would adding *more* power, unleashing even more energy over Dakkar keep the planet stable?

Unless Kakkari was growing hungry and she needed the power of the heartstones to sate herself.

That was what my own mother had always believed. That Kakkari, our goddess and protector, was a hungry being, and that as long as she was fed, she would watch over us. My *lomma* had always believed Kakkari was a goddess to be *feared*, not viewed as a goddess of benevolence and fertility and life. Kakkari was as hungry as Drukkar after all.

"And she's hungry now," I murmured to myself, blowing out a sharp breath.

Kara looked up at me, a befuddled expression on her face. "*Neffar?*"

I smiled at her. "Nothing, *saila*." My gaze strayed to the satchel still clenched in her hand. Something about the sight of it made *me* hungry. Hungry for her. Knowing that the *kana* would offer protection against what I feared. "Let's get your tea brewed and return to bed."

She blinked, the tips of her ears heating. "It's the middle of the afternoon."

In her ear, I rasped, "We should take advantage of the bed now, for we will not have another before *Dothik*."

Her breath hitched. She stilled, and her expression was as serious as I'd ever seen it, though she still couldn't hide the excitement in those eyes.

"You're taking me to *Dothik* with you?" she whispered softly, as if raising her voice would shatter the proclamation I'd made, erasing it from existence.

"*Lysi*," I said, shrugging one shoulder before guiding her back to her *soliki*. "Like you would let me go without you. I figure it's easier and safer if I can keep an eye on you, regardless."

"Safer?" she asked, finding that word curious.

My jaw clenched. "*Lysi.*"

But I didn't offer her an explanation.

And when were back at the *soliki*, back in her bed and me back between her thighs, capturing her breathy moans between my lips and tonguing her breasts until she thrashed...I decided it was better to keep her close, that she would likely not leave my sight while in *Dothik*.

Because if anything happened to her—like what had happened to Bodin—I would never be able to forgive myself.

CHAPTER 40

"That's your plan?" I asked Arik. Even though I wasn't looking at him as we rode on Syok, I knew he could hear the disbelief and hesitation in my voice. "To keep my hood on at all times and tell people I'm *diseased?*"

"Except when we are at my home," he added.

I turned in my seat to look at him, craning my neck painfully to level him a glare. "*Diseased?*"

His grin was almost enough to make my irritation melt away. Almost.

"And I'll be the only one to know how pretty you truly are," he added, as if that would soften my ire. "Something I'll relish as I peel away your little hood and cloak every night."

I huffed out a sharp breath and turned forward again.

"Don't pout, *rei saila*," he purred in my ear. Then his lips trailed across the sensitive lobe of my ear, and his hot breath there made a tingle rush down my back. "I'll make it up to you, I promise."

"There has to be a better way," I told him.

Arik sighed. His lips left my skin, and his voiced was endlessly patient as he told me, "You are a hybrid female, Kara. That's a fact. You want to know another one? Your appearance will draw attention in *Dothik*. And we cannot allow the *Dothikkar* to know that I am in the city. We need to gain access to the temple quietly and without anyone watching. And there will be people watching, Kara. There is no doubt about that."

"Why don't you want the *Dothikkar* to know you are in the city?" I questioned.

A sharp laugh tore from his throat. "You think that just because I'm a *Vorakkar* now, he still wouldn't try to have me killed?"

The blood drained from my face, my belly freezing over. I struggled to turn in my seat, Syok throwing his head back when I accidentally nudged his neck with my foot as I swung it over.

"*Neffar?*" I asked, my voice quiet.

Arik gave me a slow blink. "If he knows I'm in the city, he will take the opportunity. Make no mistake about that, Kara."

"When?" I demanded, frowning. "When did he try to have you killed?"

"The first? When I was ten."

Ten?

He'd only been a child.

"Ever since then, he thought I was dead. One of the assassins he sent..." He trailed off, a gruff note in his tone as he touched his tipped left ear. Had it been sliced off during that attempt? "Well, it doesn't matter how. The important thing was he believed the first attempt had been successful. Until I became a *Vorakkar*."

"He didn't recognize you when you first entered the Trials?" I asked quietly. "At all?"

"*Nik,*" he said. "But he knew afterward. I whispered it into his ear after he placed these cuffs on me. When he could no longer wield his power and influence over me because he'd announced me as a horde king in front of all of *Dothik*."

There was a hint of dark satisfaction edging his voice.

Then he chuffed. "And it was foolish. Impulsive. That one moment has cost me many nights of lost sleep."

I swallowed. "And was it worth it?"

His eyes pinned me. He bared his teeth. "*Lysi.*"

I shivered.

"When...when were the other times?" I asked, not entirely sure I wanted to know.

"That very night," Arik told me. "Another the next night. I left for the wildlands after that, after gathering my horde. Then he sent another during my first season, who posed as a messenger from *Dothik*, who slipped into my *voliki* during the night with a blade. None since. But if he knows I'm in *Dothik*, he will try again."

Suddenly, my aversion to wearing a cloaked hood during our time in *Dothik* sounded childish and petulant.

I took in a deep breath. "I'll wear the cloak. My tail looks Dakkari, so maybe if I let it drag behind me, people won't think twice about it."

Arik cupped my face between his palms, the rocking gait of Syok pushing me further into him. His kiss was gentle and soft.

"I'll be hooded too," he said against my lips. "At least until we reach my home. My companions will meet us at the south tunnel into the city. We will be protected. Don't worry for your safety, *saila*. I won't let anything happen to you. I just want you to be prepared in case we need to leave quickly."

"This is why you didn't want me to come?" I asked, suddenly feeling guilty for pushing.

"It was always going to be dangerous," he told me, pulling away. His hand dropped from my cheek. "But I'd rather you be safe at my side now than worry about you from a distance. And you know your *kalloma* best. The priestess she spoke of might not trust me. But if you speak with her, she will."

I nodded, swallowing thickly. "I'll do my best."

"I know you will, Kara," came his gruff reply, filling me with a sense of pride.

However, there was a question in my mind that wouldn't give me peace. Not until I asked it.

"Where..." I trailed off, biting my lip, not entirely sure if he would appreciate the question. "Where was your mother during all this?"

He'd spoken of her briefly. Hardly at all. All he'd told me was that his mother was dead and that she'd studied *Dothik's* history, passing on her knowledge to her son.

Given what he'd told me two nights ago, about who he was in *Dothik*, about the *empire* he'd created on the streets of his district, I wondered what role she'd played in all this. She must've been close to the *Dothikkar* too. Arik was evidence of that.

Arik's shoulders tensed briefly.

"She died when I was ten," he told me.

Feeling a chill skitter up my spine, I asked, "She died during the assassination attempt?"

I bit my lip, suddenly knowing what her fate had been, given the cold look on Arik's face.

"Oh, Arik," I breathed, reaching forward to place my hand over his thumping heart. Its rate was steady, however.

"She'd caused quite a stir among the *Dothikkar's* court when she was first pregnant with me, and I don't think he ever forgot that. But she'd managed to keep herself hidden for ten years. Me too. Until someone recognized her and reported her to the *Dothikkar* in exchange for gold."

The *Dothikkar's* court?

"She was among his court?" I asked softly, trying to under-stand. Her story. Arik's story. And how everything slotted into place.

"Many people think my mother was a concubine. One of the

Dothikkar's whores." The word twisted from his lips bitterly. "But she wasn't. She was highborn."

I started in surprise.

"She came from a family that was close to the court. Her father had been the previous king's advisor throughout his lifetime. An arranged marriage between my father and my mother would not have been out of the question. But another female, whose own grandfather had been a great *Vorakkar*, was chosen instead to be queen. The *Dothikkar's* advisors believed it would create stronger ties between *Dothik* and the hordes."

"His queen died though," I murmured. "And she had given him no heirs. No legitimate heirs for the throne."

Arik inclined his head. "My mother was a companion of hers. She always told me the queen had been deeply unhappy. Listless. She'd been sick, and my mother told me that the queen thought it a blessing. That her prayers to Kakkari had been answered because she *wanted* to die."

A thick knot was lodged in my throat. "That's terrible," I whispered.

"The queen passed on." His voice was a soft rasp as he admitted, "And my mother slipped into the *Dothikkar's* bed."

"But why?" I croaked.

"She had aspirations for power. Like Tanniva," he told me, inclining his head when he saw I understood. "My *lomma* was many things. Great things. And terrible things too. She wanted to be a queen. She wanted to hold power in her hands and be able to wield it wherever she saw fit. She had been raised by her father for such a thing and had expected it for nearly her entire life. And suddenly there was a position that had just opened to her, that would give her everything she ever wanted."

But it obviously didn't work, I couldn't help but think.

Arik's lips twitched as if he heard my unspoken thought, but there was no humor in his gaze.

"When she fell pregnant with me, she demanded that the *Dothikkar* marry her and marry her quickly," Arik told me. "She was having his child, and she wanted the heir to be legitimate. She wanted her son to be the next king. She was highborn, after all. She did not think he would deny her. In the end, the *Dothikkar* laughed in her face and tossed her away. He ordered her to get rid of the child. And then he banished her from his court."

My chest squeezed.

"For years, my mother held that anger close to her. That shame. That fury. She let it eat at her," Arik said softly. He shook his head, clearing whatever memory had been in his mind.

"And then what happened?" I asked. "Did her father help her?"

"*Nik,*" Arik said, his mouth pinching down. "When my mother was banished from the *Dothikkar's* halls, she caused quite the commotion about it. It shamed her father. Shamed the family's name with her actions, and he turned his back on her too."

What would that feel like? To have everything you ever knew suddenly taken from you? To have those you love ignore you like you had never existed?

I couldn't imagine the pain that would've caused.

"She had no gold, no home, no social standing, and she was pregnant," he said. "She moved to the outskirts of the city. The Southern District."

"Your district?" I asked.

"*Lysi,*" he said gruffly. "She found work at a tavern. The owner took pity on her, I think. He let her work there in exchange for a room and for food. After a while, he paid her in gold. She was charming. Beautiful. She could talk to anyone. She would stand out on the street and draw people inside. The tavern was filled every night because of her. And the owner? He's like family now. Still running the same tavern too. You'll likely meet him when we get to *Dothik.*"

"I'd like that," I said softly. When silence stretched between us, I prompted, "And what happened next?"

Arik's gaze was gentle and his smile was soft as he regarded me. "You and your stories, *saila*. You cannot get enough of them, can you?"

"You cannot begin one without telling me what came next, Arik," I said, hoping to lighten the mood. I knew what was coming. "I just want to understand *your* story. And hers."

"I was born in that tavern, in the back room up the stairs," he told me. "And after, my mother continued to work. I grew up surrounded by drunken laughter and the smell of burned stew because my mother was a horrible cook. We were even… content, I think. But my mother never forgot what the *Dothikkar* had done to her. She started going to the temple, praying for Kakkari's vengeance against him, perhaps even Drukkar's. She would use all her gold to pay peddlers on the street who claimed they could curse him with sickness or infertility or death."

My brows drew together. That was why he'd reacted with distaste when I told him of my own gift. Suddenly it made sense.

"And when she eventually spent all our gold on it, on the crooked peddlers and on the temple donations, when we had nothing left, I knew I had to get the gold for us. For both of us. Because gold is life in *Dothik,* and you are nothing without it. And so I did."

"I take it the coin you showed me is not your only one," I commented, my gaze straying to the pocket in his trews that he'd once pulled it from.

The grin he flashed me was smug. "Far from it, *saila*. Gold buys information. Gold buys silence. It buys safety, in many cases. I would be a fool not to have a stockpile of it, even though I am a *Vorakkar* now and truly have no need of it on the wildlands. But many people I consider my family still live in *Dothik*. The gold is for them. To protect them in my absence."

"Your absence?" I asked quietly. "An absence implies you will eventually return."

"Is that not what we are doing now? Returning to *Dothik*?"

He knew what I meant, but he'd dodged my unspoken question. "All right," I whispered. I thought over everything he'd told me thus far, quietly processing and pondering, though I was hungry for more. "So that's how your mother knew about *Dothik's* history. How you know about all your stories, though I still think some of them are untrue."

His bark of a laugh unraveled some of the tension I'd felt rising in him. "They are all true, *saila*. It is your interpretation of some stories that leaves much in question."

I rolled my eyes and then said, "So your mother *was* a scholar of sorts. Being from a highborn family, she must've had an extensive education. She was learning because she thought she would be the next queen. And when she was pregnant with you, was she learning even more? Because she knew her son would have claim to the throne?"

"*Lysi*," he said slowly, peering at me. "That is correct."

"And what of your own education?" I asked carefully. "You... you cannot read, can you? Did she not prepare you for that?"

It was something I'd noticed whenever I read my books to him. Like last night, our last night in the *saruk*, as we'd lounged back in my bed, resting after our mating, I'd pulled out a tome that the *Sorakkar* had supplied to me at my request. One of the few books in the *saruk*, but one I'd never read before. It was dry reading, mostly an account of crop rotations by the year, but I still found it endlessly fascinating.

I'd watched Arik out of the corner of my eye, however. I'd watched his eyes travel over the page, the inky words and noticed his focus, coupled with slight frustration. I'd started to run my finger across the page as I read, seeing his frustration lessen. But I'd *watched* his mind work. As if he was memorizing the symbols and matching them to the words that came from my mouth.

If Arik was surprised by my observation, his only indication was the slight flattening of his lips.

"Not for her lack of trying," he grunted out, looking away from me, his hand coming up to run over his jaw. I noticed he would do that when he felt uncomfortable. Just like how I'd brush through the hairs on my tail. "But when I finally took an interest in it, when I began to understand the benefit of it…she was already gone. And there were things that were more pressing than learning how to read."

"I'm sorry," I breathed, taking his wrist, wrapping my fingers around his warm skin, above his *Vorakkar* cuff.

He pulled away, making me frown.

"Don't," I said softly, pulling him back to me, reaching up to turn his face so that he was forced to meet my gaze. "It's not something to be ashamed of."

His derisive laugh made me flinch, but I wasn't intimidated. "That is very easy for you to say. You've reads hundreds of books, *saila*. What you must think of me, knowing I can't even read a single sentence on a scrap of parchment."

My brow furrowed. He was…embarrassed. Embarrassed to tell me this. Why?

"We had very different upbringings, Arik," I murmured softly, watching his chest rise and fall as he took in a deep breath. "I learned to read because there was *nothing else to do*. You didn't learn to read, but look at everything else you did learn. Everything else that I know *nothing* about. You had a different education than I did. And I consider yours much more valuable than mine has ever been."

He stared at me, his jaw gritting, but I saw my words hit home.

I gave him a soft smile, watching as it slowly melted down

his walled defenses, which I had sensed building during our conversation. Hesitantly, I leaned forward, raising my face to his, and he sighed, ducking his head to give me what I wanted. His kiss. His tongue stroked over my tongue, and I pressed closer.

"I'm sorry," he murmured gruffly when we pulled back. "It's not something I like for people to know. Because it *is* a weakness. And I cannot be seen as weak. Especially in *Dothik*."

"And is that what I am?" I whispered teasingly, thinking it strange that the word *weak* was even in this male's vocabulary. There was nothing weak about him. "Just 'people' to you?"

He groaned, murmuring something under his breath that I didn't catch, as close as I was to him.

"I'll teach you," I told him, making my decision. "How to read and write. If you still want to learn. No one else has to know."

His brow furrowed as he studied me. "And you would keep that secret for me?" he wondered out loud, his voice soft.

I looked him in the eyes unflinchingly. "I'd keep any secret you asked of me."

His eyes burned.

Suddenly he stopped Syok. Before I could blink, he was jumping down, reaching up for me, snagging me across the waist as I blinked in surprise.

Laughing, I asked, "What are you doing?"

He grunted, swinging me up into his arms and carrying me over to a rocky formation at the edge of a forest we were passing. A...boulder.

Oh.

It was boulder time already. We'd already stopped earlier in the day, only a short distance from the *saruk* we'd left behind.

When Arik dropped me to my feet, I gasped as he tugged at the laces of my trews, getting them undone in record time before pushing them down.

Then he flipped me, pushing me forward over the boulder, my backside exposed to him. The rock was startlingly warm from the sun against my tunic, and I moaned, the heaviness between my thighs growing and growing, needful and exciting.

The familiar feeling of Arik's cock pushed against my entrance a moment later, shoving into me quick and hard.

His groan met my gasp. His hand came around half of my neck and half over my jaw. When I cried out with a particularly *delicious* thrust, one where he hit a place inside me that sent sparks through my vision, he shoved a finger between my lips, keeping me quiet. I moaned around his finger, sucking and biting at it, making him curse and making his pace quicken rapidly.

He didn't speak at all, which was unusual. Normally he'd be teasing me with his voice, his words, murmuring wicked, naughty things into my ear, things that could make me come without his cock between my legs.

But this time when I came, moments or perhaps hours later, it was only from the thick, toe-curling, hot length of him. The way he stretched and filled me to the brim. The way he made me *crazed*, made my mouth water and my spine arch.

I screamed, every shaking limb tightening and tensing.

And when Arik came? He came in a rush. A flood. He groaned into my neck, biting at the back of it, leaving his mark as he was always prone to do. But I didn't mind. That morning, I'd looked at those marks in the mirror, running the pads of my fingers over every one, feeling arousal pool in my belly at the memory of each. I thought...I thought I *liked* being claimed. I *wanted* him to claim me, in whatever way he could.

When his cock was spent though twitching, he still held deep inside me as we regained our breaths.

Then, against my neck, he said softly, "I hope I don't ruin you, Kara. The last thing I want is to make you hate me. But I fear I might. I fear I *must*."

I tensed.

There was a soft, wistful tone to his voice, one that made me think he hadn't meant to say the words out loud. Did he even realize that he *had?*

Then his kiss pressed over his bite.

"Come, *rei kassiri*. Let's get you cleaned up."

My love.

I sighed, longing rising in me, even though I knew he said the words flippantly. Without true meaning, only pleasant affection. I knew he cared for me. Just like I knew that he would never, never love me.

"*Dothik* awaits."

"What about Syok?" I asked, frowning, looking back at the *pyroki* who stood beyond the edge of the forest that lined the paved road. Hidden from view.

Dothik stood just in front of me. Well, the massive wall of the city's border did. On the other side, I heard nothing. But every now and then I'd catch a boisterous laugh carrying on the wind or the sound of wheels against stone and the clanging of steel.

"My men will come out to retrieve him and lead him through the main entrance. He'll be safe here for now, I prom- ise," Arik murmured, his eyes narrowing down the road, his head tilting to the side as if listening for something.

This was what I'd always dreamed of, hadn't I? On the cusp of entering Bekkar's great city, the capital that I had read about and fantasized about for years.

While I felt excitement, crippling doubt and worry also plagued me. After Arik had informed me what was at stake if we were discovered within the city's walls, I wondered if I should've stayed behind at the *saruk* while Arik journeyed ahead. I didn't want to slow him down. I didn't want to be the reason he was caught.

Arik looked down at me, his face shadowed in the darkness, but I saw the brightness in those glassy orbs. He grinned and tipped up my chin. "You have your worry written all over your face, *saila*. I told you not to fear. I will not let anything happen to you. I will let no one touch you. You're mine, remember?"

His words brought a flutter to my belly, but mingled with my nerves, it only made me feel like running.

"How will we get in?"

"There's a tunnel," he said. "Come, I'll show you."

Instead of heading toward the wall, we went back into the forest. It was dark and eerie. Completely silent. As we passed Syok again, I ran my palm over the *pyroki's* flank, and he nudged me along, as if to say *Go—don't worry about me.*

Reaching forward, I grabbed Arik's hand, curling my fingers between his. He took mine without hesitation, guiding me through the maze of dark trees and helping me over fallen trunks. The warmth of his hand softened some of my nerves. He would make sure I was safe. I knew that. But who would be looking out for *him?*

We came to a stop near a tall, nondescript tree.

"Here?" I questioned, frowning.

Arik nodded, releasing my hand to crouch. He shuffled aside rotting leaves and black vines. There, beneath all the dead foliage, was a hatch with a black handle. Arik tugged it, and it opened with a jarring *screech.*

Leaning over it, I peered inside, only seeing black. Though I caught a whiff of something foul, and I covered my nose with my arm, making my *Vorakkar's* lips twitch.

"You will not like it down there, *saila,*" he informed me as he stood. He came to me, maneuvering my arm away from my nose and taking my cheeks in his cupped palms. "But I promise that once we reach my stronghold, I will draw you the largest, hottest bath you've ever taken."

"With soap?" I asked, brightening.

His lips twitched again. "With three different kinds of your choosing. And then I'll kiss every part of you to make up for this."

"That sounds like a great deal," I breathed.

Arik chuckled, pressing his lips against mine softly. "I thought you might say that."

I nodded, stepping away from him to peer down the blackened shaft. "All right, let's go."

"So eager," he sighed. "You are a very high-maintenance female, you know. It will take a lot of effort on my part to keep you pleased."

I knew he was only teasing. I heard it in his voice, no doubt trying to distract me from the filth that would greet me at the bottom of this tunnel.

"Because I like to be *clean?*" I asked, raising a brow.

"And you like your pretty dresses and your hair to be brushed multiple times a day. Your soaps and long baths. Your books, which are very expensive in *Dothik*, mind you," he rasped into my ear. "The things I could spoil you with here, *saila.*"

My heart skipped a beat, but I leveled him a sharp look. He chuckled as he walked to the hatch, crouching near its edge.

"When we left the *orala sa'kilan*, I left with the clothes I was wearing and a few tunics stuffed into a satchel. I'd hardly call that high maintenance."

Arik flashed me a slow grin that had my belly fluttering, and then...he jumped down into the darkness of the hatch.

I made a startled sound, darting to its edge as I peered down. I heard the squelch of his boots, his muted curse.

"Arik," I hissed.

"Now you, *saila*," came his voice from down below. I couldn't even see him it was so dark.

"What do you..." I trailed off. "You want me to *jump?* Down *there?*"

"High maintenance," I heard him tsk. "You see what I deal with, *rei kassiri*?"

I huffed, looking away from the smelly hatch and around at the darkened forest. I couldn't even see the road from here, though I spied one glittering turret of *Dothik* through the canopy of the black trees.

Muttering under my breath, I slid my legs into the hatch until they dangled.

"You're going to catch me, right?" I asked. My heart was suddenly thumping in my throat. I'd never thought myself afraid of heights—given I'd grown up in the North Lands and my tower was at the tallest peak of the temple—but it was the darkness below that made me nervous. Never-ending, it seemed to eat at the air. Like the darkness of the lake as I'd sunk.

"Of course I will," came his voice, solid and steady.

It was that voice—and the male I trusted who spoke in that voice—that had me taking a deep breath.

Then I pushed myself off the edge, a startled, muted squeal whistling from my throat as air rushed up to meet me. I fell long enough for my belly to drop out from beneath me, for panic to climb in my throat as my hair whipped and thrashed.

Then I slammed into hard arms. I heard Arik's grunt, felt him soften his knees to brace for the impact. I sucked in lung-fuls of air, trying to calm my panic.

"I never want to do that again," I informed him when I was able to speak.

His amused huff rustled my hair as he set me on the ground. I heard my boots squelch into something I'd rather not identify as a putrid smell floated up to sting my nostrils.

"I'll never be able to wear these boots again," I sighed.

"I'll get you new ones, *rullari*."

I'd never really understood why he called me *rullari*. A form of *princess* in Dakkari, though I certainly could understand the soft name right then. I was acting like a child when Arik was risking a lot to bring me here.

Pushing back my shoulders, I reached for his hand, threading my fingers through his. His hand squeezed mine, reassuring me.

"Lead the way," I told him, and I promised myself—and Arik, though it was a silent promise—that I wouldn't complain once more. No matter what lay in this tunnel, I would face it head on.

Arik pulled me forward, and I heard his hand running along the wall in the pitch black. He seemed to find what he was looking for, an object clattering.

I heard a whistling drag, and then light flared before us, making me squint, as Arik lit a torch. It was in a holder, imbedded deep within the tunnel wall, and I watched as he took it out with his spare hand, holding it before us to light our way.

"These are the southern tunnels," he told me quietly, resuming our pace as I fell into step beside him. The light only extended so far, and beyond its boundary was endless darkness. "They stretch under the Southern District and beyond."

"Did you make them?" I couldn't help but ask. The tunnels were roughened shafts. In some sections, Arik had to duck because the ceilings were low.

"We made this one to lead out to the forest. An easy escape if we need it, or to access the city," he informed me. "But the others? They've been here since *Dothik* was born. We think Bekkar had them made to easily access different parts of the city. One of the tunnels used to lead directly to the *Dothikkar's* keep, though it collapsed about fifty years ago."

"Bekkar?" I gasped out.

"*Lysi,* I thought you might like that bit of information," Arik teased.

I realized something for the first time. As jarring as it was surprising.

"It's strange to think that he is your ancestor," I commented. "That his blood runs in you."

"Is it so hard to believe I am a descendant of a great king?" he asked. Though his tone was edging on playful, I still heard a softness in it that had me regretting my words.

"Not at all," I said, squeezing his hand. "It's just the first time I'm realizing it. That there is so much history here. Formative history of our planet, and that you are very much a part of it. Truthfully, it makes perfect sense to me."

Arik looked back to meet my eyes. He regarded me carefully but said nothing. When he faced forward again, he said quietly, "It's not far, *saila*."

But just as he said the words, my vision cracked and split.

So swiftly and suddenly that it took me by surprise.

The sharp whistle of air through my nostrils must've alerted him that something was wrong.

"Kara?" I heard him ask. Through the splice in my vision, I saw him turn just as I reached out a hand to steady myself on the wall. "Kara!"

"Give me a moment," I breathed. "Don't worry. This is—"

That was the last thing I remember saying before sliding. I felt his arms wrap around me, but I was blind. The tunnel fell away. The light too. This had happened often when I was younger but not so much in my later years. While images came to me in my dreams, they were never as clear as *these* moments. When I slept, it was hard to differentiate what was a dream and what was a vision. They often mingled together.

But *these*.

These were always visions. And every single one I'd ever had had come to pass, just in the way I had seen it.

Arik's face and the familiarity of his body burst into view. It was him I focused on as the picture widened, scaling back from his face to show me the East Lands. His eyes were on me. Pinned. Yet he was so far away. There was a coldness to his features, and even in the vision, I felt a painful ache in my chest, so deep that I looked down to see if I'd been wounded.

I was wearing a dress of gray silk. My feet were slippered. The weather was so hot, dry air crawling down my bared arms. *Kalloma* was next to me. My sisters.

Everyone.

Even the *Vorakkar*. Standing together with their wives and their councils. The *Sorakkar* of Rath Hidri stood with his *Arakkari*. And next to them…

A wall of red.

So high and dense that I couldn't see through it. The pinch of fear. Endless and deep, I felt the voices pulling at me. I felt them pulling *so hard* that I swayed on my feet, though if it was from the heat or Arik's gaze or the million voices of Kakkari, I couldn't be certain.

Arik was standing on the opposite edge of the circle from me. I saw a blue flash, I felt the power of the heartstone, felt the shape of them drawing closer and closer. Broken once. Now reuniting.

"*Nik,*" he growled to me. From far away, but I heard it as if he'd spoken it directly into my ear.

When I saw the blue glow, it was coming from my own palm.

Just as I saw a gentle rounding of my belly through the silk, unnoticeable except to me.

I looked up into Arik's gaze once more.

"*Nik.* You know I would have never allowed this."

My lips formed the words, "It is my choice."

They echoed and then began to fade. Too soon. Too soon.

Nik, nik, nik, I thought, feeling the edges of the vision begin to fray and burn. *I need to see. I need to see what happens.*

But my pleas went unanswered and my back bowed as I

was pulled from it. Ripped from it, I felt the ache in my chest as I looked into Arik's cold gaze once more...and I felt the ache in my chest when I resurfaced.

The scent of putrid rot and still water swam through my nostrils and choked me.

For a moment, I couldn't move, but I began to blink. I was sprawled against the wall. *Nik*, not a wall.

Arik. He had pulled me into his lap, his arms wrapped tight against me, murmuring my name in my ear, drawing me back. In front of me were two unfamiliar males, frowning, crouching before me though they kept a respectful distance back.

When I gasped, air threading into my lungs, stinging and painful, I heard Arik's shuddered breath in response.

"Kara," he murmured, turning my face to meet his. His hand touched below my nose, and I tasted blood on my tongue. When his hand came away, it was red, but that was nothing abnormal. He was lucky my eyes hadn't started bleeding, which had once given *Kalloma* quite a fright.

I focused on breathing, drawing in one breath after the other, though the stench in the tunnels made me want to vomit. The vision made me want to vomit too because suddenly I felt dread and dismay so heart-wrenching that I wanted to curl up and sob.

The feeling passed, however. The emotions ran high, but as the moments dragged on, I felt myself calming as I processed what I'd seen.

I couldn't help but shy away from Arik's gaze, however, when he tilted my face up to his, his concern etched clearly, his nostrils flaring. The coldness of his eyes in the vision made me want to sink into the earth below the tunnel, and I couldn't stand to see them now.

But finally, I managed to find the courage to meet them.

When I did, I nearly sobbed in relief. Because they were

concerned. Warm. *Frightened.* And I never thought I'd see Arik scared.

Yet he was. For me.

"What was that?" he demanded softly, wiping under my nose again. I must still be bleeding. And he obviously didn't like to see it.

"I…" I trailed off, flashing a look at the two males that had suddenly appeared. How long had I been out? My neck felt tight. My limbs boneless. My clothes were covered in filth, and Arik's wouldn't be much better, considering I was sitting in his lap.

One of the males was older, with deep lines that ran from the edges of his eyes and around his mouth. Strong and burly, his forearms were the size of small tree trunks, and his yellow eyes scanned me curiously as his hand wiped down his jaw, a gesture I recognized from Arik.

The other was younger. Lithe but strong, his stature reminded me of that of the Killup leader I'd spoken to. Erul. He had a scar that curved around his mouth, another lining the entirety of his tail, from base to tip, that had me wincing.

"This is Bakkia," Arik murmured, gesturing to the older male. He pointed to the other. "And Kalik."

"Your family," I said softly, running my mouth before my mind caught up. But it always felt slow after a vision, like I was wading through thick water and sludge.

Bakkia's lips quirked up at my words, and I decided I liked him.

"*Lysi,*" Arik said, his voice warming, losing its tightened edge. "*Vok,* don't do that to me again, Kara."

"I'm sorry," I said, my hands curving over my belly, the memory of a swell making my chest squeeze. "I cannot help it."

"We should get to the Head," Kalik voiced. It was a surprisingly deep, gruff voice, one I hadn't expected. "The guards patrol the district more regularly at this time of night. I've been timing their rotations. They have another coming soon."

"Can you walk, *saila*?"

"*Lysi*," I said. "Just help me up first."

Kalik stood and held out his hand for me. I took it gratefully, and he tugged me up as Arik's hand settled over my backside as if to keep me steady. He stood after me, drawing me away from Kalik, which had the other Dakkari male giving him a dry, amused look.

Arik only raised his brow pointedly. Kalik sighed, shaking his head. "This way. Do you remember how to reach the Head, Serok?"

"*Vok* off," Arik scoffed.

"Who knows?" Kalik asked, shrugging. "You're a *Vorakkar* now. Maybe the wildlands have addled your mind."

I heard no venom in his voice, however.

Bakkia clipped the younger male in the shoulder with his fist, making Kalik laugh as he rubbed the spot.

Taking my hand, my horde king asked again, "You are certain you feel all right?"

"*Lysi*," I murmured, giving him a half smile that I knew didn't reach my eyes. I would think about my vision later. I'd have time to process what I saw, and I didn't have to tell Arik about it right away. "Let's go. I was promised the best bath of my life."

I saw my flippant words didn't ease Arik's concern. It tightened in his eyes because he knew me well.

Bakkia, however, laughed boisterously, the sound echoing down the tunnels in all directions.

"Where did you find this one, Serok?" he asked. "I like her."

Arik's voice was soft when he answered, "In the tallest damn tower of the *orala sa'kilan*."

Kalik's gaze widened comically.

"He broke into my chamber in the middle of the night," I

informed them softly. "From the outside. I'm surprised his fingers weren't frostbitten."

"My *deva* nearly were," Arik grumbled, making Kalik guffaw.

Bakkia snorted in disbelief even as he muttered, "Why am I not surprised?"

Chapter 42

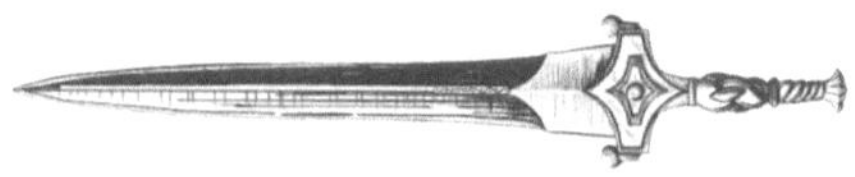

We called the entrance of the southern tunnels the Head. The main road outside, which spanned the entirety of *Dothik*, even all the way to the *Dothikkar's* palace, was the Spine. The alleys that branched off the Spine we called the Limbs, and they were numbered accordingly.

The body of *Dothik*.

And my stronghold—called the Heart—was at the very center of the Southern District.

You will find the answer in the Heart of Dothik.

The *Seta Kalliri's* message for the High Priestess of the capital.

The Heart looked just as I'd left it. As if I'd never been gone at all.

"We kept her gleaming for you," Kalik told me with a grin, clapping me on the shoulder.

I had my arm around Kara's waist, keeping her close to my side. I was still distracted by what had occurred in the tunnels. I would never forget the calmness of her face and voice as she told me not to worry. As such, I would never forget the fear and panic that threaded through me when she dropped, when she started shaking, when red blood—the color of a *vekkiri's*—had begun to run from her nostrils, staining her skin.

There my Kara was, writhing in the filth, her eyes rolled back in her head. And I'd never been more afraid.

"Good," I murmured to Kalik, peering at him from underneath my hood. "Let's get inside before someone sees."

I took to the steps quickly, feeling the weight of Bakkia and Kalik at my back, a comfort. Kara's legs still seemed unsteady as we climbed, and she'd been uncharacteristically quiet once we exited the Head. I'd expected whispered questions about the dark, cobbled streets. Excited statements about the glowing glass windows and the turrets of the palace that we could see clearly from the road.

Instead, Kara had kept her head down and said nothing.

A part of me was pleased. Relieved. The last thing I wanted to do was call attention to us. The only beings we'd encountered from the Head were weaving drunks—a few of whom I knew very well, though I'd not said a word to them.

When the heavy door of the Heart slid shut behind us and I heard Bakkia lock it, a tendril of my tension eased. The smell of the entrance hall was familiar. It smelled like rain on cobblestones during the warm season.

The entrance was dark. My home in *Dothik* was comprised of three stories above ground and two below. Before I'd decided to enter the Trials, we'd been planning to extend a tunnel toward the Head right below our feet. I wondered if any progress had been made, but I assumed not since Kalik would've suggested that path instead of taking to the streets.

Turning to Kara, I pushed back her hood to look into her eyes. A smear of blood was still present beneath her nostrils, but the flow had stopped.

And for a moment, I was angry. Angry at Kakkari.

Why her? I wanted to ask the goddess. *Why did you choose* her?

Two of the other *Morakkari* possessed gifts like Kara, and I knew the burden of them. I knew the pain. I knew the turmoil.

Kara was good. She was everything *good*. So why did Kakkari choose her to bear this burden?

"Who's here?" I asked softly, reaching out to touch Kara's cheek, tilting her face up as if inspecting her for more injuries. She was holding herself still, but she met my eyes. The filth from the tunnel covered her back from when she'd fallen. It covered all of me too. I watched Kara's nose wrinkle, and I felt a bit of relief at the small gesture.

"I'm living here. Only me, for now," Kalik told me. "The rest are gathered in the kitchens to see you."

"Who?" I asked, not certain how many people I wanted in the house, not with Kara so close.

"Vala. Ulli. Errana," Kalik said.

"And Kiro," Bakkia added. "Only the core of us. I didn't tell the others that you've come back. Not yet."

I nodded, inhaling a sharp breath. "I'll be there soon. Let me get her settled and get changed."

"What about Syok?" Kara asked, the first question she'd spoken since the tunnels.

My chest warmed at her concern for my *pyroki*.

"I'll get him," Kalik said. "I'll lead him through the east gate. I know the guard on duty tonight. He won't say anything if I slip him some gold."

"*Kakkira vor,*" I said to Kalik. "Do it quickly. Then we'll meet, *lysi*?"

Kalik inclined his head.

Leading Kara through my stronghold felt surreal and familiar. My rooms were on the top floor, where no one else was allowed to enter. My private sanctuary with some of the best views of *Dothik*. I knew Kara would like it. I knew it would remind her of her tower in the *orala sa'kilan*.

As I led her up the stairs, I could feel Bakkia's gaze pinned to my back. I could almost hear his thoughts, however disapproving they might be, but I would speak with him later. As we'd made our way to my stronghold through *Dothik's* quiet streets, I'd kept my eyes open for anyone who might notice us. I'd kept my eyes open for any that had followed us. I knew Bakkia had done the same. I knew he had my best interests in mind. That would include being wary of Kara's presence.

"It's almost as big as the temple," came Kara's soft observation as we climbed yet another staircase. "And so many stairs."

"You'll feel right at home, then," I murmured into her ear, my hand tightening at her waist.

Soon we were standing at the threshold of my rooms and I led Kara inside, closing the door behind us, sealing us in.

The first thing I did was go to the fireplace. In *Dothik*, the fire basins were built into the walls with wide stone hearths and chimneys through the tops of the buildings. There was a chill in the room, and I banished it quickly.

When the fire was roaring, I looked back at Kara, noticing that she'd immediately gone over to the books that were shelved on a case on the wall. My lips twitched, approaching her from behind, running my fingers around her neck so I could untie her cloak. She paid me no mind, her gaze completely rapt on the spines, though she never touched them.

"My mother's," I murmured to her. Though I had peered down at them in frustration nearly every single night when I lived here. I'd flipped the pages so often I wouldn't be surprised if they were a crumbled mess now. "You can read one to me tonight, *lysi?*"

I slid her dirtied cloak from her shoulders and then reached for the hem of her tunic. She was surprised when I pulled it over her head, turning slightly. When her breasts were bared and the points of her nipples were pebbled, I unlaced her trews and helped her step from them.

My cock thickened at the sight of her nakedness, but I told myself it was not the time.

"Come," I murmured, though my voice had thickened with desire. Madness, I thought. When had I ever wanted—*nik, needed*—a female this much in my entire life? Never.

Yet everything about her was perfect. I remembered thinking she was no great Dakkari beauty. I remembered thinking once that her Dakkari features clashed too strangely with her human ones.

Now?

Vok, she was so damn beautiful she made me ache looking at her. I had the strangest urge to bite her, to lay my claim, to hold her to me forever. How had she wiggled herself into me in such a short amount of time?

"I promised you your bath."

"And my choice of your soaps," she reminded me softly.

My lips curled. "*Lysi*. How could I forget?"

She gasped when I led her into the next room. All gleaming white marble—like the floors in the temple's atrium—leading to a large sunken bath in the floor.

"It's the size of a lake," she commented, and I noticed that some of the excitement I'd expected had begun to creep back into her tone. I was happy to hear it. I didn't like it when she was quiet, just as I didn't like it when she cried.

"I wouldn't say that," I murmured, chuckling. "Does this please you?"

Her shy smile had my heart thumping. "*Lysi*."

I grunted, rubbing at my chest. "Good."

Going to the bath, I turned on the gold taps. The pipes that ran through the floor started chugging, groaning and creaking, but soon hot water began to pour from them. Running water— something I absolutely missed on the wildlands.

Then I went to the chest along the wall, plucking out the

slim, long glass vials filled with different colored soap granules, before placing them next to the bath.

"As promised," I murmured to her. Then I pulled her into my arms. Her nose wrinkled from the stench of my clothes. "I want my kiss, female."

"Even though you smell like death?" she whispered, already going to her tiptoes.

I ran my fingers under her nostrils again, but the stained blood would need to be washed away.

"*Lysi.*"

"Will you join me?" she wondered, the words whispered against my lips, and I lowered my head.

The taste of her was familiar and lovely and soft. When my tongue stroked her own, the kiss took on a desperate edge, my fear and panic from when she fell pouring into her, and she gasped when I gripped her hips harder, when my touch began to stray.

But then I tore myself away, stepping back, swallowing hard.

"*Nik,*" I murmured, my voice ragged. "Not yet at least. But when I return, we'll talk, *lysi*?"

She knew to what I was referring. I watched her shudder slightly, but she inclined her head.

Unable to resist, I lowered my head one last time as I passed her. The kiss was chaste and short, though I lingered as long as I could afford to.

There was a warning rising inside me, almost as alarming as what had occurred in the tunnels. I knew what that warning was. I'd already felt it in Bakkia's gaze. I'd already felt it in nearly every interaction I'd had with Kara.

I huffed, stepping past her without a look back. Because if I stayed, I'd end up in the bath with her and I'd never want to leave it. I crossed the comfortable sitting room with the fireplace roaring to the door directly across from the washroom. My sleeping room, the furs of my bed looking cleaned and pressed, and I wondered if Kalik had seen to them when he heard about my return.

I went to my chests and dressed in clean trews and a black tunic. I pulled a fresh pair of boots from within as well, tugging them onto my feet, and then I left quickly, taking to the stairs and jogging down to the main level.

Just outside the kitchens, I heard the laughter and the murmurs. I recognized the voices within, and for a moment, I hesitated outside in the hallway, leaning against the stone wall in memory. Listening to the voices I'd known for years. They were like a balm on my soul.

I belong here, came the thought. Sudden and soft.

It was something I'd always known. I longed for *Dothik* out on the wildlands. I longed for the familiarity of my city, of the people that had made me who I was. Nassik's words returned to me.

Don't turn your back on your city.

I'd lost faith in our vision, the one we'd made as mere children. I'd thought to create our own city. Our own kingdom, like the great Bekkar. I thought the wildlands were the answer.

Now? I wasn't so certain. And it was uncertainty that would get me killed if I wasn't careful. It could get us all killed.

I pressed the heels of my palms to my eyes, breathing deeply as I tasted Kara on my tongue.

You cannot have her and have Dothik, I thought next. *You know this.*

After a moment, I steeled my spine. I wiped a hand over my face and smoothed back my hair.

When I entered the kitchens a moment later, it went quiet. Familiar faces, familiar eyes pinned me in place. I saw Kiro smirk. Vala stood. Errana was perched on the table, her thigh pressed against Ulli's arm. Bakkia stood against the ice chests with his arms crossed over his wide girth.

My family. Only Nassik was missing. And Kalik would return soon after seeing to Syok.

Then I grinned.

"Did you miss me?"

CHAPTER 43

I settled on the soap that smelled like *luria* blooms, fragrant and wonderful.

After Arik left, I scrubbed at my skin and my hair repeatedly with the granules, feeling a little guilty after I realized I'd used the entire vial.

The water was luxuriously warm, and I skimmed my pruning fingertips over the surface of the water, tracing it with my touch, though my eyes were unseeing. I felt much better than I had in the tunnels. I was clean, which always helped me focus. The water aided in loosening the knots in my shoulders and the ache of my thighs from riding Syok—*and Arik,* I thought with a flush—for the better part of the last three days.

The high emotions from my vision had evened out and leveled off. And yet...I still couldn't shake my dread.

I couldn't...

I couldn't shake the knowledge that I would be with child.

Because it was a certain thing. Never had my waking visions been wrong. A rarity in itself. *Kalloma's* own visions were unpredictable at times, and she was considered the strongest of the priestesses, a master of her gift. Some of her visions manifested. Others didn't. It made her doubt, it made her frustrated.

But mine?

They had never failed me before. So much so that *Kalloma* didn't call them visions—she called them *knowings*.

So why would one fail me now?

And if I was going to be with child, I knew whose child it would be. The only male whose child it could be, the only male I wanted. The only male I was falling in love with.

Arik's child.

A baby.

Was I pregnant already? Even now?

It was difficult to say how far into the future the vision had been. It had been hot and dry in the East Lands. *Kalloma* had always told me the climate in that region was warmer than in the others. But I thought the vision would happen soon. Considering that the heart-stones had been present, considering all the *Vorakkar*, the priestesses, and the *Sorakkar* of Rath *Hidri* had met for a sole purpose.

Which brought me back to what I'd avoided thinking about for too long...

The obvious distance between Arik and myself. I'd felt the pinching ache. The hurt in my chest. A wound that was raw and painful. His gaze had been cold. In the vision, I'd seen his *pujerak* at his side. And I'd seen Bakkia, Kalik, and two others I didn't recognize—a male and a female.

I didn't know what it meant. I strongly suspected one thing, but I shoved it from my mind because it hurt to think about it. I didn't want it to be true.

I didn't realize how long I'd been in the bath until Arik appeared at the threshold of the doorway.

For a moment, I was confused and asked, "Have you not left yet?"

His eyes narrowed. "*Kassiri*, I've been gone for over an hour."

My heart pinched a bit at the word. *Love.* An affectionate little soft name he'd taken to calling me since we left the *saruk.*

He crouched near the edge of the bath, watching as I waded near. His palm dipped under the surface of the water, and I watched ripples from his touch lap toward me.

"The water is almost cold, Kara. Come out from there. Let me get you warm by the fire."

"*Nik,*" I protested. "Come in with me. I'll warm it back up."

Arik sighed, shaking his head. "You and your baths, *saila.* I've always wondered why priestesses always looked so *clean.* Now I know it's because they spend hours soaking in their washrooms."

Still, I was pleased when he stripped off his clothes. My mouth went dry at the sight of him. All masculine, golden flesh and scarred strength. Longing pierced me, skittering down my spine, making my tail twitch beneath the water. I wanted him. I wanted him *always.*

"Do you know a lot of priestesses?" I wondered, watching as he stepped down the stairs into the bath. I went to the taps, turning on the water to heat it.

His lips quirked. He seemed...jovial. At ease. There was a lightness in the lines of his face that had me studying him closely.

"Just the ones in *Dothik.* They walk the Spine every afternoon for sunlight. And your sisters in the *orala sa'kilan,* though they very much detest me."

"The Spine?" I asked, frowning, shaking off the dreaded knowing from my vision, forgetting about the swell of my belly. Maybe, for the first time, my vision had been wrong. It wasn't out of the realm of possibility. I hadn't had one for a very long time after all. Maybe the absence of them had altered the strength of my visions.

Lysi. That had to be it.

"The main road through *Dothik,*" he informed me,

catching me around the waist, peering down at my face in a way that had me squirming in his hold. "But only we call it that."

We. Him and his...companions?

The water was beginning to warm again. And though my head still ached from the vision, there was a desperation rising in me at the feel of his cock pressed against my belly. Maybe it was my fear or my adamant dismissal of the truth of my vision —I needed it to *not* be true—but I dug my fingers into his shoulders and pressed him back toward the stairs.

A gruff sound rose from Arik's throat.

"*Nik, saila,*" he rasped, taking my wrists. A laugh threaded from his throat when I tried to sit him down so I could crawl into his lap and sink down onto his cock. "*Nik.*"

"Why?" I whispered, hearing my own desperation. And I hated it.

His brows furrowed. I managed to get him sitting in his confusion, and I slid my legs over him. He groaned when my slit pressed against the head of his cock as I wiggled my hips over his.

His hands clenched and squeezed at my thighs, but I knew it was in warning.

"*Kassiri*, you can use my cock all you like tonight," he told me, further fanning the flames in my belly. "I'll lie back on my bed and let you do whatever you want to me. But not right now."

"Why not?" I murmured in his sliced ear, brushing my lips over the flattened flesh, moving my hips. "*Hanniva.*"

"*Vok*, Kara," he said, his voice strained. "Stop. We need to talk."

A little cry of frustration growled up my throat, making Arik freeze. Then he groaned and I felt his cock pulse against me, as if he liked it when I was mad.

"*Don't* do that," he hissed at me. "Unless you want me to

bend you over the side of this bath and ensure you cannot walk in the morning!"

"*Lysi,*" I shot back. "Do that. That's what I want right now."

Arik took a calming breath, shoving my hips off him, and I bit my lip to keep my sudden tears at bay. I didn't know *why* I needed this right now.

Nik, that was another lie I told myself. I knew *exactly* why I needed this right now.

I needed the distraction of his body against mine. Because it was easier than meeting his eyes and forcing myself to confront the truth. I needed to feel the pinching pleasure between my thighs because it was better than remembering that pinching ache in my chest.

"You're different since what happened in the tunnels. I want to know why. I need to know what happened, Kara."

Biting my lip, I turned away.

Arik didn't let me, however. He waded forward, bringing me back into his arms, pressing his palms to my cheeks so I was forced to meet his gaze.

I could never hide from him. I never *wanted* to.

Except right at this moment.

"You never told me how your mother died," I whispered. He had hinted at it. But he'd never told me explicitly. It was my attempt to escape this. My last one.

Arik's gaze narrowed.

"She was murdered by the *Dothikkar's* assassins."

I stilled.

"The ones sent after me when she was recognized in the market," Arik continued, unflinching in his quick honesty. "The *Dothikkar* had given his order for my death. But also for my mother's. She died trying to protect me. She died trying to *shield* me. And they cut right through her. I can still see her falling."

I couldn't stop the tears that welled in my eyes. The horror. Unfathomable horror that he'd experienced, that he'd *witnessed,* watching his mother's murder. And here I was...wallowing because of an impending broken heart.

It made me ashamed of myself.

"The scar down my back. The one you said you saw in your dreams," he started. "I got it that night. One of the mercenaries...he didn't know he'd be killing a child and a mother. It was his partner that gave me the scar. Who nearly sliced my ear off. But it was him who let me go free. Because of him, I'm alive. And because of him, the *Dothikkar* believed I was dead."

He lowered his head, brushing his thumb against the tears that slid down my face.

"Now, *saila*," he purred. "What else would you like to ask to try to distract me? Shall we talk about the first male I ever killed? Shall we talk about how much gold I've stolen in my lifetime? Or perhaps how many females I've fucked in my—"

A sizzle went down my spine, and it broke me from my stunned stupor. "I don't care about the females that came before me," I breathed, looking him in the eye, seeing his cool surprise and the way his nostrils flared. "Because I know what you feel for me and I know that I'll be with you long after I truly am. I know that they are forgettable but *I* am not. Not for you at least."

His hand on my cheek twitched. His glare was piercing even as I cried. But I saw my words hit him. *Hard.*

"I'm a coward," I whispered. "But I will tell you what you want to know. I had a vision in the tunnels. It hasn't happened in a long time, and so it took me by surprise. I'm sorry if it scared you. I know it is a jarring thing to witness."

Arik's touch gentled on me. His voice was guttural and gruff when he asked, "What did you see?"

"You," I said, telling the truth about that at least. "And many others. The *Vorakkar*. Their queens. The *Sorakkar* of Rath Hidri. *Kalloma* and my sisters. We were in the East Lands. I saw…I saw the fog. And it is more terrible than I could have ever imagined."

There was something I recalled just now, something I hadn't truly noticed at the time. In the vision, the *Vorakkar* had all given Arik and his companions a wide berth. He'd been at the head of the oval shape we'd made. I'd been at the opposite end of it with *Kalloma*. But the *Vorakkar* had stayed closer to the priestesses than their fellow *Vorakkar,* and I wondered why.

"We?" he growled. "You were there too?"

"*Lysi.*"

His gaze flickered between my eyes, assessing. His brow furrowed. "Is that all?"

"All the heartstones were present. I could feel them nearby," I said. I hesitated, and Arik leaned forward slightly. "I…I had one in my hand. The one we took from the *orala sa'kilan.* I could feel its heat. I could hear Kakkari and her voices."

"Her voices?"

"*Lysi,* she has many," I informed him. "Millions of them."

For a moment, he looked dumbstruck. I watched his face pale, but then he shook his head, his lips pursing.

"What is it?"

Arik's gaze slid past me to the taps of the bath, still running with hot water.

"Sometimes…" he started and then trailed off. "Sometimes I think my *lomma* had Kakkari's gift."

I stilled. "Why do you say that?"

"Because she mentioned something about Kakkari's voices once. Well, more than once. She told me that she heard them and that it was like a buzzing in her mind that would never stop. Sometimes it made her scream because she said there were millions of them. That she couldn't think. Or hear. I found her once with so many scratches down her face because she said she was trying to get them out from underneath her skin."

I shuddered, thinking on his words.

Then I thought it was entirely possibly that his mother had a gift. It would explain a lot.

"People believe that the goddess is one being. One entity. But if you could hear her," I said, bringing Arik's gaze back to me, "then you would know better."

"You have heard her too?" he asked.

"I hear her in the visions sometimes. I could hear her when the priestesses were praying in the evenings if I was close enough. And I heard her in the heartstone. Those voices."

Arik took a deep breath in.

Hesitantly, I told him, "*Kalloma* believes that all of our power is connected for a reason. That there is a rhythm to that power and it ebbs and flows like Drukkar's Sea. There have been stretches of time in our history when there were very few accounts of *anyone* possessing a gift. And now? There are so many. There *is* a reason for it. There always is."

"The *Vorakkar* believe something similar."

"But you don't?" I asked, carefully pressing my hand to his bare chest, just over his heart to feel it thumping underneath my palm.

"I don't know what I believe," he told me, spearing me with a long look, frowning. "I thought I believed one thing. But since you, Kara...I am not certain anymore."

"Would you like to know what I think?" I asked him, feeling more like myself than I had since the tunnels. Having him close, hearing his voice and feeling his touch...it helped center me. It helped me refocus.

He inclined his head, studying me carefully. Then his hand moved from my cheek to slide through my wet, clean hair. As if he couldn't help himself.

"I think it's very likely your mother had a gift," I informed him.

"Why do you say that?"

"All of us are connected. We comprise an extensive network

of power that stretches over the surface of Dakkar. I don't think it's the heartstones that give us power. I think it's the people that can *channel* the power of the heartstones that truly make us strong. The heartstones are like...waypoints. They give us direction, focus. And I think there is a reason that I've seen you since I was a child."

Arik's heart stuttered beneath my palm.

"I think your mother's power was within that network and that it attached itself to me. Like roots of a tree. Leading me to her and to you," I said softly. "How else do you account for me knowing you before I ever laid eyes on you?"

Which made the vision I had all the more heartbreaking. Because the ache in my chest had felt like a *severing*. Like I'd lost a limb and I could feel its ghostly absence.

A shuddered realization bloomed within me.

"We are where we are meant to be," I whispered to him softly as his head began to descend toward me. "Right now in Kakkari's plans. And I know that you have no faith in the goddess. But I can feel her enough for both of us. I can protect you enough for the both of us."

His lips crashed down into mine, and I met him fully, threading my hands up into his hair, pressing my body to his. His heat and scent and taste were so familiar. It was a comfort even when I felt a restlessness rising in my breast.

He groaned. Against my lips, he rasped, "I think you will be the end of me, Kara."

"*Nik*," I said, squeezing my eyes against the sudden sting of tears as I thought of the swell of my belly and the child that would come. "I think I will be the beginning."

Arik stiffened, though his lips continued to move against mine. My fingers dug into his hair, trying to keep him to me. But all too soon, he retreated.

"About your vision," he began, his lips reddened from the

fierceness of our kiss, though his eyes were hardened with intent. "What are you not telling me?"

This was Arik after all. On our first meeting, he'd told me I was not a practiced liar.

"Give me this one secret. For now," I pleaded softly. He frowned, but I leaned forward to press a gentle kiss to the side of his downturned mouth. "It has no bearing on the fog. It will not put anyone in danger. I promise you."

"I don't like secrets," he said, his tone flooded with discomfort. "Especially when it comes to you, Kara."

"*Hanniva*. It's important to me."

I refused to tell him. Not yet. Because if I told him, it would make it real. It would mark the beginning of the end, and I wanted to savor him for a little while longer.

His jaw twitched and tightened. He ran a hand over the jumping muscle and then jerked his head in a nod, though it displeased him.

"Very well," he murmured. "I will allow you your secret for now. But if you think to keep it from me for long, you are very mistaken."

It was a small relief. I nodded.

"Let's finish bathing," he said. "Then I'll get you something to eat, *lysi*?"

I nodded.

Swallowing, I said quietly, "I haven't taken the *kana* today."

His gaze flashed. "Then I'll bring you hot water with your meal."

His arms slid around me.

"And then later, when I have you in my bed and you're using my cock as I promised," he murmured, "we'll test out how well the *kana* works, *lysi*?"

If he noticed the way I stiffened, he didn't comment on it. Hopefully he'd mistake it for desire.

In a flash, I pressed my lips to his when he bent down. As a way of distraction. But all too soon, I felt the familiar curl and sizzle of lust, spiraling in my belly.

The kiss turned hungry, fueled by the high emotions of the night.

A low growl rose from Arik's throat, rumbling and dark.

He led me over to the edge of the sunken bath, pressing my front to the cool marble. Behind me, I felt the prod of his thick cock against my sex, and I pushed back, eager and desperate for him.

"I changed my mind. Our meal can wait," he rasped. He hissed as my moan echoed around the washroom, as his cock sunk in *deep*. "*Lysi*, lift that pretty tail for me and get ready for your fucking, Kara. This is what you wanted, wasn't it?"

"*Lysi*," I whispered, doing as he asked, moving my tail away. My lips parted when I felt his *dakke*—the hardened bump at the base of his cock—press into my sensitive, puckered flesh underneath my tail when he thrust forward. Wicked and wonderful. "*Hanniva!*"

For a moment, I wanted to forget. *This* was what I needed. What I craved.

"And when you come for me, *rei kassiri*," came his velvety purr in my ear, and he slammed home, stretching me and filling me to the brim, "you'll scream for me."

"*Lysi!*"

"You'll scream for me," he huffed into my ear as water began to slosh from the sunken bath with his powerful, rough thrusts, "so all of *Dothik* knows that you're *mine*."

CHAPTER 44

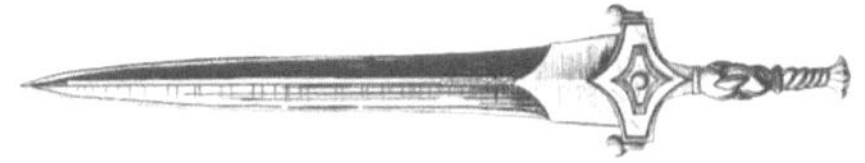

Through the window in my sleeping room, a shaft of moonlight speared over Kara. She slumbered peacefully, her breaths rising and falling in a comforting rhythm as I stroked my fingers down her back and waist and hips.

I'd lit up another fire in the room, and so we'd kicked off the furs, which had tangled around our ankles with the ferocity of our fucking, which had gone on late into the night.

In the aftermath, she was passed out next to me, her cunt still filled with my come. I was sated, unbelievably satisfied. Yet I wanted her again.

She was curled toward me, her beautiful face relaxed, her lips parted. Looking at her filled me with supreme contentedness. It filled me with *rightness*. My chest warmed when she made a little sound in her throat as her tail flicked against my leg.

She dreamed. I wondered if she was dreaming about me.

Shifting on the bed, I drew her into my arms, curling them tightly around her. She was a deep sleeper, something she'd told me once but something I'd also come to realize on my own. Nothing could wake her...which was a weakness. One that worried me. I woke at the slightest sound, the slightest movement. It had saved my life more than once.

After our bath earlier, Kara had slowly seemed to return to her normal self. She'd chatted throughout our meal, asking me about the layout of the city and if she would be able to see more of it while we were here, even if it was during the nighttime.

We would need to gain access to the priestesses' temple tomorrow, which posed an issue in itself. Ideally in the evening when that area of the city was mostly cleared out. It was near the market that Kara so desperately wanted to see, but as the sun began to set, the vendors packed up their stalls and the people of *Dothik* went in search of their local tavern or back to their homes.

The temple was still guarded by the *Dothikkar's* soldiers, however. They wouldn't allow us entry, especially if we were cloaked figures. They would demand to see our faces, and they would soon realize who I was...and who Kara was too.

We had to sneak inside, a feat that was nearly as impossible as breaking into the *Dothikkar's* palace.

After our meal, we'd sat in the sitting room by the fire. Kara wanted to dry off her hair before we went to bed—my particular little female—and so I'd turned the chair toward the flames and pulled her into my lap. She'd snagged a book off the wall and had it opened in her lap the moment I'd pulled her down. She'd settled into me as if it was the most natural thing in the entire world. As if we'd passed our evenings just like that for decades: sitting by the sparking fire after our evening meal as she read to me, sliding her fingertips across the page as my gaze tracked the strange words.

After a dozen pages, however, and once Kara's hair had dried, I'd grown impatient. My hands had begun to wander, squeezing and cupping flesh I wanted to kiss and lick and stroke. When she'd begun to stammer over her words, her gentle cadence giving way to breathy sighs, I plucked the book from her hands, placed it alongside the tray I'd brought up from the kitchens, and took her to my bed.

And now I watched over her even though I felt like I could sleep for years. I didn't think I would sleep while we were in *Dothik*. Not when she was in bed next to me. I was too fearful that I'd wake to a shadowy figure looming over my bed, a blade gleaming as it whistled down toward her.

I couldn't risk it.

Not when there were many people in this city that wanted me dead. That would use any weakness I had against me.

And Kara?

She was steadily becoming my biggest one.

A sound at my door had me freezing. Without another moment of hesitation, I slid soundly from the bed, disentangling my limbs from Kara's as I drew my dagger from underneath my pillow. Making sure the sleeping room was secure and that the window was latched, I made my way out to the sitting room, peering into every darkened corner.

A rap at the door came. Three knocks, a long pause, followed by two rapid ones.

I relaxed, blowing out a sharp breath.

Bakkia.

I went to the door, pulling it wide. If he was surprised by my nakedness or the way Kara's scent was all over me, he didn't comment on it. The male I'd known all my life, who'd given my mother a chance at a new life, who'd given her a home when she'd had none, stood at the threshold of my private quarters.

"*Lysi?*" I asked quietly.

"We need to talk," came his hushed voice. His tone made me straighten. Something about it sent a warning down my spine.

I inclined my head, gesturing for him to come inside. His bulk moved into the darkened room, and I said, "Wait here."

I left him in the sitting room to return to my sleeping room. With a brief glance at Kara, I replaced my dagger under the pillow, smoothing a hand through her hair. Then I went to my chests, pulling on trews and lacing them lazily before I returned to Bakkia.

I left the door slightly ajar, though I knew that Kara wouldn't wake. I knew I'd be back beside her long before she ever woke.

Bakkia was standing at the fire, staring down into the flames.

"Tell me," I murmured, placing my hand on the back of his shoulder when I stepped up behind him.

When he turned, my hand fell away.

"I didn't want to say anything during the meeting. I'm not even certain I saw what I did."

"And what do you think you saw?" I asked, feeling myself slip back into my old skin like I'd never left it behind. It seemed strange to realize I was anything else but *this*. It seemed strange to realize that I was a *Vorakkar*. That I was responsible for a horde, which waited for me out on the wildlands.

Bakkia said, "I think I saw Kiro and Vala leaving a meeting with Nyonnia."

A growl left my throat, physically feeling myself react to the name.

"The mercenary from the Eastern District?" I hissed softly. "The *vokking* bastard who gave up Bodin's location to the guards at the palace?"

"*Lysi,*" Bakkia said.

I took in a calming breath, though I felt the tension prickle through my shoulders. All the contentedness and satisfaction I'd felt next to Kara vanished in a single instant.

"Where?" I asked.

"At the tavern off the Seventh Limb," he responded. "Last week. Right after we heard from Nassik that you were returning to *Dothik.*"

"Why were you there?" I asked. "If anyone saw you in the Eastern District..."

"I know," Bakkia said, blowing out a sharp breath. "But I needed to get supplies for the tavern. I made sure I wasn't noticed."

"Why not get the supplies from Suava?" I scowled. "Surely there's more than enough gold in our stores to get you whatever you need from him, even if he marked up the prices again."

"Suava died," came his short reply.

"*Neffar?*" I asked, stilling.

"In his sleep," Bakkia said, shrugging. "He was an old male. His time had come. But his son doesn't have his head for business. And so I've been going to the Eastern District to get what I need."

"*Vok,*" I said quietly, rolling my neck before rubbing at the back of it. "I didn't know."

"Obviously," Bakkia chuffed.

It was strange to feel disconnected from the city, from the people I knew so well like this. Kara had spoken of a network of power over Dakkar. And while it still gave me chills thinking about what she'd said about that level of connection, I understood what she meant. Because there was a network like it in *Dothik*, the one we'd created, and it ran on knowledge, on secrets, on trust, and on gold.

That was powerful in itself.

But I'd been gone from this place for over a year now. I hadn't returned in all that time, and while it felt effortless to slip back into who I'd been all my life, things had obviously changed in my absence.

"So you saw them leaving the tavern with Nyonnia?" I asked quietly, meeting his eyes.

"I saw Kiro certainly," Bakkia told me in a low tone. "Vala had his cloak drawn up, but I recognized his gait. The limp. I'm fairly certain it was him. And they said nothing about a meeting. They know your feelings for Nyonnia. They know all our feelings about that sack of shit."

Kiro and Vala had been at the meeting tonight because I considered the two of them some of my closest allies. And they hadn't said a word.

The network was built on trust. The moment that crumbled it would all fall away.

"You think they'll try for their assassination attempt?" I asked.

Bakkia breathed in deeply. "I can see no other reason for why they would meet with him. They know Nyonnia has connections to the palace. They've made it clear they want the *Dothikkar* dead. But considering how he turned on Bodin, I don't understand how they think they can trust him."

"Have you told Kalik?" I asked. "Or Errana?"

He shook his head. "I wanted to tell you first. I wanted to let you decide what you want to do with the information."

"*Vok*," I cursed softly, running my hand through my hair.

"Welcome home, Serok," Bakkia said wryly.

I thought over the options quickly, weighing each one.

"We'll wait until after we've secured the heartstone from the priestesses," I told Bakkia. "We might need them if we have to gain access to the temple. But afterward..."

"You'll put them on trial," Bakkia finished for me.

"*Lysi*."

Bakkia inclined his head. "And what if something happens before then? What if they put something into motion and it's too late to stop it?"

My nostrils flared.

"It's the risk I'll take," I said quietly. "And it'll be on me to deal with the consequences if they actually succeed."

Kiro and Vala had been the most outspoken members of our core group about wanting the *Dothikkar* assassinated. They believed it would solve everything. They believed it would clear a certain path to the throne for me. With our supporters not just in the Southern District but in the Eastern, Western, and Northern Districts, it would be easy to take it. If not by blood right, then because I was a *Vorakkar*.

Yet they couldn't be more wrong. The *Dothikkar* hadn't recognized me as his son. He had no proven heirs. If he died without securing a successor—a *legitimate* successor—it would leave *Dothik* in turmoil and unrest. It would leave *Dothik* vulnerable.

It would be up to his council and the priestesses to secure *Dothik* in the aftermath of his death, and both groups were perhaps even more dangerous than he was.

"If the *Seta Kalliri* and the *Vorakkar* step in on your behalf," Bakkia murmured quietly, "your legitimacy will be recognized. Perhaps this is not a terrible thing, Arik. Perhaps this is—"

I cut him a sharp look.

He knew my thoughts on assassination attempts. Him more than anyone. He knew my hatred for my father. Just as he knew I would not pave the way to the throne in his blood.

"We do this the right way, or we don't do it all," I growled low.

"To Kiro and Vala, this is the right way," Bakkia said. "So you mean we do this *your* way, or we don't do this at all."

I closed my eyes, blowing out a sharp breath through my nostrils.

"Do you want *Dothik?*" Bakkia asked.

A loaded question. One that Nassik had recently asked me, though he'd phrased it differently. But the meaning had been the same.

Guilt mingled with longing. Responsibility warred with selfishness.

"*Lysi.*"

My answer was a guttural rasp.

"It would be easier to turn my back on it," I continued

quietly. "It would be easier to stay out on the wildlands and make a kingdom of our own. But *this* is my home. Every foul, rotten, greed-filled corner of this city is what I know best. And I want to build it up again. I want to make it new. I want to create the city that Bekkar always meant for it to be. And it will be the hardest thing I will ever do in my lifetime, but I know now it is what I *must* do."

Satisfaction gleamed in Bakkia's eyes.

"Then we will get it for you," came his simple answer. "You have hundreds—*nik, thousands*—behind you already. With the hordes at your back and the priestesses at your side, you will have even more support. *Dothik* is already yours, Arik. We just have to take it from within."

Swallowing, my gaze flitted to the flames. All my life, we'd waited. We'd built up a network, we'd built up support, and we'd waited some more. With a single murmured word, thousands could storm the *Dothikkar's* palace. They could flood the streets and charge at his gilded gates.

I only needed to give the word. But that could only happen when the palace was at its weakest.

Soon, I thought.

We were close. So close.

And it couldn't have come at a worse time with the fog in the East Lands.

"And I know you do not like the thought," Bakkia continued, "but his death *is* inevitable. It is the only way to move forward. It is the only way to cut the disease from this city. And after his death, we occupy the palace, we remove his council, and we have the priestesses confirm your bloodline. All of *Dothik* saw you in the *Vorakkar* Trials. They cheered for you when the *Dothikkar* placed the cuffs on your wrists. They will follow you because you have already proven yourself to them."

As if sparked by the words, the scars on my back seemed to heat. Sometimes I could still feel the lash of the whip.

"Is that all we have to do?" I murmured, flashing Bakkia a grim smile. "If I'd known it would be that easy, we'd have done it years ago."

Nothing ever went to plan, however. Not once. And I still had a horde to think about. I still had Kara's safety to think about.

Bakkia chuffed out a long sigh.

"And what about the female?" Bakkia asked, gesturing toward the ajar door to my sleeping room.

"What about her?" I murmured, quirking a brow.

He leveled me a dry look. "Who is she? Really?"

I'd never lied to Bakkia once, and I didn't see the point of starting now. "She's the *Seta Kalliri's* daughter."

His eyes widened.

"Not by blood," I added, as if it wasn't obvious. "But her daughter all the same."

"She's a priestess?" Bakkia hissed softly.

"*Nik,*" I said. "But she believes she can secure the heartstone for us from the temple. She's the reason I have the heartstone from the *orala sa'kilan*. And why the *Sorakkar* of Rath Hidri will bring his to the East Lands. She is...not to be underestimated."

"High praise coming from you," Bakkia commented, though his tone was edged in wariness. Though he'd been warm to Kara, I knew that Bakkia did not trust easily. We were alike in that way.

"Trust me on this, *lysi*?" I asked Bakkia, reaching out to clasp his shoulder. "And trust me on Kiro and Vala too."

"Have I ever *not* trusted you?" came Bakkia's pointed question.

"Only because I've never given you a choice," I returned. "But I'm giving you one now."

The male I loved like a true father swallowed, meeting my gaze, his eyes darting between mine.

"The wildlands have changed you, Arik," came his soft

observation. His gaze strayed past my shoulder. "Or perhaps the pretty hybrid female in your furs has."

"Changed me for the better? Or for the worse?" I wondered. I wondered what he saw in me that *had* changed.

His grin was soft. "That remains to be seen. But I hope it is for the better."

"Get back to the tavern," I told him after a long silence had passed, as the fire crackled between us. "We will meet at dawn about the priestesses. The fog takes precedence right now. Afterward, we'll decide on the throne. Together."

Bakkia inclined his head. "With Kiro and Vala?"

"*Lysi*, even with them. Act as if you did not see them. Say nothing about it. This will play out as it is intended to," I murmured to him, thinking about Kara's words to me in the washroom. "We are right where we are meant to be."

CHAPTER 45

My dream faded to a whisper when I woke.

"Give her strength, Kakkari. Give her the strength to survive this world because I will be gone from it soon. I will give you my life in exchange."

When my eyes opened, I winced at the sharp pain throbbing at my temple.

"Rei kassiri," came his hushed murmur. I sighed, rolling into Arik's warm body, wrapping my limbs around him tight and pressing my face into his wide, unyielding chest. "What is it?"

His voice was husky and gruff from sleep, though I knew he'd slept very little through the night. He'd woken me often to his cock slipping between my legs and his lips at my throat, possessed with desire though I'd sworn I felt restlessness roving inside him too. As if he was seeking relief, as if he was seeking to release that restlessness into me.

And I would take it from him gladly. I wanted to give him everything he wanted.

But he will not give you everything in return, came my taunting, silent whisper.

The voice I'd heard when I woke was not Kakkari's. I'd heard it before, the lilting, strange, soft voice. It was my mother's. My human mother's. Or so I'd always assumed.

It was my mother's prayer.

It was my human mother's prayer to Kakkari that had given me this gift, which sometimes felt like a curse.

My mother had sought help. And Kakkari had answered.

"Sometimes," I whispered into his skin, feeling the sharp pain in my temple begin to fade, "I think that nothing I do matters. That this gift is useless. Because all I see are memories or futures that I can never change. *Kalloma* can change her futures though. And the human queens of the hordes...you said they unleashed great power to protect those they love."

And what can I do? I thought, tired and morose from my dream. It always dampened my mood, whenever I dreamed of my mother and her beautiful voice. Usually I was alone in my foul mood. But now I was not alone. And Arik would bear some of it.

"Kara," came his voice, nudging my chin up so I was forced to meet his half-lidded gaze. "Everything you do matters. *Vok* your gift. You don't need it. Because it was not your gift that led you here. It was not your gift that secured us two of the heartstones."

"It was my gift that led me to the heartstones, that led me to realize what their purpose was for the fog," I reminded him.

He chuffed out a sharp breath. "*Nik*, you came to that realization because you've read every damn tome in the *orala sa'k-ilan* and because you have a frighteningly good memory when it comes to stories and words. And all of those things threaded into your dreams."

His gruff sentiment had some of my foul mood fading away, my heart flipping in my chest.

"And you?" I wondered. "Because when I came to that realization about the famine in the West, it was you I saw rising from the earth, with red veins under your skin and glowing eyes."

His lips quirked. "I cannot blame you for dreaming about me, *saila*. Who *wouldn't* want to?"

My laugh was surprised, the words expected and yet unexpected.

"Arrogance is no better than wrath or greed," I recited, whispering it over his skin once my laugh faded away.

Arik grunted. His eyes glimmered in the low morning light that streamed in through his window. His bed was ridiculously comfortable, plush and warm with furs so soft they felt like silk across my naked skin.

"Did your *kalloma* tell you that?" Arik murmured, his fingers curling around my hip. When he pressed close, I could feel his thick cock, hot and hard against my belly. "Because I embody all three of those things, and yet you are still in my furs beside me and you're about to feel how greedy I truly am."

In a moment, I forgot my dream. I forgot the whispered words that had pulled me from it, spoken into my ear like my mother had been right beside me in Arik's private quarters in *Dothik*, kneeling next to the bed where I slept. He broke me from the melancholy I'd felt rising in my breast, and I marveled that *this* was Arik's own gift.

When my lips met his, my horde king groaned, his fingers tightening over my hip so hard that I wanted them to leave a bruise. I wanted to be marked by him. I wanted to mark him too. With my teeth, with my nails, with my kiss, with my *love*. I wanted it to mean something. I wanted him to remember me before it was too late.

"*Hanniva*," I pleaded against his lips, ignoring the pinch between my thighs. He'd taken me more times than he ever had last night. I was feeling the effects this morning. But I didn't care.

His next groan was pained. He broke the kiss abruptly,

pressing his forehead to mine as his tail wrapped around my ankle.

"We cannot," he rasped. "I know I was rough last night with you."

"I liked it," I whispered.

His eyes glowed. "And I did too."

"Then why—"

"We also have another meeting this morning. I told everyone to come at dawn, and I cannot be distracted by you, no matter how much I want to be."

Understanding speared through me, even though I had the strangest urge to whine.

"All right," I whispered. "We? Does that include me too?"

"*Lysi*," he said, dropping one last kiss across my lips before pulling away. "I know better than to try to keep you away."

I watched him slide from the bed, and I rolled into the place where his body was still outlined in the furs, seeking his warmth and inhaling his scent. He smirked as he watched me, keeping me in his vision as he went to his chests and began to pull out a fresh tunic and trews.

I sighed. Devastatingly handsome. I wanted to look at him forever. Giddiness mingled with excitement and nerves in my belly as my gaze ran over him.

Then he ordered, "Now tell me what you dreamed."

I blinked, feeling the wave of memory mix with that familiar wash of melancholy. Only this time it was softer. Not as sharp.

"My mother's voice," I told him softly. "My birth mother."

Arik's eyes narrowed, and he paused momentarily in dressing to turn to me. "You hear her voice?"

"Sometimes," I told him, pushing up from the bed on one outstretched arm. My breasts swayed as I righted myself, Arik's gaze briefly dropping to them, to my swollen nipples he'd sucked and bit teasingly throughout the night, making me gasp and squirm. His eyes darkened, but then he shook his head, meeting my gaze once more.

"And you don't like to hear her?" he guessed.

"It's not that," I told him, not entirely sure how to explain it. "I love hearing her voice. I love every time I learn something new or when another puzzle piece of her slots into place. But I—I think she made a bargain with Kakkari. For me. I hear her prayer in my dreams often. I think she gave up her life willingly to the goddess for me to have this gift. And it hurts me to know that it was for nothing. That I don't have the power to truly *change* anything."

I'd never even told *Kalloma* this. Not only because whenever we spoke of my birth mother, I sensed it made her uncomfortable. And so it was easier not to speak of her—even about this. Even about what I knew to be true.

"*Kalloma* told me my mother brought me to the *orala sa'k-ilan* and then she left. But I don't think she ever did," I whispered to him softly. "I think she died there. In the temple. I think she took her own life there as a sacrifice to the goddess. For me. And I think *Kalloma* never wanted me to know."

Arik's brows drew down. His tunic was forgotten, his trews only half-laced when he approached the bed once more. He tugged me to its edge, his warm, calloused palms cupping my cheek.

"I'm sorry, *rei kassiri*," he murmured, his thumb stroking the bridge of my nose. "You never asked her? Directly?"

"*Nik*," I said softly. "Maybe because a part of me doesn't want it to be true. Even though I already know. Deep down, I already know."

Just like my vision yesterday. I didn't want it to be true. I didn't want Arik to turn his back on me. I didn't want to feel the crushing break in my chest.

But deep down...I already knew what would come to pass.

I gave him a wobbly smile, reaching up to clasp his *Vorakkar* cuffs, hot and unyielding beneath my palms. "Ignore me," I told him. "My dreams always put me in a strange mood. And I know today is important. I know today we need to be focused."

He'd told me we would journey to the priestesses' temple here in *Dothik*. I assumed the meeting this morning was about *how* that would happen.

Arik frowned. "Like I could ever ignore you, *saila*."

We held one another's gaze for a long time, my heart in my throat at the sentiment I heard behind his words.

He cared for me. Deeply. But I didn't know if it was foolish, or perhaps my own inexperience, to hope that he cared for me the way I cared for him.

When I turned my head, I brushed my lips against his palm. It was dawn now—I could see the rays of the sun sliding against the walls.

"Where did you put my satchel?" I asked. "The *Sorakkar* gave me those dresses. One of them is still clean. I'll wear that today."

Arik frowned, but he stepped back when I slid from the bed. "I'd prefer if you didn't wear his gifts," came his grumbled words.

Some of the tension melted away in the room with the familiar argument. We'd had it after we left the *saruk,* and we'd bickered over the nice gifts for the majority of an afternoon until Arik had taken his frustrations out on me against a damn tree.

He'd been jealous. Of the aging *Sorakkar*, who loved his queen very much.

"He should know better," came Arik's growl. "To give a female something like that, who obviously had already been claimed. Especially by a *Vorakkar*," he spat out. "It was an insult."

"Oh?" I teased, keeping my voice nonchalant though his

words filled me with an intoxicating thrill. "Is that what you did at the *saruk*? You claimed me?"

His eyes narrowed, the dangerous glint of them in the dawn light making my belly flutter.

His grin was feral. "Wasn't it obvious?"

I gave him a small smile, still standing naked next to his bed. "*You* haven't given me any dresses, so what else am I supposed to wear?"

"My own *vokking* tunics," he grumbled under his breath.

Then he scoffed, reaching into another chest, pulling out my worn satchel which had certainly seen better days. He handed it to me and watched with his hands on his hips as I pulled open the flap and fished out the shimmering, dark, silky material of the *Sorakkar's* gift. Deep blue in color and trailing to my ankles, I thought the dress would blend in with my cloak and wouldn't draw too much attention.

"I'll send for as many dresses as you like, *saila*," came his promise, making me smile though I ducked my head to hide it. "And when they come, I'll have that one shredded for fire fuel."

I barked out a short laugh as I pulled on the shift dress, which clung to my hips and breasts. It was only held up by slim straps on my shoulders, but on the whole, it was a modest dress, especially when considering the clothes I'd seen worn in the *saruk* and even within Arik's own horde. Some females had been practically naked. Some of the males, even more so.

I knew what he was doing. Trying to distract me. After my dark admission about my mother, he was giving me something else to latch onto, to pull me from that place I'd rather not visit. And it was working. I was grateful for it.

Arik *was* jealous, there was no mistaking that. But I knew he was playing it up to make me smile, to help me forget, at least for a little while.

When I was dressed, I stepped into his arms, winding mine

around his neck. His fingers clenched into the silk. Yesterday already felt like it had happened years ago.

"I'm ready," I told him.

"I haven't decided if you'll come with me today, *saila*," he admitted. "I don't want you to be upset if I decide to keep you here. To keep you safe."

I flashed him a smile, one that had his expression pinching in wariness. Because he'd told me once that he could never deny me.

"Of course," I told him. "You know I'll do whatever you say."

He groaned.

Because he knew the opposite was true, especially because we were in *Dothik*.

And I wanted to see it all.

This city *was* Arik. I could never fully understand him without understanding *Dothik*.

"I mean it, Kara," he warned.

I smiled again. Leaning forward, I brushed my lips against the middle of his chest, looking up at him beneath my lashes.

"I know. I do too."

We'd been sitting in the meeting room for hours.

Shortly after dawn, Arik had led me down the two flights of stairs to the first floor and led me through weaving hallways until we reached another stretch of rooms.

Inside, I was greeted with two familiar faces—Bakkia and Kalik—and four unfamiliar ones.

Well, not entirely true.

I'd frozen up when I recognized two. The two Dakkari I'd seen standing behind Arik in my vision—a male and a female, who I learned were called Ulli and Errana. The remaining two males were Vala and Kiro.

"Sleep well, *kalles*?" Bakkia asked me, a knowing twinkle in his eye, when we'd both stepped into the meeting room.

"Very," I replied hesitantly, confused.

Arik shot the older male a stern look, but then I watched him take command of the room. It wasn't something I'd witnessed at his horde because I'd really only seen him during the nights there.

But this Arik?

I could see why they followed him. Why they hung on his every word and obeyed his every order. Ulli had leaped up to secure me a chair, and Arik had only needed to jerk his head toward it.

Gone was my teasing, sensual, jealous, thoughtful lover. In his place was a focused, patient, driven, direct horde king who knew the maps of *Dothik*, which were spread out on a table before us, like he'd come to know my own body.

He will make a good king, I couldn't help but think.

And I knew they all saw it. They all believed it. Or else they wouldn't be here.

Like he was Bekkar in the flesh, I couldn't take my eyes off him. I hung on his every word. Whenever he spoke to me directly, asking about information about the priestesses, asking about information he actually *didn't* know, I had the strangest urge to duck my head and break his gaze in respect. As if I didn't still feel the stretch of him between my legs or taste him on my tongue from his long kiss before we left his rooms.

This was my lover. But this was someone else entirely too.

I was just now realizing it.

And it made him all the more devastating. All the more ruinous for me.

Because, without a shadow of a doubt, I knew that I'd never meet anyone else like Arik. I'd never experience another male like him again. He was it for me. He was all I would know, all I *wanted* to know.

"*Nik,*" came Arik's voice. He was frustrated. I could see it in the lines of his body, but I didn't hear it in the growl of his voice. "Unless the security around the temple has changed since I was in *Dothik* last, I know there are ten guards stationed around it at all times. Every few minutes, they walk the perimeter, *lysi?*"

"There's more now," Kalik added, leaning forward to tap on the map, gesturing toward an alleyway that I saw was titled the Twentieth Limb. "A robbery happened from here last season. Four males broke into the temple because they learned how to time the guard rotation. They took jewels, gold. Even the damn goblets the priestesses drink their *havvia* from."

I stilled.

"They drink *havvia*?" I asked quietly. "That's...surprising."

"Your priestesses do not?" Errana asked me, her eyes narrowing. I thought at first that she didn't like me. I had wondered at first if it was because I was half-human and half-Dakkari, if she didn't like the look of my face, which was decidedly human. Or I had wondered if, perhaps, she had feelings for Arik. Feelings like my own. But shortly, I'd realized that wasn't the case. It was Ulli she cared for, the male who never left her side. And it wasn't distaste for me. It was distrust.

All of them were mistrustful of me. Even Bakkia. Even Kalik. It didn't matter that Arik brought me to them. It didn't matter if Arik trusted me or not. It mattered that I was a stranger to them and that they were watching out for their leader, for the male they'd known nearly all their lives.

I didn't mind the mistrust. I understood it. Likely, I would react the same way because I, too, wanted to protect Arik at all costs.

It relieved me, truthfully. They didn't care that I was a hybrid. They didn't care that I looked different than them, that I was physically weaker and smaller than them. They only cared about Arik.

"*Nik,*" I told her, folding my hands in my lap as Arik's thigh pressed into my own. We were seated next to one another at the table, and I'd found his warm, sturdy presence comforting and distracting. "Not anymore. *Havvia* is taken in the old way of prayer. It's a..."

"Drug," Arik finished for me.

"And it can be dangerous," I added, tilting my head to the side. "The priestesses in the *orala sa'kilan* used it hundreds of years ago, until one of the priestesses died from it. It's incredibly addicting."

"Did your *kalloma* ever use it?" Arik asked me, pinning me with that gaze.

I took in a deep breath, licking my dry lips. "I know she took it once when she was here in *Dothik*, but she never drank it again. She said the experience was not something she wanted to feel. She said it made Kakkari seem further away, not closer. And if the *Laseta Kalliri* studied under my *kalloma*, then I am surprised that she allows it to be taken among her priestesses here. The *Seta Kalliri* is very much against its use in prayer."

"This is *Dothik, leikavi*," came Vala's drawl. *Beautiful one*, he'd called me. Arik gave a sharp growl of warning at Vala's address to me. *Jealous, indeed*, I thought, reaching over to squeeze his thigh with a warning of my own. Vala coughed, hiding his discomfort. "Drugs are commonplace. Especially for the priestesses. We have it on good authority that the *Dothikkar* himself takes *havvia* every night. He has the *Laseta Kalliri* deliver it to him and lead him through his prayer."

His words sparked an idea.

It sparked two, actually.

"Maybe you don't need to break *into* the temple," I said softly, suddenly excited.

We just needed to speak with the *Laseta Kalliri* once after all. To give her *Kalloma's* message.

Arik leaned forward quickly, standing from his chair to peer at the map from a different vantage point. His finger traced a road to the *Dothikkar's* temple, his brow furrowed in concentration, and I could see the way he was making a plan, a schedule in his head. But then he diverted his attention down another road. One that led somewhere else entirely.

"All we need to do is to catch the *Laseta Kalliri* away from the temple," I finished softly. "And now there are three times when you know she is not there. When she delivers the *havvia* to the *Dothikkar*, when she returns from the evening prayer with him..."

"And when she takes her afternoon walks near the western market," Arik finished for me, the tone of his voice distracted. "That's it."

Kalik rose from his chair too, beginning to pace against the stone floor. "Breaking into the temple would still be safer because we know there are no guards allowed inside. All three times she is away from the temple, she is heavily guarded."

"That may be. But at the market, she is less so," Arik argued. "When she goes to the palace, it is only her. The guards are not distracted, and so they watch over her closely. But when she is at the market, there is a crush of people. She has her sister priestesses with her. They all walk together—to show their faces, to offer their hope to the Dakkari who wish for it. The guards trail them, *lysi*, but there are many distractions."

"Many opportunities, you mean," Bakkia said, grinning.

Arik exchanged a look with him. "Absolutely."

"We would need to distract some of the guards," Ulli offered up. "And it may be better if one of us delivered your message to the *Laseta Kalliri* instead of you two. You need to stay hidden. Arik, for obvious reasons. And you, Kara, for even more obvious reasons."

I didn't take his words as an insult. He was simply stating a fact. That my appearance would draw the guards' notice.

Still, I glanced at Arik, seeing him working Ulli's words over in his mind.

"The message would have little weight coming from one of you," Arik finally said, shaking his head. "*Nik*, it must be me. Or Kara. Or both of us. The *Laseta Kalliri* cannot ignore a *Vorakkar's* presence just as she cannot dismiss Kara's, who speaks for the *Seta Kalliri*."

"What *is* the message?" Bakkia asked quietly.

"*You will find the answer in the heart of Dothik*," I answered. "That's what the *Seta Kalliri* told me to relay."

Bakkia's gaze cut to mine. Kiro and Vala exchanged a look. Kalik nodded, his spine straightening.

"What is it?" I asked curiously, sensing the change in the room.

"At least let us try to set up a meeting with her for you," Errana said, ignoring my question. "There is little risk in that. But much at risk if something goes wrong in the market."

"We run into the same problem," Arik argued. "We have one chance. If she dismisses you the moment you leave her sight or, worse yet, calls the guards, what then?"

"And if the *Dothikkar* discovers that you are in *Dothik* once more, what then?" Errana hissed.

"He cannot very well execute me in public, now can he?" Arik asked her, flashing her a disarming grin. His words made my belly turn to ice. "Even he wouldn't dare, or he'd have riots in the streets."

Then his grin died.

"Maybe he should know I'm here. Maybe I can be the distraction we need in the market, giving Kara enough time to speak with the priestess."

"*Nik,*" I said immediately, rounding on him with wide eyes. He wanted to announce his presence in *Dothik* when we were taking all these pains to try to hide it? "Are you out of your mind?"

Bakkia grunted. "I have to agree with the *kalles* on this one. That is out of the question."

Arik's nostrils flared. "Then you better think up another distraction that will take the guards' eyes off a dozen priestesses during a busy market day. There won't be many, I assure you."

"Leave that to us," Kiro said, inclining his head to Arik. "We will give you enough time to speak with her. Just make it fast."

"You know I don't like unknowns," Arik told him, spearing him with a long look before he turned his gaze to Vala. "You know I don't like it when plans are made in the dark and left unspoken."

Out of the corner of my eye, I saw Bakkia shift. There was a sudden tension within the room, one I didn't understand. One I didn't think Errana or Ulli understood either because I saw them shoot puzzled expressions at one another.

Kiro shielded his sudden stillness by leaning back in his chair, his posture open, unguarded. Vala did the opposite. He leaned forward, clasping his palms together on the table.

"We will not fail you" was what Kiro said, inclining his head. "That I promise you. Have we ever before?"

Arik's jaw was tense and tight. When I reached underneath the table to touch the side of his leg, it felt like a tree trunk of stone beneath my fingertips.

"That remains to be seen," he murmured.

The muscles in his leg loosened. Some of the tension in the room faded, and I felt like I could breathe again when Arik shot Kiro a cool grin.

"You don't want to fail me? Then don't disappoint me."

CHAPTER 47

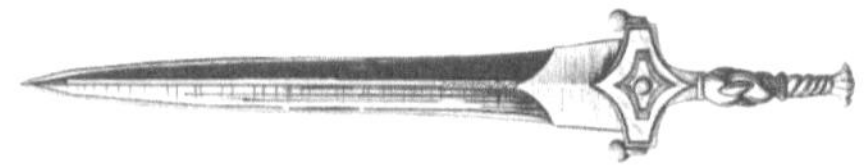

Off the Eleventh Limb, I pressed Kara back into the stone wall of the tavern, catching those golden, human eyes widening before I brought my mouth down to hers.

Despite the nerves and tension I felt threading through her, I heard her hitched sigh as her fingers dug into the tops of my shoulders. I didn't hold back my groan.

At the entrance of the alleyway, I heard a chuffed laugh and then retreating footsteps. I let out a sharp exhale and then backed off, tasting Kara on my lips.

"How much longer?" she whispered, her head tilting subtly to look at the entrance of the alley, where the Dakkari male had almost approached—before he'd realized the Limb was occupied.

"Any moment now," I told her, brushing the backs of my fingers against her cheekbone. I was still angry with myself. I shouldn't have let her come. I should've locked her up in my private quarters and had Bakkia stand outside her door to make sure she was safe. But against my better judgment, I included her among the plans.

Every glance her way, every time her head tipped up to peer at her surroundings had me tensing.

"Don't be upset," she whispered, leaning up on her tiptoes to brush one last kiss against my lips. "You know I need to speak with her. That's why I'm here."

She knew me well. Perhaps too well, the observant little *privixi*.

I could never deny her what she wanted. That should've frightened me. After today, I would need to think about what that meant. And what it meant going forward.

Now, however, was not the time. The sun was high over our heads and was just about to dip. The bustle of the market just outside the alley was at its peak. Shouts and laughter, vendors hawking their goods, a flurry of haggling and offended curses when someone got too greedy, the stomping of the *pyrokis* pulling carts. All familiar sounds.

Familiar scents, I thought too. Steamed, spiced *wrissan* meat wrapped in *ukki* leaves. The heady smell of burning hops from the tavern. The scent of *luria* and *seffi* blooms from the oil and bath salts vendor. The scent of piss in the alleyway. Of hot cobblestones during the warm season in *Dothik*.

A drop of sweat rolled down Kara's temple as if on cue. Errana had let her borrow a lighter cloak, one not suited for the harsh cold of the North Lands during the frost. Mine was made of the same material. Even still, it did nothing to help banish the sticky heat of the marketplace, made only hotter by the crush of bodies.

Outside the Limb, I caught eyes with Ulli. He lifted his chin as he walked down the main road, signaling that the priestesses were coming.

Taking in a deep breath, I looked back to Kara. "Never leave my side."

She flashed me a grin that had me wanting to push her cloak up her thighs. "I was never planning to."

Her words held a double edge. A meaning that we both

heard. It made my belly tighten with desire, with rightness…but it also made my chest ache because I knew better.

In a tense silence, we waited until I saw the first guard pass the alley, his Dakkari-steel armor clanking against the sword at his hip. Pressing Kara back into the stone, I angled my body to shield her from sight.

More guards came. Five in front of the procession. When I caught the billowing silky dress of the *Laseta Kalliri*—her head held high, a demure smile on her face, though the sharpness in her eyes had always given me pause—I murmured into Kara's ear, "She's here."

I felt her nod against my chest.

The *Laseta Kalliri* passed the alley. Then I saw the group of her priestesses behind her. All dressed in varying shades of blue and gray. Then five more guards took up the rear as they passed. Ten guards in total, not to count the ones that could dart here at a moment's notice if trouble rose.

"Let's go."

Kara clasped her hand in mine when I reached for it, and I pulled her down the narrow Limb, out onto the main road. Before us, I saw the backs of the five guards walking in a straight line behind the priestesses. Like a wall, boxing them in.

We trailed the procession, joining the group of Dakkari that had begun to follow too. Thankfully, since Kara was quite small, no one looked at her twice. It was me that got most of the strange looks shot my way. Which I would take gladly.

The market was shaped like a large oval in the center of the Western District. Vendors, with banners and tarps streaming overhead, lined the edges. Carts, laden with food and brew and baubles, stayed toward the inside, nearest the golden statue of Kakkari, which the *Dothikkar* had placed before I'd even been born. Her hand was outstretched, and I'd always imagined she was asking for gold. As a young boy, I'd always imagined climbing up her feet and legs and placing a coin into her hand, wondering what she'd give me in return.

It seemed appropriate for my father to place such a statue.

From behind the guards, I saw the five in the front begin to break away, striding toward various spots around the market. Despite their rigid postures, I watched from afar as they settled into familiar places, lulled into the comfort of another afternoon, another *normal* afternoon, one they'd experienced countless times before. Only one in particular seemed to be keeping an eye out for trouble, his head turning and scanning the growing crowds. The others...well, one went to a vendor selling gold jewelry. Another went to the cart selling steamed *wrissan*. The other two leaned against the pillars in between the archways of the marketplace, rolling their necks and crossing their arms across their chests. One stifled a yawn.

The five behind the priestesses, however, stayed in place, dutifully marching around the marketplace, circling Kakkari's statue, softening their pace when one of the priestesses stopped to pet a Dakkari boy on the head, his mother erupting into sudden, grateful tears at the gesture.

I felt Kara squeeze my hand, and then we were breaking away from the main crowd, stepping up to the base of Kakkari's statue in between two of the food carts, the vendors of which not paying us any mind.

Bakkia was stationed near the spice vendor, dipping his fingers into puddles of it, lifting the soft powders to his nose, though his eyes never left mine. Ulli and Errana were leaning back against the local inn. Two lovers, flirting and smiling, though Errana had her trusty dagger close and Ulli's gaze constantly flitted across the market to where Kiro and Vala were.

I couldn't see them from this vantage point. It was their responsibility to draw the guards' gazes. It was ours to secure the *Laseta Kalliri's* attention.

Judging from the noise, the excited chattering, I could pinpoint where the head priestess of *Dothik* was. She was just on the other side of us, beginning to walk around the statue. She'd be in view in just a few moments.

Kara's breath began to quicken. That was when I spied a guard—not one of the priestesses' guards, but one on market rotation—beginning to walk up the path toward us. He paused when he saw our cloaked figures, his eyes narrowing.

Vok.

Out of the corner of my eye, I saw Ulli reach his hand up. My jaw tightened, keeping my gaze on the corner where the priestesses would first appear. Waiting for that slippered foot, and then we would dart out.

My gaze went to the guard. He was striding toward us.

I straightened. Errana had seen him too. She was already making her way over to us, to intercept the guard before he could reach us, a determined gleam in her eyes.

A ripple of energy seemed to go through the market. A flurry of gasps and cries that relieved me because I thought, at first, that Kiro and Vala had succeeded in creating a distraction.

I was just about to step away from the statue when the sudden clattering of dozens of *pyrokis* across the cobblestones filled the marketplace.

My brows furrowed. I waited for the priestesses to appear, only they never did, and when my gaze went to Bakkia's, his lips were pressed, his scowl and the tension in his body alerting me that something was wrong. Very wrong. His gaze flitted to me, and he gave a subtle shake of his head.

"Come," I murmured to Kara. Errana had just reached the wayward guard, though his attention was directed at whatever was on the other side of the statue, and we took advantage of the brief distraction. Quickly, I pulled Kara away, rounding the road to see what the commotion was, my belly churning because the plan was not going smoothly. It never did. This was expected. We could—

I stilled on the Spine, the main road that stretched and ran through all of *Dothik*, and Kara's boots banged into the backs of mine.

A dozen *pyrokis* had flooded into the marketplace. Saddled mounts. Gleaming gold paint curling along the beasts' sides, and flapping golden banners with depictions of a familiar crest.

"*Vok*," I growled under my breath, my spine going ramrod straight. My body felt like it'd been struck with lightning. Every vein in my body felt electrified, a current of hatred and disgust flowing hot and wild.

The *Dothikkar* himself was sitting astride the largest of the *pyroki*.

All gleaming dark hair, neatly plaited down his back. Golden armor adorning his shoulders and chest, though it did little to conceal the roundness of his belly or how his spine hunched with its weight. What use did he have for armor? He'd never wielded a sword in his life. It was all for show, and he grinned down at the gathering crowd, though they could get no closer to the *Dothikkar* since the guards had jumped off their *pyrokis* and made a circle around him, swords drawn.

He's out of his palace was my first thought. *Out in the open.*

"Is that..." Kara's voice trailed off because she already knew.

As if on instinct, my gaze zeroed in on the place that had no armor, that left him vulnerable. His throat. It would be so simple. It could happen so fast, before anyone ever noticed me coming. I could reach him before his guards ever even noticed me.

I let out a low growl of frustration.

Nik.

Because then that would leave Kara vulnerable. It would leave her unguarded.

And I refused to give in to my baser instincts, no matter how much I wanted to see his hot blood run in the streets of *Dothik*. No matter how much I wanted revenge for my mother's murder and for Bodin's, for the injustices against the city I loved.

My gaze never left the *Dothikkar's* face. I tried to look for similarities between us. Unfortunately, there were many. The dark, straight slash of his brows. The way his jaw was cut into a square. The slope of his nose.

Things that were familiar to me because they were also *mine*.

The *Laseta Kalliri* stepped toward the *Dothikkar*, her face formed in a pleased, surprised grin.

"What brings you from the palace this afternoon, *Dothikkar*? Would you like to join us for our walk?" she asked him, her voice soothing, though it only made my hackles rise.

The plan was *vokked*.

Truly *vokked*.

I cut a look to Bakkia and shook my head. I flagged down Ulli and Errana, giving them the signal to return to our district. We would have to try tomorrow. Or we would have to break into the temple tonight.

We needed to get out of the marketplace before any of us were caught, especially with the *Dothikkar* here.

Turning, I went to give the same signal to Kiro and Vala.

Only my blood ran cold when I saw the look in Kiro's eyes, which were pinned to the *Dothikkar*. His hand was reaching into the slip pocket on the side of his trews, where I knew he kept his dagger on a strap at his thigh.

I stepped forward, dropping Kara's hand for the first time. Kiro and Vala were closest to the *Dothikkar* out of all of us. But it was Kiro who actually stepped forward. It was Kiro whose gaze connected with mine, his expression determined, his brow set in a solid line of resolve. Vala reached for him when he realized what was happening. With unsurprising swiftness, Kiro elbowed his friend right in the nose, Vala's head snapping back, and Kiro took advantage of the brief distraction.

It was Kiro who'd had his sister brutally taken from him. Assaulted, raped, and murdered by the *Dothikkar's* own patrol guards, whose trial the *Dothikkar* himself dismissed with a wave of his hand and a sickening smile, as if the life of a Southern District seamstress didn't matter.

He had reason to hate the *Dothikkar* and every corrupt being that the *Dothikkar* protected with his power just as much as I did.

And for a moment, I hesitated.

I hesitated as I watched him advance, snaking through the growing crowd, pushing his way closer and closer.

For a moment, I wondered if I had any right to take Kiro's vengeance away from him.

But it would cost Kiro his life if he succeeded.

That I knew with absolute certainty, and so I jerked my head over my shoulder and met Errana's gaze. She sprinted over, her boots hitting the cobblestones.

"Take her back," I growled, pushing Kara into her arms. "*Now.* And keep her safe."

"*Lysi,*" Errana said, and she took Kara's arm, already pulling her away.

"*Nik,*" Kara protested. "What are you—"

"*Go, saila,*" I hissed, darting forward to press a kiss to her lips to silence the argument perched on her tongue. "I'll come back to you soon. I promise."

Her wide eyes were panicked, but I broke her gaze, turning around swiftly to track Kiro in the crowd. My belly tightened when I saw he was close to the circular ring the guards made around the *Dothikkar.* He was edging his way to the small gap between two guards.

"*Vok,* Kiro," I growled under my breath, seeing Bakkia match my movements and my pace as I strode toward the crowd. He could reach Kiro from the other side if he was quick enough. But I feared we were running out of time. That moment of hesitation had cost me. "*Nik.*"

I didn't care about the looks shot my way as I lunged through the crowd. I didn't hear the curses at my back when I trod on toes. All I cared about was reaching my friend, my brother before he made the biggest mistake of his life. One that would likely cost him his own.

But I had only just reached the middle of the crowd when I saw Kiro draw out his dagger. Bakkia wasn't close. He couldn't reach him. Vala had begun to close in from the north side, blood streaming from his nostrils, but Kiro had weaved his way through the crush of bodies expertly.

With dawning realization, I knew I would see my friend die today if I didn't do something soon.

Just as I knew I wouldn't reach him in time.

So I stopped in the middle of the crowd and threw back my hood, ignoring the ripple of shocked murmurs when the Dakkari around me finally got a good look at my face.

"*Dothikkar!*" I bellowed out.

And I watched as my father's gaze zeroed in on mine.

CHAPTER 48

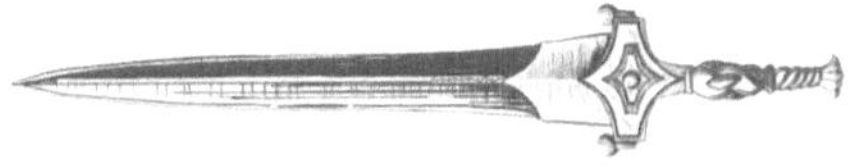

The damn fool still went for it.

The moment that the *Dothikkar* shifted on his *pyroki* to meet my gaze, I saw Kiro leap for him, taking advantage of his turned back and the utter shock of the guards at my presence.

"*Nik,*" I growled, dread curling in my belly.

Shouts from the guards erupted immediately. A lunging of bodies hurtled toward Kiro as alarmed cries and startled screams erupted from the crowd and they began to scatter. The priestesses' own guards closed ranks on them, shuffling them from the center of the action, and my gaze went to Kiro, to the *Dothikkar*, to the *Laseta Kalliri*.

The *Laseta Kalliri,* whose icy red gaze was on mine, seemingly unalarmed by the assassination attempt that was unfolding right before her very eyes. There was *knowing* in those eyes, and I couldn't stand to see it. Not right now.

I broke her gaze, pushing forward when I saw Kiro tackled to the ground, his pained cry ringing through the market, just as I heard a bone snap and a dagger clatter to the cobblestone.

The guards closed around the *Dothikkar,* who huddled in the seat of his *pyroki*.

And when I pushed forward—the crowd easily parting for me despite their sudden shock—I saw that a guard was kneeling on Kiro's back, his cheek pressed to the ground, a sword at his jugular. My friend's dark eyes were resigned, his jaw ticking with his failure. And when they met mine, they closed, as if he couldn't bear to see my disappointment. My anger.

Out of the corner of my eye, I saw Vala and Bakkia poised on the edge of the circle, waiting for a signal from me. To do anything. To do anything at all.

Instead, I met their eyes quickly and shook my head, telling them to stand down. Telling them to *disappear*.

Vala did as he was told, melting back into the crowd.

But Bakkia...

Bakkia stood his ground, crossing his arms over his chest, still much too close to the *Dothikkar* and his guards for my comfort.

One of the guards helped the *Dothikkar* off the back of his *pyroki*, who seemed to realize he was more of a target perched up so high.

Striding forward, I kept my eyes on my father. Some of the guards that surrounded him dropped their heads at my approach, but not all of them.

The *Dothikkar* ignored my presence at first. His booted feet approached Kiro. He squatted to look my companion in the eye.

Kiro struggled, and I heard him spit. The *Dothikkar* reared back, nearly toppling over from the unexpected action, but one of the guards caught him and helped to haul him up.

"You've just ensured your own execution," the *Dothikkar* hissed under his breath when he stood, his cheeks darkening with anger and disbelief. "How dare you!"

Stepping forward, I said, "Release him to me."

The *Dothikkar's* gaze flared, fire in his eyes. Hatred too.

"Never," the *Dothikkar* replied, his eyes narrowing on me.

We hadn't been this close to one another since the end of my *Vorakkar* Trials. When I'd called him a murderer and given him a cold grin. When his gaze flitted to one of his guards and then to the growing crowd, I wondered if he really *would* try to have me killed right there and then. "He tried to assassinate me. And now I know he's one of *yours*. What have you to say about that? Was he doing it under your orders?"

A rush of murmurs came from behind me.

"You insult me, *Dothikkar*," I said clearly and easily. Lifting my hands, I continued, "Did I not take the vow to protect and serve *Dothik* when you placed these on my wrists?"

The *Dothikkar's* lips pressed. His gaze flitted away from mine, as if he couldn't bear to look at me. I wondered if I looked more like my mother than he was comfortable with.

"He's a young, misguided fool," I said gruffly, my fists lowering, squeezing at my sides. "One that will be punished accordingly, but not in your dungeons. For I know all too well what happens there."

His nostrils flared at my softly murmured barb.

For a breathless moment, I actually thought that the *Dothikkar* would release Kiro. I actually thought that he'd give the order to let him up.

But then he smiled, cutting and familiar. The tension in the circle of the guards rose. My gaze flitted to Bakkia once, and I saw him slowly edging his way closer.

"We can negotiate his release at the palace," the *Dothikkar* said, his voice rising so that the crowd could hear.

My jaw clenched. Because I knew the moment he got me there, I would be trapped. He wanted this to happen away from hundreds of eyes. He couldn't very well execute a *Vorakkar*—and especially not *me*—in the streets of *Dothik*, and he knew it. I knew it. But he could do it privately.

"*Nik,*" came Kiro's voice, and he was struggling against the guard at his body. "Serok, *nik!*"

Kiro was my responsibility. He always had been. Everyone under my protection was, and I couldn't turn my back on him. I couldn't have any more blood on my hands.

"Very well," I murmured to the *Dothikkar*, meeting my father's eyes and watching them gleam. "We will settle this matter privately. In your grand hall. And then we will speak about the fog that is spreading toward *Dothik*."

At my words, the rush of voices came and the *Dothikkar* narrowed his eyes, displeased at my announcement. *Dothik* didn't know much about the fog. They'd been kept in the dark, deliberately. Only the hordes and the *saruks* truly knew the dangers. And those in the city who knew about the fog had heard it from friends and family on the wildlands, whose messages had journeyed all the way to *Dothik*.

My gaze flitted to the *Laseta Kalliri*.

"For I am in *Dothik* to try to stop it. What we need to stop it is here. In the Heart of *Dothik*. The *Seta Kalliri* tasked me with this."

Those red eyes sparked, and the *Laseta Kalliri's* gaze shifted. Her shoulders drew down, subtle shifts in her body that told me she understood. Looking at her up close gave me pause, however. The lines of her face familiar.

The *Dothikkar* gestured at one of his guards, who stepped forward. His expression was one of discomfort as he said, "This way, *Vorakkar*."

I gave the guard a cool look. "I have matters to attend to first," I told him. My gaze went to my father, who had pasted on a small, tight smile. "I will come to the palace at nightfall."

"Then I cannot guarantee what decisions are made for your friend here," the *Dothikkar* said quietly, stepping toward me. His voice was lowered so the crowd could not hear. "You come with us now. Or I will have him killed the moment we step into the dungeons."

I kept my expression neutral. Over the *Dothikkar's* shoulder,

I spied Bakkia, his gaze thunderous. But I spied the dawning realization there too, the sudden need. He began to move. Away from the crowd, keeping toward the outskirts nearer to the vendors. Away from me.

Good.

I tracked him with my gaze, watching him dart around the Dakkari who watched the scene with rapt fascination and glee. Closer and closer he drew to the *Laseta Kalliri*. The guards were distracted. No one paid him any mind. We'd needed a distraction, and we'd found one.

When the *Dothikkar* frowned and looked toward where my attentions were directed, I said, "Let's make this quick."

Bakkia was within two arms' length of the *Laseta Kalliri*. From the corner of my eye, I watched his head duck, his lips move. Her gaze dropped to the ground as Bakkia spoke to her. And then he was gone, melting back into the crowd as one of the priestesses' guards turned in place, frowning, hearing something that was no longer there.

The *Dothikkar* clapped me on the shoulder, grinning.

"What enjoyments we will have this night," he said loudly, keeping up appearances for the crowd. "And then tomorrow when you return to the wildlands, we will drink in your honor. For the glory of *Dothik*."

Instead of the merriment the *Dothikkar* expected from the crowd, he was met with unease and hushed murmurs. Already setting up the narrative for my disappearance, was he? In a week, he'd make the announcement that I'd been killed in an *ungira* or *bveri* attack as I rode back to my horde.

I grinned at the *Dothikkar*. And because I had nothing to lose—because I was backed into a corner with no options left— I corrected, "For the glory of Dakkar, *Pattar*."

Father.

Only the Dakkari in the front heard my response, but I heard the swift ripples of *knowing* as my words made their way through the crowd. Many heard the rumors in *Dothik*. They had heard them for years, especially in my district. But this was the first time I'd actually confirmed it. And so publicly at that.

And the words of a *Vorakkar*? They mattered. They held weight. I'd confirmed my birthright before the *Dothikkar,* and all of *Dothik* would know come morning. Perhaps even tonight. It would wind its way through taverns and brothels, through the forges in the Northern District, through the highborn homes in the West.

"For the glory of Dakkar, *Pattar,*" I repeated softly, holding his gaze.

The *Dothikkar's* face went purple. His eyes bugged out in shock, as if he'd never expected me to say *that* word. As if he'd never expected me to *dare* to say it.

But that was the thing. When someone had nothing else to lose, then they were unpredictable. Like a caged beast who was finally let free. And if he thought I'd go to my death quietly... well, he had another thing coming.

"I look forward to returning to my home," I said with a grin. "My *true* home. Where I always knew I'd end up. My *lomma* knew it too, didn't she?"

"Take him," the *Dothikkar* hissed at one of his guards, who came forward again. This time, he boldly gripped over my *Vorakkar* cuffs, and I allowed it. I turned, briefly meeting the *Laseta Kalliri's* gaze before I looked south.

My jaw clenched.

Kara stood there, Errana's arm around her waist with Ulli at her side. Underneath her hood, I saw her eyes were watery with tears, even from this distance. Because she knew what this meant too?

As we began to march toward the *Dothikkar's* palace, I held her eyes until I could see them no more.

CHAPTER 49

I stared at my hands pressed against the table in the meeting room of Arik's home, focusing on my breath. Where we'd been earlier this morning...before everything changed.

Kalik was pacing, though he hadn't seen what happened in the marketplace. He'd been on patrol around the Western District in case any trouble erupted on the outskirts. When Ulli told him what had happened, he hadn't said a single word. He'd exchanged a single look with Bakkia, who'd been brooding in the corner since our arrival, and then he'd begun to pace.

"*Vok*," Vala whispered. His head was dropped, his forehead pressed into the wood of the table. "*Vok.*"

He sounded tired. He sounded close to tears.

Errana's voice sounded, cutting through the thick silence.

"Do you think she'll come?" she asked. "Truly?"

The *Laseta Kalliri*.

"You shouldn't have done that," Ulli hissed again, unable to keep quiet about his opinions on what Bakkia had done, giving the *Laseta Kalliri* the stronghold's location. "Exposing us like that! What if she's loyal to the *Dothikkar*? You saw the way she smiled at him!"

"The *Seta Kalliri* has her loyalties," I said softly. "Not the *Dothikkar*."

Ulli scoffed. "And how do *you* know that? Because the *Seta Kalliri* has been in the North Lands for over three decades now. The *Laseta Kalliri* was just a girl when she left here. What would you know about her loyalties besides what your *kalloma* told you?"

"Ulli," Errana said quietly, shaking her head subtly. "Don't."

"You cannot understand the bond between the priestesses," I argued softly, meeting his eyes. "But I have seen it all my life. It is as strong as blood."

But Ulli's nostrils were flared. He glared at me from across the room. His expression made me want to shrink, but I held that gaze, my spine straightening.

"You don't seem all that upset that Serok is gone," Ulli commented, his eyes narrowing on me. "I haven't trusted you since the moment I saw you. What's your plan, exactly? Why are you *here?*"

"Enough," Bakkia growled out, stepping forward even as Ulli's words chilled my heart. "Ulli, enough. She is *his.* You don't speak to her that way."

Ulli scoffed, and I swallowed the sudden lump in my throat.

"I love him."

The soft confession stilled the entire room as five pairs of eyes darted to me.

"So do not assume that I do not fear for him," I told Ulli, my eyes filling with tears for the hundredth time since the marketplace. "Because I know that they can hurt him. I know that he is at the *Dothikkar's* mercy tonight, and I know how much that will *cut* him."

"He could die," Ulli hissed. "The *Dothikkar* won't just hurt him, *kalles.* He will kill him!"

"*Nik,*" I said softly, shaking my head. "He will not die. Not tonight. And hopefully not for a very long time."

"How can you be so sure?"

Instead of Ulli, the question came from Kalik. The first time he'd spoken. He'd stopped in his pacing to regard me. To give me his full attention.

"Because there is still something that has not come to pass," I told him. "And it will. It will happen in the coming months. He will be there. Just as you will be." I turned my gaze to Bakkia, to Errana, Ulli too. "As will all of you. Vala, I'm not certain about. He was not in my vision."

Ulli blew out a sharp breath. "Your vision. *Vok.* Now we have a truth sayer on our hands."

His derision was palpable.

"Believe me if you want. Or don't," I told Ulli. "But he will not die tonight. That does not mean we should not try to help him. And Kiro."

"Tell me something about my future, then," Ulli said, lifting his chin. "Tell me something if you wish for me to believe you."

A flurry of anger went through me, but I breathed through it. Years of patience and managing my emotions got me through that single moment.

"I don't have to," I informed him, keeping my words clipped and even as I held his eyes. "That is not the way it works, despite what your *truth sayers* here in *Dothik* tell you in the streets."

Ulli's lips were pressed into a slim line as he stared me down. Errana finally stepped between us, sliding her hands up his arms. "Enough," she whispered to him. "Arik believes her. *Arik.* And you know how he feels about such things. So I believe her too."

It was Errana's words that finally made him blow out a swift breath. It took him long moments, but he finally inclined his head in a sharp nod, his jaw ticking.

"It's growing late," Kalik noted, cutting through the tense silence. "We're losing sunlight every moment. We need to make a decision and soon. We might not be able to wait around on the priestess, even if she *does* come. We can have the word sent out into the streets. They will come for him."

Who is "they"? I wondered.

"Is there a way to get into the palace without being noticed?" I asked. "You must've discussed it with him before."

"We can walk up to the front gates," Ulli said. "I'm sure they'd let us right in."

If he expected me to rise to the barb, then he would be disappointed. I met his eyes. "If it comes to it, then I *will* walk right up the gates and let them see my face. If it means bypassing the guards and getting into the *Dothikkar's* halls quicker, then I will. Make no mistake about that."

Ulli rolled his neck, lowering his eyes from my face.

"*Nik,*" Bakkia growled out. "Arik would have our heads."

"There is one path," Kalik said, sighing, approaching the table. "But if you thought the southern tunnels were covered in filth, you should see these."

I would swim through muck and excrement if it meant reaching Arik. If it meant having him in my arms tonight, knowing that he was safe.

"Where?" I asked.

"It's deep underground," Kalik started, going to a cabinet on the wall and shuffling through a stack of parchment. He floated a sheet of it down onto the table, schematics drawn in green ink.

"This is...this is the palace?" I asked, shifting forward, my eyes tracing the bold lines.

"The dungeons," Kalik corrected, his fingers tracing a particular shaft. "Here. It's...it's how they dispose of the bodies. They transport them down here because it leads out into the Northern District where they can burn them. That's where a lot of the Dakkari steel is processed. They have access to the forges."

I shuddered, muted horror making it hard to swallow. They *burned* the bodies here? They didn't bury them?

"We know Kiro will be in the dungeons," Kalik continued. "Serok would want him out first. Where they will keep *him*, however...I'm not certain. I would think the *Dothikkar* would want him close. Just in case."

"That's not much of a plan," I whispered. "Get Kiro out and wander the palace until we find him. Dodging countless guards and trying not to get taken to the dungeons ourselves."

Kalik knew it too. They all did. It was why everyone was so quiet. Because they all knew we were *vokked*.

"We'll send out the word," Bakkia finally said. A breath whistled through Vala. "We will have our supporters flood the gates. We can have hundreds, if not thousands there by night-fall. It will be a distraction, keeping the guards' attention on the western courtyard."

"You can do that?" I asked, heart ticking up in relief. "They will answer your call?"

"They will answer *his* call," Bakkia said.

"Keeping the guards' attention on the western courtyard will be useful to get Kiro out," Kalik cut in. "But not Serok. How will we find him?"

I blew out a breath. Because I knew what I had to do, the answer coming to me swiftly.

"I have to go in alone," I said.

"*Neffar?*" Bakkia huffed. "*Nik.* Like I said—"

"He's not here," I cut in. "And this is *my* choice. I'll try to speak with the *Dothikkar* while you get Kiro out and you search for Arik. If I tell him that the *Seta Kalliri* sent me with a message specifically for him, it might offer me some protection."

"And being a *Vorakkar* should've offered Arik protection too, *kalles*," Bakkia argued.

Just then, a knock sounded.

We all froze.

It was faint, coming from down the hall. The front door of Arik's stronghold.

Bakkia was out of the room before we could take another breath. As if he set all of us into motion, we raced after him, my heart thudding a thousand times a minute, hoping and praying to Kakkari that this was what we needed. That this was what we had hoped for.

We skidded into the entryway just as Bakkia opened the door.

And there, on the front steps of Arik's home was a tall, cloaked figure. Standing alone, not a soul in sight behind her.

When she lifted her gaze, her red eyes burned into ours.

The *Laseta Kalliri*.

She'd come.

Her eyes connected with mine, as if pulled.

There was a peculiar expression that came over her features, one of longing, of *memory*.

My heart began to beat faster just as my brow furrowed. Like my body knew something my mind did not.

"Kara," she murmured.

My heart stopped entirely as she stepped inside.

"It is like seeing him again," she said, reaching out her hand and pressing it to my cheek. A jolt of power raced through me. Her voice was strange. Not present. She was far away, lost. "Your soul even *feels* like his. Just as she said."

"*Neffar?*" I breathed.

"But there is no time for memory now," the *Laseta Kalliri* said next, shaking her head swiftly, shaking off the tangle of threads in her mind.

"*Nik*, what did you mean?" I said quickly, catching her hand. All my life I'd been kept in the dark. Something *real* was here. Right in front of me. I needed to know what it was.

"We are close," she said, smoothing her hand over mine.

"Very close. And I know that he has risked much for this. You all have. As have we."

Now I understood Arik's frustration. He'd said something about the priestesses only speaking in riddles. I understood now. But I also understood what it was like living with priestesses. They saw the world in a different way. Like pieces of a puzzle that needed to be fitted into place.

People like my *kalloma*. People like me, who saw things that others could not.

Like the *Laseta Kalliri* before me. I felt the undercurrents of her power like they were tied to me the moment she touched my skin. A buzzing built up in my veins, waiting for a conduit to be unleashed. Her?

I didn't understand it. I didn't understand what was happening, but I had the strangest sensation that my *kalloma* had kept something very important from me. Perhaps her biggest secret of all, and she'd had many over the years.

"You know me," I breathed. It wasn't a question. It was a fact.

"*Lysi*," the *Laseta Kalliri* said. Easily, she said, "You are my blood. And blood recognizes blood, does it not? Can you not feel it, Kara? Because I can."

The entryway seemed to sway under my feet. I reached a hand out to the wall next to me, and I felt another hand close around my arm. Bakkia's. Strong and warm. I could feel his wariness even now as he pulled me closer to him, away from the *Laseta Kalliri's* grip.

"And you will need to feel it," the *Laseta Kalliri* continued, "to take what will be yours."

My brow furrowed. I shook my head. I didn't understand what she was implying. "My...my mother was human. A *vekkiri*."

"So she was," the *Laseta Kalliri* said, giving me a serene

smile that didn't quite match the sharpness in her gaze. "But it was my brother who you were born from too."

Her...brother?

The *darukkar* of a horde? The *darukkar*—the only thing I'd ever known about him—who fell in love with a human female?

A sharp prick came at my temple, and I squeezed my eyes shut at the sudden intrusion.

"Enough for now," she finally said. Her eyes glowed in the darkness. "We will speak later. When the *Dothikkar* is dead."

CHAPTER 50

"Once, I told the *Dothikkar* that a messenger would come to him from the *orala sa'kilan*," the *Laseta Kalliri* told me as we rode in the boxed carriage being pulled by two *pyrokis*. Toward the *Dothikkar's* palace. "That she would take her rightful place here in *Dothik* at the king's side. And that *Dothik* would flourish for it."

"A seed," I whispered. "Planted in his mind."

"*Lysi,*" she said, reaching over to grab my hand and squeezing. Her palm was warm, whereas mine felt clammy and damp. "But it may also be a truth. I did not lie to him. I did see it."

"Me?" I wanted to know.

Her gaze was frightening, but I didn't feel the urge to shrink away from it. "*Lysi.*"

"I—I always thought my gift from Kakkari was because of my mother's sacrifice," I confessed. "I held on to so much guilt, thinking that she died trying to make me strong."

"She did," the *Laseta Kalliri* said, making my heart freeze in my chest. "She gave you *her* strength. You would have already been born with a gift. In our bloodline, the possibility is strong, even likely. But Beth made yours even stronger. Visions of a certain future...I could not believe it when the *Seta Kalliri* told me that."

Beth?

Had that been my mother's given name? It was strange to think I'd never known it. Hearing her name now made me want to smile. It also made me want to cry.

"They may be wrong," I told her, swallowing the thick lump in my throat. "I have them very rarely."

"Because you choose *not* to see them."

My brow furrowed.

"When we get to the palace," she told me, switching the topic of conversation so swiftly, in a way that reminded me of Arik, "do not speak. Keep your hood up and your face to the ground. Until we reach the *Dothikkar*. But I will make sure we are alone."

"And Serok?" I asked, not using his given name, even in front of the *Laseta Kalliri*. I didn't think I'd even use it in front of *Kalloma*.

Her gaze was rapt. "Loyal to him, *rei kassiri*? I said my vision *might* be a truth. Not that it was a certainty. Only *you* have the power to say for certain."

"*Neffar?*"

She'd told me I'd be at the king's side...but had she meant *Arik's?*

"There are other paths for you. Others that the *Seta Kalliri* has seen."

"Death," I told her. "That was one of the paths she saw for me. Long and endless."

"There is life too," my aunt told me. "But you know that already."

I stilled, thinking of the swell of my belly in my vision.

"And hurt. And pain," she continued. Then she sighed, turning her face to peer out the tinted windows of the boxed carriage. "Love is a terrible thing. Power and security are what you should strive for instead. It is what we have worked toward."

"I don't believe that," I told her, shaking my head.

Her smile was serene. Her eyes were unfocused for a brief moment. "You are your father's daughter. He believed in love too. Look where it got him."

A swell of tears stung my eyes, but I blinked them back.

"The *Seta Kalliri* too, however briefly," came the soft comment. "Then she saw her true purpose."

"How does she fit into all of this?" I wanted to know, stroking through the tuft of hair at the end of my tail. It was tangled and dirtied from the marketplace, and I had only just noticed, my mind elsewhere, my mind with *Arik*. "That's what I don't understand."

"Your *kalloma* loved my brother too. For a very long time, since they were children," she informed me.

"*Neffar?*" I asked, shocked. My brow furrowed. I could not imagine my *kalloma* in love, not like what I felt for Arik. It felt strange. It felt like I didn't know her at all.

"My brother wanted her to forsake her duties. To leave *Dothik*. To live a freer life, away from the greed and from the responsibility, out on the wildlands. She nearly agreed."

"I cannot imagine that," I confessed quietly, my heart twisting in my chest because I knew what her decision had been. How it must've *hurt*.

"And in the end, she chose power over him. Because she understood that long after she was gone from this world, her influence would still be felt on Dakkar. That is true immortality. No one would remember her love. But they would remember that she was the *Seta Kalliri* that helped propel Dakkar into a new future," the *Laseta Kalliri* told me. Sighing softly, she said, "And then she felt love again. In you. For the child that she could have had with my brother. For she loved his child as if it was her own. She felt him again in you."

I looked out the window, tears beginning to roll down my cheeks, watching the buildings pass me by without truly seeing them. It was dark in the streets, the windows glowing golden, but I thought there were many Dakkari out that night, beginning to stream into the streets, following our carriage. They were striding along the streets, faces drawn. Arik's supporters. They were coming.

My heart felt like a battered thing as I listened to what she was telling me.

Was that why *Kalloma* had never wanted to speak of my mother? Because my mother's love for my father reminded her of everything she'd given up? Everything she'd sacrificed?

And for what?

As if reading my thoughts, the *Laseta Kalliri* said, "We want what your *Vorakkar* wants. A new future. We have seen the way the city has rotted from the inside out. We want to see it restored again."

"And is that all you want?" I asked. It wasn't that I didn't *trust* the *Laseta Kalliri*. She was telling me the truth. It was that there was something deeper here. An undercurrent that had gone unspoken.

"We want a seat at the *Dothikkar's* table," she told me. "To rule not beneath him but beside him. We do not want to be cast aside any longer. We have been the foundation of this city since its birth. Priestesses have helped shape *Dothik* since Bekkar's rule. But do you know of anything that we have done? Priestesses like Tanniva, who is painted no better than a whore within the tomes? When it was she that helped unite the hordes when they tried to ride against the capital? There would be no *Dothik* without her. And she went to her grave disgraced. Or Jevna, who stopped a war between the Northern District and the Western District? The city nearly starved. But have you ever heard her name?"

"*Nik,*" I whispered. "I have not."

The *Laseta Kalliri* said, "We are done living in the shadows of this city. We want to claim our rightful place in *Dothik's* history."

"He does not trust the priestesses," I told her softly.

She smiled. "He does not have to trust us to work with us. He wants a throne? We will secure it for him. But it does not come freely."

"Nothing ever does," I recited, hearing Arik's voice in my mind.

It was one of the first things he'd ever taught me. That everything had a price. He was born in *Dothik*. He knew the costs of this place better than most. Perhaps he *would* work with the priestesses at his side.

"As for your first question," she murmured, craning her head at an angle to see how close we were to the palace, "I will make sure your *Vorakkar* is in the room when we meet with the *Dothikkar*."

Relief went through me.

"Let me handle him," the *Laseta Kalliri* said, her voice serene, turning in her seat toward me, reaching a hand out to smooth over my cheek. "No matter what happens, Kara, know that tonight is the beginning. He will take his rightful place just as he was always meant to. Just as his mother always prayed for. Just as you have foreseen. And when he is on the throne, we will rise too."

"And how do I play into all of this?"

Because there must be a reason that the *Laseta Kalliri* came to us tonight. Not just because I was her brother's child and I needed her help. There was a price, wasn't there?

There was more at work here. Something I wasn't understanding.

"You are the most fortunate of us all, *rei kassiri*," the *Laseta Kalliri* said. "Because you do not have to choose. You will not have to choose between love and duty. Not like your *kalloma*. Or your birth mother. Or your father."

My breath hitched.

"For you, love and duty are one and the same," she said quietly. "Love for your king and duty to your blood."

But her words didn't quell the restlessness squirming in my belly.

Her words made it worse.

"We only came to *Dothik* for the heartstone," I whispered, my voice taking on a strange, wistful tone. Through the walls of the carriage, I heard voices. A rush of voices that began to swell and swell. I heard distant shouting. The clanging of metal.

The *Laseta Kalliri* laughed. "And does that not seem like ages ago, *rei kassiri*? We will deal with the fog in time. We *must* secure *Dothik* first. As you can see."

She tilted her face, gesturing out the window.

A banging came on the carriage window, and I jumped. Peering out, I saw hands and fists beating at the glass. Faces pressed closer, and I turned my head away when Dakkari began to shout, in fear that they would see me.

"They are his?" I asked, knowing blooming in my belly.

"*Lysi*," the *Laseta Kalliri* said simply as she peered out the window. "Your *Vorakkar* has connections throughout this entire city. He has entire districts in his pocket. What happened in the marketplace is now news to all of *Dothik*. They have come for him."

My lips parted. Another bang came on the window, and from the outside of the carriage I heard the two guards on the *pyrokis* yelling, telling them to get back. More guards, the ones riding behind our transport, moved to the sides, physically pushing the Dakkari back from the carriage.

Moments later, I saw wide Dakkari-steel gates. Thick columns and impenetrable strength. And then I saw a crush of bodies as we continued to move forward, though our progress was slow and stilted. The noise in the carriage got so loud I nearly covered my ears.

The banging on our windows stopped the moment we rolled through the gates, and I heard a loud *boom* when they closed behind us. But it didn't stop the sea of shouts and voices, so many that I couldn't understand what they were saying.

The *Laseta Kalliri* secured my hood in place.

Strangely, I found that I wasn't nervous. All I wanted was to reach Arik. I would face anything to reach him.

When a guard opened our door, I lowered my face and hopped down to the cobblestones, wondering if Bakkia, Kalik, Errana, Ulli, and Vala were right beneath my feet, working their way toward the dungeons.

I couldn't help but peer past the carriage. My breath hitched. What I saw was striking. Dakkari faces were pressed to the gates of the palace. Hundreds of faces, hundreds of eyes. Shouts rose to the sky, a rumbling thunder.

"We want our king!"

"We want our king!"

What had happened in the marketplace was merely the first ripple. This was the storm that that ripple had *created*. Hundreds and hundreds of Dakkari beating at the *Dothikkar's* gates. This was the power that Arik wielded. This was what he had built, the son of a rejected highborn female, the son who'd been born in the back room of a tavern—Bakkia's tavern— who'd only known struggle and sacrifice his entire life.

"We want our king!"

Before me, the palace of the *Dothikkar* was shimmering and beautiful. Mesmerizing in its sheer breadth and opulence. Glittering turrets rose to the sky, reminding me of the *orala sa'kilan*. There was a grand golden staircase leading up to the entrance of the palace.

A place I'd always wanted to see. And now...it made nausea curl in my belly just looking at it.

Because Arik was somewhere inside those gilded halls.

Or in the dungeons, deep underground.

Guards were rushing out of the palace and running along the watch towers high above the growing crowd. The surge of bodies was growing. And I'd seen the Dakkari streaming this way as we traveled in the carriage. More would join as the night fell. I wondered if the others could hear the cries, even deep underground.

"Get back from the gates!" one frustrated guard yelled, jabbing through the slats of metal with the hilt of his sword. A pained moan met his words. "*Get back now!*"

"Kara," the *Laseta Kalliri* said. "Come now."

When the crowd saw the priestess step from the carriage, they went even more wild.

"*Laseta Kalliri! Laseta Kalliri!*" they cried. "*Free our king! Free our king!*"

The High Priestess of *Dothik*, however, paid them no mind. She faced forward, drawing me near, and we set into motion, beginning to ascend the staircase with her name on the tongues of hundreds behind us.

At the top, the *Laseta Kalliri* told the frazzled-looking guard, "Tell the *Dothikkar* there is a messenger here from the *orala sa'k-ilan*. The *Vorakkar* of Rath Serok must also be in attendance to hear the message."

"*Laseta Kalliri*...the *Dothikkar* and the *Vorakkar* are occupied currently. And now we have the breach at the gates. If you'll wait in the—"

"*Nik,*" came her sharp tone. "Now."

Stunned silence came from the guard, and I studied the marble at my feet, similar in color to the entryway of Arik's home. My heart was racing in my chest. It seemed to swell with the raucous cries behind me, with the violence of the banging steel that only seemed to get louder and louder.

"Have you informed him about the crowd forming?" the

Laseta Kalliri demanded, her face expressionless as she regarded the male in front of her.

"*Nik*, we...we thought we could handle it."

"And can you?" she asked.

The guard's nostrils flared. "Wait here," he finally said. "I—I will inform him of your arrival."

Even though the heavy doors closed behind us, I could still hear, "*Free our king!*"

CHAPTER 51

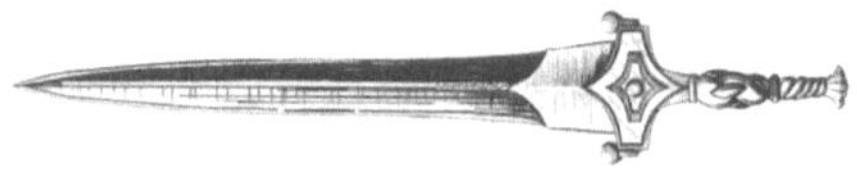

The room held all kinds of curios and collections, encased in tall glass boxes that were set up on golden pedestals around the room. A *wrissan* skull. A *privixi* claw. A gold dagger with a bright blue jewel encased in the hilt. A frayed rope with beads tied at the end, which looked completely out of place among the gleaming surfaces. Strings of green jewels. Rusted boxes. Bone shards and medallions and crumbling tomes that I knew Kara would itch to get her hands on.

We were in his private quarters, and it was unlike anything I'd expected.

Testing the restraints again that shackled my wrists and ankles, I heard them jingle and clink together, giving the *Dothikkar* pause as he lounged back in his chair that looked identical to his throne in the main hall. He sat before a flickering fire in the wide hearth, so large that it took up the entirety of the left wall, making sweat drip down into my eyes.

Large, arched glass windows sat across from me. From this vantage point, I could see the outer stretches of the city, with its flickering lights and shadowed buildings.

I spit out blood onto the white floor. The contrast was shocking. There wasn't a speck of dirt on these floors, but splatters of my blood covered it at regular intervals. Earlier in the afternoon, he'd had a female servant come to mop it up. Shortly after, he'd nodded his head to his guard—with bloodied fists and a heaving chest—and we'd begun again.

I grinned at him now, my teeth blackened with blood. One of my eyelids was swollen, drooping into my vision. My face felt like it was on fire. It hurt to breathe.

And still, I smiled at him because I knew how it enraged him. His jaw started ticking. His feet kicked out restlessly from his throne, and his tail twitched.

"What are you waiting for?" I asked quietly. "You've wanted me dead since I was inside my mother's womb. You have the opportunity now. So take it. Because I guarantee you will never get it again."

I'd felt something break in me throughout the day. But it was something I'd never expected.

It was the burning hatred. The consuming disgust. The spiteful sizzle I'd felt sparking my anger throughout the entirety of my life, spurring me forward, spurring me forward to this.

As I sat with my father in his private corner away from the rest of *Dothik*, I saw a frail, hateful, cruel, frightened, pitiful male.

As I sat there with my father, it made me ashamed to have been born from someone such as him. That his blood was mine. That I was created from a part of him. Anger had consumed my mother. Fear consumed my father.

I didn't want to be either. Angry or afraid.

It was a travesty that so much had been wrecked by this male. It was a travesty that he and his advisors had steadily driven *Dothik* into a downward path since the beginning of his rule, nearly five decades ago. Fifty years of greed and malice.

Those years sat heavy on him now. Without his armor, he looked like the beggars I would often pass on the corners of the marketplace. Desperate. Hungry. Vulnerable.

His misery was palpable. And even as he commanded his guard to beat me, even as he ordered the next guard in to take over, throughout the day I'd come to pity him.

He was beneath me. I was not like him. I knew what loyalty was. I knew what love was. I knew what sacrifice was.

He'd never known any of those things.

I was everything that he was not. And strapped to that hard-backed chair, as I watched him drink himself into a slow, miserable stupor and eat platter after platter of food, the smell of which turned my belly, realization filled me.

I felt that fire in me again. The thing that I had lost after Bodin. His death had made me doubt. His death had made me doubt that I could lead, that I could trust my instincts, that I could keep the people that I cared for most in this world safe.

But now I understood what Nassik, what Bakkia had been trying to remind me of. It burned through me with fierceness and determination, so powerful that I felt strength return to me.

This was about *Dothik*. This was about her people. This was about Dakkar.

This wasn't about me.

I could lead *Dothik,* not because of the blood that ran through my veins but because I knew this place like it was an extension of myself. I saw this city for what it was, every desperate, aching, dark place of it. But I also saw it for what it could be, restored to Bekkar's gleaming vision. *I* would make *Dothik* better for it. Not this waste of a male who pretended to rule a city while his advisors spent his gold on prostitutes and brew and weapons they would never wield.

The *Dothikkar* stared at me with unseeing eyes, swirling his goblet. I heard banging coming from somewhere, a metallic boom that echoed faintly, but I thought it was just the ringing in my ears. The *Dothikkar* didn't seem to notice. Neither did the guard, whose fists were raw and blackened. Darkness swam in my vision, and I blinked it away, realizing it was not sweat as I thought but blood.

I would stay here for as long as was necessary, but I refused to die here. I would stay here until my companions got Kiro out —because I knew they would come. I knew that they would come for me too, but I wished they would not. I could handle the *Dothikkar*. I would let him drink himself into a bleary mess, I would incapacitate the guard—he just needed to come a *little* closer—and then I would snag the key that hung from my father's waist.

Then I would kill him.

Because I saw now that I could do nothing with him standing in my way. I thought it was honor driving me to keep him alive. Now I saw it was mere hesitation and uncertainty. I was done waiting. Waiting had accomplished nothing. It had only made *more* suffer.

No longer.

It was not me that would die this night. But him.

And tomorrow, I would greet a new *Dothik*. One that was as malleable as clay in my hands once I washed through the streets—though most of the worst beings in this city resided right here in the palace.

The *Dothikkar* waved his hand, humming to himself as he took another swig of his wine. I breathed in through my tight, swollen nostrils and saw the guard approach me from the other side.

Just as he reared back his fist, the door opened.

"*Dothikkar*, the *Laseta Kalliri* is here," came another male's voice. It was tinged in wariness.

"Mmm, *lysi*," the *Dothikkar* said, gripping the arms of his throne as if to push himself up. "I will meet her in my usual rooms."

"There is someone with her," the guard said, stepping into the room. "A priestess from the *orala sa'kilan*."

My heart froze in my chest, and within my shackles my fists squeezed.

"A priestess," the *Dothikkar* said hurriedly, now struggling to stand from his throne, though he swayed a bit when he climbed to his feet. "Now?"

"The *Laseta Kalliri* says the message is urgent. She...she wants the *Vorakkar* present."

The *Dothikkar* huffed out a displeased breath, pressing his lips together when his eyes clashed with mine.

A long silence drew out in the room. I sensed the guard slowly backing away before the *Dothikkar* said, "Very well. Show them in."

"But..." The guard trailed off, his tone disbelieving. "But *Dothikkar*, they will see him. And you should know that there is a commotion at the front gates. We have guards—"

What is happening at the front gates? I wondered.

The *Dothikkar* glared, stepping forward on unsteady legs.

"They will see that I am *right* in this! This *duvna*, for he is no *Vorakkar* of mine, tried to have me killed this afternoon."

I nearly laughed. *Duvna.* He'd called me a street creature, something no better than the rodents that scurried in the gutters for food.

"Everyone in the market saw it. And what do we do to enemies of *Dothik*? We punish them. The *Laseta Kalliri* will understand. She was there. She saw it. *Kakkari* knows. Kakkari has given me permission for this. Whispered it right into my ear."

The guard knew better than to argue. Even still, he asked, "Would you like your *prikri* present for the meeting? I can send for him."

His lead advisor, who I was surprised to not have seen this day.

"*Nik*," the *Dothikkar* murmured. "The *Laseta Kalliri* will not want him present."

That was curious.

"You still have him being watched for me, *lysi?*" the *Dothikkar* asked next, his words slow and drawn. For a moment, it seemed like he'd forgotten I was there entirely. Until he stepped forward into a splatter of my blood and his gaze snapped to me, narrowing, as if it were my fault.

"The *prikri?*" the guard asked, as if to clarify. "*Lysi, Dothikkar.*"

Paranoia, I thought. I could add that trait to the growing list of why my father was no longer fit to rule—if he'd ever been fit to rule in the first place.

I had it on good authority—a guard stationed along the outer walls of the palace—that the *Dothikkar* was beginning to decline. I thought my source had meant his physical health. But perhaps he'd meant his mind after all.

"It must be so difficult for you, *Pattar,*" I murmured, watching him flinch at the title. "To be able to trust no one within these walls."

"*Silence,*" he hissed. Then he looked back to the guard, eyes narrowed and suddenly impatient. "Send them in. Quickly. Don't keep the priestesses waiting."

"*Lysi,* but *Dothikkar,* the gates are—"

"*Now!*"

Out of the corner of my eye, I saw the guard hesitate for a brief moment. But then he was gone, the door banging shut behind him.

I gritted my jaw, my eyes flashing to the keys dangling around my father's waist. The other guard was still present. But if Kara was with the *Laseta Kalliri,* as I strongly suspected, I was running out of time. I *would not* put her danger. I could play with my own life. But never with hers.

This was no place for someone like her.

But the guard never strayed closer to me, and if I didn't get him down before I got to the *Dothikkar,* I'd be vulnerable.

But pissing Dakkari off was a talent of mine. One carefully curated over years and years of practice.

"When you sent those assassins—the first ones, mind you —to kill my mother and me," I started, staring straight into my father's eyes, "did you feel anything at all when they reported that we were dead?"

A muscle at his temple jumped.

"Nothing?" I taunted, smiling, drawing the guard closer toward me. "How furious you must've been when you realized that they lied to you. How angry it must have made you to realize that you still had an heir. Alive and well, living beneath your feet, on the cusp of taking *everything* away from you."

"You will take nothing away," he said, stabbing a finger in my direction, his face going purple. "You are no one."

"But I am everything that you are afraid of. Because I am your blood. I can take your throne. I have the Southern District at my side," I growled. "I own half of the Western District and the trades in the North. Now I have the hordes at my back and the blessing of the *Seta Kalliri* herself."

He sputtered. "You lie! The *Seta Kalliri* would *never* give a blessing to someone like you."

"*Nik?*" I rasped. "Then why did she hand me the heartstone of the *orala sa'kilan?*"

A muted roar escaped his throat, and I watched him snap. Up until now, I hadn't seen the extent of his rage, but I saw it burst as his fists snapped toward me, a whirling of unexpected motion. The sickening thud of them against my face, my head reminded me strangely of the sound of the tannery in my horde, when the animal skins were stretched and pulled tight and scraped.

With no way to block the assault—I had to take it. Just as I had all day. Except there was a fury in his violence—one the guards had lacked—and so it hurt all the more. He wanted to hurt me. He wanted to *kill* me.

I didn't know how long it went on. In between the ringing in my ears, I thought I heard the guard trying to interfere. It was *him* I'd wanted to draw closer, but he was still out of reach.

Then came a muted cry from the doorway. *Kara's.*

Nik.

The *Dothikkar's* attack ended when he heard a voice, clear and crisp, ring through the vaulted room.

"Leave us," came the *Laseta Kalliri's* voice.

At her voice, the *Dothikkar* stumbled away, wheezing and winded and drunk. The *Laseta Kalliri's* voice was meant for the guard. Without a moment's hesitation, the guard left the room, his heavy footsteps echoing, jumping to follow the order of the priestess as opposed to that of his supposed king.

Then it was just the four of us. When I'd blinked away the blood that swam in my eyes, I focused them on the small, hooded figure standing next to the *Laseta Kalliri*. Dressed in the gray silk of a priestess, with a cloak to match, I spied Kara's shimmering eyes as she peered at me from the darkness of her hood. She was not one to hide her emotions, after all, and I read the horror on her face as if she'd screamed it from her throat.

She stepped forward, coming toward me, but the *Laseta Kalliri* caught her wrist, shooting her a sharp look.

Once the *Dothikkar* caught his breath, he peered at Kara's figure, a wild, excited gleam in his gaze. "Is this her? The messenger you told me about all those years ago?"

Inhaling a sharp breath, I tested the bonds at my wrists again.

"*Lysi,*" the *Laseta Kalliri* said. "But is this any way to greet a priestess of the *orala sa'kilan*? Covered in a *Vorakkar's* blood?"

The *Dothikkar*, for the briefest of moments, looked bewildered. He peered down at his blood-covered fists and wiped a hand over his cheek. "Kakkari allowed me this. Did she not show you too?"

The *Laseta Kalliri* smiled. I watched with heavy-lidded eyes, my chest heaving, as she strode across the marble, the hem of her dress dragging my blood across the floor.

"Of course," she told the *Dothikkar*, reaching forward to cup his face, pressing her thumb to a drop of my blood that clung to a deep wrinkle.

"I am right in this?" he asked her.

"Of course."

My eyes connected with Kara's again, and I could physically feel the energy buzzing off her skin. She was holding herself back, keeping herself restrained. I gave a subtle shake of my head, and she bit her lip, dropping her gaze when the *Dothikkar* took a step past the *Laseta Kalliri* toward her.

"Let me look upon her face," the *Dothikkar* said, zealous eagerness in his tone. "Let me look upon the face that will bring me greatness."

What lies had the *Laseta Kalliri* been spinning during her time in *Dothik*? I wondered.

Or what truths?

The last thought brought a fresh wave of trepidation, and I struggled against the bonds when he stepped toward Kara, his hand outstretched, a hand covered in my own blood. I felt one of the links on the chains begin to give.

"You have done the work," the *Laseta Kalliri* said. "Now let me give you what you've sought for so long."

She looked at me as she said it, however. With the *Dothikkar's* back turned, she picked up his spilled goblet off the floor, bringing it over to the gold table near the replica of his throne. Her movements were slow. Methodical. As if she walked in on him in a drunk rage every night of her life.

"*Lysi,*" the *Dothikkar* breathed. "I have waited so long."

"And you don't have to wait much longer," the *Laseta Kalliri* informed him. I watched as she pulled a purple vial from the pockets of her robes, the distilled liquid inside shimmering.

Havvia.

She poured it into his goblet and filled it halfway with wine from the glass decanter.

"But first, we must meet with Kakkari, to seek her guidance," the *Laseta Kalliri* said, drawing the *Dothikkar's* gaze away from Kara. With relief, I felt him retreating, his greedy eyes fastening on the goblet.

"*Havvia?*"

"*Lysi,*" she murmured, holding her hand out to beckon him forward as if he were a child, eager for a treat. "Come. Drink."

Kara had been right. It was an addicting drug. I could see the lust for it in my father's eyes, the way he stumbled in his haste to reach it.

The *Laseta Kalliri's* head tilted, turning her ear toward the darkened arches of the window behind her.

"Your supporters are here, *Dothikkar.*"

For a moment, I didn't understand what she meant.

"Can you not hear them?"

Supporters?

Was that what I'd been hearing, what I thought was simply the throbbing pump of my heartbeat? When the ringing of my ears faded, I finally heard what she was referencing. The banging, *lysi,* but as I focused intently on the glass, I heard something else.

Voices.

Voices as one. Chanting, crying, shouting something to the sky that began to grow and grow.

With wonderment, the *Dothikkar* went to the windows that overlooked the front of the palace. The closed gates with the guards stationed on the towers. And beyond...I knew what he saw. *Dothik.* The west and the south of the city. The towering height of the priestesses' temple. He might even be able to see Kakkari's statue in the marketplace from here.

In my mind, I saw the roads and paths leading to here. I traced them in my mind as Kara quickly came to my side.

The banging grew louder and louder. The voices too.

The *Dothikkar* gasped.

"Oh, Arik," Kara whispered, tears in her voice.

"Listen how they call for you, *Dothikkar*," the *Laseta Kalliri* said. While I felt Kara's hand come to my cheek, I watched as the *Laseta Kalliri* simply plucked the keys to my shackles off the *Dothikkar's* belt. His eyes were so wide on the scene before him, a grin of glee on his face, that he didn't even notice. Or care. "They know she is here. Kara, your queen. Just like I told you."

I froze, meeting the *Laseta Kalliri's* eyes when she stepped forward, handing the jangle of keys off to the female she spoke of. Kara paid no mind to her words. Instead, determination stole over her face as she went behind me, jamming one of the keys into the lock at my wrists.

Kara, your queen.

The *Laseta Kalliri* smiled at me, and I had the strangest sensation that she knew exactly what I was thinking. That I was remembering my mother. That I was remembering her songs and stories.

Kara, your queen.

The chosen, curious thing.

Who will make you a king.

The chanting from the outside grew even louder. The banging at the gates began to sound as if they were being beaten down.

"Look at them," the *Dothikkar* breathed. A laugh broke from his throat. "Look at them, here for me! What are they saying? I can't make it out."

"'We want our king,'" the *Laseta Kalliri* told him softly, touching his forearm, bringing the goblet between them.

The shackles from my wrists dropped to the floor. When the *Dothikkar* started to look toward the sound, the *Laseta Kalliri* lifted the goblet to his lips, cradling it between her palms like an offering. The shimmering purple that mixed with the wine.

"Seek Kakkari now," she said quietly. "Listen to your people. Let them guide you as the *havvia* takes you closer to the goddess."

"They want to see me?" the *Dothikkar* asked, lowering his lips to the thick rim of the goblet. "Let them see me. I am here."

"Drink it all, *Dothikkar*."

Kara came to kneel at my feet. Her hands were steady, and she got the key in quickly. A quick twist of her wrist and the shackles released from my ankles and the end of my tail.

I rose quickly, feeling a stabbing pain in my side that reverberated down my legs. Ignoring it, I dragged Kara behind me, stepping forward.

The *Dothikkar's* head turned, and I saw the *Laseta Kalliri's* gaze snap, saw her lips pull down.

"*Dothikkar*, the *havvia*," she said, trying to direct his attentions toward it.

But when my father met my eyes, his own widened in disbelief. His hands grappled for the key at his waist, a key that was no longer there.

"I will do this, priestess," I told her, knowing that a king's death should not be on a High Priestess's hands, regardless of what she might think. "This is my responsibility, not yours."

But when the *Laseta Kalliri* pressed the goblet toward him again, he slapped it away. It clanged onto the marble floor with a ricocheting echo, the shimmering, thick *havvia* swirling in the thin wine.

"What is this?" the *Dothikkar* gasped, his eyes turning to the *Laseta Kalliri*, realization bringing clarity to their reddened depths. "You—you freed him? You did this? Do you know who he *is?*"

CHAPTER 52

"Lysi," the *Laseta Kalliri* said, straightening, her lips pulling back into a serene smile. "I do."

"Then you know what we must do," the *Dothikkar* growled. "I have had the others killed. He is the only one that remains!"

"I understand," she murmured, reaching out her hands to smooth them over the tops of his shoulders.

"Kakkari showed me the path!" the *Dothikkar* continued, seething, his face going red. "*I* will be the last king of Dakkar. Bekkar's line ends with me! It is my name that will echo through the wildlands, just as Kakkari intended. But perhaps it is *you, Laseta Kalliri,* who has lost that vision."

Arik stepped forward. Though he was bloodied, he stood strong. Unlike the *Dothikkar,* who was swaying beneath the priestess's palms.

"You would rather have *Dothik* crumble to the ground upon your death, encasing you like a tomb," Arik growled out, "than have it survive without you. What madness has overcome you, *Pattar?*"

He spit out the last word like it was filled with venom.

The *Dothikkar* shoved himself out of the *Laseta Kalliri's* grip, and I saw his hands scramble for the dagger at his waist. The blade flashed gold. The jewel-encrusted handle sparkled.

"I will have to do this myself," the *Dothikkar* growled.

"Listen to them," Arik said, watching the *Dothikkar* advance. "Do you hear what they are saying? The people of *Dothik* know who their rightful king is. They know."

"Because of your whore of a mother, no doubt!" the *Dothikkar* bellowed, kicking the heavy, spilled goblet across the floor. "Spreading rumors like she spread her legs."

Arik didn't rise to the words, though he went deadly still at the barb.

"They want their rightful king. They want me on the throne. Thrones are not taken on battlefields. They are not taken in great bloody wars. They are taken in small rooms, just like this one. They can be taken over the course of *years*. And they can be taken in single moments. So I give you this last chance, *Pattar*. Recognize me as your rightful heir tonight, or watch me take the throne by force, with my supporters battering at your gates, with my people infiltrating your palace, and with the swords of the hordes and the *saruks* on the wildlands."

A furious cry left the *Dothikkar's* throat, and I barely suppressed my shout when he lunged for Arik, moving surprisingly quickly.

The dagger flashed out. Arik dodged, nearly stumbling back into the *Laseta Kalliri.*

"*Recognize me!*" Arik growled out in a rough voice. "Or you die in this room."

"*Nik,*" I whispered, seeing a shimmer begin in the center of my vision, beginning to bloom outward. "*Nik,*" I breathed, stumbling back against the wall.

Not now. Hanniva, not now, I pleaded with Kakkari.

Two visions in the span of two days? When I had not had one in *years?*

"Get her out of here!" Arik ordered the *Laseta Kalliri,*

gesturing to me when the *Dothikkar* swung the blade wildly at him, crashing into a glass case, toppling it over. Shards of glass scattered across the floor.

Arik didn't have a weapon. I had no doubt in my mind that in a battle of strength, Arik would win. But the *Dothikkar* was not in his right mind and likely had not been for years. He was unpredictable, and that made him incredibly dangerous.

My vision began to blur. The movements of bodies began to sway, but I fought against the vision, knowing that for Arik's sake, I could not fall. It would leave me vulnerable. And by extension, it would leave *him* vulnerable.

Pain throbbed at my temple. My knees began to tremble.

"Kara!" Arik growled out, his gaze darting to me, narrowly dodging another of the *Dothikkar's* wild swipes at him. The older male lashed out quickly again, catching Arik by surprise when his attention was on me, and I watched more blood bloom when the blade connected with his forearm.

Nik.

The *Laseta Kalliri's* slippered feet were crunching over the glass toward me, the sharp shards puncturing the blue silk. In my ear, voices began to whisper. Building and building. I squeezed my eyes shut.

The *Laseta Kalliri* told me that my visions were unpredictable because I tried to suppress them. But what if the vision would *help* Arik? What if it was just the distraction that he needed?

"*Dothikkar,*" I cried out, my eyes flashing open.

I gasped when a sharpness hit me in the chest. When nausea roiled in my belly. Something powerful was rising. Coming to the surface.

"Let me feel it," I whispered raggedly, clutching onto the wall, my nails pressing into the stone. "*Let me feel it.*"

Distantly, I heard the *Laseta Kalliri* say, "*Dothikkar,* she is having a vision. It could be what you have been seeking!"

I felt her cool touch at my temple. I heard her gasp, felt her quick retreat.

The dangers of fanaticism gleamed in the *Dothikkar's* eyes as he sprinted toward me. Greedy and hungry. Forgetting about Arik entirely. Forgetting about the *Laseta Kalliri's* betrayal...or perhaps he had not yet realized it was a betrayal.

I saw his brief recoil just as the vision bloomed. But it was strange, unlike anything I'd experienced before. Overlaid with the present. Two images at once, happening in conjunction with one another. I saw the *Dothikkar,* his breath heaving, a bloodied dagger in his fist, staring down at me with a mixed expression of eagerness and fear and trepidation.

"She has *vekkiri* eyes," he growled, the words ringing hollow. "What is this?"

"The *Seta Kalliri* does not doubt her," I heard the priestess say. "Dakkar will change with her. Just as it has changed with the others. You know this."

Next to the *Dothikkar*, I saw Arik. But not the Arik that was in the room. My *Vorakkar's* face was drawn in anger in the vision. Looking at me, right through me. When I lifted a hand to my face, I was crying. But I couldn't determine if it was in my vision or our current reality. The two were one and the same.

The Arik whose temple was bloody and whose face was bruised pushed over another of the glass pillars. In the room, glass shattered, and I watched him pluck something from its depths. A dagger. With a blue stone in its hilt.

The *Dothikkar* didn't even turn to regard him. He didn't even seem to hear the glass break.

"Show me!" the *Dothikkar* ordered, a drop of spittle adorning the bottom of his lip. I watched it hang as my knees finally gave way. I crashed to a heap on the floor, saw Arik advancing from the back of the room, a dagger gleaming, his brows drawn. "Show me her will!"

"*Show me,*" I whispered. But it was a request I made of

Kakkari, whose power I felt strumming in my veins, tight and raw. Unbridled and frightening.

At my request, I screamed. My eyes squeezed shut, and I blocked out the world as pain—unlike I'd ever felt before—coursed through my body.

I thought every bone in it was breaking. Snapping over and over again. I thought my innards were being twisted and plucked. My skin felt heavy, hanging off me, as if I'd drawn inward on myself, retreating away from it.

"*Kara!*"

I heard Arik's roar. But then it was lost in the millions of voices that screamed in my head. Her voices. I thought of Arik's mother. I thought of what she must've felt or thought. I'd heard Kakkari's voice before, but *this*…this was terrifying.

I was screaming. I must've been. Because my throat felt scratched raw and I couldn't draw in a breath without it feeling like I was inhaling fire. If tears were streaming from my eyes, they were of blood. This pain was killing me from the inside out. This pain would be the end of me.

Was *this* what *Kalloma* had been afraid of? Was *this* what she'd seen in her own vision? Death. Long and painful.

Nik, I thought, gritting my teeth as my back bowed. I felt a hand on my forehead, hot and strong, and I focused on that touch as I sorted through the mess of voices filling the entirety of my body. Words were scraped across my skin. They scraped at my mind, my skull, and imprinted themselves deep in my bones.

"*Show me,*" I pleaded, but my voice was ragged and aching and I was sobbing through the words.

The pain never retreated, but my vision cleared. It might feel like I was being ripped apart, piece by piece, but I saw Arik next to me, the dagger forgotten at his side. The *Dothikkar* was hovering close too. I was on the ground, and he was kneeling at my feet, gripping my ankles and bowing his head over them. I felt his hot breath against my flesh, and it felt like a brand, sizzling and tormenting.

The *Laseta Kalliri* was standing. Far away. She was watching me, her spine straight, her fists curled at her sides. Watching me with fear but also...recognition. Pride.

"Can you not do something?" Arik bellowed at the *Laseta Kalliri*. "She is *dying!*"

"*Nik*, she is not," the *Laseta Kalliri* said, her voice *awed*. "She is being tested."

"Show me her will," the *Dothikkar* was saying at my feet, pressing the words deeper into my skin, and I wanted to twist away and scream. "If she is channeling herself through you, then show me *your* will."

I lifted my hand. In it, I saw the heartstone, glowing in my palm. I was in the East Lands. The dust streaked across my face, and the heat felt oppressive. Suffocating.

"*Nik*," Arik said, but it was my vision. Returned to me. Beginning again from where it had ended previously. His gaze burned into me, but even his eyes helped quell the pain. The ache in my chest was nothing compared to the fiery whips inside me, and I focused instead on the splintering of my heart.

In my hand, I held the heat of the heartstone. *Nik*, there were two. In my hands.

And another, I thought. *Another* I could not see. There was a heavy weight at my back.

A sword.

The sword.

I saw the glow of the other heartstones. And in my vision, I felt the burst of power, the dizzying rush of it, though it didn't bring me fear. I *was* that endless power. I could hold it in my hand and not be afraid of it, though others might've been.

And in the next moment, I watched the heartstones crumble. I watched them turn to dust in my hand, picked up by a strong breeze that seemed to lash at the land with violence, rumbling the earth as shouts of alarm rose into the sky.

"*Kara!*"

Arik's voice was far away. I felt the heat of his child in my belly. Anguish speared through me.

In my vision, I turned to look for him. Only when I turned, I turned into a room in the palace of *Dothik*. I saw the throne. Empty and waiting. Arik's back was to me now, and he was standing on the outside terrace, framed by the arches of the columns that peaked into points at the very top.

At his side was Bekkar's sword, as familiar to me as Arik was. Only a stone I didn't recognize glittered in its hilt. White and shimmering. A stone I knew was not there.

"Show me her will," the *Dothikkar* told me, and the vision broke. Snapped like a tether—and when I returned to my reality, I tasted blood on my tongue and my vision was darkened red.

Kalloma would tell me to breathe through it. I felt a longing for her build in my breast, and I cried more until my tears ran clear.

"Kara," Arik was saying. His hand at my face. But I began to feel numb. The longing for *Kalloma* faded away. My fear for Arik. My trepidation that this pain, that this moment would change me forever. "*Saila*, look at me."

"Show me her will!" the *Dothikkar* said.

In a flash, I reached out to take the *Dothikkar's* hand, tearing it away from my ankle. I acted on an instinct I didn't know I possessed. But something powerful was coursing through me, something I couldn't control. "Then take it," I said.

The *Dothikkar* began to scream the moment my flesh met his. Just like I had.

"I can feel her!" he bellowed. The sound he made was terrible, a mixture of a laugh and chilling shout. Terrible enough to make me want to recoil. When I tried to take my hand away, his pressed down harder, gripping. To the point that I thought he'd break my bones. "I can hear her!"

Blackness shrouded my vision. I felt my muscles giving. I felt a rage growing. Thick like the fog in the East Lands. *His* rage. *His* turmoil. I felt the *Dothikkar's* every will and whim in that single moment, and it *terrified* me. It channeled into me like a current. Every dark, desperate place in him...I saw it all. I felt it all.

"*Kara.*"

His voice. He was just *right there*. Above me. I could sense Arik near. I could smell him. Taste him.

And so I gripped him. I gripped him like he was the only good thing in this growing darkness, and I didn't let him go.

I need you, I thought. *I need you now. I need you to keep me safe.*

His hands were strong and sure on me. Guiding me through it.

When the pain ended, it ended so abruptly that I nearly blacked out from it. Or perhaps I did. Because when I came awake, my vision was bleary. My mouth felt dry. My bones felt hollow, and when I tried to move, everything hurt. Arik's bloody face was hovering above me, a strange expression on his face, though he closed his eyes in relief when he saw me awake.

It was silent in the room.

So silent that I thought I couldn't hear anymore. I couldn't hear anything at all.

"Kara," came his soft voice, and I was so relieved that I began to sob. I was so relieved that the pain was gone, that the vision was gone, that Arik was *here*, that the *Dothikkar* was—

My breath whooshed from me, and a chill raced down my spine.

Because I saw a heap on the floor.

The *Dothikkar*.

On his back, staring up at the ceiling of that gilded, terrible room. A trickle of black blood ran from the seam of his mouth. Dark veins crawled across his flesh. His chest was still.

The king of Dakkar was dead at my feet.

CHAPTER 53

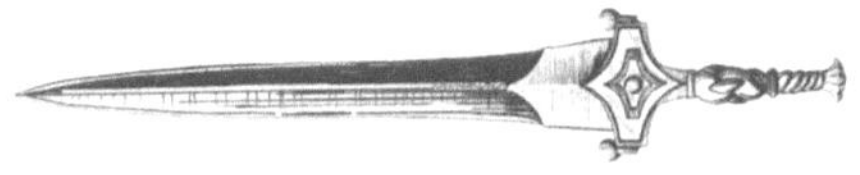

"Kiro is dead."

I said nothing at Bakkia's announcement. I turned away from him, my footsteps echoing in that grand room that I only wanted to tear down. The stillness made me restless.

"The healer said he took a turn in the night. That his injuries from the dungeons were too great. Vala was there with him in the end. Ulli too."

I squeezed my eyes shut, grief already battering at my chest.

"And I should've been there too," I said softly, running a hand down the stretch of my face.

I hadn't slept in days. The taking of a city was not for the faint of heart...or the weary.

"*Vok*," I breathed. Louder, I bellowed, "*Vok!*"

The word seemed to echo endlessly throughout the throne room of the palace.

After Kiro had been taken from the marketplace, the *Dothikkar* had had him sent to the dungeons. But just as I'd assumed, he hadn't been merciful. There'd been no negotiation for Kiro's release. The guards had been cruel, just as they had been with Bodin.

Kiro had been alive when Bakkia and the others had reached him through the tunnels. But just barely.

"Vala is..." Bakkia started and then trailed off. His heart was heavy. I could feel its heaviness from here. "He left. To clear his mind. I'm not certain where."

"Let him go," I told Bakkia. "He'll come back to us in his own time. Once he's ready."

We hadn't spoken about what Bakkia had seen in the Eastern District. About Kiro and Vala meeting with Nyonnia.

And now? With everything that had happened the last few days and with Kiro's death...it wasn't important anymore. Not in the least.

What *was* important was securing *Dothik*. And it hadn't been easy. After the *Dothikkar's* death, I'd needed to act quickly. I'd ordered the *Laseta Kalliri* to send for her priestesses, to have them here in the palace to dissuade a potential uprising from the guards. I'd done nothing to stop the Dakkari at the gates from beating it down and streaming their way into the courtyard and the palace, using them as a distraction in the aftermath as I'd tried to locate Bakkia and the others...and to locate the *Dothikkar's* advisors and have them secured and watched.

My other main priority had been to get Kara to safety. To get her out of the palace and back to my stronghold where she would be protected.

I didn't trust the *Laseta Kalliri*. Not one bit. But she'd been a tremendous force that night. Not only after the *Dothikkar's* body had been discovered by the guards but in helping me secure the palace and get Kara back to the Southern District.

The guards that were still loyal to the *Dothikkar*—to my father—had fought against us, trying to keep the palace from falling into our hands. But with my companions at my side—as they had always been before—we'd cut through them swiftly. Those that had surrendered in the end we'd had gathered up and sent to the dungeons in the Northern District to await sentencing.

Blood had been spilled that night. Some of which was still being scrubbed away by the palace keepers—who seemed afraid that their livelihoods would be threatened and who seemed eager to do my bidding, if only to show their new allegiance.

There were too many within these walls who I didn't trust, too many who were not vetted and whose loyalties I couldn't rely on. But there was no time to weed them out. Not now. Nassik would be here any day—leading my horde back to *Dothik* from the wildlands, a decision that I knew would disappoint many. The failing of a horde was commonplace. Mine had failed...within the course of a single night. In its stead, I'd gained a kingdom. And truthfully, I didn't know how I felt about that. It still didn't seem real.

What felt real to me was returning to the Southern District in stolen hours of the morning. What felt real to me was drawing a listless Kara into my arms, feeling her face press into my chest as I pleaded with her to eat something, as I pleaded with her to look at me, to speak to me. It hurt like hell, seeing her like that, but at least it felt *real*.

"How is she?" Bakkia asked, as if reading the direction of my thoughts. Because these days they always seemed to travel back to Kara.

"Not well," I told him, running a hand down my face, my mind still lingering on Kiro too. A moment from when we were young, sitting on the rooftops of the Northern District and watching the steel being melted down. I could still smell the fumes, stinging my nostrils, and feel the heat on my face from the forges. Kiro's sister had been alive then. He'd been lighter then. More carefree. He could watch the metalwork for hours. A spear of grief thudded into my chest. "I am thinking of sending for her *kalloma*. If only to help…see her through. Because I fear I cannot. Nothing reaches her."

"Does the *Laseta Kalliri* still come to her every day?" Bakkia asked.

I heard something in his tone, and it brought another pang to my chest. Because I could not handle one more thing, one more mention of information that might derail everything. "Why do you ask?"

Bakkia shook his head. "No reason. Just that…maybe she could help her in a way that we cannot."

I regarded him carefully. He was lying to me. But right then, with Kiro's death, with Vala's retreat, with a whole *vokking* kingdom resting on my shoulders, and with what had happened in the *Dothikkar's* private rooms…I didn't want to know what he was lying to me about.

Not right now.

"Where is Kiro now?" I asked gruffly.

"In a room in the west quarters. The healer has begun the washing ritual."

"*Nik*, we will…" I trailed off, feeling my throat tighten. Clearing it, I said, "He will be cleansed in the Southern District. Our home. He would not want it to happen here. And then we will have him buried in our own territory, the territory we all built together. With his sister. With his family. With Bodin. We will cleanse him ourselves. And dig his grave ourselves. For we are his brothers and his sisters now. *Lysi?*"

I heard Bakkia's hard swallow. "*Lysi*," he said quietly. "He would want that. I'll see that the preparations are made."

"*Kakkira vor*," I said softly, inclining my head.

Bakkia hesitated before he left the throne room. "What are you doing in here anyway? All by yourself?"

I just need a brief reprieve, I thought. The throne room was quiet. Empty. Desolate, even. And yet the views from here were some of the best in *Dothik*. There was a wide terrace that stretched the length of it, and I'd just needed some air. I'd needed to feel the wind and the setting sun on my face. Just for a moment.

Every moment since the *Dothikkar's* death had been harried. I'd been running around the palace, solving one problem only to be thrown into the next, meeting with the *Laseta Kalliri* and ambassadors from the highborn families, having a scribe send off *thesper* after *thesper* to the *Vorakkar* of the hordes and the *Sorakkar* of the outposts, who would need to come to the capital at such a precarious time.

My birthright needed to be confirmed if we wanted a peaceful transition, one that didn't set a dangerous precedent. Some of the highborn families had agreed to testify about my mother's pregnancy, those that remembered or who were still alive—for a price, of course, which included preferential treatment among my courts. But then, again, everything had its price.

There'd been unrest in the Western District when word of the *Dothikkar's* death had reached them and when my own name was being whispered in the streets. The Western District was home to a lot of the highborn families. Their influence would be necessary for the foreseeable future, a fact that I'd known for quite some time. Not that I was pleased about it. Not that I was pleased that I would need to smile at the same families that had turned their backs on my own mother when she'd needed help and who'd happily spent the *Dothikkar's* gold when he'd paid for their silence.

But the structures and foundations and corruption of *Dothik* would not change overnight. There were sacrifices on my part that needed to be made to ensure that I remained in power.

Once my position was secured, however?

That would be a different story entirely.

Bakkia was still waiting for my answer. In the end, I didn't give it to him. Instead I said, "Have the meeting with the priestesses pushed back until later tonight. I would like to pay my respects to Kiro. And then I need to check on her, *lysi?*"

After the grief of seeing my friend—of knowing that his death could have been prevented—I would need to feel her against me. I needed to smell her skin and her hair and feel the way she still wrapped her tail around my leg, even though she could hardly meet my eyes.

Bakkia inclined his head. "*Lysi.* I'll have it done."

"*Kakkira vor, Prikri,*" I said, testing the word on my tongue. *Prikri.* The *Dothikkar's* lead advisor. The *prikri* of my father was still locked away in the upper floors and guarded, especially after he'd tried to flee this morning.

Despite the tension and grief of Kiro's death, Bakkia shook his head. "Not a chance, Arik. I'll leave that position to Nassik. He'll be thrilled."

I chuffed out a short breath but couldn't find it in me to smile.

"*Saila.*"

My eyes went from the tray of half-eaten food—*progress*— to her turned back at the window.

She was still dressed in what she'd gone to bed in the night before. The softest tunic of mine that I could find, one that reached her knees.

I laid my sword on the table next to the tray. Ulli and Errana were downstairs, keeping watch over the stronghold while the rest of us were at the palace. We wouldn't be disturbed.

When Kara heard my voice, she turned. Briefly, her eyes flickered to mine, but then they lowered. Even still, she strode to me as if pulled, and I met her halfway in my private quarters. Drawing her close, I cupped her cheeks in my palms and tilted her head up.

"Look at me, *rei kassiri*," I murmured. "*Hanniva*. Let me see you."

But she closed her eyes even as her hand reached up to grip my wrist tightly, holding me to her. "*Nik*."

"Why?" I asked.

"I'm afraid at what you might find, Arik," she whispered, "if you look too close."

My brow furrowed. "*Neffar?*"

Her head dropped into my chest, her forehead pressed between my pectorals.

What happened in that room?

The question that had been poised on my tongue for the last few days was at the ready. And even now, I couldn't make it come.

And yet...

I remembered the female that sat crying on the back of Syok as we journeyed to my horde. I remembered the fire in her gaze, the anger, the *life,* and I vastly preferred *that* to the fear that had taken root in Kara. A fear I didn't even know how to name or identify because she'd told me nothing.

And because I have not pushed her, I added silently. I had been exceedingly gentle with her. Careful with her because I'd seen how fragile she'd been in the aftermath of that night. With tears of red blood streaking down her face and a body that seemed to be made of glass for the way she'd winced with every step.

Her strength had seemed to recover, though her appetite had not, and I worried about her sunken cheeks and her exhaustion.

I should've been afraid of the extent of the power I'd witnessed that night. But all I saw was my Kara. With her wide, sad eyes.

I'd been gentle, but perhaps she needed me to be something else for her.

"*Nik*," I murmured, drawing her away from my chest. I pushed all thoughts of what I still needed to accomplish tonight at the palace away, and instead I focused solely on Kara—where I had longed to be all day even though seeing her like this brought a sharp ache to my chest. "None of that. We will speak of this, *lysi*? Now."

Her brows drew down.

"Kara," I said. "Look at me, *rei kassiri*."

Rei kassiri.

My love.

Since when had that soft, teasing, affectionate name started to sound more and more like a truth?

A soft inhale whistled through her, and then her eyes were on mine. And I held them fiercely, sensing a knot begin to unravel in me the longer she held my gaze.

"Tonight," I murmured, smoothing a hand down her neck before skimming over the tops of her shoulders, "I want to take whatever it is that has been hurting you."

Her eyes went stricken. "*Nik*," she whispered. "I don't want you to."

"Then help me understand," I said.

She inhaled a shuddering breath and then pushed out of my arms, walking back to the window. She crossed her arms over her chest, hugging them to her body. I waited. And I waited. I would wait as long as was necessary, as strangers' voices carried up from the street below, as laughter poured from a nearby tavern.

There had been offerings placed outside the Heart when I'd returned to the stronghold. With messages I couldn't read scrawled across scraps of parchment and attached with roughened twine. Bottles of brew, mostly. Small, glittering trinkets that I was surprised had not been stolen. I assumed what the messages said. Messages of hope. Messages of blessing.

My gut twisted, thinking I could not be weak. I had to strong for the people of *Dothik*.

But just like I'd always known, Kara was my weakness. She always would be.

"I killed him."

The words hung in the air between us, so softly spoken that I'd nearly missed them entirely.

It was the first time she said it out loud. The first time it was acknowledged. Even the *Laseta Kalliri* had not said a word, even to me in private when we met.

"I killed the *Dothikkar*," she continued. "Your father. The *king* of Dakkar."

I shook my head as I felt discomfort churn in my belly.

"*Nik*, you did not." Still, I said, "I hate that his death would cause you this pain. He is not worth this turmoil, Kara. He is not worth—"

"I know," she said softly. Then her shoulders sagged. "And still, I can hear his screams in my mind."

"He wasn't screaming, Kara," I said after a brief moment of hesitation. She turned to look at me, her brows drawn. "Only you were."

I saw the way my words hit her. I saw the way her face crumpled, and I strode forward quickly when silent sobs began to rack her body.

"*Rei kassiri*," I whispered, everything twisting in me at the sight of her.

"*He was,*" she cried softly. "He was—I heard it!"

She cried into my chest when I pulled her close, running my shortened claws down her back when I felt the way she trembled.

"It was you that was screaming, Kara," I said, the words spit out gutturally. I didn't like thinking about seeing her as she'd been. It'd been terrifying. "You were twisting and screaming in so much pain, and then you had moments of quietness, moments I think Kakkari was speaking to you or you were seeing something that we couldn't. Then it would begin again. All over again, and I thought—"

I cut myself off because I couldn't say it. I couldn't say it out loud.

I thought the pain would kill you, I finished silently. *I thought you would die right there in my arms.*

I'd never seen anything like it, and I *never* wanted to see her like that again.

"Then," I tried again gruffly, "the *Dothikkar* reached for you. And you placed your hands on him. He went very still. Then he was laughing. He said that he could feel her, that he could *feel* Kakkari."

"He was screaming in my mind," she whispered into my skin, shuddering.

I traced her spine with the side of my thumb, and that shudder turned into a shiver. I dipped my head, pressing my nose into her hair and inhaling her scent deeply.

"He backed away from you," I told her. "He broke the connection, and he was spinning in the room, like he could see what you were seeing."

"He did?" she asked softly.

"*Lysi,*" I said. "*He* broke the connection, Kara. He was speaking to himself. Or maybe he was speaking to Kakkari, I can't be certain. He was saying *nik, nik, nik*—over and over again. The next thing I knew, I heard him fall. Blood began to seep from his mouth, and he was clutching at his chest. The *Laseta Kalliri* felt his heart stop, *saila.* It stopped in his chest, and that's why he died."

"But I—"

"If you channeled Kakkari's power into him, then he was not strong enough to withstand it," I said sharply. "But *he* wanted to feel it. *He* reached for *you.* When he broke the connection, he was still alive. Do not forget that."

It was silent between us as I continued to stroke her back.

"I should've told you what happened in that room," I said. "I should've told you this days ago. For that, I am sorry, *saila*."

"I was in no state to hear it," she whispered finally. "You knew that."

Needing to feel connected to her, I kissed her. She made a small sound in the back of her throat—a needy sound though it also sounded like a sob.

Then she was kissing me back, desperately, her hands digging into the tops of my shoulders, and I growled, feeling *her* need fire in my belly.

Then Kara broke the kiss abruptly, turning her face to the side. Her cheeks were wet, I realized. She'd been crying, and it felt like a dagger to the chest.

"It's not only that," she whispered raggedly. "What I felt that night...it was...it was terrible, Arik. I felt Kakkari at her worst. I...I had always believed Kakkari to be a giving goddess. A merciful one. She's the goddess of life! She gives us bounty, she protects us from the worst of Drukkar's wrath. But that wasn't the goddess I was connected to that night. I've felt her before but never like that. She is angry. She was not benevolent or kind, and I felt her rage. And it *scared* me. It's made me question everything I've been taught. Everything I believed to be true. I fear her now. When before I had only loved her."

I understood what she was telling me. What she'd felt that night had changed her entire perspective. No wonder she'd not been herself for the last few days. She was hanging in the balance of what she'd known and what she *now* knew.

"But she offered me great power," she told me. "And a part of me was very tempted to take it. A part that I am ashamed of."

I swallowed, my nostrils flaring. I couldn't imagine the price Kakkari would demand for that kind of power. And I didn't want Kara anywhere near it.

"What did you see?" I asked her.

Her golden eyes met mine, and I couldn't help but lean down and brush a soft kiss against her tear-streaked face.

Vok, this female…

Had I ever expected her when I'd climbed that damn tower of the *orala sa'kilan?*

"I saw you on the throne."

Slowly, I pulled away, hearing something I didn't expect in her voice. Resignation. Despondency.

"With Bekkar's sword at your side."

A beat of silence passed between us.

"Did you see anything of the fog?" I asked.

"We will defeat it," she said, not quite meeting my eyes. "We will wipe it away from this land like it had never been."

A bright relief burst in my chest, the seemingly permanent knot that had been tied within it *finally* loosening.

I smiled. "*Lysi?*"

"*Lysi*," she said, though her voice did not hold the same relief as mine. When she met my eyes again, she told me, "And then your work in *Dothik* can truly begin."

My relief dimmed.

"And what is the price of all of this?" I asked slowly.

She took in a deep breath. "This will be our last chance. Kakkari will give no more after this."

"I don't understand," I confessed, shaking my head.

"I fear that if Dakkar becomes unbalanced once more, we will all meet the Kakkari I felt that night. The vengeful one. And she will be merciless."

CHAPTER 54

"Where are you taking me?" I asked Arik.

He only continued pulling me along beside him. Kalik trailed us, though he kept a respectful distance back. My own guard. The one Arik had assigned to me when I'd returned to the palace. To live here with him so he didn't have to constantly travel to the Southern District when the time was better spent elsewhere. Arik didn't trust anyone else—except his core group—to watch over me in his absence, of which there had been a lot. He was incredibly busy, pulled in so many directions by so many different people as he tried to get his footing. I understood that. And so I took advantage of the moments we were together, savoring them as best as I could.

It was a week later. And only in the last few days had I begun to feel more like myself. The aching, empty pit in my belly was still there, but it seemed to lessen each day. My hands didn't tremble whenever I tried to eat anymore. Food didn't make me feel nauseous. My bones didn't feel hollow anymore. My strength was returning.

But I still hadn't looked at myself in a mirror. Hadn't met my own eyes since the *Dothikkar's* death because I was still afraid of what I'd see in them.

And I hadn't prayed to Kakkari. Not once. Because I feared opening that connection again. Every moment, I lived in fear that another vision would crash over me. That I'd feel that terrible pain again.

I tried to hide it from Arik, however. I smiled at him whenever he was with me. I sighed into his kisses and clasped him to me when we were intimate. When we had sex, it was the only time I allowed myself to be unafraid. Because when I was with him, he would help keep me steady.

And right now?

I needed stability.

I needed to pretend that everything was all right.

That didn't mean I hadn't sensed the change in Arik, however. A change that only heightened my anxiousness and turmoil whenever I allowed myself to think about it too deeply.

He was away from me for longer and longer hours of the day and night. Two days ago, I'd not seen him at all. The indent in bed next to me was the only indication that he'd been there, however briefly. From our private rooms in the northern wing, I could just make out the comings and goings of the front of the palace. I saw how many Dakkari showed up, seeking an audience with their new king. I saw the *Laseta Kalliri* and her priestesses come and go. I swore I'd even seen a *Vorakkar* or two—with their hulking bulk and painted, battle-bred *pyrokis*—journeying all the way from the wildlands to meet with Arik.

I'd seen members of the court—including beautiful Dakkari females—coming to offer their allegiances and loyalties to Arik. Seeing them hadn't filled me with jealousy. Instead, they had filled me with an ache of doubt. Doubt that I could be the female that Arik needed at his side to help build a new *Dothik*.

A mere vision had crushed me. Had made it difficult to stand on my own two feet again. How could I expect to stand by Arik, who needed unwavering strength at his side?

I'd always felt like I had to prove myself. I'd always felt like I would never be enough for the Dakkari. Compared to the females of our race, I was small and weak. A hybrid. What could I really offer a *king?*

Arik's hand squeezed around my own as he came to a halt outside two grand doors.

Kalik stopped down the hallway to give us privacy, but I saw no other soul in sight. Arik came up behind me, wrapping his arms around my waist as his lips dropped to my ear.

"I have it on good authority that these were Bekkar's private offices," he murmured.

I stilled, eyeing the handle of the door. "Truly?" I whispered.

I could feel the curve of his smile against me. I could hear it in his voice when he said, "*Lysi.* And wait until you see what Bekkar's son turned them into after his death. Open it, *rei kassiri.*"

The handle was hot under my palm. The door was heavy and creaked open on old hinges. But when I saw what was within, my breath left me. I felt the glimmer of the female I'd been before rise. I felt her rise, eager and excited, exuberant in her surprise.

I laughed, delighted.

It was a library.

A grand library with floor-to-ceiling windows that over-looked the wildlands.

Thousands of books and ancient tomes and papery scrolls were stacked and shelved. There was a familiar smell in the air, one that reminded me of *home*, of the quiet hallways of the *orala sa'kilan,* and I breathed it in greedily.

"It hasn't been touched in quite some time," Arik's voice sounded behind me. He sounded...uncertain? Like he thought I *wouldn't* like it? "I had it cleaned for you yesterday. You should've seen the layers of dust. It would have sent you running for your beloved bath."

I spun into him though I never wanted to take my eyes off the books.

"You like it?" he asked me gruffly.

"Only as much as I like you," I whispered, feeling tears prick the backs of my eyes. His gaze flashed, and maybe it was how overcome I was with sudden emotion but I added, "Meaning I don't just like it. I *love* it."

I love you was what went unspoken.

Arik's eyes didn't change. He looked at me steadily, his hand curving around my hip, holding me against him. My heart was beating in my throat, and I saw my reflection in those fiery, beautiful eyes.

"Good," he rasped, swallowing. But then his gaze darted away, and I swore I sensed his discomfort before he covered it with a grin. "Good, *saila*. I had hoped you would."

But his reaction made me feel off-balance again. I hid my disappointment when I turned to regard the shelves, not quite seeing them anymore. Slipping out of his grip, I walked up to one, running my finger over the spines and the scrap of faded red fabric that held one scroll together.

"I know I haven't been with you as much as I would like to be," came his voice after a tense silence.

"I know how busy you've been," I told him. Over my shoulder, I met his eyes and said, "My offer still stands. I can help with correspondences or *thesper* messages. I can help you with whatever you need."

Arik stood close to the door. He hadn't stepped into the library, and I had the stray thought that he would disappear at any moment.

"I know," he murmured. His jaw tightened, but he looked me squarely in the eyes as he added, "But for now, I'd like to keep you out of it."

"Why?" I asked quietly, though I feared I already knew.

It hadn't gone unnoticed by me that he kept me *away*. Away

from the guards, away from the Dakkari that worked in the palace, away from the kitchens, from the hallways. Away from the throne room.

Away from anyone who might *see* me.

At first I had assumed it was because he sensed I needed the space to pull myself back together. To heal, just a tiny bit, each and every day. I'd been grateful for the reprieve.

Now, however?

I wasn't so certain. And I was beginning to feel alone. *Lonely.* On the way here, we'd walked through the hallways quickly. I hadn't seen *anyone*, as if Arik had ordered everyone out of his wing.

Was he trying to hide me away? As if my presence here would spark unease? I hadn't thought that the way I looked mattered to Arik. Now that he was the king, I didn't think the secrecy mattered. The whole point of us hiding my face in *Dothik*, originally, had been because we'd feared the *Dothikkar* discovering us, discovering Arik.

So why did it matter to him now?

And if it did, why hadn't he just kept me in the Southern District? Away from prying eyes?

"It's safer" was what Arik replied. "Until we feel more secure."

Who was *we?* And was I included in that?

"Kalik will be just outside the door when you wish to return to our rooms," Arik said. "I wish I could stay with you, *saila*, but the *Laseta Kalliri* is waiting for me. We have trials today for the guards in the northern dungeons. And for the previous *prikri*."

I nodded. Turning to Arik, I gave him a small smile I didn't feel. "Of course. I understand."

He lingered in the doorway. It looked like he wanted to say more as he ran a hand down his tired face. Two days ago, I'd told him he needed to sleep more. That he was drawing himself too thin.

What would you have me do, Kara? he'd snapped at me, his tone harsher than I'd ever heard it. *There is not enough time in the day. I will sleep when the kingdom is secured.*

He'd apologized to me later, whispering it into my ear in the early hours of morning. The last thing he wanted to do was take his frustrations and stress out on me...and I'd forgiven him with a kiss, letting it go.

Just as I was doing now, even though I wanted to demand answers from him.

Arik glanced at the tomes behind me before meeting my eyes. "You'll be all right in here?"

I was beginning to feel like a child, one that needed constant tending. I hid my frown and inclined my head. "It's a room full of books, Arik. In a place touched by Bekkar. I think I'll be fine."

The selfish part of me wanted him to worry about me.

The other part of me didn't. Because I didn't want him to be distracted. This wasn't about me. This wasn't about *us*.

This was about what was best for Dakkar. *Arik* was what was best for Dakkar, and he needed to be levelheaded for the task ahead.

So when those selfish instincts rose, I needed to remember that.

He looked at me for a long moment. I likely wouldn't see him again today, and so I took full advantage. I looked at him right back, studying the strong set of his shoulders and thinking how I wanted to trim his hair when a dark lock dipped down into his eyes.

He pushed it back impatiently but said, his voice gentle, "I'll see you later this evening, *saila*."

I nodded.

Then I watched him leave.

And as I looked around at the library in his absence, I could no longer feel that glimmer of excitement I'd felt before.

CHAPTER 55

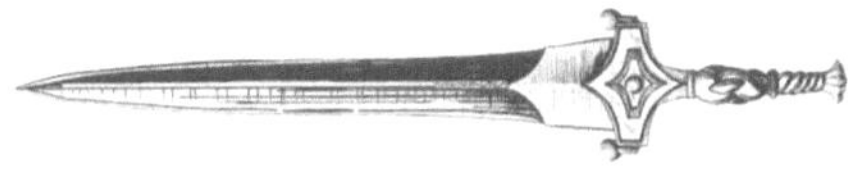

"The temple has the gold required," the *Laseta Kalliri* informed me, tapping at something on the parchment she'd placed in front of me. I stared down at the figures and words in silence, tracing the symbols wordlessly. "We can rebuild the Northern District. We have the land there. The space necessary for more buildings. For homes."

"The *Sorakkar* have already agreed to open up their *saruks* to new members," Bakkia told the *Laseta Kalliri*, shaking his head from his spot against the wall in the room I'd claimed as my office. "The population in *Dothik* is too high. You may not see it in your gilded temple, but the streets are overflowing with Dakkari. We need more hordes in the wildlands. More *saruks*. The city walls are our boundaries. We cannot build much more within them."

"Then break down the walls," she said simply, shrugging. "What threats does *Dothik* have now? The Ghertun are gone. The Killup—"

"Were never our enemies," I finished for her sharply. "I will grant them their own kingdom in the North Lands if they agree to the terms we have laid out for them."

"And the *vekkiri*?" the High Priestess of *Dothik* asked. "What of them? You say they are building a *saruk* of their own. Will they adhere to the same terms as the other *saruks*?"

"*Lysi*," I told her. "They must."

"Do you trust that they *will*?" she asked.

"I do," I said softly, spearing her with a hard look. I couldn't get a read on the High Priestess. Some days, I thought that we were on the same page. Others, we were at odds. She tested me at every turn, and it was beginning to grate on me. She was toeing the line of respect, pushing her boundaries. "The hordes are working closely with the *vekkiri* responsible for the *saruk*. And I have faith in the *Vorakkar*. I have faith in their judgment."

The *Laseta Kalliri* rolled her shoulders. Nassik mirrored her motion, though he did it with his neck, no doubt feeling the tension building in the room. My *pujerak* had arrived two days before, dusty from the wildlands with the rest of my horde in tow, and I'd been relieved to see him. We'd waited for him to lay Kiro's body to rest, after all, and now our friend was finally at peace in the Southern District with his family, where he'd always wanted to be.

"Very well," the *Laseta Kalliri* said easily, flashing a small smile, turning her back on us to walk to the window that over-looked the Southern District. It had the best view of it, one of the reasons I'd chosen this wing for my office. "And what does Kara think of creating more hordes? Of more *saruks* instead of building and expanding *Dothik*? Is she in favor of it?"

My brow furrowed. I frowned, leaning forward on my hands which were pressed into the table. "Why do you ask?"

"Well, she will be your queen, will she not?" the *Laseta Kalliri* questioned.

I stiffened at the unexpected words, at the certainty I heard in the priestess's voice.

"Does the queen of *Dothik* not get a say in important deci-sions made solely by her king?"

Bakkia's arms uncrossed, and I watched him step forward.

He had the *Laseta Kalliri* pinned with a hard gaze. Nassik, on the other hand, only looked as bewildered as I likely did.

"Kara is..." I trailed off, uncertain at what I would say. At a loss for words, which was unlike me. Instead, I huffed out a sharp breath. "I am in no hurry to claim a queen, *Laseta Kalliri*. I think the security of *Dothik* comes first before such matters."

"And a queen at your side, one with the blessing of the *Seta Kalliri* herself, will guarantee the security of *Dothik*," the *Laseta Kalliri* argued. "*Dothik* has not had a queen for quite some time. I think the city will breathe easier through this transition of power with one standing beside you."

I exchanged a look with Nassik. What the priestess was saying made sense. However...

My fists clenched on the table.

I was not ready to announce Kara's presence. Just yesterday, there had been a breach in the palace. A disgruntled guard, who'd given me his loyalties in the aftermath of the siege, only to turn on me in a single moment. He'd reached the staircase that led up to the northern wing—to *our* private rooms, to *Kara* —before he'd been apprehended. He'd had a long sword, freshly sharpened, and three daggers in his possession. And I still shuddered to think what he would have done had he found Kara. The guard might not have expected to find her in my rooms. He'd been looking for *me*, after all. But to find my female in our bed...there was no mistaking what *could* have happened.

I had waking nightmares just thinking about the scene that would have greeted me had he succeeded. Of red blood, lifeless golden eyes staring up at me.

I'd narrowly restrained myself from killing the guard myself. Right there and then.

Yesterday, I'd nearly had Kara sent back to the Southern District. I'd been enraged at the possibility that there were still guards within the palace that wanted to do us harm. Then again, I had no choice but to place my trust in the ones that remained.

If I announced Kara to *Dothik*, I would present her as a possible point of weakness. *She* was my weakness. Anyone who wanted to hurt *me* only had to hurt *her*.

And I couldn't bear the thought of it.

"So why wait to announce her as your queen?" the *Laseta Kalliri* continued. "I can write to the *Seta Kalliri* and request her presence here. She can give her blessing to Kara before all of *Dothik*, which will help soothe concerns over her bloodline, of course. It would be a simple thing."

Bakkia cut into the conversation. "We will discuss this later. We have more pressing issues right now, don't you think, *Laseta Kalliri*?"

"He's right," I said quietly. "It's not the right time to be discussing this."

The *Laseta Kalliri's* nostrils flared, but in the end, she inclined her head. "Of course, *Dothikkar*."

My fists squeezed at the title, not yet used to it. Whenever I heard the word, discomfort filled me. Because it reminded me of my father.

"Whatever you wish."

"I need to speak with you."

I looked up at Bakkia, who remained in the room after I'd dismissed the others.

"Obviously," I murmured, throwing him a quick smile, though it died when I saw the expression on his face. "What is it?"

"It's about what the *Laseta Kalliri* brought up earlier. About you taking Kara as your queen."

The back of my neck went tight.

"Did you know?" he asked me, looking at me steadily. Studying me. "About her bloodline?"

My brow furrowed. "*Neffar?* About whose bloodline?"

"*Kara's.*"

I went still, hearing the hesitancy in Bakkia's voice.

"Her father was the *Laseta Kalliri's* brother. Your female has a direct ancestral line to the priestesses. To highborn families, right here in *Dothik.*"

A breath pulled from my lungs. My hand spread out on my desk to steady myself as I stood. "*Nik,* her father was a...he was a *darukkar.* In a horde."

Bakkia simply looked at me, and I felt my chest begin to knot once more.

"The *Seta Kalliri* knew. Didn't you think it was odd? That she took a hybrid child into the *orala sa'kilan* from a *vekkiri,* simply because she asked? They would have never even seen a *vekkiri* in the North Lands before. Not at that time. *Nik,* she took the child in because the *Laseta Kalliri* asked her to. Because the child was her brother's. And they raised her there in secret, without anyone knowing. Why is that?"

Growling, I asked, "Why are you telling me this *now?*"

"I wanted to tell you before. But we found out the night the *Dothikkar* died. When the *Laseta Kalliri* met with us at the Heart," Bakkia explained. He ran a hand over the back of his neck. "And in the aftermath...I didn't want to burden you with this."

"*Vok,*" I growled, turning from him, thinking about the implications of his words.

Had Kara known? And if she had, why had she not *told* me?

Bakkia's jaw tensed when I met his eyes again.

"Who else knows?" I asked.

"Just the core," he told me. "Kalik, Vala, Errana, and Ulli."

I blew out a harsh breath. "I wish you would've told me.

And I know the exact moment when you were thinking about it too."

When he'd caught me alone in the throne room.

Vok.

Stepping forward, though we were alone, Bakkia lowered his voice, "I want you to be careful, Arik. You know what the priestesses are like. You know how they warped your mother's mind in the end."

Discomfort rose in me. I'd pieced together that the *Laseta Kalliri* had known my mother. The High Priestess had repeated things that my mother used to say. How well they'd known one another, I didn't know.

"And after today, there's no doubt in my mind what the *Laseta Kalliri* is trying to do," Bakkia said. "We worked too hard for this, Arik. We worked too hard for the priestesses to try to wiggle themselves into power through *vokking* bloodlines. To help see their own desires and wants for *Dothik* through."

I closed my eyes.

Because there it was.

Spelled out clearly.

The *Laseta Kalliri* wanted her own niece as my queen. She wanted her own bloodline on the throne of *Dothik*. Because the throne held immense power.

How far she'd go to *use* that power, that influence, remained to be seen.

Finally, I understood the *Laseta Kalliri's* price for her help in securing me the throne, for keeping the circumstances of the *Dothikkar's* death private, for setting up meetings between the highborn families and myself and having her priestesses publicly show me their support in the aftermath of that night.

But the question was...could I allow it?

"I know you love Kara."

I bit out a soft curse, opening my eyes to regard Bakkia at his hesitant words.

"I know you do. I *see* it. And I've known you your entire life, so don't try to tell me otherwise," he told me quietly. "But if you make her your queen, then you risk the throne. You risk *Dothik* falling into the priestesses' control."

"They want everything that we want," I tried to argue.

"And how long will that last?" Bakkia asked. "How long will that last before you and the *Laseta Kalliri* disagree on something, like you did this afternoon, and she tries to use Kara to sway you? And how many females in *Dothik's* history have wielded their power from the *Dothikkar's* bed? *Many.*"

"She wouldn't do that," I growled softly, anger pulsing through me at the words. That Bakkia would lump Kara in with females like Tanniva. "She would never do that."

Bakkia inclined his head. "I trust in your decisions, Arik. You know that. I'm just...I know how power can change people. I've seen it. You've seen it. And the throne of *Dothik*? That's the most power anyone can have. Kara may have a full heart, but there will never be a shortage of people trying to take advantage of that. That's all I'm trying to say."

His words brought a heavy lump to my belly.

There was a thought that was bubbling in my mind. One I'd pushed aside at first, but one that kept returning.

Send her back to the North Lands.

At first I'd played with the idea because I feared for her safety. My attentions were called away for long hours of the day and night, hours I couldn't be with her. I trusted very few to keep her safe in my absence. I thought that sending her back to the North Lands, at least temporarily, would be the wisest decision.

Only my own selfish need for her had kept me from doing so. Because when the day grew long and frustrating, the only thing that could help soothe me was having Kara near, feeling her warmth against me, her touch down my spine, and her whispered words in my ear.

But now...

Bakkia was right to fear the *Laseta Kalliri's* motives.

Bakkia was right to be concerned about Kara's own loyalties.

Because blood is blood, I thought, my fists clenching at my sides. And Kara had long desired a place of her own among the Dakkari. To be recognized as the *Laseta Kalliri's* own blood, with the *Seta Kalliri* claiming her as a daughter...Kara wouldn't have to fear for her future. She could do whatever she wished. She would be protected wherever she went.

"I don't envy you, Arik," Bakkia said softly. "But I know you will do what is best. Not just for yourself but for us all. *Lysi?*"

I had many others to think about. Not just my own wants and desires.

Meeting his eyes, I said gruffly, "*Lysi.*"

And already I felt like I'd been stabbed in the chest, thinking about what I had to do.

CHAPTER 56

When Arik found me later that night, I was still in the library.

Tucked into a hide-covered chair that faced the tall windows, which overlooked the wildlands. Kalik had started a fire for me in the hearth when night had come. The soft flicker of the light was just enough for me to make out the words on the page, though my eyes were beginning to go bleary.

"Kara."

I jerked my head toward the door, surprised to see Arik standing there.

Even though it was pitch black outside and I could see the constellation of Bekkar's sword hanging just above the window, I murmured, "You're done early."

Kalik was hovering in the doorway behind Arik. There was a strange energy rolling off of both of them, which made me close the dusty tome quickly and straighten.

"What is it?" I asked, my heart beginning to thud in my chest.

"Get some rest," Arik told Kalik.

Kalik inclined his head and then disappeared from view,

leaving Arik and me alone. He stepped into the library and shut the door behind him.

"Is something wrong?" I asked softly, rising from the chair to regard him carefully. Dread was beginning to pool in my belly, dread I'd felt before.

Arik's gaze went to the pot of water that Kalik had ordered up for me. I'd still continued taking *kana*, even after all this time. The sad part of it was that I knew the longer I could put off the pregnancy, the longer I could be with Arik.

My hand fluttered to my belly and I pressed gently, wondering if it was already too late.

"Your father," Arik said, "was the *Laseta Kalliri's* brother."

My brow furrowed. That was the last thing I'd expected him to say.

Then when I truly understood what he wanted to know, fledglings of guilt built. Because I hadn't told him what the priestess had revealed to me that night. We'd barely spoken about that night, for good reason.

"*Lysi,*" I said softly.

"Did you know?" came his soft growl.

He was...angry?

"*Neffar?*" I asked quietly, rooted in place next to the chair, the heavy book hanging limply in my hand. "*Nik*, of course not. Not until that night. *Kalloma* always said my father was a *darukkar*. She never told me who his family was or that he was born and raised here in *Dothik*. I just assumed..."

And partly because I hadn't *wanted* to know. I'd pushed all thoughts of my birth parents from my mind because I'd known I'd never get a straight answer from *Kalloma*. So many years of secrecy. And for what?

I didn't understand it.

"And why didn't you tell me afterward?" Arik wanted to know, holding himself stiffly in the center of the room. We were still a great distance apart, and this was beginning to feel...terrible. The ache that was building in my chest was beginning to make me panic.

"Because I didn't think it was important," I said quietly.

"That's a lie," he rasped. "Don't *vokking* lie to me, Kara."

I swallowed hard. "Arik—"

"You didn't think that I would want to know—that I would *need* to know—that you were of the *Laseta Kalliri's* bloodline?"

"I—I don't see why it matters!" I argued, not able to stand the distance between us anymore. I crossed the room to him, tossing the book onto the small table that held my cooling tea. I took his wrists in my palms, still covered in his *Vorakkar* cuffs. "I was going to tell you. Just not now. Not when you have so many other things that require your attention."

The *Laseta Kalliri* still visited me. Nearly every single day. We sat and spoke about her—*my* family. She promised to introduce me to them, telling me they would be so happy to have me among them because it would feel like my father had returned.

Her words...I couldn't deny that longing had pierced through me during our conversations. To belong. To have a family—one tied to me with blood.

Arik's jaw tightened.

"And we've barely seen one another," I added. "When you come to me at night, I can see how tired you are. It's not an important conversation—at least I didn't think so."

There was a subtle coldness in his expression, something I hadn't seen for quite some time. It was that coldness that seemed to freeze my own heart.

"Arik," I whispered.

I had the impression he was holding himself back. I had the impression he was deliberately *not* touching me, even if he *wanted* to.

"What's wrong?" I demanded. "What's this really about?"

Because I couldn't understand it. I didn't understand where this sudden anger was coming from.

I thought...I thought he might even be *pleased* with my ancestry. That I shared blood with the High Priestess of *Dothik*, who came from a highborn family. I thought it might make it easier on him within his courts.

But maybe that was my frustrating naivete speaking. I'd done something wrong in not telling him, and I couldn't understand what that was.

"Blood is blood, Kara," he murmured to me, his voice softening ever so slightly when he witnessed the drawn expression on my face. His nostrils flared again, and it was then that I saw it. The pain. The discomfort in his own gaze. It made my stomach drop and hollow. "And blood ties are strong. Especially here."

"*Neffar?*" I asked.

Relief whipped through me when he cupped my face between his palms. Because I thought that it would be fine. That we would work through this. That he would make me understand.

"You are the *Laseta Kalliri's* niece," he told me. "And she wants power of her own in *Dothik*, even more power than she already has. Having you at my side is not something I can risk."

"*Neffar?*" I breathed.

Those words didn't hurt. Not yet. It was a delayed reaction, like that moment when I'd cut myself on Bekkar's sword in the *orala sa'kilan* and I'd been in shock at the sheer amount of blood that had begun pooling from the small wound. It hadn't been until much later that I'd actually felt the sting of pain.

That was what was happening right now. I couldn't feel the pain. Not yet at least.

"I've had Nassik send a *thesper* to the *Seta Kalliri*," he informed me, his voice hard and unyielding. His hands dropped away from my face, and he blew out a harsh breath, turning. His gaze went past me to flicker out over the wildlands. "I wanted to inform her that you would be returning to the North Lands."

My hand flew to the table that was at my side. To hold me steady when my knees felt weak.

"You...you don't mean that," I said. My tone was certain. I laughed, but the sound was hollow and empty. "Arik, what are —what are you *doing?*"

Panic was rising in my breast, and it made me want to vomit.

He ran a hand through his too-long hair. His movements were fidgety—completely unlike him—but his face was so, so cold, his mouth pressed into a firm line. There was no warmth in his eyes besides that brief flash of pain.

This was the Arik I'd witnessed in his stronghold. The leader of his district. Unbending. As stable and strong as an ancient pillar.

And now...he was the *king* of Dakkar.

His eyes were like Dakkari steel. Like ice during the frost in the North Lands. Unbreakable.

I turned from him to regard the library he'd shown me just this morning. He'd wanted me to like it, hadn't he? So where was this coming from? Why had he made this decision so quickly when just this morning I'd woken to him between my legs, full of need but gentle? He'd peppered kisses across my face as he'd stroked deep, groaning and murmuring words of his awe and desire across my flesh.

I'd never felt so *wanted.*

Just remembering this morning made my chest splinter. It felt like the little bones protecting my heart were being snapped and torn.

"*Nik,*" I breathed, shaking my head. "I'm not going."

His eyes narrowed. "What do you mean you're not going?"

"I don't know what you've been told, Arik," I said, my spine steeling, "but you can't just turn me away. You can't *do that.*"

"I'm your *king,* Kara," he growled, making me freeze, stepping close to me. "I can make you do whatever I want. And you cannot disobey me. Do not forget that! If I tell you to return to the North Lands, then *you will go.*"

The last three words were clipped. Harsh. Unfathomable hurt crashed down into my body, making me feel heavy, like my limbs were made of stone.

The worst part of this situation was that I'd *known* this would happen. I'd seen it. Maybe not *this* moment, but I'd seen the aftermath of it. I'd looked into Arik's eyes in my vision of the East Lands and seen coldness. I'd seen detachment.

All because I was the *Laseta Kalliri's* blood?

I still didn't understand.

But if this was what it took for Arik to turn his back on me, then how deeply had he even felt for me?

But there is a child, my mind whispered.

"In my vision, I was pregnant."

The words slipped from my lips before I could stop them. Even still, I cringed at the desperation I heard in my own tone. Tears were beginning to sting the backs of my eyes. This wasn't just about me. There was a child. Even if I sounded desperate and panicked, I needed to make him understand that he couldn't just make me *leave.*

"*Neffar?*" he asked quietly. He'd gone still. Deathly still.

"There's a child," I said, though my voice sounded pleading.

"*Nik*, you've been taking the *kana*. I've ensured that you've taken it every single night. Without fail. There is no child."

Was I to be so easily dismissed? My word was no longer worth anything to him? So he only believed me when it suited him?

Did he think I was *lying?*

"I'm telling you the truth!" I cried out. "You can't just—"

"Kara, *enough!*" he bellowed, slashing a hand through the empty space between us. I sucked in a sharp breath at his harsh tone. "You're hurt. I understand that," he continued, seeming to make the effort to soften his voice when he saw the tracks of my tears running down my cheeks. His expression twisted briefly, his hands clenching at his sides. "You think this is easy for me to do? You think I like to see you in pain?"

Never had I thought that Arik wouldn't *believe* me when I told him about the baby.

The possibility had never even crossed my mind.

But if he didn't believe me—if he thought that I would *lie* about a child just to stay in *Dothik* with him—then what other horrible things must he have thought I was capable of?

I didn't recognize this male.

This Arik.

This wasn't the Arik who had pulled me back from the brink after the *Dothikkar's* death. This wasn't the male whose voice softened ever so slightly whenever he called me *rei kassiri*. This wasn't the male who kissed away my tears and murmured in my ear that he would protect me. I'd felt safe with that Arik. Cherished. Loved.

I felt none of those things right now.

"It certainly seems easy for you to do," I whispered, staring at this stranger of a male with tears streaming down my face. When I turned away, I looked at the shelves and stacks of books along the walls. The shadowy corners that seemed more menacing than they'd been before. "This is about more than who my father was. You just won't admit that."

It has to be, I thought.

I'd begun to dream about a life with Arik here. In *Dothik*. Even though it was foolish. Even though I knew where my future truly was, I couldn't help it. I'd dreamed of waking next to him. I'd dreamed of making this palace my home. Walking in the marketplace. Studying in the archives, learning everything I could about the history of Dakkar.

I'd dreamed of giving him children. Starting a family. Something that up until quite recently had seemed out of the realm of possibility for someone like me.

And now I was seeing those foolish dreams slashed like a blade slicing through parchment.

It hurt so much more than I was expecting. The disappointment. The grief. The heartbreak.

That was why I knew it had to be about *more* than just my bloodline, more than my connections to the priestesses, both here and in the North Lands. He was just using it as an excuse to turn me away.

Arik didn't believe I was suitable to be his queen. Whether that was because I was only half-Dakkari or because of my upbringing, I couldn't be certain. He'd called me naive once. Perhaps he still thought that I was. That I could never be what he needed me to be.

And *that* hurt.

It hurt more than I expected it to, and I'd even been *prepared* for this.

But then I reminded myself that I was the daughter of the *Seta Kalliri*. I took pride in that because I'd grown up with accomplished, intelligent, and independent females all my life.

As the silence stretched out between Arik and me...I decided that I wouldn't beg. I wouldn't beg to stay if he wanted me to leave. I had more pride than that. It welled in me, flooding my entire body.

If Arik didn't want me as his queen...then I would leave.

And I love him enough to do just that, I thought suddenly.

I stifled a sob at the painful realization, muffling it against the back of my hand when I turned away. I heard a sharp sound break from his throat, but I stepped toward the stretch of windows when I saw him reach for me.

I loved him enough to *leave*. Because I wanted him to succeed in *Dothik*. If I wasn't in his plans for the future of Dakkar, then it was for a reason. A reason only he could see.

And he was right. He was the king. The most powerful male

on this planet now. More powerful than all the *Vorakkar* and the *Sorakkar*.

He had the world on his shoulders. I didn't want to add to that burden. I wanted to help alleviate it.

I cried silently as I looked out over the wildlands. Arik was hovering behind me—I could feel his presence like a touch, and it only made me cry harder.

"Kara…" he murmured. I waited for him to take it all back. I waited for him to say it was a mistake, that he wanted me to be here with him, to stay.

The moments ticked by.

In the end, he said nothing.

I'd thought that he could love me. I'd thought I'd seen it, I'd thought I'd *felt* it…but I'd been wrong. Because if he loved me, how could he do *this?*

And so, I could love him enough for the both of us.

See this through, I couldn't help but think. *See the vision through.*

"I'll go," I whispered, wrapping my arms around my waist, hugging them to me.

The words felt like glass as they scraped across my tongue.

"I'll go back to the North Lands. If that's what you want, *Dothikkar.*"

Chapter 57

It was strange the way my mind and my body protected me against an unfathomable thing.

But as I descended the grand staircase down to the main courtyard of the *Dothikkar's* palace, I felt numb. I could not feel joy, and I could not feel pain. I could not feel the sting of excitement, and I could not feel the crushing despair of heartbreak. There was static in my mind, but it felt like a comforting buzz, filling it, consuming me so I wouldn't focus too deeply on anything else.

Like Arik, who was standing close to the group of *darukkars*—ones from his own horde—already astride their *pyrokis*. Errana and Kalik were also accompanying me back to the North Lands. Despite the lack of close confidants Arik trusted within the palace, he was still plucking them from their posts to guide me back to the *orala sa'kilan*.

Errana was watching me, a twist of something I thought resembled pity on her face. Kalik was looking at Arik, his brows slightly furrowed. And Arik was looking at me, but his expression was wiped clean and he held himself stiffly, his hands clasped behind his back. Even his tail was still.

We'd been apart for two days as preparations had been

made for the journey. This was the first time I was seeing him since the night in the library, and the pain that began to wiggle in my chest *almost* broke me out of my numbness. But then I thought of the quiet of the temple. I thought of the wind that whistled through the columns of the atrium when we left the door open. I thought of the quiet hum of the priestesses' prayers, lullabies to me because I'd heard them all my life.

There was one last matter to speak of, however.

And so when my booted feet met the stone of the courtyard, I walked to Arik, though I kept my gaze on the notch of his throat, smooth and golden and strong. I stopped when there was a reasonable distance between us. Close enough so that he could hear me. And far enough away that I wouldn't be able to smell him, so I wouldn't be tempted to throw myself into his chest, to breathe him in, to beg him to let me stay.

Dignity. This was about my dignity. He'd already crushed it under the heel of his thieving boots, but I'd tried to pull myself back up in the last two days. I'd hardly cried. I'd hardly done *anything.* The only thing I'd done was make plans as I'd sat in my chair in the library. I didn't touch a single tome when I was within, an oddity in itself which always made Kalik, my guard, frown.

I simply looked out the window at the wildlands, and I traced the paths back to the North Lands in my mind. I planned how I'd tell *Kalloma* about the child, wondering if she—and the other priestesses—would allow me to stay in the temple. If they voted against it, despite *Kalloma's* wishes, I could journey to the *saruk* of Rath Hidri. He would allow me entry to his outpost. I could live there. I thought I could even be content there. One day.

Then I planned for the East Lands. I counted the heart-stones in my mind. One. Two. Three. Four. Five. We would need all of them.

But I knew something that no one else did, not even Arik. That this act of eradicating the fog would destroy them all.

They would turn to dust in my hands. Sacred stones that had been prayed over for centuries. Gone in a moment.

If anyone knew that the heartstones would be destroyed in the process, I wasn't certain they would wish to continue. A sad truth. One I never would've thought possible had I remained in the temple all this time.

Now, however, I'd seen the desperation, the greed in people. I'd seen it even in the *Laseta Kalliri's* face. She'd been furious when she'd learned of Arik's plan to send me away. She'd come to me at dawn the following morning, urging me to speak with him again, urging me to change his mind in whatever way I could.

She'd grown frustrated by my listlessness, by my lack of response. She'd tried gentling her tone. She'd tried raising it. But she could not get me to react. And it was then that I'd seen it. Her own fear. Her own anger.

The *Laseta Kalliri* had lost her way, driven by the greed of this city, driven by her need for power.

That morning, I thought I could finally understand why Arik was doing what he was doing. I could see it take shape in my mind, like a wispy cloud on a clear day. The edges of it were blurred, but it was tangible. I could *see* it. Though I might not fully understand it.

He was stronger than I was, that was for certain.

Because I thought I'd burn a whole city down for him in my own weakness.

In the end, the *Laseta Kalliri* had left in a stiff anger. I didn't tell her about my vision. I didn't tell her about the heartstones. Truthfully, I didn't even think I'd tell *Kalloma* once I reached the North Lands. Not because I didn't trust her, but because I was afraid she'd try to *stop me.*

Arik looked at me steadily now. I could feel his hardened gaze roaming my features though I kept my own down.

"The morning after the black moon," I told him, my voice sounding far, far away. "We will meet you on the plains of the East Lands. Inform the other *Vorakkar* and the *Sorakkar* of Rath Hidri. That is when it must be done. *Hanniva.*"

Please.

I added in that word as an afterthought because I realized I was speaking to the *Dothikkar* of Dakkar after all...whose predecessor I had murdered.

I flinched, my breath hitching, the thought threatening to break me from my state of calm. And I couldn't allow that. Not now. Not now.

"*Nik,*" came his voice. I furrowed my brow, not expecting that word. "You will stay in the North Lands. The *Seta Kalliri* will come to the East Lands, but I want you nowhere near the fog, Kara."

It stung. The bitter part of me, the part that *wanted* to make him hurt as much as I did, wanted to remind him that he didn't care what happened to me. Giving such an order made it seem like he did.

"I will be there," I informed him, hardening my voice, feeling a spark of anger which was vastly preferable over hurt. "Or will you give me your *Dothikkar* order to stay behind?"

"I will if I must," came the words.

Kalloma *will respect my wishes,* I thought to myself. If Arik wanted me to stay in the North Lands, then he would have to ride there personally and chain me up.

Knowing he wouldn't do that, I simply said nothing.

The distance between us felt like miles and miles of dangerous wildland.

I would see him again, *lysi,* but would we ever speak again? And if this *was* the last time we spoke...I didn't want it to end on this note.

Softening my tone, I said, "I know that you will do great things here, *Dothikkar*."

I tamped down my own pain into a tiny box inside me, stuffing it until the seams threatened to burst.

Arik stilled.

"I believe it," I whispered, briefly meeting his eyes. Those molten eyes that I had so desperately wanted to see when he'd come to the *orala sa'kilan*, eyes I'd only ever seen in my dreams. "With everything I have in me, I believe it."

When I turned toward the *pyroki* that Errana had prepared for me, I swore I caught a brief flash of panic on Arik's face.

"Kara," came his soft murmur, so quiet no one else could hear.

Stilling, I turned my head to look at him. My heart seemed to wiggle in my chest, shifting beneath the bones that protected it, trying to break free. As if it didn't want to be a part of me anymore.

In a brief moment of desperation, I pleaded with him silently.

Say you didn't mean it.

Say you want me to stay.

Say you believe me about the child. Our *child.*

Say that you love me.

In the end, he said none of those things.

"Be safe, *lysi*?" he murmured. He stepped back, and the disappointment I felt almost made it impossible to breath.

Looking away from him, I scanned the courtyard for the last time. It was early morning. Dark still. As if he hadn't wanted anyone to see me leaving the palace. Had he even told the *Laseta Kalliri*?

This early, no one stood at the gates, though it had become common these days. Dakkari passing by would press their faces between the steel, if only to catch a glimpse of the new *Dothikkar* through the windows of the palace. His supporters gathered almost every day at the entrance, as if they were ready to battle again for the throne.

Still hiding me away? I couldn't help but wonder.

Then I nodded, accepting it, feeling that knowledge slide down my throat like acid and settle in my belly like a stone. All of my insecurities and fears wrapped into a single thought: that he was ashamed of me.

Then I took a breath.

My lips quirked in a small smile I couldn't quite feel.

I wasn't ashamed of me though.

And that knowledge felt like a comforting balm as I stepped toward the *pyroki*. I pulled myself up onto its back. The creature was smaller than Syok, more comfortable for me to ride, and yet...strange. I was so used to Arik's *pyroki*, that gentle beast I'd grown so fond of, who was being treated like a prince in the *Dothikkar's* own enclosure.

I looked at the palace behind me. Golden light seeped from some of the windows, but the majority of the palace was dark.

Then I looked at Arik, though he'd stepped back in such a way that it cast the majority of his face into shadow.

Swallowing, I faced forward. Forcing myself to look away before I withered with my despair.

"Are you ready?" Errana asked me quietly when she pulled her own *pyroki* up to mine, side by side.

"*Lysi*," I said without a moment's hesitation.

She sighed.

"Let's get you back home," she said.

Chapter 58

The *orala sa'kilan* was just as I'd left it.

A quiet fortress, shrouded in ice, high in the mountains of the North Lands.

I thought it strange that the cold bit at me bitterly now when I'd lived here all my life. But the winds wove through my cloak and made me shiver violently—and the frost had long passed. This was the warmest it would ever be, and I felt frozen.

Our travel pace had been merciless. Partly because of me. I hadn't wanted to stop. I'd barely slept. I ate on the back of my *pyroki*, who I didn't want to name because I knew she would not be mine. The others were exhausted. I was too. And yet my own pain was driving me to reach home. To reach *Kalloma* and my family. To reach my tower. To reach my bed.

The gates parted when we stopped before them, the sound like a sharp crack as it echoed through the pass. The *pyrokis* were restless, but the *darukkars* urged them forward as Kalik and Errana went to either side of me, their necks bending and turning, seeking out dangers that I knew were not there.

As we stopped in the courtyard past the gates, I saw the door open at the top of the stairs.

For the first time, I realized how much the *orala sa'kilan* resembled the palace. With its tall columns, its glittering turrets and towers, and its grand staircase that led to ornate doors.

Kalloma stood on the threshold, her slippered feet stepping beyond the temple and already making her way down the stairs. The *Seta Kalliri*—the High Priestess of all of Dakkar—and her face was pinched with worry, relief, and desperation to reach me again.

A tightness in my chest released at the sight of her, and suddenly my exhaustion crashed down on me, threatening to unseat me from the *pyroki's* back when I nearly slid down her side.

Kalik caught me, his lips pinching down into a frown. We had been traveling for only a week. And I could see he was still concerned about the nausea that had begun to plague me toward the end of our journey.

So soon, I thought, remembering the bile at the back of my throat. *And not soon enough.*

Kalik helped me slide down to the courtyard on trembling legs.

"Are you all right, Kara?" he asked me, his expression unusually somber.

"*Lysi,*" I whispered, but my eyes were on *Kalloma.*

She'd just made it to the bottom of the stairs, and I broke free of Kalik's gentle hold, striding toward her quickly, my legs moving faster than I thought possible.

And when she caught me up in her arms, uncaring that the travel party could see her weakness or the tears I caught shimmering in her gaze, I buried my face into her neck and breathed her in. She smelled of our soap. She smelled like...

"Home," I whispered, squeezing my eyes shut when the tears began to slow and wet her neck. "I'm home."

Kalloma didn't say anything.

She only held me as I began to cry, as the shield of numbness I'd held close shattered into a million pieces in her familiar embrace.

That was when the wretchedness of loss, of heartbreak finally hit me.

And I crumbled.

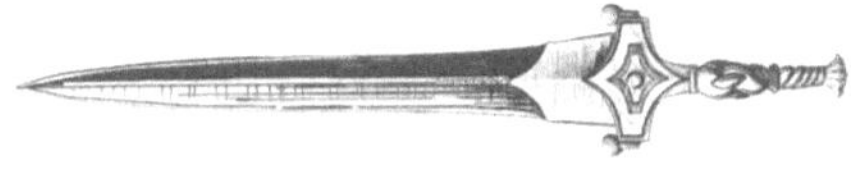

Two weeks later...

"Is this the final list?" I asked Nassik, looking over the parchment with what I knew were scrawled names. Some of which I could actually recognize as I traced my gaze over the writing.

"*Lysi,*" Nassik murmured, running his finger down the column of sixty new names we would be adding to the guard rotations. Fifteen members from each of the districts—Northern, Southern, Eastern, and Western—and no more. Handpicked, tested, and studied with their loyalties cemented.

And, most importantly, not a part of my father's old force.

"With room for more, should we need it," Nassik added.

The *Laseta Kalliri* was not in attendance at today's meeting, for which I was grateful. Nassik still didn't trust the priestess. Neither did I, but I could not deny that she was useful to me. Despite her obvious rancor at Kara's sudden departure, she'd attempted to move beyond it.

A sharp pain went through my chest at the thought of Kara,

as it always did. I rubbed at the spot, catching Nassik's gaze on me, and then I straightened.

If he'd noticed my increasing restlessness, my shortness with some of the guards or the way I'd refused to have my private rooms touched by the palace staff...he hadn't mentioned it. Though I knew it was only a matter of time before he barged into my rooms and washed the damn furs on my bed himself.

But then Kara's scent would be gone. Permanently.

And I couldn't have that.

It was already fading, day by day. Even with my sharp senses, it was growing more and more difficult to catch her familiar and comforting scent.

Kalik came into the room then, the door shutting heavily behind him.

He tipped his chin up at me, meeting my eyes.

"*Thespers* are sent," he informed me. He slid to his usual place along the wall, leaning against one of the tall chests that held a variety of maps—taken from the Heart, where Bakkia had moved in in my absence. "Are you certain you don't want the *darukkars* to accompany us?"

He meant to the East Lands. Which we would depart for come morning. And there was still so much to be done here in *Dothik*.

"*Nik*, they should stay behind. And you sent a *thesper* to the *orala sa'kilan* too?" I demanded quietly, shooting him a quick look. The one I'd had Nassik write out, ordering the *Seta Kalliri* to keep Kara at the temple.

Kalik rolled his neck, a sharp crack sounding at the movement. "*Lysi.*"

He'd just returned from the journey north not four days ago. They'd made it to the North Lands in a single week, he'd informed me. It had made my temper flare, wondering why they'd kept such a punishing pace with Kara in tow. But then Kalik had informed me it was *Kara* who hadn't wanted to stop...

Which only made that familiar sting in my chest all the more apparent. Guilt, perhaps. An ache so deep that sometimes I thought I couldn't breathe.

Because I knew that *I'd* driven her away. That she'd wanted to keep going because she couldn't wait to put more and more distance between us.

It kept me up at night. I hadn't had a good sleep since before the *Dothikkar's* death, but my exhaustion had grown even worse in Kara's absence. Food was tasteless. I ate mindlessly to maintain my strength. I tossed and turned in bed at night, and the only thing that could make me sleep—even if only for an hour—was to find her scent among the cushions that lined our bed. I dragged it into my lungs, my hands curling for her though she was not there, and it felt like a *vokking* blade dragged through my gut *every damn time.*

I couldn't remember her smile. I couldn't remember her laugh. All I could remember was her glassy, astonished, pained gaze when she realized that I was turning her away.

That was what haunted me at night. Not the unrest in the Western District over my rise to the throne. Not the overflowing dungeon in the Northern District, the lines of Dakkari that were still awaiting trial. Not the overwhelming amount of positions that needed to be filled within the palace and throughout *Dothik.* Not the *Laseta Kalliri's* apparent derision. Not even the damn fog.

Lack of sleep had made it difficult to function.

I was nowhere near ready to leave *Dothik.* And I would have to trust the *Laseta Kalliri* of all people to keep the peace in my absence. At least on the eradication of the fog, we both agreed. And when we saw that through…I would have more room to breathe. Afterward, we would hold the ceremony for my coronation, cementing it before all the eyes of *Dothik.* We would begin the expansion of the city toward the north and rebuild the canal that stretched from there toward *Drukkar's* Sea, which hadn't been maintained for over fifty years.

Afterward, I would take to the wildlands to meet with the *Sorakkar*. To meet with the *Vorakkar*. I would meet with the *vekkiri* who were building their own outpost in the South Lands, and I would meet with the Killup in the North.

One thing was for certain...I refused to rule like my father. A *Dothikkar* should embrace the old ways of our people, the old traditions. The way of the hordes and the *saruks,* and I would give them the respect that they deserved and the space to grow, if they so wished.

But for now...

For now, we needed to deal with the fog.

And in the morning, we would begin that final journey to the East Lands.

I couldn't get Kara's words out of my head. About how the fog was our last warning. That this would be our last chance to rebalance Dakkar. I still didn't know quite what she'd meant by it, but I could hear the unwavering truth in her voice. Whatever she'd seen...it had perhaps shaken her more than my father's strange and sudden death.

The black moon was in seven days.

We would have to ride fast and hard to reach the East Lands in time.

Chapter 60

I watched the dust trickle and glisten in the spear of light. Pausing for only a moment, I watched it dance and sway. Then I was moving again, winding down the stairs to the vault below the atrium.

We would journey to the East Lands soon. Despite *Kalloma's* urgings for me to stay, I knew that no one could convince me not to go.

And so I journeyed deep underground to the vault.

At the door, I pulled the key from my dress and slid it into the lock, twisting that ancient, rusted thing until I heard it pop open.

Inside, it was just as I'd left it a few days prior. I'd resumed my duties around the *orala sa'kilan*, even though I saw the way *Kalloma's* eyes narrowed in worry. I smiled and laughed with the others. I recounted my brief travels across Dakkar for Trissa and Avala. But whenever they asked me about "the *Vorakkar*," as they called him, I said nothing, giving glib, meaningless answers.

Though I tried to hide the way my belly was beginning to grow, I'd caught the *Niva Kalliri's* speculative gaze on me just the morning before when I was reaching to clean a window and my dress had plastered itself to me.

I was rounding already. More quickly than I'd ever expected.

I'd been back at the temple for two weeks already, and I had told no one. Not even *Kalloma*. And I wasn't even certain *why*. I would find comfort and safety in her arms, and yet...I couldn't help but feel like a fool. The oldest of stories. A heartbroken female with a child in her womb. Just one more for the books.

The vault was dark, and I lit the sconces on the wall with the torch I'd brought. It was a small space, a square room with stone walls and ancient weapons hanging from carefully spaced steel brackets.

The axe of Hari from the horde battles over three centuries ago. Nevriam's shield, who was the great protector of the South Lands. A dagger of gold, said to be dipped in Drukkar's own blood and imbued with his vengeful power.

Yet surrounded by ancient things, each with great and terrible stories of their own, my eyes went only to one.

Bekkar's sword.

I walked to it, reached out to smooth my fingertips over the flat of the blade which I knew was still sharp, even after all this time. The scar across my palm and on the back of my shoulder reminded me of that.

My gaze went to the hilt, reminded of something I'd seen in my vision of Arik. He'd had Bekkar's sword, and I knew it was because I would take it from the vault. It would be gifted to its next owner, to its next keeper and protector, to Bekkar's own blood. One who was actually worthy to wield it.

I remembered seeing a stone in the hilt in the vision. White in color and shimmering.

Only there was no stone in the hilt.

There was a decorative, rounded piece of gold where I'd seen the stone. And for the first time, I inspected it closely, running the sharp tip of one fingernail around the edge, seeing if it would catch anywhere. When there was no give, I went to the gold dagger that hung next to the sword, lifting it off the wall.

Prodding the razor-thin tip along the rounded edge, I pressed, careful not to scratch the gold even as I twisted the dagger.

Finally the dagger sunk slightly. There was an edge, and I snapped my wrist, prying the piece of gold up.

It thudded to the ground, heavy, landing only once before it stilled.

My breath caught. Because underneath that plated protection, a white stone gleamed in the torchlight. A stone that had likely not been seen for centuries. Hidden away in plain sight.

I knew what it was. To be certain, however, I gently pressed my fingers to its surface. Preparing myself.

A gasp wrenched from my throat as the stone began to glow. Not blue, however, like the others, but gold. A gold so yellow that it looked like the sun.

And I heard her. Kakkari's voice. Those millions of voices that whispered in my ear became one. A voice that was pure. A voice that was real.

There was no pain this time. There was no fear. I met her without hesitation, focusing on the stone, imagining that I was pushing myself into it, enveloping myself there. I poured every bit of my doubt, my disappointment, my grief, my sorrow into it. But not for Arik. For Kakkari. The way *she* had made me doubt.

There was a touch on my shoulder, but when I turned there was no one there. I felt another touch. And another. And another. Until it felt like hands sliding across my body, weaving into my hair, pressing into my belly.

I heard my own voice in my mind.

You were chosen for a reason. Remake the Five again. The Five will help remake Dakkar anew.

A sob tore from my throat. My face was wet with tears, and it felt like the air was sucked from my lungs.

I didn't know how long I stood there, my fingers pressed to the hidden heartstone, but eventually I lowered my hand.

Staring at the sword with unseeing eyes, I dragged in a slow, careful breath. I had not prayed to Kakkari since the *Dothikkar's* death. I had seen her vengeance. I had seen her anger. But this Kakkari was a different form of her. The one I'd known all my life. Guiding and giving.

It was her words in my mind. Her voice as mine. Her will and my purpose.

Calm settled deep into my bones. Relief too. It felt like a sodden bandage had been ripped from my wound, and finally, *finally* it would be time to heal it.

The Five.

The *Rivalla Lo'Kilan.*

The five heartstones?

Or the five priestesses?

I didn't know what it meant. Not yet. But I would. I would understand everything.

Carefully, I reached up and took Bekkar's sword from its place on the wall. Crouching, I plucked the gold casing from the floor and snapped it back into place, concealing the heartstone once more.

This sword had helped remake Dakkar once before, in a different time.

It would do so again. With Kakkari's blessing encased in its hilt.

Taking a deep breath, I wiped my hands over my cheeks, dashing away the evidence of my tears. Then I left the vault, locking it behind me with the sword's heavy hilt in hand.

When I reached the atrium once more, I found *Kalloma* walking with the *Niva Kalliri.* They were just ending their evening prayers and were likely dispersing to the archives for the night.

When *Kalloma* saw me, she waved the *Niva Kalliri* onward and approached me, her gaze going to the sword before searching mine.

She didn't say anything about the sword. Instead, she took my hand and led me back to the *sa'kilan*, where Kakkari's heartstone once lived, before she'd given it to me and to Arik. Now it was with him in *Dothik*, transported by his horde back to the palace.

Silently, we entered her office, and I breathed in the familiar smell of books and the warm spices of the tea brewing on her desk. Ready and waiting, as if she'd known we would be here tonight. Perhaps she'd been looking for me.

After a wave of her hand, an unseen force snapped the door closed behind us, and I laid Bekkar's sword gently across a chair. My eyes caught on the hidden heartstone. Concealed for so long. I wondered if *Kalloma* even knew.

I sank down into another chair as *Kalloma* poured me some tea. There was so much unsaid between us. So much that I had not asked her because I'd been afraid. So much that she had kept hidden herself.

With Kakkari's voice still lingering in my mind, I found myself asking quietly, "What really happened to my birth mother?"

Kalloma didn't even flinch at the question. She brought my small goblet to me with a steady hand and then perched herself on the chair closest to her desk so I was in full view of her.

"Was she here? In the *orala sa'kilan*?" I asked.

"*Lysi*," *Kalloma* said. "For a time."

"Did she…did she take her own life?" I asked next. "An offering to Kakkari? Because that's what you told her to do, to keep me strong?"

Kalloma's eyes widened, and I felt relief prick through me.

"Of course not, *rei kassiri*," she whispered, the words harsh from her lips. "Of course not. I *never* told her that."

"Then what happened?"

Kalloma blew out a sharp breath.

"Kakkari was within her," she finally told me. "I told you that, long ago. I told you about how she made the journey here but it was with Kakkari's help. Your mother was blessed, Kara. Like you. Like me. Like so many on this planet in its current state. She came into that blessing through love for your father or love for you—or both."

"You both loved the same male," I murmured. I watched her flinch. "The *Laseta Kalliri* told me that you chose your duty over your love for my father. Is that true?"

"*Lysi*," she whispered. And in that single word, I heard the despair, and it made tears prick the backs of my eyes. "I both hated and loved your mother, Kara."

That wasn't what I expected her to say.

"I hated her because she had everything I'd given up. Your father. A family. A child. But your mother was impossible to hate. Even in her grief, she was selfless and kind. And you...you are a perfect recreation of her."

"How did she die?" I asked.

Kalloma shook her head, her face twisting. "I found her in the *sa'kilan*. Late at night when you were perhaps a year old. She was collapsed on the floor. The heartstone had been within her palm. That was how I found her."

I pressed my fingers to my throat, feeling my swallow.

She'd lived in the temple for longer than I thought. And to think that she died in a place that I walked within every single day...it made my belly twist.

"Later that night when I came to you," *Kalloma* said, her voice quiet and careful, "your eyes were shining blue. Like you had two perfect heartstones for eyes. And you were looking up at me, with that faraway look I know so well, and I swear on

Kakkari that you were having your first vision. Perhaps even of *him*."

My brow furrowed.

"There is always balance in the world, Kara," *Kalloma* told me, as she had *always* told me. "There must be. And I saw it that night. Kakkari took your mother from you, but she gave you something in return. There is…"

"A price that needs to be paid," I finished for her, glancing at Bekkar's sword.

"*Lysi*," *Kalloma* said quietly. "Your father was a great male. A strong, honorable warrior. And for his mate he chose an equally strong female. Their love story is tragic, *lysi*. So much loss and grief. That is not what I wish for you. It was what I tried to protect you from, by keeping you here. By keeping you safe. Because in my own selfishness, I believed that *you* were the price *I* would have to pay for my own ambitions, for my own past mistakes."

Silence lapsed between us as I processed her words.

Eventually she said, "You are changed, Kara."

Glancing up at her, I saw she was watching me with a sad smile.

"I can see it and I can feel it," she said, clasping her hands tighter around her own goblet of spiced tea. "Do you love him?"

There was no hesitation when I answered, "*Lysi*."

"Does he love you?"

I swallowed. The pain at her question cut me into ribbons.

I didn't answer her.

Kalloma sighed, taking my silence to mean that he didn't. But all I had in the *orala sa'kilan*—besides my family—was *time*. Endless time to think, to remember, to analyze. Arik was a skilled liar. He'd told me so himself. But even I didn't think he could lie so well and for so long.

Wind rattled the windows outside. A crackle sizzled in the

fire basin. And I made the words come even though I hated to see the disappointment on her face.

"I will have his child," I whispered.

Kalloma looked at me steadily.

Then she returned, "I know."

"You have seen it?" I asked, though I was not entirely surprised.

Her head dipped in a small incline. "I saw it when he first appeared here. I was angry then. And I wanted him gone. I didn't want him anywhere near you."

"But you let me go," I said, my brows furrowing. "You let me go with him."

Her small smile made my heart stutter. "You would have gone regardless. He is yours, remember? Your dream. Your fate. It was not my place to interfere, though it was the hardest thing I've ever had to do. Even above leaving your father in *Dothik*. Because *you* are the love of my life, Kara. Never forget that."

Standing, I went to her. I kneeled next to her chair. She reached out a hand to cup my cheek.

"And you will know the love I speak of. When you bring your own child into this world. You will know the incredible joy. The overwhelming fear. The highs and the lows of that love. You will be even stronger for it," she told me.

I pressed my lips to her cheek, which felt thinner and softer than I remembered it.

"There is a reason that priestesses are forbidden from having children, lovers or husbands or mates. Because then we forget," she told me. "We forget that we are here to serve. We forget that we are here to protect. How can we serve Kakkari, how can we serve the beings on this planet if our hearts are already full, if our minds are already occupied and our love already taken?"

My brow furrowed. "What are you saying?"

She smiled. "I am stepping down as the *Seta Kalliri*. Soon I will leave the *orala sa'kilan*."

I stilled. "*Neffar?*"

"You made me realize that I have done a great disservice to Dakkar. And you were right to confront me about it. I thought only of myself because I was consumed with my fear. I can no longer continue down this path knowing that I did not put Dakkar first. Because I wished to be a mother above being a priestess."

My lips parted. "Who will take your place?"

"The *Laseta Kalliri*," she told me, eyeing me. I swallowed, not sure how I felt about that decision. "I believe it is the right choice. She needs to remember. She needs to remember what it is to follow in Kakkari's path, not to claw her way down her own."

Realization sank into my belly as I eyed *Kalloma*, who saw more than I realized.

"This place has a way of humbling you, of centering you," she said softly. "And if the *Dothikkar* truly wishes to pave a new way for Dakkar, then my gut tells me that the *Laseta Kalliri* should be out of his way."

I thought...that was probably for the best.

"And where will you go?"

"Wherever you go. Back to *Dothik*, perhaps. I long for the warmth of the West Lands again," she told me, her tone tinged with knowing. When I opened my mouth, frowning, she said quickly, "I will not leave for some time, Kara. A long transition is needed once the *Laseta Kalliri* is here. We have time. But I have made my decision. It is done."

CHAPTER 61

We reached the East Lands before anyone else.

A handful of *darukkars* from the nearest horde of Rath Rowin had escorted us from the *orala sa'kilan,* though I'd seen more than a few frown in my direction, hesitant. Whether that was because I was a hybrid female or because Arik had issued his own warning to the *Vorakkar* of Rath Rowin against taking me...I didn't know. But I was betting on the latter, even as I climbed onto the back of my own *pyroki* with effortless ease, Bekkar's sword strapped down my spine.

I'd looked at the *darukkars* steadily, practically daring them to dismount me. In the end, none had said a word and we'd left the North Lands behind shortly afterward.

For four days we rode.

On the third day, I saw the fog for the first time, from atop a cliff that I scaled that night as the others rested by the fire. I couldn't help but seek out the constellations of Tanniva's hand and Bekkar's sword in the night sky, feeling a sharp pang and ache when I spotted them, hearing Arik's teasing laugh and rich voice in my ear in memory.

Then I shook it off—I shook *him* off—and looked east.

In the dark, it had looked like a dark mass against the land. I'd mistaken it for the shadows of a valley but then realized that the fog had overtaken the *entirety* of the valley, that it had swallowed it up whole.

And when we reached the East Lands, on a bright, hot afternoon, the air had been thick. Breathing felt like sand scraping up my nostrils. We were greeted by a wall of red. So high and deep that even craning my neck back, I couldn't see the end of it.

Kakkari's punishment—Kakkari's last chance for us all, I couldn't help but think. But in all her facets, her many dimensions, her many faces...I could still feel her *hope.*

Lovely and light. Just as her vengeance was terrible and violent.

Because she was both things. She was all things.

Slowly, the others came.

Over the course of two days, our makeshift camp only grew, a temporary horde of its own.

The *Vorakkar* of Rath Kitala came first with his queen at his side, who looked at me with knowing eyes, as if she could see the face of her hybrid child within mine.

Then came the *Vorakkar* of Rath Drokka, of Rath Tuviri, of Rath Rowin, and of Rath Okkili. The *Vorakkar* of Rath Loppar was the last of the horde kings to arrive. The aging male was seeking to create a *saruk* in the West Lands, was looking to place his roots in Kakkari's earth, his time as *Vorakkar* coming to an end.

As for the last *Vorakkar,* the horde king of Rath Dulia, I'd heard his horde had been recalled to *Dothik.* He'd been the only one to remain loyal to Arik's father. As such, the *Vorakkar* of Rath Tuviri had informed me that Arik had ordered Rath Dulia back to the capital after he'd heard reports of him encroaching on a human village far to the northeast.

The *Sorakkar* of Rath Hidri arrived shortly after Loppar, and he'd greeted me with a fond smile. I could sense the power of the heartstone in his pocket. A male true to his word.

The night before the black moon, the human queens of Rath Rowin and Rath Drokka found me. Mina and Vienne were their names. I'd been standing at the edge of the fog, peering into it. Still *trying* to understand, after all this time, wondering what it was that Kakkari wanted from us.

As if hearing my thoughts, Vienne told me, "You'll never know."

The white-haired beauty had stepped up beside me just as Mina dragged her hand through the curls and wisps of red. I'd heard they were immune to the fog. That they could step right into it, breathe it in. I wondered if I could too, but I had yet to test that theory.

Most here believed that it was Vienne that had created the fog. That her use of a heartstone—the first use of one since the plague over two centuries ago—had unleashed it.

There was a hum between the three of us. I wondered if they could feel it too. It made me uncomfortable. It felt like my skin was itchy, that it was crawling with...with *power*.

"Do you feel it?" I finally asked, rubbing at my skin.

Mina's gaze had shone knowingly. Then she sighed, looking deep into the fog as if she could see beyond it. As if she could see something we couldn't. Her green eyes were bright. Earlier, I'd seen the way they'd shone up at her husband as a small, dark curl of a smile crossed over his features. Love. They were in love. And it made my chest feel like it was shredding all over again.

"When I was under the Dead Mountain for the last time, the night that it fell," she murmured, rubbing at her own arms, "there was a Dakkari witch there."

Lysi, I'd heard the account. From her *Vorakkar* himself.

"And I felt her power. I felt it clash with mine," she continued, shuddering slightly. "Like nails dragging through my scalp. And I thought that she was just like me. That had I been weaker, I could have been just like *her*. Using this gift for all the wrong reasons but thinking those reasons were *right*. That they were *just*."

Vienne reached out a hand to place on Mina's arm. In comfort. And when Mina reached out to take my own hand, I gasped, feeling the hum and thread of power connect through us all. Like a reverberation that spread through the entirety of my body.

Like a connection. Like knowing.

Like roots, I reminded myself. Roots of a tree.

"When she died," Mina told me, "I felt her death. I felt it inside me. I felt my own power responding to it."

She sighed.

"So yes," she whispered. "When you ask if I can feel it, feel *you* and Vienne. If I can feel the *Seta Kalliri*. If I can feel the *Vorakkar* of Rath Drokka. And they can all feel us, congregated in this small place. I think it's a beautiful but frightening thing."

"The five heartstones," Vienne said. "We can help channel them. We want to help you."

"Our husbands don't want us to," Mina said, exchanging a glance with Vienne, "but I know, as well as you, that there are not five priestesses here who have the gift, at least one that is strong enough. There is you. And there is the *Seta Kalliri*."

"I am not a priestess," I informed her.

"No, you are not," Vienne said. "You are something else entirely."

Those violet eyes peered at me, and I shifted on my feet, dropping the connection of their touch.

"Are you not afraid?" I asked her. "Afraid to use the heartstone again?"

"Yes, I am," Vienne told me, her lips lifting in a small, but sad smile. "But I am the only one alive that has before. I know what to expect. I know that it can be done. My only fear...my only fear is that I will make it *worse*."

"You won't," I informed her. "Kakkari *wants* us to succeed."

"And she did not before?" Mina asked quietly.

How to explain it? When I didn't even think I understood it myself?

"We all know that Kakkari is not one entity. She is not one being. She is the soul of this planet. The soul of us all," I told them quietly. "When you hear Kakkari, you *feel* that. And if she is us, then she feels the suffering that has happened here too. She feels the souls of the *vekkiri*. She feels the unrest of the Dakkari and the Killup. The consumption and fear of the Ghertun. Not all the Ghertun had evil in their hearts. Many were living in fear, just as you were. And now their souls are gone too, and there must be a price for that."

I took a deep breath and continued, "But if Kakkari is us, if she feels these things deep in her core, all the suffering and despair and greed...then she also feels hope. Love. Like the love you have for your husbands. The love you have for your children and your future children. The desire for change, for a better life for us all. The drive to see *good*. The need to be kind and understanding. I have seen what happens here. I have seen what will happen. The fog will be no more. We have the power to defeat it, and we will. Life will continue. This will fade in our memories. A new king will rise. But after this...I believe that she will intervene no more. At least not from what I've seen. This is our last chance. And we have to set Dakkar *right*."

I felt the power surge within all of us. Mina and Vienne looked at me in knowing.

Then I whispered, "We will not have the heartstones anymore. So if you truly wish to help, if you wish to give the last of your power, then know that this is the price she demands. This will deplete us all. And only then can we begin anew."

On the morning after the black moon, just as dawn was breaking over the land, Arik finally arrived.

CHAPTER 62

*K*alloma squeezed my hand. I felt her strength seep into me even as I caught Arik's eyes across the clearing.

It was just as I'd seen. Everyone in their places, in a half oval that the wall of red fog intersected. There was a noticeable tension, a quiet in the thick, hot, suffocating air.

As if the fog felt the power of the five—*nik*, six—heartstones near...I sensed its restlessness. A *pull* that I remembered from my vision in the dark tunnels of *Dothik*. I closed my eyes just as I felt a hushed murmur of voices in my ear.

Kakkari.

In all her forms. Every last soul of her.

Bekkar's sword was still strapped down my back, the hilt visible behind my left shoulder. I felt the hum and pulse of that heartstone...just as I felt the one clenched in my palm. *Kalloma* had already collected them from Arik. Both of them. The one she'd given us from the *orala sa'kilan*—which I clenched tightly, just as my mother had as she died—and the other from the temple in *Dothik*—which was in the *Seta Kalliri's* possession.

Vienne held one. The same one she'd used under the Dead Mountain, retrieved from the ancient tree where she and her husband had hidden it once more. One was in Mina's possession, from the outpost of Rath Okkili. The last was in the *Sorakkar's* possession.

The *Vorakkar* of Rath Drokka—the Mad Horde King, or so I'd heard him called—was pacing the edge of the fog, his heavy boots crunching over the dead earth.

"Give me a heartstone, *Seta Kalliri*," he called out, breaking through the tight silence. "My wife will not venture inside it. I will take her place."

Vienne walked to him, placing a hand on the center of his back to still him. They had twin children, but they had stayed behind at their horde. Safe, though I knew the distance was grating on them both. She bent her head and whispered in his ear.

Kalloma looked at me, and I shook my head. She pursed her lips.

"*Nik, Vorakkar,*" she told him. "You have Kakkari's gift, *lysi*" —I heard Drokka's scoff at the word—"but your wife is better suited to withstand the goddess's power. It is her she has chosen for this. Not you."

"There are five heartstones," Drokka argued, beginning to stalk to the *Seta Kalliri*, though the aging female held her ground, tilting her chin high. "If you think the three of you can withstand such power, you do not know what you are dealing with. But I have seen it. I *remember* it, and it nearly killed my wife!"

At his words, the *Vorakkar* of Rath Rowin—Mina's husband —stepped up beside his queen, his palm clenching around her waist. I watched her tilt back her head to look up at her horde king, but she smiled. There was an entire conversation that passed between the two—one held in silence—and eventually, I saw Rowin's head dip. I saw his subtle nod.

Drokka thought that only the *Seta Kalliri*, his wife, and Mina would be bearing the weight of the heartstones.

"It is my daughter who will bear the final two," the *Seta*

Kalliri announced quietly to the half circle, looking straight at Rath Drokka as she slid her hand to my shoulder. I'd told the plan to *Kalloma* last night. I'd finally told her what I'd seen, and it was only after my reassurances that she had agreed to this.

"*Nik.*"

The word was rough but firm.

And it came from Arik, growled out in the clearing, stilling all murmurs that suddenly erupted among the *Vorakkar* and their wives and their council members.

The *Dothikkar* stepped forward, his eyes pinned on me. But staring into them too long made my heart begin to curl in on itself, and so I looked down. To find my palm glowing from the heartstone. To find the gentle swell of my belly beneath the gray silk of my dress.

It is coming to pass, I thought. *Just as I saw it.*

"*Nik,*" Arik said again, and when I looked up, he was pointing his finger at my *kalloma*. "You *know* I would have never allowed this."

"It is my choice."

His jaw tightened when he heard my voice. His nostrils flared as we stared at one another, the first time we'd spoken since the morning I left *Dothik*, sent away on his orders. It still felt raw. That pain. That hurt. Even as I felt myself *aching* for him, *needing* him.

"And you will not interfere with this, *Dothikkar,*" I said quietly, the voices becoming louder in my mind. "You have no power here. Not when it comes to Kakkari's will."

As we regarded one another across the clearing, I'd never felt the distance between us more. Behind him, I saw the faces I'd come to know well. Kalik. Errana. Ulli. Bakkia.

"*Kalles,*" came another voice. It was the *Vorakkar* of Rath Kitala, stepping toward me. "He's right. One heartstone alone is too much to bear. Two would kill you. Surely."

A snarl erupted from Arik's throat at the mere mention of it.

The bitter part of me wanted to ask why my safety mattered to him. Because he'd been resolved to never see me again, to dismiss me, just as he'd dismissed the thought that I was carrying his child.

But I knew that wasn't fair. I knew that he cared for me. Just not enough to want me at his side.

I leveled my gaze on the *Vorakkar* of Rath Kitala. If he knew that I would have to withstand *three* heartstones, he would balk. If *Kalloma* knew what I needed to do, then she would forbid it too. Even after my reassurances.

The heartstone in my hand began to heat. I reached out to grip *Kalloma's* wrist when I felt a particularly strong pull from the fog. Even this far away, it felt like it was seeping into me, calling me closer.

"I assure you, *Vorakkar*," I said quietly, "I will survive. We all will. The fog will be gone soon. The East Lands will be restored. But first we must do this."

When I stepped forward, I found the *Sorakkar* of Rath Hidri with my gaze. I walked to him, drawing in deeper and deeper breaths. The fog was cloying. Drifting into the air like a sickness across the land. I was surprised I hadn't been able to feel it from the North Lands.

"The heartstone, *Sorakkar*," I murmured to him, holding out my palm.

Arik stepped up behind me. I could feel his heat. I could scent him too—that scent that reminded me of wonderful, wonderful things. Frost and fire and earth. I tried not to remember.

"Kara," came his voice, dropped and soft. "I said *nik*."

The *Sorakkar* looked down at my open palm and then met my eyes, indecision written across his face. The tension in the half circle rose even more.

"*Hanniva*," I murmured to the *Sorakkar*. At his side, the *Arakkari* placed her hand on his arm. "Trust me in this."

"*Hanniva*," Arik murmured behind me. "Kara, *hanniva*."

In the end, the *Sorakkar* placed a wrapped cloth in my hand.

"I hope you know what you are doing, *leikavi*," the older male finally murmured.

He plucked the cloth away, and the heartstone tumbled against my skin. I swayed, the voices rising until I could hear nothing else. I closed my eyes, the world swaying beneath my eyelids, overwhelming. There was a hint of the pain I'd felt in the *Dothikkar's* chambers the night I'd woken to find him dead at my feet. But only a fragment of it. A small piece that I could manage.

Then I felt Arik's touch.

I felt his touch pulling me back from the brink, and I wanted to sob at the rightness of his warmth, of his steadiness.

Loss and grief spilled into me again when I resurfaced. Then I stepped away from underneath his hand because it hurt too much. When I turned and met his gaze, his own jaw clenched. A flurry of shocked murmurs flooded the clearing.

Against my back, I felt Bekkar's heartstone heat and begin to throb against my skin. Like a second heartbeat.

"Everything I have done," came Arik's ragged whisper, dipping his head low to peer into my eyes, which...which I thought might be glowing *blue*, given the reflection in his own, "was meant to keep you safe."

"*Nik*, it was meant to keep you whole," I corrected quietly. His brow furrowed at my strange word. "Because you broke me a little to keep *yourself* safe. You took from me and gave nothing of you."

Except for the child in my belly.

A flurry of raw pain flashed in his eyes, surprising and sudden. "You believe that?" he asked me gutturally.

I didn't answer him.

My lungs felt tight. This was not the time or the place for this conversation, but the pain was still raw. It was unspoken, roving through me like a hungry beast. I wondered if it would ever be sated.

Stepping past him, I walked through the half circle, aware of the whispers about my glowing eyes.

"I want this done," I said softly. "I want this mended."

But my gaze was only on the fog, and I strode toward it. There was a breeze that began to flow in, blowing away the suffocating air, giving *life*. The ground began to hum with every step I took, like the connection I'd felt to Vienne and Mina. A connection to the earth, to its very core, to the roots that flowed wild beneath us.

Kakkari was here. I could feel her. I could feel her life inside me. I could feel her fingers running down my arms and her whispers in my ear.

"Kara, *nik*," came a growl.

Arik caught my hand, to keep me away again, and I knew I could not let that happen. It was now or never. It needed to be done. A wave of energy—not unlike the power *Kalloma* harnessed—pulsed out from me, and his grip left me. I heard him fall, a heavy thud on the ground when that wave sent him flying back. He could not stop this. I could not let him even if he thought he was keeping me safe.

Because didn't he understand?

I was trying to keep *him* safe. I was trying to keep us *all* safe.

"Get her back," came Arik's order. Kalik moved toward me even as I saw *Kalloma* step up to the fog. Vienne and Mina were coming too, approaching. "Get her back now!"

Do they feel what I feel? I wondered. There was an *elation* inside me. A *revelation* too. Something sliding into place, and I felt it *boom* through the entirety of my body. Booming in time with my heartbeat. With *all* of our heartbeats, which began to feel like one, heartbeats I could sense and feel like they were pulsing beneath my feet, like they were pulsing into Kakkari's earth.

Kalik never reached me. Whatever it was that was protecting me kept him back too. And Errana. And Ulli. And Bakkia. And Arik, when he tried again. They never reached me.

And when I slipped into the fog?

When I stepped past the edge of that reddened border, the thing that had taken life, the thing that was meant to humble us, to punish us, to restore us?

I didn't feel fear.

I felt hope.

"*Kara!*" I heard his roar shake the land.

I had one heartstone in each palm. I had Bekkar's sword at my back. When *Kalloma* stepped up next to me, I felt her clasp my wrist, and that power flowed. When Vienne and Mina joined us, as the fog weaved and slipped and floated before us, I knew that this was the end.

This is the end, I thought.

When the power built up inside me, I didn't fight it. Not like I did that night Arik took the throne. I felt that power build me up from the inside out. Like the wind, it shifted and flowed and sped and slowed. And I attached myself to it, dipping and gliding with it.

A hum of power.

Kakkari's voices, becoming so loud that they were all I could hear. But I didn't scream in terror. Not this time.

This time, I joined her. I added my own voice into her fray, joining my soul with hers.

It was like a key slipping into a lock.

And when I turned it...all of our power unleashed itself across the East Lands.

This is the end, I thought, a blue light exploding in my vision as the heartstones grew so hot in my palms and as I drew Bekkar's sword from its place at my back.

This is the end so that we can begin again.

Chapter 63

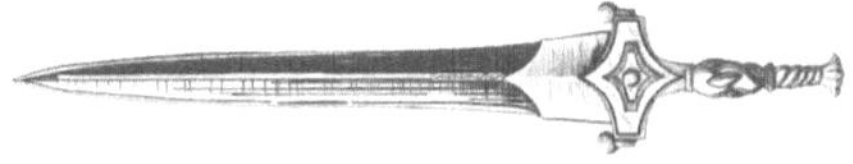

The burst was blinding.

Wincing, I shielded my eyes as I saw a golden light shine from within the fog like it was a second sun, hot and violent.

Panic and fear swam in my veins as a ripple of energy boomed across the land. There was a quiet stillness, so quiet that I swore I could hear both Kalik's and Bakkia's hearts next to me, before a sound began to groan and move. Hurtling toward us from the direction of the fog.

"*Brace!*" came Rath Rowin's sharp command, whose wife was within the fog too. But unlike me, he seemed resigned in her decision. Accepting. "*Brace now!*"

Whatever force it was that came flying at us, it hit my chest. It made the air whoosh from my lungs as I was knocked back off my feet, a hundred times more powerful than whatever Kara had done to me before.

There were grunts and cries from all around me. It stole my breath, and I dragged air deep into my lungs as the deadened earth began to vibrate and rise up. Next to me, I watched as invisible tendrils swirled skyward from the ground, lifting soil and red dirt and rocks. Hundreds of thousands of them until it looked like the East Lands were floating, a shimmering reddened landscape.

Rath Drokka was up first, and I watched him stalk at the edge of the fog like a prowling beast, tugging at the ends of his hair as a bloom of light glowed from within the fog. I had the impression that he was holding himself back. I knew he was immune to the fog. I knew he could venture inside it. This was something else. There was a helplessness to his actions as he waited. Waited for his wife to come back to him. A helplessness because he knew she needed to do this? A helplessness because he knew that she could not be stopped?

I growled, pushing up from the ground, seeing Kalik do the same next to me, his eyes pinned to the fog.

"*Arik, look,*" came his guttural voice.

I looked to where he was pointing with a bloodied hand, from where it'd scraped across the rough earth.

Deep in the fog, there was a beam of golden light, shooting straight up into the sky.

The edges of it were rough, like crackling lightning bolts were being pressed together, forced to conform to the cylindrical shape. One bolt cracked across the sky, and I watched with a tight gut as the fog began to *move*.

It suddenly grew dark over the East Lands as the fog stretched so high that it temporarily clouded over the sun. The sky turned red, the cast of it stretching over our flesh as the earth began to swirl more violently around us, the wind whipping dirt and rocks across our flesh.

Out of the corner of my eye, I saw the other *Vorakkar*. Rath Kitala was shielding his wife, as was Rath Tuviri, his golden hair whipping with the violence of the sudden wind. Rath Okkili only held his female—Maeva was her name—close to his chest, his arms bracketed tight around her, though they were both peering at the fog.

Behind us, the makeshift camp was in tatters. Some of the *darukkars* and council members that had traveled with their *Vorakkar* were running around, trying to secure the temporary tents they'd staked into the ground. Fire basins were rolling away. Tatters of the hide sleeping rolls were dancing in the wind. Other *darukkars* were simply staring at the beam of light, an expression of awe and trepidation on their faces.

As for the priestesses, they were huddled into a circle, their hands joined, eyes closed. *Praying.* Praying to Kakkari, their mouths moving in unison though I could not hear their voices over the punishing, howling wind.

When I looked back to the light—wondering where it had come from, wondering what was *vokking* happening within the fog—I saw that it was growing. *Widening.* Spreading more rapidly than any of us could have predicted, in all directions but from the same source.

"Get back!" Rath Kitala bellowed, his booming voice nearly lost in the wind and the crackling energy I felt pulse like a heartbeat across my flesh. "Get back before it—"

That was when I heard a pained scream, familiar and soul wrenching.

Kara.

I didn't think. I only knew that I needed to reach her. The fog be damned. It could prowl over this land for centuries. I didn't care anymore. I just needed to know that she was safe.

I sprinted forward, rocks and debris cutting slashes across my cheeks and arms as I ran, but I paid them no mind. The wind was whipping faster the closer I drew to the edge of the fog.

Nik, the wind was approaching the fog, I realized. Drawn in toward the beam of light, beginning to circle around it. Like a cyclone.

Another pulse of energy boomed across the East. And just as

I plunged myself into the red, I was thrown back once more, suspended in the air before I hit the ground *hard*.

On my back, dragging in lungfuls of hot, gritty air, I saw everything begin to change.

The fog began to swirl. Slow at first but then whipping up rapidly, tightening. Like a tornado, it was drawing in on itself. The golden beam of light was lapping at it, consuming it as it dragged it in closer and closer.

The earth in the air began to swirl too. The dead, red earth, though I swore I caught shimmers of gold too.

"Serok!" came Kalik's voice from behind me. "Get back!"

Nik, I thought. Drokka had been tossed a short distance away, his face cut up from the rocks, the scar running down his face appearing even more red. I exchanged a look with him. *Nik,* I would not leave her. Just as he would not leave his wife.

The shaft of gold was growing and growing. The fog was wrapping itself around it. Trying to swallow it. Trying to suffocate it. Trying to *defend* itself against it. But it was losing. It was destroying itself.

And then the fog began to lift from the East Lands. It lifted from the ground, rising into the sky. Instead of a fog it was a mist, becoming more and more translucent by the second. It seemed to scream across the land as it was consumed, the sound foul and endless.

That was when I saw her. When I saw *them*.

Their clothing had been seared away from their bodies, leaving them vulnerable and naked to the elements. The four of them stood in a circle, with clasped hands, with their heads thrown back, blue light encasing them like a bubble. They were silent. They were still, with the exception of the *Seta Kalliri's* lips, which were moving in what seemed like a silent prayer, likely in time with her fellow priestesses.

But it was Kara who held my gaze. Because she had a sword

pointed toward the sky, a blinding, shimmering stone in the hilt.

She was responsible for the beam of light.

She was channeling *all* of their power into her and using the sword as a conduit to defeat the fog.

Kakkari chose her when she was only a child.

That was what the *Seta Kalliri* had told me before we left the *orala sa'kilan*. That moment seemed like a lifetime ago. But now I understood what she'd meant.

Was this what Kara hadn't told me? Had she seen this in her vision? She'd kept something from me, pleading with me to allow her one secret.

More and more of the East Lands were revealed. Right before our very eyes. The place where the Dead Mountain had once stood proudly now lay in a crumbled heap of stone. One day, I wondered if trees and grass would cover it, if it would be forgotten in memory, another hill against the majestic landscape, where so much suffering had occurred, where so much death had been rooted.

And then, without any warning...I watched as the last of the fog was consumed.

I watched as the red disappeared from the sky even as the vortex of the wind continued to whip at Kara and the others.

The beam of golden light grew even more, searching the sky, throwing its tendrils out wide.

A light so bright that I held my hand up to cover my eyes in fear that they'd be seared in my skull.

Then all at once, the East Lands went quiet.

The wind ceased abruptly.

The swirling, violent earth dropped away, tumbling back toward the land, a rumble of clattering stones and puffed dirt, leaving us covered in grit and dust.

The light was no more.

And when I looked back to Kara, I saw the others had fallen away and only she remained standing.

"Vienne!" Drokka growled, already pushing up from the earth, his voice too loud for the sudden silence.

The *Vorakkar* of Rath Rowin was on his heels, his eyes fastened to Mina, who was curled on the ground.

Kara's eyes were still glowing blue. Though the *Seta Kalliri* was crumpled at her feet, I watched her *kalloma* reach out a hand to touch her ankle. *That* evoked a reaction from Kara, and I watched her body shudder. I watched her eyes close.

"*Saila,*" I murmured, scrambling up from the ground, earth spilling from my clothes, from my hair and flesh as I ran toward her.

Drokka had a still Vienne cradled in his arms when I reached them. Mina was stirring as Rowin hunched over her, whispering something into her ear.

The sword hung limp in Kara's grip, and she stumbled, her back arched forward in fatigue.

I lunged for her just as she began to fall. I hit the ground hard, a large rock digging against my knee, but she landed in my lap, unharmed.

"Kara," I whispered, turning her head in my palms so I could gaze down at her. My heart was beating in my throat, panic making it difficult to breathe. "Are you hurt?"

I looked down at her body, looking for injuries that I knew were not there. My gaze skimmed her arms, her chest, her stomach, her legs—

Her lower belly was rounded. Subtle but noticeable because I'd memorized every inch of her. She lived in my mind, at all moments of the day and night.

Disbelief. Despair. Joy. Guilt. Awe.

They all crashed into me in a single moment, and all I could do was meet her eyes.

She'd tried to tell me, I thought woodenly.

And I had turned her away.

I had turned her away.

"A gift," she whispered as she looked up at me. As her eyes began to well and shimmer, no longer shining blue but returned to their beautiful golden color. I thought she'd meant the child, but instead I felt her grab my hand and tuck it around the hilt of the sword she still hung on to. "Returned to Bekkar's bloodline. Worthy of a *Dothikkar* who will not be afraid to wield it."

My brows furrowed. It was Bekkar's sword. The sword she'd used to eradicate the fog.

And I couldn't care less about it. It clattered to the ground just as I sensed others drawing near, making my hackles rise. But it was only her sister priestesses, who went to the *Seta Kalliri*, covering her nakedness with a cloak, the *Niva Kalliri* helping her sit up.

"*Sika*," came another priestess's voice as she approached us, frowning in my direction though she was careful not to meet my gaze. "*Sika*, can you stand?"

Sister. The priestess, whose voice was shaken at what she'd witnessed, held her hand out for Kara.

"*Lysi*," Kara said, turning her head away from me, reaching for her even as my arms tightened. "I think I..."

But her voice faltered, her eyes closing, a wave of fatigue crashing into her.

"Where are the heartstones?" came the *Niva Kalliri's* quiet voice.

The heartstones were the least of my worries.

"Where are they?"

"Gone."

The tired word came from the *Seta Kalliri*. Her voice sounded like it had been scraped raw.

"What do you mean they are *gone?*" the *Niva Kalliri* demanded, her tone pitching higher in fear.

"It was Kakkari's price," Kara whispered in my arms, looking up at me. "Except one. Except yours."

"Kara, stay with me," I pleaded, dread swirling in my belly. Unlike anything I'd ever felt before.

Then her head lolled, her body went limp, and she tumbled into oblivion.

CHAPTER 64

When I woke, it was to the familiar surroundings of *Kalloma's* library.

My eyelids felt heavy, and my body felt weak. Like I'd just woken from one of my deeper dreams.

"*Rei kassiri,*" came *Kalloma's* gentle voice, and I heard her chair push back from her desk. "Oh, you're awake."

The relief in her voice was palpable.

As the world rushed back in, I shielded my eyes against the light streaming in from the large windows. I was lying on *Kalloma's* bed, the furs making me sweat, tucked tightly underneath my chin.

"The child," I rasped immediately, my brows drawing tight in concern, trying to move my arms, to bring my palms to my belly.

"The child is well," *Kalloma* told me, hurrying toward me though her movements were slow. Her voice trembled as she said, "The *Morakkari* of Rath Okkili has been watching over you. She left just yesterday. But she said the child is fine. Healthy."

Potent relief made the backs of my eyes prickle. It had been my biggest fear, though I knew what needed to be done.

"What were you thinking?" came *Kalloma's* drawn, tight

voice, though I also heard the relief in it. "*Goddess*, Kara, you are...you frightened us all."

She trailed off as she came to sit on the edge of my bed, reaching out to stroke a hand through my hair.

Though my movement felt sluggish, I grasped her wrist and held it to me.

"Are the others all right?" I asked. "Vienne? Mina? No one was hurt?"

"*Nik*, they have recovered," she told me. "All except you."

I swallowed. "What happened? How are we here? How long has it been since—"

"Over a week now," she told me, and I processed her words, trying to force my sluggish mind to get its bearings. "You collapsed on the East Lands. But we fought to have you brought back to the *orala sa'kilan*."

They...*fought?*

Suddenly, I knew what she meant.

Arik.

"He is here," *Kalloma* told me, answering my unspoken question. She frowned as I began to sit up, but instead of pushing me back, she cradled my arm in support. A wave of dizziness made the room sway, but I gripped her tight as she helped center me.

"In the temple?" I asked.

"*Nik*, outside in the courtyard," she told me, a tinge of annoyance coloring her tone, and I wondered what had transpired while I slept. "He has been there since the East Lands. He will not leave."

I didn't know how that made me feel, and I didn't have the energy to figure it out.

"He wanted to bring you back to *Dothik*," she told me gently. "To have you tended to by his healers. He was...displeased when we brought you here."

Lysi, I could only imagine how he'd reacted.

"He might be the *Dothikkar* now, but you are still *my* daughter," *Kalloma* told me, her tone fierce, smoothing her hand down my hair. "And I knew the *orala sa'kilan* would help you heal. There is still magic in this place, even without the heartstone watching over us."

"You did the right thing," I whispered, swallowing. The furs fell away as I slowly swung my legs over the bed. I was dressed in light blue silk that tangled around my ankles. "I'm...I'm just so relieved that everyone is all right."

"Do you remember?" she asked me quietly.

Did I remember what happened in the East Lands?

A sharp bloom of pain spread at my temples when I tried to focus on the fragments of memory. I remembered the pain, but I also remembered the *ease* at which I felt that power flow through me. The frightening depth of it. The allure of it.

"Not much. It's probably for the best," I told her. A half-truth. Though a half-lie as well. Lowering my voice, I asked, "And the fog...is it gone? Truly?"

"*Lysi,*" she told me gently, her mouth pinching down as if she'd heard the untruth in my voice, like I could hide anything from her for very long. "A few scouts from each of the hordes have remained in the East Lands. Watching over it for now. Seeing if anything stirs from the quiet."

Gently, I placed a hand over the small swell of my abdomen, staring down at it.

"It's quiet there. Like even the earth is waiting too. Like us, it will take its time to heal."

I nodded.

"Oh, *rei kassiri,*" she breathed. Suddenly I was in her embrace, and I pushed my face into her neck, breathing her in. "You scared me. So much. I'm so glad you've come back to us."

Tears pricked my vision, but I squeezed my eyes shut. Focusing on *Kalloma's* heartbeat. Focusing on her scent and her heat and her wonderful embrace.

I didn't know how long we stayed like that, but eventually *Kalloma* dragged in a deep breath and shifted, rising to stand on unsteady legs.

"I'll send for some food and water," she told me, worrying her lip. "You must be hungry."

It was on the tip of my tongue to protest, but then I thought I needed the time alone. A brief moment of reprieve and assessment.

"*Kakkira vor, Kalloma,*" I said quietly.

She had already started toward the door, but at the words, she stilled briefly. Turned to regard me, her eyes flitting. "Are you certain you're all right, *rei kassiri*? I can send for another healer. Or call the *mokkira* back."

"*Nik,*" I said quietly.

Truthfully, it felt like I'd been scraped raw from the inside out. My body felt strong, especially as I shook more and more of the heaviness from my mind.

But my soul...

It felt weak.

Torn.

"*Nik,* I'm fine," I assured *Kalloma.*

She hesitated again. "Would you...would you like to see him? I'll need to inform him that you've woken, but if you'd like to speak with him too—"

"*Nik,*" I said quickly, a flare of panic rising. "I—I'm not ready to see him yet."

She nodded. "Very well. Whatever you need, *rei kassiri*. I'll keep him away."

"*Kakkira vor.*"

My eyes closed with relief and longing and torment as she left the room.

I wondered when I would feel whole again.

CHAPTER 65

"He's still here, Kara."

I didn't pause in my transcription, though the word I was writing looked wobbly and warped from the sudden intrusion.

Avala stood on the threshold of my tower room, carrying a golden box in her arms.

"He nearly battered down our doors just now."

My fingers tightened on the quill.

"But, oh, *look* what he left for you, Kara," Avala said, her voice hesitant even though I heard her struggle to contain her delight. "Aren't they lovely?"

Another gift? I thought, dragging my gaze away from the parchment, my curiosity getting the best of me even as I felt a pang echo in my chest.

It had been a week since I'd woken. And still, I was being a coward. Hiding in my tower, numbing myself against the inevitable pain of seeing him again.

But Arik had made his presence known. Time and time again. Climbing the stairs to the door of the temple every morning, afternoon, and evening to see if I would speak with him. Sleeping in the courtyard—in the frigid, icy nights—even though he had his gilded, luxurious palace back in *Dothik*. Beyla had told me that he bathed in the ice river not far from the entrance. What she didn't tell me was that she'd begun to sneak out hot meals to him from her kitchen. *That* I had learned from Avala. Whose voice, hardened against him, had begun to soften throughout the week.

Even *Kalloma* was beginning to feel sorry for the *Dothikkar*. Even though she would not admit that, I knew her well. And I saw her pity etched in the lines of her face whenever she returned from speaking with him.

Standing from my desk, I walked to my dearest friend and lifted the lid off the golden, intricate chest, bracing myself for what I would find.

My heart panged when I saw what was nestled in the protected confines. Wondering what poor soul Arik had summoned from *Dothik* to bring this all the way to the North Lands. There must've been a road now, trodden by *pyroki* hooves, from the gates of the city to the temple.

Smooth, plush parchment greeted me when I lifted the lid. Sheets and sheets of it. Thick and luxurious, made of the finest of fibers. My quill would glide effortlessly over it. My ink wouldn't bleed and feather. My hands nearly shook with the want I felt until I made them snap the chest closed.

"Oh, Kara," Avala said, her voice pinching when I turned. She thought I was going back to my desk, but instead I was reaching for my cloak. This needed to stop. "He's obviously sorry for—"

My chest squeezed. "You can give the parchment to the *Niva Kalliri*. I know she wants some for her own transcriptions."

The gifts had started coming even before I'd woken from my week-long sleep and had only continued since.

A beautiful carved box filled with expensive vials of *luria*-scented soap, which had been my favorite from Arik's stronghold in *Dothik*.

A chest full of silk dresses, dresses he'd once promised to me when he'd been jealous of the *Sorakkar's* own gifts.

A gilded brush. A handheld mirror. A memory from the *saruk* of Rath Hidri when we'd mated for the first time. Seeing those had only made me shiver, remembering his rasping words in my ear when he'd told me, *Look at how pretty you are, rullari. You like to admire yourself in the mirror, Kara? You vokking should.*

Then he'd begun to hit me where it *really* hurt.

Because then the books had begun to arrive. The first of which had made me gasp out loud because it had been a perfectly preserved copy of Bekkar's history, the edges of the parchment gilded, the pressed hide cover perfectly smooth and unblemished. I didn't know how he'd managed to find it in *Dothik* because I'd thought that the one in the *orala sa'kilan* was the last in existence.

But I should not have been surprised by Arik's tenacity and determination. That one had been particularly painful to have to turn away. That had been the only gift that I had been sorely aching to keep clasped in my greedy hands.

But in the end, I had sent it away. I didn't know if Avala or Trissa or *Kalloma*—whoever came bearing my gifts that particular day—returned them to Arik or kept them secured somewhere. I didn't care. I just didn't want to see his gifts, which sparked the memories.

Yesterday he'd given me three rounded ink pots filled with the blackest of *kreki* inks. Now it was the parchment.

I sighed, grabbing for my cloak. It was time. It was past time.

He needed to return to *Dothik*. Every moment he lingered here took him away from the city. His throne was so new that it would put him in a dangerous position, a position I knew he could not find himself in at such a precarious time.

He needed to return to *Dothik* to reassure his people.

He did not need to be sleeping in the courtyard of the *orala sa'kilan*, waiting.

"Are you going to speak to him?" Avala's quiet voice came, tinged in what I thought sounded like hope as she cradled the chest of parchment close.

"*Lysi,*" I said, swallowing, steeling my spine. "This has gone on long enough."

Avala said nothing as I began to descend the stairs.

There was a fluttering in my chest, the first true emotion I'd felt all week. Nerves. Anticipation. Hurt. Grief. I didn't know.

Strangely, it felt good. Truthfully, I'd begun to worry. That I couldn't *feel* anything.

I made short work of the stairs, sensing Avala trailing me. Though when I reached the hallway at the bottom, she stopped, no doubt giving me the privacy I needed to speak to him.

I glided through the hallway, turning down the next one, not a soul in sight. When the atrium came into view, I eyed the door, which had been opening and closing a lot in the past two weeks.

And Arik was just on the other side of it.

When I opened it, the steel groaning loudly, I saw his turned back at the top of the stairs. Bekkar's sword was strapped there, the familiar hilt with the white stone twinkling against the smooth metal.

His hands were on his hips, his hide trews encasing him in a way that made another sensation spear through me. Unexpected and yet...I grasped it tight. With both hands because I *wanted* to feel something.

Even if it was desire for a male who'd broken my heart and turned me away.

A guttural sound left Arik's throat when he saw me there. He'd expected *Kalloma*, possibly. Or Avala.

I stepped from the atrium, wrapping my cloak around me tighter though it was not as cold outside as I'd expected.

I'd shocked him, it seemed. He stared at me, frozen in place. As handsome as always, possibly even more so. His hair was still long, and I remembered that just weeks ago I had wanted to trim it, that I had lovingly run my fingers through it, gasping into his mouth as he teased me with his tongue.

Then he was moving.

Coming to me swiftly.

The way his arms wrapped around me was familiar and right. Another gruff sound escaped his throat, and then his palms were encasing my cheeks and he was bringing his forehead down to mine, breathing me in.

"*Saila.*"

There was a wiggling in my chest. Something wanting to break free. Beating at the bones of its cage.

"This has to stop, Arik," I said softly.

He stilled.

Slowly, he pulled back to regard me, and I took advantage of the small opportunity, pressing back against the door I'd just shut, putting distance between us.

His hands dropped to his sides. I noticed he no longer wore his *Vorakkar* cuffs. He'd had them cut from him.

I heard his swallow the same moment I saw his eyes drop to my belly, his gaze running over me, assessing.

"You have a duty to Dakkar," I continued, ignoring the way my heart sped at his determined perusal. "And you turn your back on it every moment you are here."

"I don't see it that way," he rasped, those molten eyes returning to mine.

I frowned. "You've been away from *Dothik* for weeks. When the city needs you the most. How do you not see it that way?"

"Then return with me," came the quiet words. "Come with me, and we will return this very moment."

My bewilderment coupled itself with a spark of anger.

"Why are you doing this?" I asked him, aghast, holding his

eyes because I *needed* to understand. That wiggling in my chest was only growing, strengthening. "*Dothik* is all you've ever wanted. It is what you've always chosen."

Was that a small flinch?

"And..." I trailed off, uncertain where the sudden overwhelming desperation was coming from. My shoulders sagged. "And I *understand*. I truly do, Arik. I don't want you to have to choose because I know what is best for Dakkar. I'm telling you that I understand why you did what you did. You don't need to feel guilt for it."

There was a flair of panic in his gaze when I began to turn. He caught my wrist. "Kara, let's speak of this, *lysi*? Just...stay. Stay with me."

"Go home, Arik. Return to *Dothik*," I told him softly, meeting his eyes once more. "You should not be here."

"I should be wherever you are," came his adamant words. "And I'm done trying to fight that."

The relief and honesty in his voice gave me pause. It made my belly flutter, but it also made my chest squeeze tight, so tight that I felt like I couldn't breathe.

I was wrong.

I wasn't prepared for this. Because all I wanted was to run back up my tower and barricade myself in there. My hand was already searching for the handle of the door, grappling with it, which Arik saw, and he lunged, trapping me.

"*Saila*," he growled down at me, stilling my hand, the hilt of Bekkar's sword flashing over his shoulder. "*Saila*, come back to *Dothik* with me. *Hanniva*. I will get on my knees and beg you right here if that's what you wish. But I'm not leaving here without you."

The want in my heart was tremendous.

And yet...he hadn't even apologized. He hadn't even apologized for the callous way he'd hurt me, the coldness in his voice when he sent me away, the ease with which he'd done it.

"*Nik,*" I said, struggling to break his grip. "I don't want that. I just want you to leave."

He shook his head.

"No more gifts," I continued, feeling panic rise. "I will only send them back to you. No more sleeping in the courtyard with Syok when you have a bed elsewhere."

"*Lysi,*" he murmured, his jaw clenching. "Yours. *Ours.*"

My stomach squeezed.

"No more of this, Arik!" I finally hissed, feeling that wiggling in me break, a flood of emotion pouring out in a rush, spilling over. My eyes pricked with tears and my throat went raw as I said, "You sent me away from *Dothik* because you didn't want me! Don't you remember that? Because I remember it every single moment of every single day and night. So don't make this harder than it needs to be! Return to your city, *Dothikkar*, because *I* don't want you here. And if you cared for me at all, then or now, *you will go.*"

His eyes flashed. An expression of anguish—so clear and overwhelming—crossed his features. I nearly froze at the sight of it.

Then his face changed again. "Think of the child, Kara."

I froze.

My lungs squeezed, and my hand shifted protectively to my growing belly. "You mean the child that you denied? Even when I told you what I saw?"

A rough sound came from his throat. Torment crossed his features. "And I can never tell you how much I *vokking* hate myself for it. Every moment, I think of it. *I am sorry, rei kassiri.* I am so *vokking* sorry for that moment. It was my own weakness, my own fear. But *hanniva*, think of our child."

"I do," I breathed, pushing at his chest. "*I am.*"

"Then don't take our child away from me to punish me!"

My fingers pressed to my lips as my heart gave a pitiful,

aching throb. In shock, I stared at him. "Arik...I'm...I'm not. I'm not trying to punish you."

Was that what I was doing?

Had I been doing that without even realizing it?

"Aren't you?" he rasped, his voice guttural, his eyes going surprisingly bright and glassy.

Blowing out a shuddered breath, I felt him push away from me. His back turned, and his shoulders moved with his deep inhale.

"*Vok*," he breathed, scrubbing a hand down his tired face. Softly, he said, "*Vok*, this was not how I wanted this to go. This was not what I wanted."

I felt his exhaustion and his anguish in those words.

"I never wanted to hurt you, Kara," he told me gently. "Not *ever*. But I did it anyway. You have every reason to hate me for it."

A sound escaped my throat.

Was that what he thought?

That I *hated* him?

He couldn't be more wrong.

When he turned to meet my eyes, I said quietly, "The *Laseta Kalliri* told me in *Dothik*, the night that I...the night that the *Dothikkar* died, that I wouldn't have to choose between duty or love, not like my *kalloma* had to."

His brows furrowed.

"Because she told me that they were one and the same," I whispered. "That my duty and my love were *you*."

"Kara—"

"But she was wrong," I told him, shaking my head. "They are not one and the same. The duty that the *Laseta Kalliri* spoke of? It was her own ambition forced onto me because of a bloodline. So in the end, I chose love. You may not see it now, Arik, but I am choosing to stay away *because* I love you. Because I do not want to compromise the one thing that you have worked toward your whole life."

I was crying now, the tears tracking down my face, and I was *glad* to feel them. It felt good. To finally cry again. To release something.

"*You* chose your duty," I told him. "And I cannot blame you for it. You were right to choose it. Now let me help you. Because without me at your side, you will not be tied to the *Laseta Kalliri*. You will not be tied to anyone. You will be free to rule as you see fit. And you will be an even better king for it."

It had taken a long time for me to realize why Arik had done what he'd done. But in the end, I had understood. Perhaps I was still harboring hurt over it...but with time, I hoped that it would lessen. I hoped that I would come to terms with it, that I would accept it.

But I refused to let the *Laseta Kalliri* treat me like a pawn, whether she was of my blood or not.

I turned from him because I couldn't bear to see the knowing on his face.

"So *hanniva*, return to your city," I murmured, my hand resting on the handle of the door. "Take Bekkar's sword and use it to create a better world for us all. For the hordes, for the *saruks*. For the Killup and the *vekkiri*."

Over my shoulder, I met his eyes.

"*Hanniva*, Arik," I whispered. "Take your rightful place on the throne and do what you were born to do. Take a queen who will be strong enough to lead beside you, who *Dothik* will accept with open arms, who you will not have to hide away. Forget..."

My voice broke. It felt like shards of glass were ripping me up from the inside out.

This was what I'd been trying to numb myself to. This exquisite, tormenting pain.

"Forget it all, Arik," I pleaded quietly, a sob breaking from my throat. "Forget me, forget us. And one day, you will see that this is the right choice. You will see that this is what's right for Dakkar."

With that, I turned away from his stricken expression. I stepped inside the atrium.

When the door closed behind me and locked, I nearly crumbled to the ground in my grief.

And as his fists pounded on the door behind me, my name a bellow on his lips, I walked away for us both.

CHAPTER 66

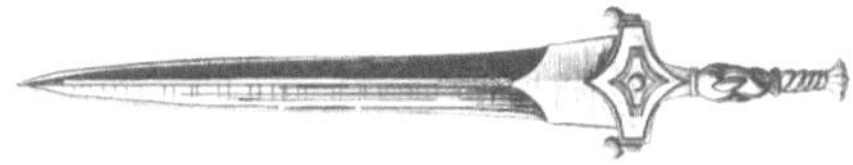

It was a familiar feeling.

Freezing my damn *deva* off in the North Lands, my hands prickling and numb and covered in ice. My gut felt like I'd swallowed a boulder. My heart felt even heavier than that.

I was so *vokking* angry at her.

I was so *vokking* over my head for her.

I was so *vokking* torn up and guilt-ridden and sorry.

I'd made a complete mess of things. But I was determined to fix it.

She thought I could return to *Dothik*, knowing what I knew now?

Nik. I refused to leave the North Lands without her.

Had I truly driven her to this?

To make her think that she was *forgettable?*

And did she really think me capable of turning my back on her and our child?

You did before, came the hateful thought, and I nearly growled out loud, a fissure of incredible guilt and turmoil nearly splitting my chest wide open.

Every jumbled, tormenting thought only made me climb faster and harder, scaling the western tower in the dark of night. Because I was done waiting. My *saila* was inside this tower, and I would stop at nothing to reach her. To make her understand.

Something I should have done weeks ago.

My stomach bottomed out when my hand slipped on an ice-covered ledge, but I managed to right myself. Just above me, I could see the golden light pouring from her window. I was almost there. Almost to her. And I refused to leave her tower until I made her understand.

When I finally found purchase on the ledge outside her window, I reached up and nearly ripped the glass right off its mountings.

Her surprised, watery gasp met my ears when I launched myself inside her room, landing with a crouch on the rug-covered floor. Dripping ice onto it as I sealed the window shut once more before all the heat was sucked out.

"A-Arik?"

When I turned to face her, I saw that she was curled up in her bed. She'd been on her side, facing away from the window, but now her neck craned toward me. Tears were tracking down her swollen face, making me growl, making discomfort prowl in my chest. Her human eyes were bloodshot, the tip of her nose red.

Had she been crying all this time?

Determination filled me as Kara struggled to sit up, staring at me with shock.

My fingers went to the metal fastening of my cloak. When I tugged it, the thick furs fell to the ground in a wet heap, steam curling from its surface. Next was Bekkar's sword, unsheathing Kara's gift to me and laying it carefully against the ledge of the window. A sword we still needed to discuss. Then my belt of daggers joined it.

"What...what are you doing?" came her voice, her tone tinged with bewilderment and...trepidation.

I toed off my thieving boots, and Kara's eyes went wide—those glassy orbs looking slightly panicked—as I peeled off my sodden tunic, which landed with a wet slap against the rug.

When I unlaced my trews and pushed them down, I felt considerably warmer as my naked flesh met the warmth of her room.

My hands were tingling as feeling began to return. As I prowled toward her bed.

But at least her tears had stopped in her shock. Her face was still wet and splotchy, but I would dry it.

When I stood at the edge of her bed, I pulled back the furs, seeing her dress pushed up to her upper thighs.

"What are you doing?" she whispered, her brow furrowed.

Her scent was everywhere. Heaven. Perhaps this place truly was the *orala sa'kilan*—the frozen haven. If she was here, it was.

"You said your piece, *saila*," I informed her, slipping into bed beside her, a sharp intake of air meeting my ears as my chilled flesh met hers. When she began to retreat, I bracketed my arms around her, holding her to me. "Now I will say mine. *Lysi?*"

Her spine stiffened. She pushed at my chest, but I held tight, gritting my teeth.

"You need to leave. I told you to—to go back to *Dothik!*"

"*Nik*," I growled softly. "This is where I belong. *With you.* You will not tell me otherwise."

Her tears were returning, but they were angry. Frustrated. I hadn't lost my touch. I could still make her mad. Strangely enough, I felt a flurry of relief at that thought. In the East Lands, she'd only shown me her indifference. Earlier this morning, she'd shown me her despair.

I could make her mad. I could make her use her claws and teeth against me. But I only wanted her to soften for me. I only wanted to see her smile, hear her laugh.

Because it had been too damn long since I'd heard it last.

She was struggling against me, but I was holding her tight. When her neck flashed, I acted on instinct. With a gruff growl, I leaned down to bite at the flesh, holding it gently between my teeth.

Kara froze, and I ran my wide, warming, calloused palm up her back, feeling the press of our growing child against my abdomen. So damn *right*.

A knot loosened in my chest. A swell of pride mixed with my awe.

Releasing her neck, I brushed my lips gently over the mark, feeling her shiver against me.

"You know me better than anyone, Kara," I told her softly. "Even Bakkia. Even Nassik. Kalik. So did you truly believe that I would leave without you?"

Her whisper was ragged against me. "You made me leave you without a second thought."

I flinched. Pulling away from her neck, I clasped her cheeks in my palms, holding her gaze.

"I made a mistake, Kara."

She stilled at the ragged, raw pain she heard in my voice.

Swallowing hard, I said again, "I made a mistake, Kara. The worst damn mistake of my life. And I'm sorry for it. So *vokking* sorry for hurting you. I wish I had not given into my fear. But there were other factors to consider. And truthfully, I was thinking of sending you back to the North Lands even before I knew of your true bloodline."

Her eyes went stricken, and her struggles resumed.

"*Nik*, Kara," I growled, restraining her. "Listen to me. *Hanniva!*"

With apparent effort, she stilled though her glare was pinned to me.

"There were those in the palace that wanted to do me harm," I told her. Her brow furrowed, but her frown never let up. "Guards still loyal to my father. Who saw my taking the throne as a slight against *Dothik*. Even now, there are those that do not recognize me as *Dothikkar*. There have been threats against the palace. Threats *inside* the palace, even when you were there."

She had at least stopped struggling as she listened.

"I was thinking of sending you away to keep you safe. I even had Nassik write out a *thesper* message to your *kalloma*," I confessed to her. "But I was too damn selfish, and I never ordered him to send it. Because I wanted to keep you close to me. I wanted to see you and hold you and feel your warmth against me. You were the only thing getting me through those days without me losing my *vokking* mind. You were the only thing bringing me peace."

Her lips parted.

"There was a guard, armed with weapons, who had made it past the others. They caught him on the stairs that led up to our private rooms, Kara. On the *vokking stairs*. Only moments away from you. And if he had found you..." I trailed off gruffly, watching some of the color drain from her face. I couldn't finish the sentence. Instead I admitted, "The next afternoon...that was when Bakkia told me about your connection to the *Laseta Kalliri*."

"You found the guard the day before you showed me the library?" she asked. At my nod, a desperate sound escaped her throat. "You...you wanted me out of the city."

I swallowed. "And if I had to make you hate me to do it... then I would."

Understanding went through her gaze even though her body was still stiffened in my arms.

"Don't misunderstand," I told her. Discomfort swam through me as I admitted, "Your connection with the priest-esses was still a large concern. Bakkia made me realize that." She frowned. "Because he saw what I felt for you. He feared that you could bend my will to theirs. And he reminded me of my responsibility to *Dothik*. To the promises I'd made, long before I ever met you."

"I wouldn't have done that," she argued, her anger rising again. "*You know that.*"

My lips lifted in a humorless smile. "He was not wrong in his worry. There is a part of me that wonders if I *wouldn't* do anything you asked of me."

She blinked in astonishment.

"And when I realized that, I gave in to that fear," I told her. "At the expense of hurting you, at the expense of hurting myself, I sent you away. My only relief was that I *knew* you'd be safe in the North Lands at the very least. Even if you hated me for it."

She brushed her fingers over her lips, pondering over my words.

"Were you ever planning to see me again?" she finally asked, her eyes flashing up to mine, narrowed. "You were so cold and detached that night."

My mood sobered considerably, thinking over the weeks since I'd sent her away.

"After you left," I murmured, "it took every last *vokking* scrap of discipline in me not to come after you." My lips curled in a smile I didn't feel. "I've barely slept, *saila*. I barely remember to eat because I have no appetite. I won't even let anyone touch my damn furs because they still have your scent on them."

A sharp inhale whistled through her nostrils.

"And every *vokking* night as I tried to sleep, I buried my nose in the cushion you slept on. To breathe you in, to remember you. Because it was the only way I could find a moment of peace, the only way I could sleep for an hour or two. Only if I could imagine that you were still next to me."

Her eyes welled with tears. Could she hear my anguish? How much I'd missed her? How much I'd craved her?

"You think it was easy for me, *rei kassiri*?" I asked gutturally. My throat went tight. "You think it was *easy* for me to send you away? *Nik*, it was the hardest thing I've ever had to do, made even harder because I could *see* your pain. I could feel it like a blade in my gut. And believe me when I say that I would have preferred a blade to your pain, Kara."

"You don't mean that," she whispered raggedly.

"You know I do," I rasped, smoothing my thumb over the tear that fell, shaking my head as my other arm tightened around her back. "*Lo kassiri tei*, Kara."

Her soft gasp met my ears.

And I had never said it before in my lifetime, but I said it to her now.

"*Lo kassiri tei.* I love you, *saila*," I told her, holding her eyes so she would see the truth in them. "I loved you even when I hurt you. And I will spend the rest of our lives trying to make amends for that, if you'll give me another chance."

"Arik..." she whispered, shaking her head.

I remembered her other concerns, which she'd made abundantly clear to me earlier this morning. Every last one made my hackles rise.

"You think that I could so easily take another queen? If you understood how *wrong* that idea is to me, then you would not even suggest it. I have not even thought about another female since I met you, Kara. You hold my attentions and desires captive. *Only* you."

That made her pause. That made her chance a peek up at me as she nibbled at her bottom lip.

Gruffly, I said, "And you think I was trying to hide you away in the palace because I was *ashamed* of you, *saila*?"

I scoffed, my arms tightening around her.

"Never," I said quietly. "*Never.* I wanted to show you off to all of *Dothik*. I wanted to parade you around in the marketplace so everyone would know that you were mine. And yet I could not risk your safety. The less that the guards knew of you, the better. At least until I could secure the palace and select guards of my own."

"I thought..." she whispered. Her words trailed off.

Against her back, my fists clenched. "I know what you thought. And I did nothing to help assuage your fears."

Very subtly, I felt her body begin to soften. To relax. And it made my heart *vokking* soar, and I struggled to contain my hope.

"As for your last concern," I murmured, tipping her chin up so that she met my eyes. "That you would not be strong enough for *Dothik*...I cannot think of a queen who would be stronger."

CHAPTER 67

A *queen?* I thought, a small gasp escaping my lips before I could help it.

There was that familiar wiggling in my chest as my eyes flitted back and forth between his own. The want. The need. The hurt. The joy.

Arik told me he *loved* me.

The words had been as sweet and heady as wine. They were...overwhelming, truthfully, swirling in my mind like a thickened mist. I knew he cared for me. But never had I thought he *shared* my feelings. Never had I thought he felt the same as I did.

Then again, given what he'd told me already tonight, I wondered what else I'd missed in my blissful ignorance—like the threats in the palace. I'd had no idea. No idea how much danger I'd been in.

Though I didn't agree with *how* Arik had gone about sending me back to the North Lands...a part of me understood better now. That was all I'd wanted. A reason why. A reason that made sense.

He was afraid of my connection to the priestesses.

And he'd wanted to keep me safe.

He'd been cold during my departure because he couldn't waver. He'd had to do what was best for him *and* for me. I might not have seen the reasoning then, but I could see it now.

"I don't care about your bloodline," Arik growled softly. "I was a fool to let it influence my decision in the first place. Turn my head whichever way you wish, *rei kassiri*. Steer my views toward yours. Whisper into my ear what you want for the city. Because now I know that you will be its biggest champion. *We* will make those decisions together. You care not for power. You care not for politics or for pandering. You want what I want. And that's to build *Dothik* back up to its original glory. Without the corruption. Without the greed. We can make it great once more."

Could I give him another chance? I wondered, my lips parted, my heartbeat throbbing.

"I want you, Kara," he said finally, softly, as he leaned his forehead against mine. My lashes brushed the tops of his cheekbones when I blinked. Desperate elation slid down my chest, like a tiny ball of fire warming me from the inside out. "I *need* you. I need you because I love you. I need you because these last few weeks have been the purest of hells without you. I need you because I cannot imagine waking up without you, not a single day more. I can't, Kara. I *won't*."

A ragged sound burst from my throat, raw and aching. "You drive me to madness. You know that, right, Arik?" I whispered.

"I know," he told me, one hand coming to my hip under the furs, squeezing. "But I always have. Ever since I first stepped foot inside this very tower. But we work, Kara. We work so well, even when we're fighting, when we're arguing. And I can freely admit that I need you—when I have never needed anyone before in my life. I will gladly tie myself to you in whatever way I can. If you can find it in yourself to forgive me. If you can find it in yourself to love me again."

When he first burst into my tower and began stripping his

clothes off…I'd been bewildered. Shocked at his sudden intrusion. Wondering if it wasn't a dream. I hadn't had time to steel my defenses. I'd been raw from crying most of the day, nursing my broken heart and cradling the growing child that would be my only memory of Arik.

So when he came into my tower…I'd felt *relief*. I'd felt the same need he spoke of. It had mingled with so many emotions—the bad and the good.

Then reality had crashed back into me, and it had nearly stolen my soul.

But now…

Now…perhaps this building heat and fluttering in my chest was him giving it back to me. Perhaps this was him rebuilding what he had broken inside me.

And I needed to decide if I would let him.

I needed to decide if I thought I could be the female that he needed. The queen at his side. The mother of his children. The love of his life.

And I needed to take responsibility for my *own* part in this.

I didn't want to be this broken thing.

Because I have done so much already, I thought to myself, pride swelling in my chest.

I had set the plan of the heartstones into motion against the wishes of the priestesses. I had had enough courage to leave the only place I'd ever known, to travel across the dangerous wildlands with a *Vorakkar* at my side, all for an unknown. I had seen his horde. I had seen a *saruk* and convinced its *Sorakkar* to help us.

And *Dothik*…

Regardless of how Arik had tried to comfort me in the aftermath of that night, I knew that I was responsible for the *Dothikkar's* death. While it hadn't quite been an assassination, I'd known that he would die that night, whether it was from the *Laseta Kalliri's* hand or Arik's…or mine.

I had given Arik a throne. I had given him his father's throne.

And it was me who'd found Bekkar's hidden heartstone. It was me who had channeled its power, combining it with the remaining heartstones, which had crumbled like dust in my palms, to defeat the fog in the East Lands.

Gone.

Destroyed.

And during that moment, as the power of not one, not two, not three but *six* heartstones flowed through me, I'd had my last vision for the last time. But it hadn't been a vision of the future. It had been an opening into the past.

It had been of Lessa. Bekkar's queen. In that moment, I had seen the history of the sword. A sword from Bekkar's own father, made new when Lessa—his love, his wife—had a white, shimmering stone placed in its hilt. A stone she'd had since she was a child, found on the banks of a nearby stream that she played in as a young Dakkari girl. A gift for her. Kakkari's gift.

She'd had the sword remade. Reforged once more. Strengthened.

Because of her, Bekkar had become even stronger. Because of her, Bekkar had become great.

And so with the blessing of Lessa, with the strength and protection of Vienne and Mina, with the guidance of the *Seta Kalliri*, one of the most powerful females on all of Dakkar, and me, a hybrid born from love and raised with love, *we* had ended the fog.

The Five.

The *Rivalla Lo'Kilan.*

Once, I'd believed the *Rivalla Lo'Kilan* referred to the original five heartstones in the ancient texts, the ones that had been used by the priestesses of old to save Dakkar over two centuries ago.

Now I knew that *we* were the Five.

Five females spread across time, across great distances, across different generations. Five females who had come together for a single purpose, guided by Kakkari's hand toward a single moment.

We had saved Dakkar. We had restored the balance, we had made the sacrifice after years of bloodshed and war at the hands of the Ghertun *and* Dakkari. After years of greed that spilled out from Dakkar's capital, like poisoned fingers dragging through the soil.

We were given another chance. One we could not squander.

So perhaps the question was not if *I* could be the female that Arik needed, if I could be a strong queen at his side.

With startled realization, I puffed out a soft breath, feeling his heartbeat against my shoulder.

Perhaps the question should've been...was *Arik* worthy of *me?*

Was he the male that *I* needed at *my* side? For the rest of our lives?

"You hurt me," I whispered.

"I know," he growled, his voice guttural and raw, as if I was dragging a blade through him right then. "Allow me to make amends for it, *saila.*"

"And how will you do that?" I wondered, feeling the icy walls around my heart begin to melt. Like rivulets of melted hurt beginning to slide away.

"To start," he rasped, "I will never let you doubt what I feel for you again."

"That would be a good start," I whispered in agreement.

His sharp intake sounded between us. His scent was all around me. His warmth.

"And you may not like it, *saila,* but I will shower you with gifts. For if I was still a *Vorakkar,* my chosen queen would expect her *deviri.* Her bride's gifts. And as such, you will have gifts fit for a *Lakkari.*"

There it was.

A *Lakkari*.

The queen of *Dothik*. The queen of Dakkar. The queen of the *Dothikkar*.

"I...I did like the books and the parchments and the soaps," I confessed softly.

A gentle sound left his throat. Not quite a chuckle. Not quite a sigh. Something in between.

"And you will have more," he told me. "I will give you libraries of books, all your own. Books that you will read to our children. Books of Dakkar's history. Of Bekkar's and Lessa's love. Of constellations in the night sky. Books of how their mother saved Dakkar, for surely there will be tomes dedicated in her honor."

My throat went tight as tears welled in my vision. Because I wanted that. Not the glory, not the accounts of what happened in the East Lands—I wanted to read to my children. To *his* children. Instilling in them the great love I had for words and story.

I could picture it so easily in my mind. Had dreamed of it even when I was in *Dothik*.

"I will have a statue of you placed at the entrance of *Dothik*, so that all that pass into our city will know who truly rules it," he whispered. "So they will know who truly rules its king."

For the first time in what felt like weeks, a soft laugh fell from my lips.

Arik breathed it in, closing his eyes for a brief moment as if he were *savoring* it.

"There it is, *rei saila*," he murmured. "There it is."

He meant my laugh. He'd been *waiting* for it. And that only broke through even more of the pain—chipping, chipping, chipping away at it.

Deciding to play along, I whispered, "Not only a statue of me. One of *Kalloma* too. Of Vienne and Mina. And of Lessa."

He swallowed, those eyes flashing open. "Of Lessa too?"

I would need to explain it to him. With time, I would. We would have to speak of the East Lands. Of Bekkar's sword. Now, however...*this* was only for us.

"*Lysi*, of her too."

"It will be done," he proclaimed, not even hesitating for a moment. "I have kneeled before no one, but I will kneel before you, Kara."

"Will you?"

Then, to my surprise, he was pulling us from the bed, swift on his feet. It took me a moment to realize that my tears had long dried. That the way he held my hand filled me with longing and hope, not loss and anger.

We stood by the window he'd burst in from, next to his drying pile of clothes on the floor.

Well...I stood.

Arik dropped to his knees before me, which stole my breath. His hands cupped my hips in a gentle grip, his thumbs skimming the swell of my belly. All beautiful, naked, scarred, golden flesh and unyielding, formidable strength.

He stared up at me with determination, though there was a fissure in his armor. A vulnerability that was only for my eyes.

I will be the only one to ever see him like this, I knew suddenly.

"I have kneeled before no one. Not as the head of the Southern District. Not as *Vorakkar*. Nor as *Dothikkar*. But I will kneel to you, Kara," he began. "I will kneel to you. Because *you* are who I will worship until the day I die and beyond even that. As my love. As mother to my children. And I hope as my queen. As my wife."

A puff of air left my lips in a soft sigh as the heat from his palms sank into my belly.

"I will give you children, Kara. I will give you sons and daughters who will grow up in a Dakkar that will be greater than the one we lived in."

"You've already begun," I whispered, knowing the child in

my womb was a sensitive thing for us both. Still, I took one of his hands, pressing it to the swell, seeing the emotion rise up in his eyes, hot and wanting.

"*Lysi*, our son," he said raggedly. He bent his head, and his forehead pressed into the swell, which only made my heart rise to my throat. His voice was raw as he said, "The first of our line."

Our line.

"And if it's a girl?" I asked.

Arik shook his head, pulling back to look at me. I heard his audible swallow, and then those molten eyes were fastened to mine. I felt a shiver run down my spine as he said, "My *lomma* told me that our first child would be a son. Our next will be a daughter. Then another son. Then two more daughters."

Five.

Five children.

"How...how do you..." I trailed off, thinking of the certainty I'd heard in his voice. "Your mother?"

"*Kara, your queen,*" he murmured. *Nik,* recited. "*Kara, your queen. The chosen, curious thing. Who will make you a king.*"

"She said that?" I asked quietly. Was I surprised? *Nik.* Not at all. "She foretold that?"

"When I first heard your *kalloma* call you Kara, I dismissed it. Because how could it be? How could she have known your name? But now...*vok, rei kassiri.*"

My love.

"You were right in your theory. That Kakkari connected *all of you* through her power, to steer us to where we were all meant to be," he finished quietly. "My mother found you in Kakkari's aether. Attached herself to you and by extension, you to me. By Kakkari's design. We were fated, Kara. You and I. We have always been written. I know that now. And so I do not doubt the things my *lomma* foretold to me. Not about you. Not about our children."

The feeling of rightness swelled in my breast. The last of the ice melting away. I felt so warm that I could burst. Buzzing with so much of it that I thought I could send a wave of energy rushing through the North Lands, banishing ice and cold, making it eternal summer.

Was Arik worthy of me?

Lysi.

The answer was quick. I felt it reverberate in the soul that was taking shape and taking form.

Arik was mine. I was his. Our lives and souls had been inter-twined since I'd had my first vision of him.

It was a heady feeling to have the *Dothikkar* of Dakkar, the most powerful male on this entire planet, kneeling at my feet.

But it didn't make me happy.

And so I dropped to my own knees in front of him.

Even kneeling, he towered over me. And he regarded me carefully as I took his hands into mine, smoothing my fingers over his roughened callouses and scarred knuckles.

"Let me be your husband, Kara," he rasped softly. "Because I do not think I can wait a moment more to have you as my wife. Say that you'll have me. Say you'll give me just one more chance, and I swear on Bekkar"—my lips twitched a little because he knew how seriously I would take that oath—"that I will love and cherish you, that I will fill *Dothik* with your laughter, that I will protect you and our children and forge a new path for us all. That is what I offer you."

"A word of advice, Arik," I began, my voice soft but my words purposeful, "never reveal your hand before a deal has been made. Isn't that what you taught me once?"

He'd said it in this very tower. Upon our first meeting when he told me that everything had a price.

He blinked in surprise.

Then I saw understanding dawn.

Leaning forward, I brushed my lips across the back of his hand, feeling his warmth, watching his gaze heat and soften.

"Because I would have accepted just your love," I informed him. A ragged laugh tore from him. The edges of my lips curled even as a sharp lump lodged itself in my throat, as I struggled to keep the raw emotion at bay. "But now I want everything. And I will demand nothing less. The gifts, the libraries, the statues, all five children."

"The laughter," he reminded me. "And the worshipping."

"*Lysi*, especially those," I whispered, my eyes locked on his.

"*Vok*," he breathed, nudging my hands away so he could cup my face in his. "*Vok*, I could not love you more, *saila*."

I didn't think I would ever tire of him saying that. It soothed a wound inside me like a balm. My own self-doubt when I never should have doubted.

"You will forgive me?" he asked quietly.

"*Lysi*," I said, swallowing the lump in my throat. "*Lysi*, I forgive you, Arik."

And I meant it. If we were going to begin again...then I needed to put the hurt behind us. It had no place in my heart as we moved beyond it.

A gruff sound escaped his lips, and then he was leaning forward.

I met his kiss halfway.

Desperate and eager and hard.

I gripped his shoulders, swaying under his kiss as we devoured one another. Hungry and aching.

"I missed you, Kara," he growled against my lips, his taste on my tongue, his grip unyielding around my waist. "So *vokking* much."

"I missed you," I whispered back, the world behind my closed eyes swaying as a wonderful smile spread over my lips. "*Lo kassiri tei.* I love you too."

He pulled back, his breathing heavy. Leaning his forehead against mine, he rasped, "Again."

"*Lo kassiri tei.*"

"Again," he pleaded.

I stroked my hand down his strong jaw before brushing my fingers over the scar at his lip. "*Lo kassiri tei.*"

A shiver went through him. Perhaps *he* needed to hear those words just as much as I did.

"No male is allowed to stay within the temple," I couldn't help but tease. "If *Kalloma* knew…"

"Your *kalloma* will be returning with us to *Dothik* soon anyway," he said gruffly, knowing in his voice. "And after all we've been through, *rei kassiri*, I think Kakkari will allow me this one night. Don't you think?"

Then he was kissing me again, and I sighed.

He laid me back on the rugs, pulling me into his arms. His warm, naked skin pressed into me, and I widened my legs so he could sink in.

"*Lysi*, I think she will," I finally said, smiling.

One moon cycle later...

"L*akkari,*" came one of the palace keepers' greetings as I passed. The Dakkari female inclined her head, and I reached out to squeeze her hand, noticing that she was holding a dusty cloth in it.

"Kina," I returned. She smiled when I used her given name, her yellow eyes lifting to find mine. "Have you seen my husband?"

"He's in the throne room," Kina replied.

She leaned in subtly, casting a look over at my two guards, handpicked by Arik himself. Kalik had volunteered to be my shadow as we settled into the palace, but I knew that Arik needed him on his council. And so my two guards—a tall, broad female named Deria and a male named Illo, who was considered one of the best swordsmen in *Dothik*—trailed me every moment that Arik was not with me. I understood the need for it. After we returned to *Dothik* from the North Lands, there were precautions put into place for my safety. While they might've seemed excessive, I knew that Arik's priority was to protect me. And to protect the child growing each day in my womb. Just as he'd promised he would.

"He's still meeting with a male from the Eastern District."

Ah, *lysi*, Arik had said something about that when he left our rooms this morning. The leader of Arik's rival network, when he was at the head of the Southern District. But I was surprised the meeting was still going. It was nearly the middle of the afternoon.

"Did it sound like it was going well?" I asked, quirking a brow.

Wisely, she didn't say anything, but she matched my expression, and I chuckled.

"I see," I murmured. "Maybe I should go rescue the poor soul."

"Perhaps," she giggled lightly.

I squeezed her hand again, giving her one last smile, and went on my way.

When I first returned to the palace, I thought my presence had surprised many of the guards and the palace workers. Not because I was a hybrid female, however. Not because I'd lived in the *orala sa'kilan* all my life or because I could claim the *Seta Kalliri* as my mother.

But because my temperament was so different than Arik's. In all that I encountered those first few days, I could practically see the wheels turning in their minds, wondering how we worked together. How we fit.

When, truthfully, Arik and I were perfectly matched. A fact that was only reinforced to us every single day. He calmed me down when I was overwhelmed—a steady, strong presence I sorely needed. And I reined him in when he got that little bloodthirsty gleam in his eyes when yet another highborn family boldly questioned his decision to disband the courts in the palace. He would kiss me when I found myself worrying about the child, when I found myself chattering on about my fears that I wouldn't be a good mother. And I would distract him in similar ways when I felt he was taking on too much stress, pulling him out of his offices if the hour grew too late, leading him by his tail to our bed, which only ever stoked his desires.

We worked.

Just as we'd known we would.

And every night as I lay in his arms, I was struck by how incredibly grateful I was that he hadn't given up on us, even when I'd wanted to. For two weeks, he'd stayed outside the *orala sa'kilan*, if only to speak with me. After he sent me away from *Dothik*, I'd been strong when he'd been fearful. But after the East Lands, he'd been strong when all I'd wanted to do was hide.

I loved him even more for it.

"*Lakkari*," came another greeting from two guards I passed. I inclined my head and smiled at them, winding my way down familiar halls. The palace was incredibly large, but we only utilized a small portion of it, keeping some of the wings and passages locked entirely until we found better use for them. The whole of the dungeons below had been shut away and would never be used again. Arik wanted to have them destroyed entirely—he still thought about Kiro's death more often than he admitted to me, and I later learned it was also where Bodin had been murdered under his father's orders—but it was a project for another time. One I hoped would bring him a small semblance of peace.

Running daily palace life was not unlike running the *orala sa'kilan*. I just had to speak with more people throughout the day. It was a lot more given names and faces to know, but I didn't feel right *not* interacting with everyone who came through our doors on a regular basis. The guards and the palace keepers knew to come to me for certain issues and to my husband for entirely different ones. But each of us contributed to keep the palace running smoothly.

Kalloma helped where she could too, but I thought that there were those still struck by her constant presence in the palace, too awed to directly ask her for anything. Though she was no longer the *Seta Kalliri*—that position now lay with my father's sister high in the North Lands—some of the palace members still treated her as such.

I thought that a large part of *Kalloma* was relieved to be back in *Dothik*. There was a radiant warmth that had returned to her skin. She could actually step outside to enjoy the sun on her face without a heavy cloak. She could walk in the marketplace, her arm linked with mine, and absorb the sounds and smells. She gave me a tour of the *Dothik* she'd once known, her favorite sitting spot, her favorite place for quiet and reprieve, where she'd lived with her family as a girl before studying in the temple—she hadn't been born into a highborn family, but rather she'd been raised by a mother who'd tirelessly worked in the marketplace selling thick slices of *hibri* bread to provide for her child—and where my father and she used to meet when they were young.

I saw a different side of her in *Dothik*. One that made me realize that my *kalloma* was growing older. I was glad that she could experience a contrasting life, away from the temple and its weighing responsibilities. It didn't mean she still didn't journey to the temple in *Dothik* every day to say her prayers. It didn't mean that she still didn't seek Kakkari's hand whenever she felt she needed it. But there was a noticeable, marked difference in her faith after the East Lands.

We never really spoke about what happened in the fog, if what she'd felt flowing through her had been different than what I'd felt.

But sometimes I still caught her waving her hand toward a door, expecting it to close with the gust of air she thought she'd channeled toward it, similar to how she'd extinguished the fire I'd inadvertently lit on Trissa's dress all those months ago.

Only the door would remain open and there'd be a look of confusion on her face, brief but apparent. Then realization would come. Longing came next. She'd walk to the door, close it herself, and I wondered if it ever felt like a missing limb to her. Tangible but simply...gone.

But I knew she would do it again, if given the choice.

She'd made mistakes, certainly. We all had when it'd come to the fog. But she'd been determined to make them right...and so she had.

The closer I veered toward the throne room, the more guards and palace keepers I passed. All of them greeted me, inclining their heads, stopping in their tracks as I passed. And just when I caught sight of the grand doors leading to the throne room, I heard Arik's growling voice, though I couldn't make out his words.

The next moment, a male—dressed in black trews and thieving boots—left the throne room with a scowl on his wrinkled face, ready to be escorted out by Arik's guards.

The male didn't see me, and I watched his back curiously as he strode down the hall toward the front gates. I watched him until he disappeared.

I sighed. Arik regularly met with tavern owners, vendors, seamstresses, metal workers, more so than he met with the highborn families. But one thing was apparent...corruption was steeped in this city like a plague, and it would be hard to cut out. Businesses were used to bribing the *Dothikkar's* palace so that the guards would look the other way.

Still a long way to go, I thought. While I didn't know if Arik could stamp out the greed and corruption that flowed into the streets of his city entirely...I thought that he could get relatively close. But nothing would ever be perfect in a city of this size. Arik knew that better than anyone. The inhabitants that had grown wealthy under his father's rule battled against him at every step.

Nothing was easy as *Dothikkar*...and he had to fight tooth and nail to gain an *inch* in the city *he* ruled. Thankfully, he had the hordes and *saruks* at his back, bestowing their support. He had the support of the priestesses—*Kalloma* and my aunt included, the latter placated with her promotion in prestige in the *orala sa'kilan*. For now. And he had the whispered rumors that his queen had helped defeat the fog in the East, rumors that he allowed to circulate.

Without these things, every new law and every rewritten one would have been an uphill battle for him.

All was quiet in the throne room, and I nodded at the guards to open the doors. Over my shoulder, to Deria and Illo, I said, "Stay out here. *Hanniva.* I won't be long."

They faded back as I stepped into the throne room.

Quiet and vast, it was an impressive space. Imposing columns of marble stood tall. One side of the room led to a long, open-air terrace framed by arches, revealing an expansive view of *Dothik* below.

The doors closed behind me as my gaze fastened on my husband.

Stilling, I felt a prickle at the back of my neck, a short breath whistling out from me. I had wondered when I'd see this last vision from Kakkari. But here it was. The vision I'd seen months ago—on the night of his father's death, the night that had changed everything—of Arik standing at the banister of the terrace, looking out over the city, Bekkar's gleaming sword at his hip.

It felt like a completion of sorts. A final piece slotting into place.

What *hadn't* been in my vision was when Arik turned to

regard me, a softened grin stealing over his expression. His eyes slid to my belly. I saw a flare of pride there, and no matter how often he pressed his lips to the rounded bump...there would always be pride coupled with awe in those eyes. As if he didn't believe that we were real.

"I heard you were being difficult again, *Dothikkar*," I teased softly, reading the lines of his body and knowing that while his shoulders were tense and there was a crinkle of annoyance between his brows, I could easily pull him out from his darkened mood.

A scoff left his lips, and Arik turned, leaning back against the banister, watching my slow approach. *Nik, admiring*, savoring, I realized, feeling my cheeks flush with knowing. It would be another couple months until the child came, according to the *mokkira* who tended to me. Even still, Arik acted as if I would give birth at any moment, sweeping me up into his arms if he thought a distance was too great for me to walk, making sure I ate seemingly five times my bodyweight in food every day, and drawing me long, hot baths in the evenings, making the time to join me for the vast majority of them.

He took my hand when I neared, pulling me into his arms. I sighed, pressing my face into the soft hide of his strapped vest, the familiar line of his daggers present there. Drawing him into my lungs, I heard him murmur, "He'll live with the new laws. Or he can leave and join a *saruk* or a horde, who have no use for the gold he clearly loves."

Pulling back, I reached up to push a tuft of hair away that had fallen into his eyes. He was so incredibly handsome, which was made even more apparent to me whenever I saw some of the palace keepers nearly swoon as he passed, as they were left giggling in his wake. Witnessing it had only ever made my own lips twitch in amusement instead of jealousy.

"It's not even like I'm asking him to *stop* his network," he grumbled, his shoulders tensing again. "I know what it's like. I know they will always find ways to make their purchases, to sell their goods, to shuffle their gold around. I'm just asking that he be a little more discreet about it. You would have thought I'd sentenced him to mine the Teru Gulch by the way he was acting."

"*Kassiri*," I whispered, cupping his cheek in my hand, forcing him to meet my gaze. *Love.* Between us, our child bumped his abdomen, and I saw his eyes soften, felt his shoulders relax once more. "Change will come with time. But you are going about it in the right way *now*. Trying to blend the old and the new, taking smaller steps along the path instead of giant leaps. We will get there. I have faith in that."

His face turned, and he pressed his lips to the center of my palm before grasping it in his own.

"Were you worried for me, wife?" he wanted to know, his eyes beginning to gleam as they always did when he referred to me as such.

We hadn't waited to make our vows.

We hadn't even waited to reach *Dothik*, though very few knew that.

Over a moon cycle ago, Arik and I had left the *orala sa'kilan*. *Kalloma* would join us in *Dothik* a week later, but on that journey, it had been just the two of us and Syok.

And we'd barely even left the North Lands when one night, under a clear sky, we decided to exchange vows of our own, tying ourselves to one another without another Dakkari in sight. The vast darkness of the wildlands, Syok, and a skittish *privixi*—a four-legged watchful, harmless creature who had been drawn to the warmth of the fire that night—were our only witnesses.

And as we'd exchanged the vows and promised our love to one another, as he'd taken me into his arms afterward and I'd watched the way the firelight had played over his naked flesh, as I'd gripped his wide shoulders and our cries had joined together in the night, I had felt a familiar warmth flow through me, sparking through my body. Familiar power. Kakkari's touch. Mingling with the desperate desire, the need to join ourselves together after so long, the need to touch and claim and kiss and stroke.

We'd been blessed. We'd been fated, ever since the beginning.

I was Arik's wife and he was my husband before we ever stepped foot back in *Dothik*. And while the ceremony for his throne and the subsequent public blessing of our joining by *Kalloma*—which announced me as his queen to all of Dakkar—followed shortly after, we would always remember our quiet, private vows in the middle of nowhere, somewhere in the Northwest of the wildlands. And the aftermath of it, the wildness with which we'd needed one another.

My knees trembled even now, remembering it, especially when Arik's eyes went molten with memory.

"Not worried for you," I corrected. "Worried for the other male."

His brief chuckle filled the terrace. It was a hot afternoon, deep into the warm season. Soon the winds would change. Though the climate would always be more forgiving in the West Lands once the frost came, I knew that it would still come. And it would come sooner than we would like it.

"Truthfully," I murmured, knowing it was a delicate subject, "I was coming to ask you about the traveling party we'll be taking with us. The *bikkus* are beginning to prepare food for our journey, and they wanted a final count."

Arik inhaled a deep breath.

We would be doing this once a season, so he'd better get used to it. But we had argued already over my joining him. With the pregnancy, he worried that riding a *pyroki* would be too strenuous for me, would be too *dangerous*. But as his queen, I needed to show support to the hordes and *saruks*, to the Killup we would meet in the North Lands and the growing *saruk* of the humans we would meet with in the South Lands. Arik refused to be like his father, sitting on his throne in *Dothik*, ruling a planet without ever seeing it. This was important to Arik, to remain connected to those that lived beyond the capital. The journey would take weeks. But it was necessary, and I was determined to remain at his side throughout it all.

Seeing my resolve and my stubbornness, he'd finally given in. But we were taking two *mokkiras*—two master healers— along with us, and I'd be traveling in a carriage pulled by two *pyrokis*. A compromise. One that worked for me, though he grumbled about it whenever he got the chance.

"Twenty in total," he informed me. "Kalik and Bakkia will be joining us."

I inclined my head, holding his eyes. Then I leaned forward, brushing my lips across his. "I'll let the *bikkus* know."

He growled. "I still do not know how you talked me into this, Kara."

I beamed up at him, and immediately his small scowl softened.

"That's how," I whispered, delight threading through me. He would give me anything I wanted. I knew that. But I also knew better than to abuse it. So I picked and chose my battles accordingly.

Leaning forward, I kissed him more fully. Feeling his arm tighten around my back, a gruff sound escaping his throat.

"You'll be happy I came with you," I vowed. "And who knows? Maybe we can find another lake to enjoy. I think you owe me another lake experience to make up for the first, don't you think?"

He groaned, shaking his head as he buried his face into my neck. Did his cheeks feel a little hot?

"Are you *blushing?*" I asked in disbelief.

He groaned again.

And my laugh filled the throne room.

Another promise he'd made good on.

"*Vok, saila,*" Arik rasped. He moaned before biting his lip, his head falling back, exposing the thick, golden column of his throat. The tip of his uncut ear twitched, something that always made me squeeze my thighs together.

I didn't think I'd ever seen anything more erotic than my husband responding to the way I pleasured him. With my hands, with my tongue.

The position was awkward at first, and he'd fussed with thinking the rocks would dig into my knees too hard. But I'd silenced him by dragging my tongue up the underside of his cock, humming around the tip as he froze and *finally* reclined back along the lake's bank on his elbows, allowing me to kneel between his splayed thighs.

I bobbed my head, taking his cock deeper. He was so thick, however, that I could only ever get a third of the way down his shaft. The rest I squeezed and stroked with my fists, just the way I knew he liked it.

We'd only been traveling for a few days, but already the need had grown into something ravenous. Pregnancy, I realized, only made me needier when it came to our intimacy, something Arik had gleefully taken upon himself to satisfy. And back in *Dothik*?

He satisfied me *very* well.

Traveling with a large party, however?

It didn't leave much privacy. Or time to be alone with one another.

As such, the moment we'd come across the lakes, Arik had announced we'd make camp here. And after a strict order to his guards to stay back at camp—ignoring Kalik's knowing smirk

—he'd led me down a long path, far from the others, to one of the moonlit lakes, the silvery orb high and full above us. And I'd followed him with a fluttering belly, nearly bouncing on my heels in excitement, hardly able to wait to get my hands on him.

"*Vok*, do that again, wife," he pleaded, groaning, his hips tilting up.

And I nearly smiled at his encouragement but then focused instead on sucking on the sensitive area just below the head of his cock. A spot that always served to drive him *crazy*. When I did it a second time, I did it hard, and he froze, his tail flicking rapidly back and forth. He held his breath, and I could feel how close he was to losing control.

"*Nik,*" he growled, his hand cupping under my jaw, feeling it work as I continued to lazily suck. Then he was gently tugging me off. "*Vok*, you nearly made me come right then, *saila*. Need you too much. Slide up. I need your slick, needy cunt right now before I lose my *vokking* mind."

He didn't have to ask me twice. I licked my lips, tasting him there, and crawled up his body, straddling his hips.

I was too far gone in my desire to worry if we could be heard. If our echoing moans would reach the encampment. I didn't care. All I knew was that I needed Arik and I needed him *now*.

"*Lysi,*" I moaned when he thrust up, sliding all the way inside in one swift, hard movement. "*Lysi, Arik!*"

Pleasure zapped down my spine as I rested my hands on his wide chest, rocking over him, desperate and greedy to meet his thrusts. Swirling my hips, trying to press my clit to his *dakke*, though the swell of my belly never *quite* let me reach it.

He knew what I needed and tilted his own hips in a way that let me feel it, and I tossed my head back, crying out.

The lake lapped at my knees and feet, the cool water a startling contrast to the warm night and the incredible heat I felt building within my body. Stoked like a fire, and Arik was making it roar.

His eyes were on mine, half-lidded in his own pleasure as his hands dug into my hips.

Mine, I thought.

"All mine," I whispered, though I nearly choked on the words.

Those beautiful eyes melted at my words. It always heightened his desires...my possessiveness. "*Lysi?*"

"Mm-hmm."

His dark grin was punctuated with his increasing, powerful thrusts. "Then take what's yours, *rei Lakkari*. And I'll take what's *mine*."

My queen, he'd called me.

Another desperate cry tumbled from my lips as he picked up his pace, the wild slap of his flesh against mine echoing across the smooth surface of the still lake. Moonlight cut across his body, casting him in various hues of silver and gold.

Then he was growling, pushing up off his back so that he could meet my lips. He kissed me and then trailed his mouth down my jaw, my throat, ducking low to nip and suckle on my growing breasts before moving back up. The change in position made me sink lower onto him, our child tucked safely between us.

"*Almost there, kassiri,*" I whispered, feeling the telltale signs of my orgasm beginning to crest. "*Ohhh!*"

His fingers slid down my hip, roving toward my clit. When he pressed there—the roughened pad of his thumb *sublime*—when he sunk in particularly deep, when a loud groan vibrated his chest, and when he began rutting with wild need...my vision momentarily blackened.

Bright stars and streaks lit up behind my closed lids as beautiful pleasure pulled and tugged at me. He felt me tighten. He felt my demand that he join me.

His loud bellow made me grin. I was intoxicated by him. Mesmerized. Besotted. Heat spilled inside me, wonderful and familiar.

In the aftermath, as we regained our breath, I found myself tucked against his side. The rocks along the lake's flattened bank were smooth. Polished little surfaces that conformed to my body. It was surprisingly comfortable. So much so that I thought I could fall into the deepest of sleeps. Even with the cool water lapping at our bodies.

Arik was tracing his fingers down my back, making me shiver, making my tail twitch, which only brought a small, endearing smirk to his face.

"Tired?" he wondered quietly.

I nodded against his chest just as I felt his strong hand spread over my belly.

Safe.

He always made me feel safe.

And I smiled into his skin, brushing my lips across a scar there. One of many. But I knew every story of every last one.

"*Veekor*," he whispered. "Sleep, *rei kassiri*. I'll watch over you."

"Mmm, you won't let the lake creatures get me?" I teased sleepily.

A husky, surprised chuckle filled the air.

"I didn't let them get you before," he murmured, pressing his lips to my hair. "I certainly won't let them get you now."

I smiled. My eyelids grew heavy. The water lapping at me felt like an embrace. But it was Arik that soothed me, calmed me.

"*Lo kassiri tei*," he murmured to me.

I grinned.

Over the wide berth of his chest, I saw our discarded clothes. I saw Bekkar's sword glinting in the moonlight, the white heartstone gleaming. *Waiting.* Because Kakkari had left us one, after all. A heartstone to create a new Dakkar.

My gaze flickered back to Arik.

My husband. My lover. My king.

Connected to me through magic and fate.

Entwined as one.

Between us, our child moved, and Arik grinned.

I whispered back, "*Lo kassiri tei.*"

Want to hear about new releases, exclusive giveaways, and get access to **bonus content,** like extended epilogues and character art?

Sign up for **Zoey Draven's newsletter**:

www.ZoeyDraven.com/newsletter

If you're already subscribed to my newsletter, access all bonus content here:

https://zoeydraven.com/bonus-content/

Desire in His Blood

Brides of the Kylorr #1

OUT NOW!

We call the Kylorr demons. *Monsters*. Never in a million years did I expect to call one *husband*...

I'm drowning under the weight of my father's debts. Working myself to the bone, I know that if I don't pay them off in time, the sadistic creditors will take everything: our home, our respected name, and, worst of all, my two beautiful sisters.

To save my family, I agree to do something reckless: marry a wealthy and mysterious stranger, who offers me a wicked bargain I can't afford to refuse.

However, his bargain comes with one terrifying catch. Because my husband-to-be is a Kylorr. One of the most fearsome alien races, the Kylorr

549

are beastly monsters, all muscle and menace, with powerful wings, depraved cravings, and berserker-like rages. The worst part?

They survive on *blood*.

Cold and cruel, Azur of House Kaalium, the High Lord of Laras, demands me as his blood bride. To feed from me. To use my body in whatever way he wishes.

But if Azur expects a demure, submissive wife, he'll be in for a rude awakening. My new husband might crave my surrender but there's one thing I'll never give him.

My heart...even if he wants to shatter it into a million pieces.

CONNECT WITH ZOEY

SCAN THE QR CODE WITH YOUR PHONE TO ACCESS HER LINKS:

Kraving Dravka

Kraving Tavak

Brides of the Kylorr:

Desire in His Blood

Craving in His Blood

Hunger in His Blood

Hordes of the Elthika:

The Horde King of Shadow

About the Author

Zoey Draven has been writing stories for as long as she can remember. Her love affair with the romance genre started with her grandmother's old Harlequin paperbacks and has continued ever since. As an Amazon Top 50 and USA Today bestselling author, now she gets to write the happily-ever-afters—with an otherworldly twist, of course! She is the author of Sci-Fi and Fantasy Romance books, such as the *Horde Kings of Dakkar* and the *Brides of the Kylorr* series.

When she's not writing, she's probably drinking one too many cups of coffee, hiking in the redwoods, or spending time with her family.

Website: www.ZoeyDraven.com
Facebook group: Zoey's Reader Zone